JEANNIE SAKOL

HOT
30

DELACORTE PRESS/NEW YORK

Published by
Delacorte Press
1 Dag Hammarskjold Plaza
New York, N.Y. 10017

Manufactured in the United States of America
First printing

Designed by Oksana Kushnir

LIBRARY OF CONGRESS CATALOGING IN PUBLICATION DATA

Sakol, Jeannie.
   Hot 30.

   I. Title.
PZ4.S153He   [PS3569.A455]   813'.5'4   79-23372
ISBN 0-440-03394-2

HOT
30

For Stephanie Bennett
a friend in deed

The truth can make you dead.
   —L.A. graffito

"All literature is gossip. All journalism is gossip. All novels are gossip."
   —Truman Capote

Acknowledgments

A good many more than thirty people aided, supported, and comforted me in the creation of this novel, among them: Steve Tisch and John Avnet, Tova Laiter, Roger Price, Patti Gilbert, Charles Hulse, Judith Plowden, Liv Faret, Jack Gillihan, Peter Nicklin, Marty Davidson, Gene Winick, Leif Pedersen, Michael Kosser, Jerry Minkow, Gerry Ament, Madeline Amgott, Barbara Bernard, Emily Pattner, Madeleine Morel, Mel Lewinter. I want to thank Bill Grose for saying, Go ahead. And my parents, my sister Phyllis, and especially, Miriam.

Acknowledgments

"Here's looking at *you,* kid!" Lou Dexter mocked himself in the rearview mirror before turning his car over to the Ma Raison parking valet. "A born-again Bogart," Jennie Bliss Sternholdt had called him in an excess of the vintage movie lust young women have for men with bags under their eyes. "Battered—" she had crooned. "But beautiful."

He wished he could live up to her vision of him. He did not feel like a born-again Bogart. He felt, as Raymond Chandler would say, like an amputated leg. Cut off from the main body of life. He would need more than Bogart bravado to get through the next few hours. The gala celebration of Dorrie Bridges's thirtieth birthday only served as another reminder of his own failure and professional disgrace.

It was four years since the Russians sentenced him to death and then expelled him unshaven and in chains. Four years since the State Department turned its back on him and the *Washington Press* canned him "for cause" and without severance and his ex-wife the princess divorced him on the grounds that she could no longer hold her head up in Bloomingdale's.

Several book publishers had offered him big bucks for his side of the story, which he refused. No other news organization would hire him. As a result, after twenty Pulitzer prize-winning years in the same league as David Halberstam and Woodward and Bernstein, he had walked around jobless and on the balls of his ass broke, until last week. Canadian press lord Kevin Marceau wanted to beef up his West Coast bureau of *The Weekly Insider,* a publication slightly below the intellectual pretensions of *The Star* and *The Midnight Globe.*

"I'm afraid all I can offer is Newspaper Guild minimum."

Lou's last remaining pair of Daks were paper thin at the seat. "My name still means something—"

"Your name is mud, Dexter, but I don't care. I admire you. That's why I'm willing to take the chance. But do yourself a favor. Forget the Pulitzer and all that crap. We've got ten million readers waiting to be entertained. News isn't news anymore. It's show business."

Instead of SALT and OPEC and Camp David, he was now assigned to the Tits and Ass beat of southern California. His job to track down juicy rumors of sex, scandals, and corruption. His listening posts the Polo Lounge, the Palm, and the various other celebrity tip joints like Ma Raison.

He had taken the job. Tonight's party for Dorrie Bridges was his first assignment. It put his new identity as a journalist into humiliating perspective. She was the total news media personality. Her daily column was read by millions in 420 newspapers. Her weekly television report out-rated "60 Minutes" and "20/20" combined.

With her prim Walker Evans face and soft southern drawl, she was hailed as the Angel of Truth by those she helped and the Angel of Death or worse by those she destroyed. *Time* called her the Madonna Communicator, while *Women's Wear Daily* dubbed her Scarlett O'Horror.

What's more, while Lou Dexter was somewhat past forty and literally fighting for his life, Dorrie Bridges had more power and influence than he had ever had and was almost young enough to be his daughter. In fact, she reminded him of his daughter—his "ex-daughter," as Lisa now preferred to be known. It was the eyes: the solemn, direct eyes that suffered neither fools nor dissembling.

He would be meeting Dorrie in person for the first time tonight. They had spoken by phone once. On his return from Russia, she had tracked him down to ask what really happened on the historic journey to Ekaterinburg/Sverdlovsk with the enticing Sonya Boris.

"It's all in the trial records," he had told her.

"Now, Lou," she had cajoled. "You know I can't read Russian."

"There's a translation."

"You know every good story loses something in the translation."

Call it a perverse sense of honor or boyish sentimentality. Remind him it wouldn't matter in a hundred years. Whatever anyone told him or he told himself, he had felt the necessity of keeping his mouth shut then and during all the months of harassment and scorn that followed.

Sure of this one thing if nothing else, he had put on a Braggi tan, a black turtleneck to hide his sagging neck, and the Stanley Blacker blazer Jennie had charged to her Saks Fifth Avenue account this very morning.

"Fuck it. I can't face it." Overwhelmed by shame, he had collapsed on Jennie's bed in a fetal position with a bottle of Jack Daniel's. "I can't go."

"You have to go."

"I can't. How can I tell Dorrie Bridges I'm covering her birthday for *The Weekly Insider*?"

"She'll probably fall madly in love you—"

"Oh, Jen—"

"I'll kill her if she does."

"I'm through, Jennie. Stop wasting your time on me. I'm a tired old man."

"Think Bogart—" she had teased.

"Humphrey Bogart is dead! He went out on the crest. Some people live past their time—" His voice had broken.

"Lou—" Jennie cradled him to her young breasts.

"Jesus H. Christ—" His eyes had filled with angry tears. "What do I do, ask Dorrie Bridges if she sleeps in the nude? Or if she and Sonny Syntagma play love games to keep their relationship exciting? Or how it feels to be thirty years old in a youth-oriented society? I shouldn't be here at all. I should be in Geneva—"

"I'm glad you're here."

"Or covering the Middle East—"

"There are more Arabs and Jews on Rodeo Drive—"

"I shouldn't have taken this job. I'd be better off digging ditches—"

"*Lou!*" She pistol-pointed her finger in mock warning.

"*You!*" He responded in kind to the small ritual they had evolved in their brief relationship.

In the garbage dump of his life, Jennie Bliss Sternholdt was a daisy. In her mid-twenties, her entire consciousness was conditioned by film. She could recite movie credits going back to *The Birth of a Nation* and act out from memory whole scenarios of such classics as *Casablanca*. A graduate film student, she earned her living finding locations for features and TV commercials while trying to break in as a director.

Her mythic hero was Humphrey Bogart. "As a man. As an actor. As a cultural original." She had managed to see every one of his seventy-five feature films from *A Devil with Women*, made in 1930, to his last, *The Harder They Fall*, in 1956.

"Bogie was a giant among midgets and so are you! Would Bogie be scared of Dorrie Bridges? Call me and let me know how it goes."

"Am I staying with you tonight, Jen?"

"Bogie wouldn't ask. He'd know."

"Am I, Jennie?"

"Call me from the party."

Humphrey Bogart would have walked out and kept going until he reached Tierra del Fuego. Lou Dexter drove to Ma Raison. The garden had been cleared of tables and tented with a blue velvet sky spiked with crystal stars. Covering one entire side was a photo mural of the famous HOLLYWOOD sign retouched to read D-O-R-R-I-E-W-O-O-D while the recorded voices of the Mormon Tabernacle Choir sang, "Dorrie, Dorrie, Hallelujah" very softly.

Along the other sides were blowups of Dorrie in familiar stages of her life. The time a certain Irate Starlet slammed a cream pie in her face. The very moment a certain Hopeful Politician stuck his tongue out at her behind her back. The walk in the London rain with Prince Charles that started the marriage rumors. The chaste hand-holding with superstud Sonny Syntagma, who was supposed to be her future husband any year now. Sharing the dais with Marva Burnside the night they raised a million dollars in twenty minutes for the socialite's pet project, a new Children's Hospital.

Now that he was there, he was feeling better. As his old Aunt Fanny always urged, if you take on a job, do it well. Dorrie had not yet arrived. The first person he wanted to find was Marva Burnside. She and her husband Norris were Old Money, not directly connected with the entertainment world. When Dorrie first arrived in Los Angeles over a decade before, the Burnsides had taken her under their wing. Marva would be good for some personal anecdotes and she might also be able to shed some light on a rumor Jennie had told him just as he left.

Jennie had heard at the tennis courts that Dorrie was about to break the biggest story of her career. "She's going to blow the whistle on a heavy. It's supposed to be so big and so hot, it'll drive energy and Kennedy right off the front page!"

It was still early, and so far only the Early People had arrived. Animated, well-dressed, and vaguely familiar, they appeared to be trucked in from a central depot like movie extras to function as a backdrop when the heavies finally showed up. TV cameramen with minicams and press photographers from all over the world prowled around with the self-importance of gods.

"Have a Beverly Hills Egg Cream?" The waiter offered him the latest rage, an alcoholic egg cream made with crème de cacao and Perrier. At the rate people were drinking Perrier, they'd have to have a mineral spring the size of the Atlantic Ocean.

"Jack Daniel's. Double. One rock in the shape of an isosceles triangle."

The Coast.

When you said The Coast, nobody thought you were talking about the Hamptons, the Gulf ports or the shores of Puget Sound. Everyone knew you meant the amorphous land mass and mind set of southern California where dreams came true, the good died bad and if you wanted some orange juice, all you had to do was stick out your hand and pluck a fresh can out of the freezer.

Here, the operative word was *hot*. Hot property. Hot agent. Hot director. Hot studio. Hot personality. Hot restaurant. Tonight's party for Dorrie Bridges was the hot party of the year if not the entire twentieth century to hear all the talk. The hot people would be here. There would be plenty of hot gossip and hot rumor and maybe even some hot hard news. It was going to be up to him, poor over-the-hill dirty old man Bogart bastard, to find it.

The trick lay in understanding the California life-style. A masterwork of contradiction, it was for most people a Longfellow nightmare of empty dreams and things not being what they seemed. Coast people played life cool but functioned hot.

If this was one of the hot A-parties, all he could think was that it was just as dull and stratified as the international political and diplomatic circuit. Clustered together in one corner was the Hollywood Establishment, the embalmed cadavers of a bygone day, preserved in an aspic of nostalgia and the mutual reassurances of eternal youth and talent. A few yards but a whole generation away were the Young Hollywood Brats in beards, sneakers, and thrift-shop chic, wearing in some cases the 1940s discards of the veterans smiling at them with such hostility. Mingling among them were the stars of television, rock, and fashion plus the agents, writers, lawyers, gynecologists, plastic surgeons, and everyone else who either had or wanted a piece of the action.

He could smell the California Perfume, the suffocating attar of envy, greed, spite, sweat, musk, and fear blended with hate, Joy, cunt, Aim, spunk, talc, Russian Leather, Scope, and raw, suppurating ambition.

"Where's Dorrie? Anyone seen Dorrie?" Something was wrong or about to go wrong. It was after ten, long past the expected arrival of the birthday girl. The action had come to a standstill. Camera-ready smiles had gone soft at the edges. The small talk had dried up. The music had switched to disco but nobody was dancing. They were all intent on watching the entrance.

It occurred to Lou that he had been unable to find any of Dorrie's inner circle. Not Marva or Norris Burnside. Not Andrew Van Kennan, her secretary. Nor Tom Jennings, the colorful Nashville newspaper publisher who first recognized the teen-age Dorrie's talents. Or Glitz Dreamburg, the flamboyant agent and hostess of the Malibu Bitch House who had once lived with Dorrie in New York. Or Sonny Syntagma, who, according to local intelligence, owed his stardom to Dorrie.

Astonishingly, among the people he did recognize in the crowd were several of Dorrie's victims. It struck him as odd that they should attend her birthday party. Hoagy Harris? She had confronted him with his shameful secret on live television. Viktor Varvanza? After a Dorrie exclusive, his ballerina wife had swan-dived off the top of the Empire State Building. Connie Michelin? The publisher of *Newsmagazine* was known to blame Dorrie Bridges for her declining circulation. She had given Dorrie her first by-lined column and Dorrie had thanked her by leaving her in the lurch.

Lou Dexter did not like notebooks. He preferred a thin sheaf of typing paper folded in half and in half again to form a writing surface two inches wide that fit neatly into his palm. While waiting for Dorrie, he would explore one of Kevin Marceau's current editorial obsessions. Youth. "Being thirty is the beginning of the end in California," Marceau had informed him. "That's why Dorrie's birthday is significant. I want quotes. Streisand. Minnelli. Jackie Smith. Mork and Mindy. How do they feel about getting old. What can we learn from them."

In newspaper tradition the numeral 30 meant the end of a story. Maybe he would use that as his lead. Too subtle, he concluded. *Insider* readers wanted quotes, not cultural parallels. Dorrie herself had expressed her feelings in this morning's paper, her column headed ON BECOMING THIRTY.

I write this in advance of the Big Day. By all counts, this is the final day of my youth. I'm thirty years old and I have been checking out my body and my mind for signs of senility and decay. I feel conflicting emotions. That I have just begun to live and that I have lived long enough. That I know all there is to know and that I have learned absolutely nothing.

When I was growing up in the sixties, the rallying cry was "Never trust anyone over thirty." Now I'm about to be that person. Should I trust myself? Was Scott Fitzgerald right when he said he didn't want to live past thirty? Are Elizabeth Taylor and Ali MacGraw sucking wind, as we say down home, when they assure us older is better? Not that they, or I, or anybody has much choice in the matter.

I found my first gray hair last week. I yanked it out and wondered how soon I might risk cancer by tinting my tattletale locks. The gray is gone for the moment but I know it will be back and will bring a few friends.

To me, Emily Brontë is the finest woman writer I know. She was thirty when she died. When you read this, I will have crossed the line.

I will be thirty. No longer will I be able to blame foolish mistakes on youthful ignorance. On this personal New Year's Eve, I resolve to start my exercises. Again. And stick to a healthful diet. I resolve to rethink my priorities and put first things first.

As it is written in Ecclesiastes, "To every thing there is a season, and a time to every purpose under the heaven. A time to be born and a time to die. A time to weep and a time to laugh; a time to mourn and a time to dance. A time to keep silence and a time to speak."

Now it is coming up to my season to be thirty. What will it be like? I'm afraid I won't know until it happens.

Dorrie Bridges sounded like quite a woman. Maybe Jennie Bliss Sternholdt was right. Maybe Dorrie would fall madly in love with him. Maybe they would do a May-September Act. The public liked incongruity. Beauty and the Beast. Mariel Hemingway and Woody Allen. Dorrie and Lou? It sounded like a neighborhood beauty parlor.

"Lou Dexter?" A chiffon balloon with a vacuum cleaner nozzle for a mouth tried to suck him into her embrace.

"I'm—sorry—"

"I'm Fawn Roberts—and I want you to meet little Winnie!" Hearing her name, a small girl dressed like Rita Hayworth in *Gilda* held a brown More cigarette in a pearl holder to her glossed lips. "Got a *wight?*"

Ten years old and as *wovvable* as Kool-Aid in Guyana, *Wee Winnie Woberts* was America's first Weather Child. Her nightly appearance brought KLA-TV's Six O'Clock News the highest ratings for that time period in the Greater Los Angeles area, many of them mothers of other little ten year olds who were far more *wovvable* than Wee Winnie if given the chance.

"Isn't she fantabulous?" Fawn's voice trembled, tears matting her double fur lashes. "It makes up just a little bit for Dawnette, doesn't it?"

The penny dropped. Here was another of Dorrie's victims. How could Fawn Roberts explain her presence at Dorrie Bridges's birthday? Perhaps, to survive in California, you needed a selective memory.

The exploitation of children always reminded him of Jonathan Swift's classic description of the Irishman who regarded a healthy child as the most nourishing of food "whether stewed, baked, boiled or served as a fricassee!" Swift would have had a field day with the Dawnette Roberts story.

Even in Moscow, Lou had read about Dawnette. *Tass* had seized on the tragedy as an example of capitalistic corruption. At age twelve the girl had possessed the sublime combination of Hollywood fantasy, the androgynous body of a Botticelli angel and the sensuous face of Messalina in heat.

After several soft-core porno films, she appeared in her first TV movie as a young heiress kidnapped by terrorists and raped with a broomstick.

"I was born sexy," the child had told reporters. "I loved being touched. Why do you think babies scream to have their didies changed? They want to be wiped. And powdered. And oiled. In *all* the little creases!"

For *Playboy,* she recalled turning on a family friend at the age of two by lying on the floor with her nightie pushed up and her legs in the air. "He picked me up and gave me a horsey ride on his lap." At three she had masturbated to orgasm and had her first actual sexual intercourse at five. With a boy of eight across the street.

Furthermore, she didn't see what all the fuss was about. As her mom always told her, the female body was a musical instrument "made to be played."

Unhappily, the TV film had inspired a real gang of terrorists who were also religious zealots to abduct her to their Arizona desert commune where they raped her with religious artifacts including a cactus crucifix.

For four media-filled days, Fawn had kept vigil until an Air Force helicopter found the hideout and brought the ravaged victim home.

Horrifying as this was, it was as nothing compared to what happened next. After a week of convalescence and hourly bulletins like those outside Buckingham Palace during times of royal illness, the ladies and gentlemen of the press were invited to the Roberts swimming pool.

"Dawnette will be out to greet you *momentito!*"

A delay beyond the conventional Star Wait was ended by a piercing scream. Nobody seeing Fawn Roberts's demented face would suggest a publicity stunt. Dawnette had disappeared again.

Police, neighbors, and two hundred members of the Dawnette Fan Club searched the woods, knocked on doors, and made daily headlines. A week later, while little Winnie was showing yet another reporter around, he pointed to the corner of the garage. "What's in there?"

"Our old freezer. We don't use it anymore."

"Then why is it plugged in?"

The frozen body of Dawnette Roberts was a princess in

aspic. The distraught mother blamed the terrorists for seeking revenge for their leaders' arrest. She sold exclusive rights to photograph the body in living color for fifty thousand dollars. Only one reporter knew the truth. Dawnette had written a letter. "I'm scared. Mom keeps saying it's great publicity. She says I have to say it hasn't killed my appetite for sex—" She had mailed the letter to Dorrie Bridges and stepped into the freezer.

Dorrie broke the story on television. "Fawn Roberts is a butcher who treats her offspring like meat. There is a hideous justice and a warning to all who sell young flesh like that beautiful child in the freezer."

"Dawnette loved Dorrie Bridges. That's why she addressed her last mortal words to her," the mother sighed. "That's why I brought Wee Winnie to meet her and show her the torch has been passed on." She pushed the child against Lou's groin. "Just look at my baby! Wouldn't she make a wonderful cover story for the *Insider*?"

"Well, I'm new and—"

She kiss-kissed the air. "Why don't you come see us? See how Winnie *lives*. How she *sleeps*! How she *eats*! How she *plays*!" She stooped to embrace her child. "We'll show Mr. Dexter *everything*, won't we, dearest?"

He fled to the men's room where he relieved himself in more ways than one. "Jennie?" he said into the phone.

"Yes—" She sounded pissed off.

"Jennie Bliss Sternholdt?"

"Yes, Lou—" As long as he lived, he would never understand women.

"Where, may I inquire, is the loving woman who sent me off to war about an hour ago? What's wrong?"

"Nothing's wrong."

"Did I do something? Leave the seat up?" His ex-wife the princess never forgave him for that.

"I don't believe we're having this conversation."

"I was only kidding."

"You're always kidding."

"Okay, okay. Let's start again. 'Jennie, baby, this is your born-again Bogie, speaking to you from the—' "

"Don't call me baby!"

"Maybe it would be better if I don't call you at all."

"Suit yourself." Something was up. It would have to wait. The decibel level outside had suddenly risen.

Andrew Van Kennan reminded Lou of Edith Sitwell's description of Lord Darnley, whose hands were "like silk gloves filled with wet sand." The classical perfection of his features was as out of date as his view of the world. Born as World War II began, he was twenty years out of sync. In the Depression years, his pale and perfect face might have made him into another Robert Taylor on screen. In the ethnic sixties and seventies of Elliott Gould and Jack Nicholson and Charles Bronson, his beauty was nauseating and his personality didn't help.

In his function as Dorrie Bridges's office manager and general factotum, his power had increased in direct proportion to hers. Anyone who made the mistake of calling him Dorrie's secretary could be sure of never getting through to her again.

His blond hair disheveled, his Italian cotton suit creased, he looked almost human. "Dorrie! Is she here?"

"What's happening?" The cry spread with the gleeful expectation of being an eyewitness to the unexpected. The same crowd had gathered at Calvary and on the outskirts of Vesuvius and across from Parkland Hospital in Dallas.

"Where is she?" A stern young woman grabbed Andrew by the elbow and shoved a microphone in his face.

Andrew looked as if he were going into surgery without benefit of anesthesia. "She'll be here."

"Something's happened, hasn't it? What's happened to Dorrie Bridges?"

"Give me a break—" Andrew tried to shake free.

"This way!" Lou straight-armed a path backward into the men's room and slammed the door.

"I can't understand it. She said she'd be here." When Van Kennan went to pick Dorrie up for the party, he had found a note instead. "She went out to the beach house. A little sun. A little quiet. She said she'd meet me here—"

"Why don't we call her—"

"Why don't you stick it in your ear!" The beach house had no phone. It was isolated on a small peninsula that became an island at high tide.

The door threatened to cave in. Van Kennan climbed out the window, Lou after him. "So then, where the hell is she? Maybe she did elope with Sonny Syntagma."

In the restaurant kitchen, the pastry chef was putting the final touches on the thirty-tiered birthday cake. In addition to the usual caviar, shrimp, roast beef, and salmon, there was a Tennessee collation of ham, yams, fried chicken, collards, and red-eye gravy. One grill was reserved for lamb chops for those on the Scarsdale Diet.

"Quit following me, turkey!"

"What are we going to tell the people?" Lou had sipped too much Jack Daniel's. It was beginning to leak out of him. He swayed against the other man.

"Fuck off."

To the frustrated guests, Andrew Van Kennan was both class and charm. Nodding to the woman with the microphone, he apologized. "Sorry I couldn't stop. Nature called." A pause for the laugh track. "I'm certain Dorrie wants me to apologize for her lateness. As we all know, she doesn't make a late entrance on purpose. Like some people." More laugh track.

"Just tell us where she is and cut the bullshit!"

"Dorrie took the day off. She spent the day at Trancas. I just checked the Pacific Coast Highway. There's been a tie-up. An oil truck—" He rolled his eyes upward.

The crowd moaned, appreciatively.

"I should have stayed home and watched 'Mork and Mindy,'" a petulant voice complained in the neighborhood of Lou's chest.

"I, for one, am glad you're here," he said gallantly. She looked up at him, her mouth open in a rehearsal of a smile, a walk-through of a smile, a zephyr of Dentyne rising while she tried to decide if he was worth the effort of a full no-holds-barred smile. "What do you do?"

Clearly she hoped he would be a famous producer, director, screenwriter, or powerful agent with a direct link to fame.

"I'm West Coast Entertainment Editor of *The Weekly Insider*." It was like pumping air into a balloon. Her breasts swelled up and out of her bodice like muffins baking in his Aunt Fanny's kitchen in The Bronx. "And you are—?"

She had a Suzy Starlet name and she was an actress though of course she didn't expect him to have heard of her. Yet! So far all she had done was two pilots.

"Which airlines!"

Her fierce little terrier face reminded him of Jennie Bliss Sternholdt's constant warning not to make jokes. "I'm sorry. Go on."

And an *Our Town* showcase at UCLA in which she played Emily, of course.

"Of course." The Jack Daniel's was now pouring down his throat like spring rain. Her breasts looked to him now like separate cream custards. He wondered if she would take out one, just one. He wouldn't even touch it. Well, maybe one small feel.

"The only trouble is—" she was saying. The Starlet's Lament. He struggled mightily to keep his eyes in focus. His head pitched forward. He wanted to rest it in her cleavage. "If only—" she was continuing. Something about finding the right agent and the right part. "My shrink—" He had only to nod while she iterated the assurances given by her astrologer, holistic coach, and a quiz in *Cosmopolitan* that she had star quality. "If only—"

They were back to "If only—"

"If only what?"

If only an important newspaper like the *Insider* would do a little story about her. "You know what I'm saying?"

He knew what she was saying.

"Do I turn you on," she wanted to know.

Turn him on. In the dyslexia of his mind, he was living in a place called *Fornicalia*. He was a goddam leaky faucet, never entirely turned off. *Fornicalia, Here I Come!* On the Sunset Strip a billboard demanded he think pink. At a health bar his salad was served with phallic loaves of bread punctured with hot oozing butter.

Last weekend a neighbor's toddler had offered him some chewing gum with liquid centers. "Want some cum gum?" A porno movie house advertised *Beavers of the North Country* for three days before discovering it had booked a Jacques Cousteau nature flick in error.

With Jennie in the crowded Saks elevator, the operator had asked a hesitant brunette, "Do you want to go down?" When the passengers including Jennie laughed, the woman blithely nodded. "Only if you say you love me."

Jennie. Why had she turned against him? He did not understand women. Nausea rose in his throat. He felt like the old joke about Hell, where everyone stands chin-high in shit. *Don't make waves.* He held himself upright. Laid back in the Fornicalia style but definitely upright.

"What's the matter? You sick?" Suzy Starlet asked.

As if things weren't bad enough, coming through the crowd in his direction was the final killer blow to his shattered ego. Peter St. John, the runty little pisspot of an Englishman with the dear boy wrists who fucked like a stoat and wrote rings around everyone and was also several years Lou's junior. And incidentally, was the correspondent who had replaced him in Moscow.

In his present condition Lou knew that if he came face to face with Peter St. John, he might do something really disgraceful like piss his pants or burst into tears.

"Look, dear—" He backed away from Suzy Starlet. "Let's —let's talk about this some other time. Okay?"

Her withering glance confirmed that he was a wimp and she had wasted her time after all. "Stick it in your ear."

If Lou had any sense, he'd stick it down his throat. Back to the men's room. A moment's release and he was dialing Jennie's number. "What now?" she wanted to know.

"No sign of Dorrie."

"Oh, really?"

"I'm coming home."

"No—"

"What do you mean, 'No'?"

"I told you. Go to your own place."

"Ice cream. Don't you want some ice cream? You love ice cream. Don't you remember—?"

"Not tonight, Lou."

"It's Bogie—I need you—" He whistled through dry lips. "Remember? You were Baby. You said if I needed you, I should whistle—"

"Lou—" She was being patient.

"You—"

"I'm into distancing tonight. I need space."

"I need you—"

There was a dire pause. She took a deep and audible breath and let it rip. "You're like all men! You act like you're the only person who has troubles. I'm tired of hearing about your rotten luck and your lousy job and your crazy wife and—"

"You're really tough, aren't you—"

"You bet your sweet ass I'm tough. I've got calluses on my calluses."

"Okay, so you're tough. You can lick any man in the joint—and have!"

"Jokes. Why are guys your age always joking? Life is not a joke!"

So why was he dying laughing? *Au contraire,* life was a

joke and he the biggest joke of all. Hiding in the men's room from his younger successor, pleading with a woman who was on a Humphrey Bogart trip to let him into her space.

"Please, Jennie. I need to be with you. I'm not looking to get laid."

"That's not the point. God, you don't understand anything!" She was right. He did not understand. "Okay. Forget it."

"Look, Lou. I relate to you. I dig your body. I dig your mind. I'm sorry you got thrown out of Moscow. I'm sorry you're writing shit for a living. But suddenly—I've got a little trip of my own."

"Is it me? Am I the problem?" She couldn't be wanting to marry him so soon, not after two weeks. Or was she tired of playing Bogart games? In this town the women made the moves. The first time he saw her was in Swensen's Westwood. He had just bought a double cappuccino chocolate cone with sprinkles when this tawny creature in the Annie Hall fedora assaulted him. "Mind if I lick your cone, stranger?"

Her pink tongue had darted at him through moist red lips like an erotic party favor. He had gallantly bought her a cone of her own and, after a tour of the book bins, jeans racks, and movie lobbies of Westwood Village, walked her back to her apartment on Lindbrook.

"No, Lou. Why would you think you're the problem? That's some ego you have."

Correction. He had no ego left at all. "Please, Jen—" The men's room was crowding up. "Okay—I'll—call you tomorrow—" He had to get out. Into the fresh air.

The parking valet was incredulous. "You're leaving?"

"That's why I want my car."

"But Dorrie didn't get here yet."

"My car, please—"

He had bought the white XKE Jaguar at a Sepulveda lot because it was cheap and because it was like one he had driven in England during the Swinging Sixties.

"Mister? You look weird—"

"Be back in a minute." Lou lurched around the corner of the restaurant and threw up neatly, without splashing, one of the few remaining skills of which he could be proud. He stood for several moments waiting for his body to stop heaving and the ringing in his ears to go away.

"Hey—*you!*" The girl was tense with determination, a California *Pube*, one of the fierce and floating army of pre-adolescents who swarm over places where something big is happening. This one looked about twelve, her face a wizened mask of malnutrition. She wore Coke can tabs on her fingers, a Rod Stewart T-shirt, and frayed jeans with a pink satin vagina appliquéd in cherries at the crotch.

"Yes—?"

"Are you somebody?" She stabbed at him with her autograph book. It was green plaid and had a quilted kilted kitten on the cover.

"Another time—" he muttered.

"Come *on*. I ain't got all night!"

Caught up in her desperation, he searched his throbbing brain for a name to please her. *Humphrey Bogart?* This gentle bud might not know who Humphrey Bogart was. Besides, Humphrey Bogart was dead.

"Lou *Dexter?*" The Pube recoiled. "What *is* this?" Her ball-point pen thrust in his hand, Lou had impulsively signed his own autograph. With the rage of a child who expects toys and finds socks, she clawed out the page and threw it at him. "Thanks for zip, turkey. You're a fucking nobody!"

From the mouths of babes. In his depressed state he had to get away fast, before Dorrie Bridges showed up. In a way he was glad Jennie Bliss Sternholdt needed space tonight. He needed space, too. He would go back to his hotel room and sleep. Tomorrow he would decide what to do tomorrow.

His car was standing unattended. As he drove off, the parking valet ran after him shouting and waving his arms. "Catch up with you next time!" Lou called. How he got himself to the Freeway he didn't know. Nor which Freeway. Nor what direction he was heading. *Call me pisher!* If Herman Melville were writing today, he would set *Moby Dick* in Southern Fornicalia and make Ishmael a man like himself. Good old Herman. He wondered what Kevin Marceau would say if he wrote up tonight's party in Melville style. If Marceau ever even heard of *Moby Dick,* he probably thought it was an adult sex aid. The notion gave him comfort.

A bug touched his ear. He shook his head. It came back. He brushed at it with his hand and found himself in the grip of another hand. "Lou?" Suzy Starlet had stashed herself in the narrow jump seat. "Don't be mad."

"I'm not mad. It's a good thing you're here. I'd be on this Freeway till doomsday. Where do you live?" From the look of her, there would be no problem about letting him into her space. She climbed in beside him, fumbled in her bag for a phial, and dry-swallowed a handful of pills.

"You got anything to smoke?" She lay against his arm. He indicated the glove compartment. She fished out a crushed package of Camels. "I said smoke, man. A joint."

"Sorry. I don't do drugs." Another sign of old age.

Reaching behind her back, she unhooked her wired bra and spun it around her head like a slingshot. "Wheeeeeeeeeee—" she cried before letting it fly into the air. A car behind them skidded wildly and then straightened out. Another nutball. Why couldn't he find a nice quiet girl who liked books and records!

"Sit still, dammit!"

She took one of the Camel cigarettes. "Okay, so I'll get cancer. Got a light?"

He pushed in the car lighter.

"This an English car?" Her hand had found his inner thigh.

"Okay, sexy. Cool it." He removed her hand. "Let's get this buggy home."

She pulled out the lighter. It was cold. "Got matches?"

"Be careful," he warned, giving her a Ma Raison matchbook.

She struck one match and used it to ignite the rest. The matchbook exploded into a fiery torch. "You first!" She thrust it at his face.

"You crazy?" He batted it out of her hand. It fell past his thighs to the floor. She dove across his lap to retrieve it. In trying to stamp out the flames, his foot grazed the brake. He could hear himself screaming as the car bucked and swerved. A passing driver tapped his horn and made the A-OK sign. The son of a bitch thought he was getting a blow job.

In control of the wheel at last, he grabbed the girl's hair and yanked her upright in the seat beside him.

"You're hurting me!" she howled.

He pulled into an emergency parking lane and opened her door. "Out!"

She threw her arms around his neck. "Let's get it together. You know what I'm saying?"

"Out before I kill you with my bare hands."

"I get it now. You're *gay*—"

He shook her so hard, her teeth rattled. When he let her go, she turned on the radio as if nothing were amiss. "You get FM?"

"*. . . Dorrie Bridges's beach house near Trancas . . .*"

"Ugh . . . talk!" She turned the knob. "I want disco!"

He lost several precious seconds finding the station. "*. . . birthday festivities at Ma Raison. . . . To recap, superstar media person Dorrie Bridges missing and feared dead in fire stay tuned for update and now back to disco—all r-i-i-i-g-ht!*"

All r-i-i-i-ght? What the hell did that mean! *All r-i-i-i-i-ght,* a woman is missing and feared dead, everybody dance?

The poor little bitch. They'd got her. Whatever that big story she was chasing, whoever the Biggie she was trying to nail, they'd got her first. He could see it all. A setup like what had happened to him in Russia. *Meet me alone where we can talk undisturbed.* She had fallen into the oldest trap, lured by the scent of truth. As many an investigative reporter had discovered, the truth could make you dead.

Where did that leave him? Sitting in the middle of nowhere because of oafish pride and a giant-size case of self-pity. Whatever his feelings about *The Weekly Insider,* he was first and foremost a reporter. At that very moment he should be at Ma Raison, asking questions, picking up reactions, trying to get some leads.

It was four years since he'd covered a story. He could feel the old excitement, the old machinery gearing up, the dormant juices pumping through his veins. Old dogs don't need to be taught new tricks because they know all the old tricks.

"You know Trancas?"

"I'm not sure." She grinned archly. "Why don't you hum it for me—"

He caught her soft white-bread Starlet face in his strong rye-bread Bogart hand. "Get me to Trancas." He squeezed her cheeks so hard that her mouth burst open pink and damp as a Greek fig. "Get me to Trancas fast!" As her eyes stared wide, his tongue traced the inner lining of her lips before pushing through her teeth to the panting cave beyond.

"Get me to Trancas now!" He growled into the walls and roof and floor, jabbing, darting, testing all the surfaces before withdrawing his tongue and coming to rest with his lips pressed commandingly to hers. "You know what I'm saying?"

It was Friday morning and just about time for the *Roper Valley Echo*, "East Tennessee's Fastest Growing Weekly Newspaper," to go to press. Dora June Bridges had worked through the night and was enjoying a voluptuous yawn when she noticed Jesus Man Suggs cutting a path through the press room like Moses himself at the Red Sea.

"Jim Ed, just look at what the cat threw up!" she observed with all the smart sophistication of her sixteen-going-on-seventeen years, a sophistication she employed primarily for the benefit of Jim Ed Loomis who was working beside her at the ancient makeup stone.

"That man's got more nerve than a turkey gobbler on Christmas Eve," Jim Ed bristled with the fury of the true defender caught unprepared for combat. His hands were full. His entire adolescent height and weight were concentrated on holding a heavy metal page form in position while Dorrie inked it with a hand brayer, smoothed a sheet of newsprint on the surface, and hammered a wooden planer across it to achieve a proof.

"Read it real careful, darlin'!" Grandpa Jeb bellowed from between the twin Mergenthaler linotypes that he had just switched off after a night of setting type. In the deafening silence that followed, his next chore was to coax the old Miehle flatbed cylinder press into a congenial readiness to print. He shifted a five-stick wad of Juicy Fruit to the lonely space on the right side of his jaw which gave him the comfort if not the bite of the forbidden plug tobacco.

The tympan sheet needed changing. He filled the ink trough and dragged the cartons of newsprint into position for the first press run, all the while keeping a tender eye on Dorrie's sorrel mane braided down her back and caught in a red rubberband.

She was his one, his only, his precious grandchild but he knew her high-and-mighty disdain for the Social Notes Pages and that whatever she felt, why Jim Ed was even more fierce and proud about feeling exactly the same way. Neither one of them could get it through their heads that stories about President Johnson were real fine and stories about student riots in Berkeley, California, and civil rights marches in Selma, Alabama, made real fine reading, but it was the Social Notes and Church News that attracted the local readers, especially the womenfolk, and it was the womenfolk attracted the advertisers, and without the advertisers there would be no *Roper Valley Echo*.

As usual of a Friday morning he was as nervous as a

longtail cat in a room full of rocking chairs. He glanced at the electric wall clock above the faded Martha White "Hot Rize" calendar for 1964. He kept meaning to take the damn thing down. Seven o'clock. Right on schedule. All that remained was to get the paper printed, dried, folded, counted, and stacked for the boy carriers who would be shrieking up the alley on their bicycles the minute school let out.

From where he was working, he did not see the intruder until Jesus Man spoke. "Good morning, neighbors. Praise God!"

Ever since Buford Suggs had forsaken seasonal labor for the riper pickings in the orchards of the Lord, he had become a man of fine impatience. To waste his time was to throw a spanner in the Lord's machinery. Nor could he truly understand how anybody, especially a young female of the susceptible teen-age, could ignore him as Dora June was ignoring him right now. Not with his saintly smile. Not in his white drip-dry suit that glowed in the shadowy tent when he preached, a fortuitous result of metallic threads in the polyester fabric and a judicious baby blue spotlight.

"Dora June, I'd 'preciate a minute of your time."

Dora June sucked in her breath. Slippery as okra, that man was. She knew why he had come. He would just have to wait. Jim Ed's eyes covered her with adoration, like fresh cream butter on a hot biscuit. Early this very morning, he had presented her with a bar of headline type. The type was raised and backward but when she pressed it against her arm, it said, I LOVE YOU, DARLING.

"Sorry to keep you waiting, Brother Suggs. As you can see, we're about to go to press!"

Grandpa Jeb sallied forward long enough to tip his Coca-Cola baseball cap courteously and nod. Dorrie had surely slipped one past him. Her signed editorial had stirred things up some. Nevertheless this was a newspaper and while he damned near died when he read her piece, he would, like

Voltaire, defend to the death her right to say it. That one time, anyways, if not again.

"Help yourself to some coffee and doughnuts, Preacher. Out yonder in the Classifieds."

"Thank you kindly, but I figure to wait right here and watch Dora June at her work. You don't mind that, now do you, Dora June?"

"Don't blame me if you get ink on your clothes." She was loop-legged tired and she had things on her mind. Momma, for one, had been acting peculiar, telling her she wanted to have a little talk and then finding an excuse not to, including dropping bacon fat on her foot. Jim Ed, for another, was trying to make her a prisoner of his love, acting pained and left out when she locked herself in the shed to write her stories and when she spent hours and hours gathering local farm news for the *Nashville Times* "Country Roundup" column that paid a dollar an inch to stringers.

"You're too ambitious, Dora June," Jim Ed frequently said.

"Yes."

"The way I see it, you'll take over the *Echo* when Grandpa Jeb dies and I'll teach comparative literature at Tennessee Eastern and we'll be happy as bugs in a rug."

More than Momma or Jim Ed—or Jesus Man Suggs—was the botulism scandal that had started in Nashville and looked to be spreading statewide. As usual, the night before the *Echo* went to press, they had worked straight through. These were the last few minutes for making final corrections and she and Jim Ed had their hands full. This didn't stop her mind from angering with Grandpa over the front page.

Where she had wanted FARM HAND DIES HERO DEATH IN VIETNAM, Grandpa Jeb said it didn't count as news because LeRoy Burns was a nigger, and put the high school honor roll in its place. Then, there was her new article about the "Jesus, the Beatles and Long Hair" controversy inspired by Brother

Sugg's sermon, and which brought in more than fifty pieces of reader correspondence. Mostly for Jesus and against the Beatles.

"Controversy," she had beamed.

"Bad for business," Grandpa had rejoined.

Her piece had mysteriously gone into overset during the half hour she had gone next door to Min's Truck Stop for supper with her mother, who worked the midnight shift.

Worse yet, the botulism deaths at the Nashville Orphan School had been reduced to one paragraph and used as filler on the Farm Equipment Sales page despite the fact that it was front-page above the fold in the *Nashville Times* and hinted at high-level government scandal.

You could tell something was rotten when Senator Bob Joe Bingham interrupted his golf long enough to come weeping and sniffing over the tiny small caskets and whispering into the microphone brought to the cemetery by his own secretary: "We are as Rachel weeping for our children and we will not be comforted."

There was more to the story than some poisoned cans of bonita tuna fish. If the *Nashville Times* ran it front-page, why couldn't they?

"They're looking for scandal," Grandpa reminded her. "We're looking to stay alive." He had grown up in the Great Depression and could still conjure up the taste of Poor Boy Pie. Although the general economy was good, not too much of it drifted into the southern mountains. To supplement the *Echo*'s meager profits, he did most all of the other local printing: business cards and stationery, auction handbills, trespass notices, wedding invitations, flyers for Kurtz's Dry Goods and A-1 Auto Repair plus the Roper High *Lariat* and all three church newsletters, which were more trouble than they were worth but were his civic duty.

Jesus Man showed no visible inclination to leave the press room. He hovered over Dorrie like a great white eagle ready to strike. Grandpa deserted his station for the moment. "Come on, Preacher. Let's us go get us a cup of coffee." To Dora June, he repeated, "Read it careful now. Don't want Lorinda Crull comin' in here with a shotgun."

The girl nodded her assurance. "No need to fret, Grandpa." He still worried she might do one of her little jokes, like the time she wrote a formal birth notice about Vonnie Mapes's new litter of pigs. That was last summer. She'd grown up since then.

. . . a shimmering satalustra gown, featuring a Queen Anne neckline, full bishop sleeves with French chantilly lace and a chapel sweep train . . .

Jim Ed grinned at her the way he did the times she let him slip his bare hand inside her blouse. "You'll be a much prettier bride than Rose Edna Crull."

And a much older bride, too, if she could help it. Not for a long time would there be a fingertip veil of French illusion attached to seed pearl Camelot headpiece. Nor a radiant bride carrying a cascade of yellow roses surrounded by baby's breath—

"Baby's breath? Now that is what I call significant—" Jim Ed sniggered.

If he expected his beloved to laugh, he was doomed to disappointment. Her eyes were reading but her mind was on the day ahead. She had to iron a fresh blouse for school, practice her French verbs, and phone in her farm news to the *Nashville Times*. This week she stood to make herself six to eight dollars, for sure. Soon she would have enough money to enroll in the Famous Writers School in Westport, Connecticut. She had cut their advertisement out of *Life* magazine and pasted it on the back inside cover of her spiral notebook as a constant reminder of her goal to become a famous writer, herself.

Pasted on the inside front cover was the letter from Thomas B. Jennings, Managing Editor of the *Nashville Times*, welcoming her services as a rural correspondent and encouraging her to keep her eyes open for big stories for which there would be "commensurate rewards and compensations."

At times, she prayed for a plane to crash or an earthquake to swallow up the town so she could be the only reporter on the scene, and then she would be ashamed of herself for wanting to profit from death and destruction.

"I'll walk you home," Jim Ed declared when they had locked up the Social Page.

"You go on. I've got to have a word with Jesus Man."

"Don't you go stompin' him to glory. You look meaner than an Arkansas mule," Jim Ed teased.

Out front in Classifieds, Loretta was shouting into the phone. The old Bakelite radio on her desk looked like a decayed fudge cake. Through the static came Roger Miller's "King of the Road."

"Brother Suggs?" Whether his head was bowed in sleep or prayer she did not know nor did she care. All that she wanted at this moment was to get her poor body home.

Jesus Man took her two hands in his and looked at them as if he had never seen hands before. "Such pretty hands should be doin' the Lord's work instead of the Devil's."

The radio had changed from music to news. ". . . two more orphans die of botulism . . . unconfirmed rumor that the company that sold the defective cans to the Nashville orphanage is owned by Senator Robert 'Bob Joe' Bingham, who could not be reached for comment. . . ."

"Praise God!" Jesus Man raised his eyes skyward.

Where was God when orphans were dying of the botulism? Why wasn't God's lightning coming down and striking those responsible? She stared disdainfully at Jesus Man until he dropped her hands. "You want to see me?"

"Dear child—"

"If it's about my editorial—"

"The Beatles are the Devil's own messengers!"

"Because of their *hair?* That's not logical, Brother Suggs, and you know it."

"God himself has told me, Sister Dora June. The Beatles are part of the Communist conspiracy to *deni*grate, to *dese*crate, to *de*generate fine Christian children."

Dorrie's editorial entitled JESUS HAD A BEATLES HAIRCUT had run a week after Jesus Man's revival meeting in Roper. By the time he heard about it, he was across the state in Memphis. She couldn't see why he was excited. There had been scant reaction to the editorial except for a petition at the high school to change the dress code and permit longer hair. Only one reader complained—Aunt Belle Kinkaid, who was crazier than a screech owl and beginning to look like her brood hens.

"The Beatles are not Communists. They're English."

He gazed at her with pity. "The Devil works in devious ways. You have but to look at the Beatles and know that they are Communists. Yes, *Communists.* And *Jews.*"

She had been raised to be courteous. "They are not Jews."

"Aha, young woman. Where are your eyes? Have you looked at Ringo Starr's nose? Now, if that ain't a Hebrew nose, then praise *God,* I don't know what it is."

A primal yawn contorted her face. Tears of exhaustion fogged her eyes. "I'm sorry, Brother Suggs. I've got to get some sleep. Thank you for calling by."

Before she could prevent it, he clasped her hands in his once again. *"Pray* with me, Dora June!"

"Let me go!"

"Pray for forgiveness."

"And you pray for understanding!" He was making her mad. "All I said was that Jesus had long hair and so do the Beatles."

He pulled her closer. Stale sweat assailed her. At this close range she could see tobacco stains on his teeth, sleep crumbs on his eyelids, and scabs of scurf through the crew-cut nap of sandy hair. "Devil talk. The Devil has got your tongue." His eyes bore into hers as did his hips, grinding now and bumping against her, a hardness like a rolling pin battering against her. "Lilith! Woman of evil—"

Politeness went just so far before exasperation stepped in. "Horse manure!" She pushed him aside and hurried into the street. Aunt Belle Kinkaid was pulling into Min's Truck Stop Diner to deliver fresh eggs. "Mornin', Miz Kinkaid."

"Mornin', Dora June." The old woman smiled, a battered man's fedora shading her eyes. The smile was not for Dorrie. "Well, now, if it ain't Reverend Suggs. You learning this girl the truth about Jesus?"

"Just doin' the Lord's work, ma'am. Praise God."

Aunt Belle pointed to the woman in a cotton head scarf slumped in the passenger seat of her pickup. "This here's my daughter, Lil. Come to visit a spell—"

"Now, Momma!" The woman's voice warned. She ducked her head and slumped even lower in the seat until only the head scarf showed.

Dorrie seized the opportunity to shake Jesus Man and do Aunt Belle a Christian service. "I know Aunt Belle wants to tell you how much she enjoyed your sermon, Brother Suggs—"

As she walked swiftly past the pickup, the younger woman raised her head and stared straight at her. There was a lot of hurting in Lil's eyes and something strangely familiar. She couldn't think what it was. She was so bone tired that if she didn't lie down, she would fall down.

It was just another six months to summer vacation. By then she'd have enough money to take the Famous Writers correspondence course and some left over to take the bus into Nashville and go meet Mr. Jennings. She had never seen the inside of a big-city newspaper.

The distance between the *Echo* and the small frame house back of Main Street was less than a mile. About halfway there, Aunt Belle Kinkaid pulled up beside her. "Hop in."

Grateful, Dorrie obeyed, scrooching into the cab beside Lil. "Ma—you promised—" Lil hid her face in Aunt Belle's shoulder.

"Never you mind, Lil. I know you don't want folks to know you're visitin'. Bein' rude to Brother Suggs like that. Whatever he must think, I'd hate to know."

"But—"

"Now, hush up. I'm just provin' to Dora June that a good Christian can perform a Christian act of kindness to a sinner woman who wallows in smut—"

Dorrie's head was so heavy, it fell forward. She fought to keep her eyes open until she could reach the sweet cool of her bed. From circumstance, her eyes dimly focused on Lil's clasped hands. They were smooth of skin, the nails long and skillfully shaped and lacquered, a matched diamond engagement ring and wedding band bigger than the ones in Levy's Fine Jewelry & Repair, and a slender watch like the ones in the magazines on her wrist. You didn't have to be James Bond to see she didn't keep hens for a living.

"Y'all come out and see us, now," Aunt Belle Kinkaid said as Dorrie got out.

"Momma—*please*—" Lil whimpered.

"Just being *polite*, Lil. Don't worry yourself. She's not comin' all the way out to our place."

That was for sure, Dorrie sighed. Nothing worse than mother and daughter at each other's throats. She tiptoed into the darkened house. Mallie's door was closed. There was cold fried chicken and slaw on the kitchen table. If Mallie didn't eat her meal at the diner, she was allowed to tote it home. More often than not, at two or three in the morning when she usually ate, some lonely trucker would treat her to supper for the pleasure of her company. A handsome woman with a ripe body that gave more contours to her waitress uniform than the designer intended, she took pride in two things: that she worked hard to support herself and her fatherless child and that she looked much too young to have a sixteen-year-old daughter.

By habit, Dorrie stepped out of her shoes, unbuttoned her skirt, and shrugged off her blouse, enjoying the nakedness of bra and briefs before slipping into the pink flannel wrapper she had made on the portable Singer that nearly lost her a finger when the needle jumped.

Her own room was little more than a storage porch tacked onto the kitchen, just wide enough for a raw frame bed and dresser. The old Kelvinator coughed, burped, and farted sparks from its bottom, warnings of explosion Dorrie expected but hadn't come yet. She took up the milk bottle in both hands, enjoying the cool on her palms, and drank long, convulsive gulps.

"Now, ain't that a pretty sight?" The man was ass naked, his body skin pale and patched with bramble hair. His face, neck, and left arm a fried okra, the trademark of long-haul truckers who drive with their arm out the window.

"Jerry Lee—get the hell back in here!" Mallie in a chenille bathrobe pushed the man back into the darkened room, slammed the door, and faced her daughter. "I'm sorry, darlin'."

Dora June put on her pink flannel wrapper.

Tears streamed down Mallie's face. "It's what I've been tryin' to tell you, honey. I'm getting married, Dorrie." She fumbled for her daughter's hand and squeezed it. "I've been lonely too long."

That wasn't exactly the case, the lonely part, but, still, fourteen years was a long time to be a widow and especially seeing as how Mallie hardly got to know Dorrie's father before he went off and got himself killed and in fact would never talk about him except to look sad and lonely if anyone commiserated with her being a widow woman and so young.

"Tell me you're glad for me, Dorrie."

"Of course I'm glad for you, Momma." Having a man

paying the rent, Mallie wouldn't have to be working so hard. Maybe she could quit the diner entirely and stay home and make pies. It would make things easier for Dorrie, too. As soon as she finished the Famous Writers course, she'd be leaving Roper to become a famous writer and maybe work in Nashville or even New York, Jim Ed or no Jim Ed.

"His name's Jerry Lee Perkins."

"That's real nice." She yawned. "I'm sorry, Momma. I really mean it, honest. A real nice name. We're going to get along real fine."

"Oh, baby—" Mallie clutched her into a fierce embrace, pressing her streaming face into the girl's braided hair.

"What's *ailing* you, Momma? It's going to be *fine.*"

"We're leaving Roper, darlin'. He's taking me down to Mississippi. Pass Christian. On the Gulf. He's got a house there and a fishing boat and he's going to leave his baby brother to drive the long hauls and—"

"But, Momma—I can't leave here—" She had everything planned. She couldn't pick up and go.

Mallie's face told her she wasn't going anywhere.

"He's a young man, darlin'. Twenty-seven years old. Why he wants me, only the good Lord knows. He wants children and a new life together. Please try to understand."

Dorrie had read enough stories and magazines to know she should be feeling pain and anguish but all she could think about was the need to lie down and sleep.

Mallie followed her to the sleep porch. "Don't turn from me, darlin'—"

"We'll talk about it later."

"You'll be happy stayin' with Grandpa until you and Jim Ed get married and set up in your own place—"

Dorrie lowered the rattan blinds and fell on the narrow bed, pulling the patchwork quilt over her head. "Later, Momma—"

"Dorrie, precious? Baby darlin'? Listen—there's something else—something I've got to tell you—"

"We'll talk later, Momma—"

As sweet sleep gathered her into a soft, caressing mist, she remembered that Aunt Belle Kinkaid's daughter Lil had got her picture in the *Roper Valley Echo* on the occasion of her appointment as social secretary to Senator Bob Joe Bingham and that she had heard whispers at the diner about Lil being his lady love, too, and that there'd be hell to pay if her husband found out.

Lou Dexter's heart was not in his work. It was in his mouth
along with the bad taste of fear. At this precise time he'd
have gladly traded in his press card to be in Jennie Bliss
Sternholdt's king-size bed with Jennie Bliss Sternholdt's fierce
ficus standing guard and Jennie Bliss Sternholdt's bare and
brawny leg clamped across his lap like a seat belt.

Viewed from the doorless doorway of the Navy helicopter,
Dorrie's tiny house looked like the grand opening of a super-

market. Powerful searchlights crisscrossed the steaming hash-brown ruin of a house. Tinny voices crackled from speakers. Colored flares shot into the sky like firecrackers and fell into the black Pacific waves.

The copter banked hard as if trying to shake a pebble out of a shoe, adding a foamy head to his nausea. He did not appreciate the sight of dead bodies, especially burned bodies and least of all the gingerbread corpses of baked females. If he had been on the Rouen beat that May 30 of 1431, he'd have called in sick and let someone else cover Joan of Arc at the stake.

Some of his favorite women had died in fires. Zelda Fitzgerald taking the ultimate revenge on Scott. Linda Darnell trying to rescue her niece, who was already safe. They broke his heart. He did, however, enjoy the fiery justice meted out to evil women in fiction. Miss Havisham getting hers in *Great Expectations,* Mrs. Danvers in *Rebecca,* Mr. Rochester's wife in *Jane Eyre.*

A great-aunt he had never met had died in the sinking of the Morro Castle! A veteran reporter who befriended him on his first job as a copyboy had covered both the Cocoanut Grove disaster in Boston and the famous circus fire in Hartford and shown him the pictures that were too gruesome to use.

Now he was the veteran reporter and it was this cunning that had brought him to the scene of the disaster ahead of any other newsperson. Within moments of hearing the radio bulletin, he had realized the story was not at Ma Raison, where everyone was waiting for Dorrie Bridges, but at her beach house, where she was last known to have been.

"Who the hell are you?" the officer in charge greeted him.

In other circumstances it was a simple enough question. In California the problem of who you were was not to be answered lightly. He could not, like his snot-nose daughter in her forty-dollar Adidas, inform this particular authority figure that he was trying very hard to find out who he was.

"Dexter. Lucas Jay—"

"Credentials."

He had tough-talked his way onto the chopper with a defunct Navy press card. The only defense being an offense, he demanded, "Have you found the body? What caused it? Arson? Any statement you'd care to make, sir?"

Lou held out his folded clutch of paper as if he were Moses taking notes on the Mount. The officer was not impressed. "This operation is off-limits to civilians. Including the press."

Stretchers and body bags lay on the ground nearby. Some half-dozen men were working in the rubble, the searchlights providing intermittent beams of light.

"Fine job you're doing, sir." From the looks of it, these guys couldn't find a beer can on a Saturday night.

Captain Queeg's culture clone evidently did not respond to flattery. "You're not supposed to be here. It's restricted."

"That's funny, it doesn't look like a country club."

"Move it, mister—" The officer jabbed his finger in the direction of the helicopter whose pilot took it as a signal to lift off. "Come back, you motherfucker—"

Lou's eyes were sympathetic. "Good help is hard to find."

The officer looked at him as if he were a cold fried egg. "You are under arrest."

In an age of napalm and industrial wastes, this fire at least had the style to smell good, the seasoned wood mingling with the salt air like an old-fashioned beach party barbecue. When South Seas cannibals barbecued their enemies for supper, they called it *long pig*. He thought of Dorrie Bridges crisp and brown and dripping juices.

"What's the matter? You sick?"

Before he could reply, an agitated sailor interrupted. "Sir. We've found something!" Lou's sphincter lurched. He had seen all manner of corpses in all manner of conditions. The sight still sickened him.

All that remained of Dorrie's beach house were three stone steps. The roof and walls had caved in. The gutted interior was like a Samuel Beckett set, a bleak monochrome of formless lumps and silent figures.

"There!"

A sailor holding a huge pair of tongs like a divining rod had cleared the area around a charred object.

"Holy Christ, it looks like a human head!" the officer said gleefully. While another sailor held a flashlight, the tongs opened in a wide embrace and moved toward the object of its desire. Lou's horror threatened to strangle him like diphtheria closing his throat. *Schmuck! She can't feel a thing.*

The metal arms closed in with the spastic greed of a carnival gypsy machine. At the carnival, the idea was to maneuver the gypsy's hand to lift the gold cigarette case out of the jelly beans but the gold cigarette case always slipped through. The same thing happened now. The tongs closed in around the treasure and raised it slowly off the ground.

"That's it, sailor—"

The tongs slipped. The object fell to the ground and bounced toward them. The officer screamed. "Back, everyone!"

What did the little turd think it was going to do, bite them? Lou watched in foul fascination as the sailor wiped his hands on his thighs, gripped the handles again, and with a deft motion secured the errant object. "Ready for inspection, sir!"

The son of a bitch was bringing it to them like a cat with a savaged bird. Staring at it, Lou thought he could see Dorrie's dead eyes staring back at him.

"Watch out, you idiot! You'll drop it." From his mouth to God's ears. A break in the floorboards pitched the sailor headlong toward them. The tongs slammed closed, hurling the object at them like a shot put.

Lou's attempted backflip was aborted when his toe caught in his own pants leg. He fell hard, his face smashing into the top stone step just as the cause of his panic landed beside his cheek with a sickening *thwack*. Warm slime splattered him like a "Gong Show" pie. *Oh, God; her head split open!* He clawed at the dreadful stuff, holding his breath, his facial orifices clenched against so much as a drop entering.

Poor bitch, the poor bitch— Sobs gagged in his throat, forcing his mouth open to gasp for air. "Get it off me!" He spat with revulsion. "Please—for God's sake, somebody—" Suddenly he stopped. Suddenly he opened his eyes. Suddenly he licked his lips. Suddenly he scooped his hand into the oozing mess and raised it to his mouth. "It's a melon, you fucking assholes!" he howled. "A melon, you twats." He ripped off chunks of hot charred rind and pitched them at the terrorized rescue team.

"You're under arrest!"

"What for? Identifying a melon? Don't worry. It's one of ours."

"You are interfering with the United States Government."

"Bull*shit*. You're spending taxpayers' money. Where's the body? What caused the fire? What going on—?"

A gun barrel flashed. "I said you are under arrest."

Rule of Survival: Never argue with a waitress carrying hot soup or a jerk with a gun. The search continued until dawn. Net result, a melted typewriter, the wrought-iron frames of two chairs and a sofa, some unidentifiable kitchen utensils, and some bone chips. Except for the melon, the rest was ashes.

The sailors filled the body bags with debris. "We'll run this through the lab," the officer explained.

When the helicopter deposited them at the staging area the Navy had set up on the main road, the waiting press corps were kept at a distance. For the past several hours they had been forced to content themselves with Dorrie's abandoned car. The TV mobile units had photographed it from every angle and in each increasing brightness of the new day. Personalized license plates are a challenge to the imagination in California. Dorrie's was a permutation of Thornton Wilder's *Bridge of San Luis Rey*, ST LURAY. Fascinating as this might be, there was just so much you could do with an automobile.

A reporter recognized him. "Hey, Dexter—it's Lou Dexter. What's going on—?"

"What's the big idea?"

"Where's Dorrie?"

The press corps as one surged toward the landing party.

"Sorry, folks, I'd love to stop and chat—" Two sailors force-marched Lou to a waiting vehicle.

"What'd you do, Dexter? Give us a break!"

"The Chinese got her—" he shouted before the car door slammed. "Correction: a UFO!" He thrust his head out the car window. "Purple. With flashing red lights."

While Lou Dexter languished in Navy detention, the press ran wild with conjecture, speculation, rumor, and anything else they could muster to disguise the fact that there were no hard facts. No body. No signs of a body. No notes of any kind, suicide or ransom. DORRIE DISAPPEARS IN MYSTERY FIRE one headline ran. AMERICA'S MOST HATED WOMAN FEARED DEAD ran another, more greedy for circulation. It didn't take long for the opportunists and crazies to stake out a piece of the action. A Venice psychic said Dorrie had been kidnapped by Manson disciples. She had escaped but was suffering from amnesia. A ninety-year-old shut-in said Dorrie had spoken to her from beyond the River Styx, saying she was happy in the Land of the Dead except that she missed hamburgers and fries.

An English hairdresser just starting on his own in La Jolla described on television how he had personally changed Dorrie's appearance by cutting and frizzing her hair. Though he had sworn not to tell, he felt it his sacred duty to reveal all, including the address of his new salon.

A "Friends of Dorrie" committee offered a fifty-thousand-dollar reward for information leading to her whereabouts, dead or alive. The Los Angeles police accused the Navy of a cover-up. Ma Raison wanted to know who was paying for the birthday party. A TV talking head read an open letter to Dorrie in prime time, concluding with tears in his eyes, "If you're in trouble, Dorrie, don't try to work it out alone. We love you and we want to help you. Call on us, dear. We'll respect your privacy." The phone number he gave was answered by a machine.

It took *The Weekly Insider* lawyers a week to arrange Lou Dexter's release. It coincided with two things. The Navy made its official announcement that there were no human remains in the ashes. *New West* magazine, desperate for an angle, front-covered the old *Tass* photograph of Lou in chains with a blood-red blurb: DID THE KREMLIN TRADE HIS LIFE FOR DORRIE'S?

"That's quite a picture of you." Kevin Marceau was making his regular stopover in the Los Angeles office.

"If you like black eyes and a fat lip. I hear I'm an S and M pinup."

He was trying to be jocular but he wished Marceau would piss off. The *Insider* being a weekly, he had two days to develop a fresh approach to the Dorrie Bridges story. He had the edge of having been on the site during the investigation. After milking that, he had nothing more to reveal than anyone else. He could speculate that she had fled the fire and drowned in the ocean. Maybe one day soon, her body would wash ashore or be picked up by Japanese fishermen. Weak stuff. There'd been enough speculation.

Folders of Dorrie Bridges clippings spilled over his desk. He decided to ignore Marceau. Somewhere in these articles by Dorrie and about her, there was a new angle or even a hint of what may have happened.

"How you going to tackle this?" Marceau asked mildly.

The idea came to him like a newborn colt, a bit shaky on its feet but ready to run. "I want to start my story where Dorrie's story ended."

"How?"

"Thirty—"

Marceau stared at him. "So? She was thirty years old—"

"Don't you see? Thirty! A mystical number. A meaningful

number. Symbolic. Eerie, the more I think about it—" The idea was growing as he spoke.

"Tell me."

"Okay—take the number thirty. Now tell me. What is it that reporters always used to type at the end of a story?"

"Thirty."

"Right. And what did Dorrie Bridges write about in her final column? She said that being thirty marked the end of her youth. Thirty was over the hill. The end. *Finito.* Okay?" He was getting excited as the elements fell into place.

"Okay, so then what?"

"So then, I've been going through the files and I've come up with thirty—count 'em—thirty victims of Dorrie Bridges's ruthless climb to fame and fortune. One for every year of her life. I'm going to track them all down—"

"Some of them are dead."

"Of course, some of them are dead!" Lou was sweating as he improvised. "But think of the survivors, the family, and close friends and how they feel about Dorrie. The media are calling Dorrie Bridges America's most feared and hated woman. Maybe one of her victims put out a contract on her. Maybe one of them bumped her off personally. Maybe I'll get lucky and someone will break down and confess.

"But whatever happens, I am going to illuminate the real Dorrie Bridges through the lives of the thirty people she most affected." Lou Dexter patted the mountain of clippings. "*Variety* called her the hottest journalist in all media. These are her hottest stories. She even disappeared in a mysterious fire. I want to call my series 'Hot Thirty.' You see, it all ties in!"

Lou felt stirrings of professional excitement he had not expected to feel again. He was on to something new. Tom Wolfe and Hunter Thompson had invented the New Journalism of the sixties in which the reporter was more important than the story. Now it was time for another breakthrough in personal journalism. He would create a jigsaw-puzzle portrait of Dorrie Bridges. Each of the pieces would be a minute portrait complete in itself. How he assembled all the parts would result in a whole equal to more than the sum and substance of the pieces.

"Sounds good, Lou."

There was a memorial service the following morning. He would start there. Energy surged through him. He felt the secret smugness of all who survive a more successful rival. She might have been hot but now she was stone cold somewhere. No matter what he had been through, he was alive. And well. And living in Fornicalia. It occurred to him that Dorrie might turn out to be his savior, that her death might start him on a new professional life.

"There's only one problem," Marceau said.

"What's that? Expenses? It wouldn't cost more than a few grand to track these people down. Most of them are still in California." What did it matter? They were rolling in money. "Hot 30" would double their circulation.

Marceau smiled. "The trouble is, you're fired."

"Wasn't expectin' no visitors," Aunt Belle Kinkaid clucked like one of her best hens when Dora June found her behind the house in the shady part of the yard, canning peaches. An ancient fifty-pound lard can skittered on top of the cook stove as she lowered the filled mason jars one at a time into the boiling water, setting them carefully on the slatted wooden rack with at least an inch of space around them.

"Why don't I make myself useful?"

Aunt Belle wiped out the inside of her fruit funnel with her apron before using it to point at a mound of broken glass and fruit. "That's what happened the last time someone 'round here made themselves useful." She glared before continuing. "I warned her. I said, 'Lil, darling. You've been living in the city and you might likely have forgotten how to set jars.' So what does she do, her with her fancy fingernails, so afraid of breaking them she wears gloves to wipe her behind, that fine fancy daughter of mine sets those jars so close, they damn well explode, scare the shit out of my hens, and spoil a good ten quarts of peaches!"

Lil sat behind her mother at a trestle table, her face hidden inside a faded sun hat, washing, peeling, pitting, and halving peaches. Her lips sang a silent song. Dora June pulled up a broken kitchen chair and joined her. "Jim Ed had to give some tutoring to the Bennett boy, so I thought I'd come visit for a while." After church and Sunday dinner at his house, Jim Ed had dropped her at the main road and would come by to pick her up in about an hour. By then, she hoped to know what she had come to find out.

"Now don't go wasting half the fruit like *some* people," Aunt Belle cautioned. Lil mewled like a skewered kitten. "All *right*, Momma!" Water poured down her cheeks like the Cumberland Dam. She threw down her paring knife and ran weeping toward the orchard.

"Good riddance! She's been down to Nashville too long to come back here getting in my way. 'Scald them peaches!' I tell her, nice and pleasant. Oh, no. She's too fine and mighty to stand over boiling water. No, she wants to peel them. 'Lose half the fruit that way—' "

"She looks distressed—"

"So'd you if your husband was down in Juarez, Mexico, divorcing you."

"Divorce?" Maybe the rumors were true. Maybe her husband had come home early and discovered her with Senator

Bingham and maybe the shame was more than he could stand and he was divorcing her.

"Now don't you go writing down my words, Dora June. Don't let me catch you printing my daughter's private shame in the *Roper Valley Echo!*"

It was not the *Roper Valley Echo* she had in mind. It was the *Nashville Times.* And it wasn't a divorce story she wanted, it was Senator Bob Joe Bingham's connection with the cans of bonita tuna fish that poisoned those poor orphan children. It was a hot story she was after, one that would run on the front page and several columns on an inside page, paid for by the inch and maybe—it was too exciting to think about—maybe even a by-line.

"I brought you some nice lemonade." Dorrie found Lil sprawled on her back in the peach orchard, her hands covering her face, sobbing.

"Go away—"

Dorrie set down the pitcher and the tin cups. She eased Lil up into a sitting position and fed her the cool drink as if she were an invalid.

"Aunt Belle didn't mean anything—"

"I know—" Lil sighed, her eyes brimming over.

Dorrie gathered the sobbing woman to her. "It's all right, it's going to be all right, you'll be all right, everything's going to be just fine, you'll see, no need to fret, it'll be all right, just you rest now and stop your crying—"

The sobs diminished. "What do you *want?* I know you want something! I'm not supposed to be seeing people."

"I just wanted to visit with you, have a little talk is all, talk about a few things, that's all—"

Lil sat up and released her last sob with a deep and tremulous sigh. Her eyes gazed steadfastly into Dorrie's. "What did you want to talk about?"

Dorrie's mouth went all rusty. Her heart leapt in her chest like a Mexican jumping bean. This was the test of whether she would ever be a famous foreign correspondent, able to ask anybody any question, without falling to pieces. "I want to talk about botulism—"

"Sweet Jesus!" Lil whispered. Obviously shaken, her eyes never wavered from Dorrie's.

"The deadliest form of food poisoning known to man. A toxin so lethal that a millionth of a gram can kill and a pitcherful like this"—she raised the pitcher of lemonade— "could wipe out the entire human race!"

"I—"

"Do you know what happens when you get the botulism?"

Mesmerized, Lil could only shake her head No.

"You can't taste it and you can't smell it but a little while after you eat it, you begin to see double. And then you get the nausea and the pain. And you go blind. And then the paralysis creeps up your legs and your arms and you want to scream with the fear and the hurting but you can't scream—"

Lil swallowed hard, her voice gravel. "You can't?"

"Those little orphan children could not scream because the botulism paralyzed their throats. They died like that, Lil, with their eyes wide open with fear and their poor little tongues sticking out like they were sassin' but they weren't sassin', they were dead, Lil, dead from tuna salad sandwiches made from bonita tuna fish from cans with leaky seams—"

"Please—I don't want to think about it—I'm not feeling well—"

"Have you ever seen a passel of dead children? Poor little things laid out on pallets. Poor little twisted faces. Stone dead so somebody could make a quick profit from selling contaminated food!"

"It wasn't his fault! He swore to me he didn't know it was poisoned. He's got young ones of his own, Dora June. He just thought—"

"What did he think? That it didn't signify that the cans were all bashed in and rusty and leaking at the seams—"

"He said—" Lil closed her eyes as if to keep the secret

locked inside her. "Oh, Dora June, it's all bottled up inside me like those peaches over yonder. If I don't talk to someone, I'll explode."

"What did he say, Lil?"

"He said it wasn't his fault. He's got this-here dummy corporation that owns the Fort Nashborough Distributors that's got all the contracts to supply food for all the schools and hospitals in the state. He's not directly involved, Dora June. It's the damn fools he had working for him. They told him they had the chance to buy a warehouse full of bonita tuna fish from a cannery that went out of business. He said they told him the creditors wanted a quick sale so's they could get some return on their loss. That's all there was to it. He swore it to me."

"So why are you hiding out here?"

"He said he didn't want me to get hurt. Especially with the divorce and all."

"Did he pay your husband to divorce you?"

Lil pursed her mouth in a semblance of righteous pride. "My husband is a fine man. He agreed to do anything that would make me happy."

Dorrie's eyes would not let Lil get away with this self-deceit. Her resolute gaze demanded more.

"The Senator cherishes me and has a high regard for my reputation. He is seeing to it that those responsible will be punished. Discreetly, he says. No need for a big public scandal or destroying the public's confidence in their elected officials." She smiled tentatively. "We all know how much Bob Joe Bingham has done for this state. We wouldn't want one little error of judgment to destroy an illustrious career, now would we, hon?"

"If you call killing orphans a career."

Dora June stood up and brushed herself off. She would walk back to the main road and wait for Jim Ed there. She needed some quiet time to think.

"Promise me you won't put nothing about this in your

paper, Dora June." Freed from Dorrie's demanding gaze, Lil reverted to wheedling and charm.

"I can promise you that, Lil. Not one word will appear in the *Roper Valley Echo.*"

The phone she had figured on using was occupied. The *Echo* being officially closed to business on Sunday afternoon, she had looked forward to some privacy when she gave her story to Tom Jennings. But wouldn't you know, there was Loretta in Classifieds, yapping and giggling and winking at Dorrie all nice as pie.

"Let's go," Jim Ed said, as if that was that, as if the phone being occupied meant she didn't have to bother phoning Nashville.

"Jim Ed, this is important."

"More important than me?"

He looked more like a banished puppy than a near-grown man of seventeen. Despite the chattering presence of Loretta, she put her arms around Jim Ed. "Oh, darlin'—"

"Dora June!" He gathered her to his eager body, his heart pounding to beat the band.

She whispered, "You've got to understand."

"I do understand."

"No, darlin', you don't understand. That's the trouble between us. I'm a reporter and a writer. I want my chance to fly, Jim Ed. I want to work on the *Nashville Times* and maybe someday, if I'm real good, I want to go to New York City."

"But what about us? What about us loving each other and getting married and having our family?"

Dorrie sighed. "I'm only sixteen years old."

He thrust her from him, his hands crushing her shoulders. "How long you suppose I can wait, Dora June? I want you so bad, I can't eat or sleep or hardly do anything. I'm a man and you're my woman. I want to marry you and love you."

She had been thinking about this problem for some time. Sincere and genuine love was not a sin, she had decided.

"We've grown up together. We love each other truly and sincerely. So I don't see why—"

"—why we don't get married right away—especially now your momma's getting fixed to move to Pass Christian—"

"What I was saying, Jim Ed, was that we should—" She lost her nerve. She could not say it in words. "—love each other—give ourselves to our love."

His body stiffened. "You mean—without us getting married? That'd be a mortal sin and you know it!"

"You don't believe in mortal sin any more than I do, Jim Ed. We've talked about that!"

"But—how could I respect you? You'd be like Bertha Martin, flat on her back for fifty cents." He dug his thumbs into her shoulders as if trying to rip her arms off.

Having made the decision to give herself to him, she had fondly expected this moment of declaration to be sweet and loving. "I'm disappointed in you, Jim Ed. You talk about classical lovers but you're afraid of love yourself."

"I don't want our love to be cheap and sinful. I want our loved to be sacred and sanctified by marriage."

"What you want to do is tie me down. You talk about literature but you're like any red-neck plowboy. You want me barefoot and pregnant and tied to the bedpost waiting for you to get home."

"Would that be all bad?"

She turned from him and shouted at Loretta. "Get off the goddam phone!"

Loretta had never heard Dorrie speak like that. "Gotta go, now. Bye!" She gathered up her things and left.

The phone smelled of Loretta's horehound drops. "Operator? Rachel? Are you there?" She jiggled and shouted with mounting desperation until, at last, there was a click and a nervous voice, "Central?"

"Where's Rachel? Who's this?"

"Millie. Rachel's ailing." A case of Saturday night white lightning, more than likely.

"Can you put me through a call to Nashville?"

It took close to an hour for Millie to figure how to put through the call, an hour spent by Dorrie writing her story so she could tell it better when she got Tom Jennings and an hour of pretending not to notice Jim Ed slumped over Grandpa Jeb's *Treasury of Southern Folklore*. When at last the *Nashville Times* answered, Mr. Jennings was not in, Sunday and Monday were his days off, and they could not give out his home number.

Usually she gave her report to the Farm News Editor. Now she didn't know what to do. If Tom Jennings was away until Tuesday, she reckoned it could keep until then. She would mail the story in, for his private attention.

"Would you drive me over to the junction?" There was a Sunday night RFD mail pickup that would get her letter to the *Nashville Times* Tuesday morning sure.

"You satisfied now?"

They sat in the quickening dusk, the sweetness of honeysuckle beckoning from the open meadow. "Let's take out the backseat and watch the stars come out."

Jim Ed screwed up his mouth and stared straight ahead.

"Come on, Jim Ed." She nuzzled his cheek. "Don't be shy. I know you've done it with other girls."

"You're *not* other girls!"

"Now what's the logic of that, Jim Ed? You love me but you give your loving to other girls?"

"That's not loving, that's—" He choked up.

She opened the back door of the car and began to drag out the backseat by herself. "Are you going to help me or am I going to have to do this all by myself?"

Jim Ed remained where he was, stiff as a gatepost, staring straight ahead, the sole sign of agitation a tapping foot, while Dora June tugged at the backseat, using her hipbone to keep the car door open. "Don't think I've changed my mind," he said, which caused both of them to grin and then roar with laughter.

"That's what the girls always say," Jim Ed gasped.

"The times, they are a'changin', certain sure." She felt a curious sense of achievement, of having reached one rung up a ladder and of resting awhile before moving to the next.

They found a secluded place and covered the car seat with an old picnic blanket Jim Ed's grandmother had crocheted. They lay side by side, close but not touching, watching the night sky grow black and the first stars appear.

"This has been a day and a half," Dorrie said, taking Jim Ed's hand. He did not resist nor did he cooperate. At last, he said, "I'm proud of you, Dora June."

"And I'm proud of you, Jim Ed." She placed his hand inside her blouse, pressing it to her breast. Between his flesh and hers was the thin cotton of her bra. Respecting her as he did, he had hitherto accepted the gift of her breasts as she had offered them, never presuming to remove the barrier.

"What in hell are you doing, damn you!" He pulled his hand free and turned his back on her, burrowing his face in the blanket.

"Jim Ed, I love you."

"If you loved me, you'd marry me. If you loved me, you wouldn't be thinking up ways to leave and you wouldn't be poking your nose in places where you don't belong."

"Hey! There's Cassiopeia's Chair!"

"Where?" He rolled over.

"Up there!" She pulled him to her and put his hand back inside her blouse. "Jim Ed—"

"You're going to be like one of those stars in the heavens. Out of reach."

"Jim Ed, listen to me—"

"I'm listening."

"You're the most important person in my life. I love Grandpa but he's old and he doesn't understand what I'm talking about most of the time. And Momma. Oh, Momma, she's so lonely and now she's found herself a new husband and moving to the Gulf Coast. That's all my kin. And then there's you, closer to me than either of them. My best friend. My dearest love. Can't you see that?"

The hand on her breast neither held her nor caressed her. It lay there, lifeless as a baseball mitt. Now she knew what she must do. She pressed her fingers against his lips, a gesture which always caused him to make canine growls and pretend to chew her hand. He did nothing. She danced her fingers down his chin, jumped to his chest, and proceeded briskly to his belt buckle. The Maginot Line beyond which was No Man's Land. "Mustn't ever go down yonder. Could get my hand blown off at the wrist," she would tease, returning to the belt buckle base.

Tonight was, as they both knew, different. She ran her fingers over the belt buckle and then clutched it in her palm. "I love you, Jim Ed," she repeated. Her fingers released the buckle. She eased the belt open and gently opened the top button of his trousers. The zipper sounded as if it could be heard clear over to the next county. Her fingers slid through the porticullis and found the inner gateway through his undershorts to the hard plateau of his belly.

She had never touched a man. It frightened her and excited her to be feeling her way through the foreign country of his garments, wanting to hold him and stroke him, worrying what he might think and what he might say and what he might do and feeling giddy and strangled by her clothes, especially her breasts swelling against their confinement and wanting him on top of her and around her and inside her.

Her fingers crept through a snarl of silken curls to the hard throbbing that leapt into her hand, smooth and bumpy as a summer squash. "Dora June!" He jumped like a scalded cat, falling on her, clawing at her blouse and ramming his hand up her skirt. "You want it; you're going to get it!"

Desire changed to fear. She fought him off. This wasn't what she wanted. "Please—what are you doing?" Knees, nails, teeth, her weapons were of no use against his superior animal strength. With a growl of triumph, he straddled her, her arms pinned above her head, his free hand ripping through the elastic of her panties. The face looming over her in the starlight was not human. "Dora June! I'm going to—Sweet Jesus, what am I doing?"

He collapsed on top of her, sobbing. "Forgive me, darlin'. Please forgive me. You hurt me so. I wanted to hurt you. I could never hurt you. I'm sorry. Please, please—"

She held him in her arms and comforted him. They would have to wait to consummate their love. It was strange, this difference between men and women. When a woman loved a man, she wanted to give herself to him. But when a man loved a woman, he didn't want her to. It would take some figuring out.

"It's all right, Jim Ed. I love you, darlin'."

"I know you'll be going away, Dora June. I can feel it. You're going to be famous and I'll never see you again. But I want you to know you're the only woman I'll ever love."

It felt good to be in the cool night air with his full weight on top of her, heavier than a quilt. A shooting star rose in the eastern sky. A year before, she'd have wished for love or a bicycle.

Tonight, in Jim Ed's arms, she wished for Tom Jennings to like her story and pay her a commensurate reward and compensation.

In the circumstances, the last person Lou Dexter wanted to see was Jennie Bliss Sternholdt. A walking corpse, an Emmenthal of holes, he nevertheless did not want her to Jesus Christ him back to life. He shrank from her compassion and vegetarian pity. He did not want her to help him get in touch with his anger or to ease his pain with a philanthropic hump.

There she was in Westwood, hustling up a special non-vegetarian dinner to celebrate his first day back at work. Having so brusquely rejected him the night of Dorrie's birthday party, she had made a point of formally inviting him to stay over and tomorrow they would attend the memorial services for Dorrie at the Getty Museum. She had been happy this morning, washing his hair in the shower, spitting grapefruit pips over the top of his L. A. *Times*. Causing a woman happiness made him very uneasy. Causing her unhappiness made him feel worse.

As in most of life's private crises, i.e. women, he took the coward's way. Instead of calling her to explain or cancel out, he did nothing. She would hate him and then she would forget him and that would be that. As for getting in touch with his anger, he didn't need any help. Being canned by Marceau was a double humiliation. With his credentials, he should not have taken the job in the first place, regardless of need. As his ex-wife the princess would certainly concur, it was his own goddam fault. He had asked for it. Oliver Twist on the gruel kick: *please, sir, I want some more.*

Being a mature, civilized man, his impulse had been to take Marceau's severance check and shove it down his throat and then use him as a battering ram to smash all the typewriters and computers before stuffing him into an auto compactor. Instead, he couldn't remember quite how, he got out of the building and drove to the Sunrise Apartments bar. His immediate goal orientation, as Jennie would say, was to get his brains fried and his ashes hauled by some faceless female with a limited vocabulary and no opinions on urban decay, culture lag, or health. She would giggle and be slip-slidy and he would ride her and ram her and ream her tighter than a rawl plug.

It was the only thing he could do. If he so much as said Jennie's name on the phone or heard her voice say "Lou, it's *you!*" he would damn well break down and cry, or worse.

By seven o'clock, Jennie had coated her breasts and inner thighs with musk oil and set the coffee table with candles and a centerpiece made of daisies, pecans, and papaya. They would recline on cushions, Japanese style, or was it ancient

Roman style—a little of each. It was ditsy, she knew, to be laying this *Cosmo* girl trip, but she didn't care. She could feel every inch of her skin and every bone in her body and it all felt together and good.

Tonight was a celebration for her as well. She had got three new assignments: two commercials and one feature film. In six months her Pushy Person Service had become operational. While her ambition was still to be a director and she continued her courses at USC, she made her living tracking down props, locations, and people for advertising agencies and TV and movie production companies. At first she had specialized in houses, everything from a sunny kitchen for a food commercial to sinister hovel for a caper. She had named this service *Sherlock Homes; You Name It, I Find It.*

Expanding to Pushy Person, her promise *You Want It; I Get It* was dramatized on her answering machine with a background recording of "If You've Got the Money, Honey, I've Got the Time." Today's assignments were to find a New England farmhouse, a fifty-mile stretch of road that looked like an Australia outback, and a Mel Brooks look-alike for a kosher diet-food commercial.

"Dis is de butler!" the actor's answering machine cried. "De Rhett Butler!" What a way to earn a living! By the end of the workday, she had booked the actor, found the New England farmhouse, and had three promises of Australia outback.

By eight o'clock her euphoria was cooling down; her breasts changed from straining to sticky. She was like an airliner at the end of the runway, waiting to take off and no word from the tower and no place to go and nothing to do but sit and wait. She was starving, too. Where the hell was he? She snitched equal amounts from the two crab cocktails and removed the candles and centerpiece for looking suddenly and revoltingly Doris Day.

She was hardly the little woman waiting for big strong caveman to come home. She had done that trip and it was the pits. She was every bit as free and equal as Lou Dexter.

Cooking dinner for a man was a sentimental throwback. It was the last time she would get trapped in her own conditioning. She had better things to do than juke around a kitchen.

At eleven o'clock she congratulated herself on her ability to deal with the situation, turned on the news, and ate the remaining crab cocktails, all four baby lamb chops, most of the hash browns, the tossed salad with blue cheese dressing, and the Swensen's jamoco ice cream that was a nostalgic reminder of their first meeting. The hell with him. She was tired of damaged men. Tired of men who were falling apart at the seams. Tired of putting them together with safety pins and getting stabbed in the process.

She had thought Lou Dexter would be different from the men her own age, the passive aggressives who said they admired her independence but deep down feared it. Twenty years her senior, Lou would be mature, worldly, past all the infantile bullshit. Moreover, in a ruthless California society which judged her failing twenty-six-year-old body for signs of sag and cellulite, she had further thought Lou Dexter to be above such superficial sexism and even flattered by the interest of a younger woman.

Clearly, she was wrong. Lou Dexter was like all the rest. Selfish. Childish. Boring. At midnight, she could stand the uncertainty no longer. She called his office. The Night Editor said, "Sorry. Dexter is no longer here."

"You mean he left for the day? When—?"

"No, dearie, the Pulitzer prize winner is no longer with us." There was no mistaking the sneer of the underachiever. "He's been terminated. Axed. Fired—"

Speaking of selfish, how could she have been so involved in her own ego not to realize that something like this had happened. Lou was in shit city. Ashamed to face her. He needed her and what was she doing but feeling sorry for herself!

The operator rang his room. No answer. "Could he be in the bar?" she asked. The slight hesitation told her all she needed to know, doubtless protecting Lou from what sounded like a barracuda wife. Poor thing, he would be pissed out of his gourd, crying into his beer, alone with his grief and despair, needing her desperately but ashamed to face her.

The bar was deserted except for a corner table where Lou Dexter was force-feeding a maraschino cherry to a Sunset Strip kewpie in a miniskirt. Proud of her keen director's eye for the pertinent detail, Jennie instantly noted a pair of purple bikini panties on the table and Lou's hand between his guest's widely parted thighs.

Emergencies cleared her head. She paid off the girl, the bar tab, and Lou's hotel bill. She packed his few things, checked him out, and brought him home, the cave woman with a battered trophy. In no shape to resist, Lou swayed like a marionette on twisted strings, the smell of the girl strong on him. *Why?—goddammit!* Jennie had been this route before. Why was it that when a man was in trouble, he went looking for strangers? Why hadn't he come running home to her? Got drunk in her arms? Sought peace between her legs?

Collapsed on her couch, his face looked curiously boyish despite the gaunt Lincolnesque hollows that accentuated his nose. He was a discard, one of those old pieces of furniture left in the driveway or sent to the flea market. She assessed his virtues with the clinical eye of an interior decorator. In bad shape, his veneer chipped, he was still better than most of the contemporary models. All he needed was a little fixing up.

In a way, he was like her antique brass bed. When she found it at a garage sale, it was a disassembled pile of metal tied together with clothesline and propped against a tree. A previous owner had painted it vomit green. She had bought it for five dollars, spent fifty to have the paint removed, another hundred for springs and mattress, and two weekends of muscle power buffing the virgin brass to its current mellow patina.

The bastard. Showered and wearing the Kafka T-shirt she preferred for bed, she returned to the living room for a final body check. Bastard. She bent over him to kiss his eyelids. He

stirred and clasped her to him. Bastard. He thought she was
the kewpie doll.

"Jennie—"

Lucky son of a bitch. He felt good under her, like a raft.
Except if he did turn out to be her life raft, she would do the
steering. Cool night air licked her bare behind. To cover up
would have meant moving. She stayed where she was.

A celebrity death creates a special kind of high, particularly
among other celebrities. In contrast to the survivor guilt common to ordinary mortals, celebrities feel survivor triumph.
Once more the gods have blessed them personally. Once more
they have been chosen to continue enjoying life's riches while
another famous person has been canceled.

In California, the country of eternal youth and beauty,
death has been described as nature's way of saying slow down.
A Beverly Hills widow is said to be the one wearing the black
tennis togs. Old-timers still quip about John Garfield's final
fadeout in a woman's arms as an extreme case of *coitus
interruptus.* Success rather than cars killed James Dean, Ernie
Kovacs, and Jayne Mansfield. Loneliness rather than drugs
killed Marilyn Monroe and Janis Joplin.

In this fairy-tale land where the happy ending and unhappy
ending have become synonymous, even cruel fate has its
compensations. Freddie Prinze blew his brains out but at least
had experienced the exquisite joys of stardom and fatherhood.
Diana Hyland's cancer gobbled up her innards but at least
John Travolta held her close in his adoring arms until the
final dissolve.

"What the Lord giveth, the Lord taketh away." The Reverend Dr. R. Taylor Price concluded his prayer of invocation
for the mourners gathered at the John Paul Getty Museum at
Malibu for the memorial service honoring Dorrie Bridges.
The late billionaire's edifice stands on a cliff overlooking the
ocean where, officially, Dorrie Bridges lay, presumed drowned
while presumed fleeing from the fire.

The museum is a faithful copy of a first-century Imperial Roman villa. Its size may be judged by the enclosed reflecting pool, which is over two hundred feet long or like a twenty-story building lying down. At the western end of the pool, nearest to the sea, were the podium and gilt chairs for the guests. Photographers and TV remote units were banished to the surrounding colonnades and had to focus through the Italian pomegranate trees and topiary hedges.

The sun sliced through Lou Dexter's brain like a rusty knife. He squinted through mirrored sunglasses. "Why am I here?" His head felt like Dorrie's melon.

"This is a major cultural event." Jennie had had the foresight to pour some Fernet Branca into a small medicine bottle. Holding it to Lou's lips, she smiled wanly at those nearby, begging their compassion for this clearly ill mourner.

"Dorrie Bridges would have loved covering a story like this." Tom Jennings, publisher of the *Nashville Times* and executor of Dorrie Bridges's estate, began the eulogy. "She would be proud that so many important people in every field of human endeavor are here to honor her memory. The Vice-President of the United States, the Ambassador from Great Britain, the governors of her home state of Tennessee and her adopted states of New York and California. The most talented and creative people from the world of entertainment. And the competitive members of her own profession, all here, all petty rivalries forgotten. All of us joined together to write a final obit to the touchingly short and amazing career of a rare communicator."

A single engine plane flew over, trailing a streamer that proclaimed, PETE'S PIZZA OPEN TIL DAWN.

Jennings managed a laugh. "That's about the only form of communication Dorrie Bridges didn't master. She was an amazing study in contrasts. She loved fried ham and red-eye gravy. She loved bagels and Nova Scotia. She spoke English with a Tennessee mountain accent and French like a Parisian. She rolled her own cigarettes—Bull Durham, not marijuana as some supposed, though she thought that was her business and smoking dope was up to the individual and not the government—and we all remember how she kept them in one of those tin boxes from Tiffany's and how she got busted coming across the Canadian border at Windsor.

"These are things you all know. Charming things like her little habit of marking ink dots on sugar cubes and using them for dice. A high roller"—his voice cracked—"until the recent night we will none of us ever forget.

"But there are things about Dorrie Bridges you may not know. Things I'd like to share that will illuminate her innocence and her sincerity—"

"She and Catherine de Medici," Jennie whispered. The acoustics double-crossed her. A *shhhhhh* reared up and threatened to smother her.

"I first met her fourteen years ago in my office at the *Nashville Times.* She was sixteen years old and looked about twelve, an extremely serious young woman come to see me about a job." He chuckled and sighed. "Her name was Dora June then and it was her first time in a big city. She sat herself down in my waiting room with her white gloves folded in her lap and her big brown eyes determined. She told my secretary she would wait forty days and forty nights, all day and all night, if necessary."

Lou Dexter had read this story in many variations in Dorrie's clippings. How she had come down to Nashville from Roper where her grandpa ran a hot-lead weekly, how her widowed mother had married a rigger and gone to live on the Gulf, how Dora June had arrived at Jennings's office with a cardboard satchel and a scrapbook full of her articles.

Jennie's Fernet Branca had switched his brain on and cleared his vision. While Tom Jennings developed the familiar theme of the country girl making it in the big city, Lou, the big-city guy who failed wherever he went, scrutinized him. Tom Jennings was favored by nature to look like the scion of a southern publishing family. Older than Lou but in infinitely better condition, his hair was a thick palomino thatch, his square Celtic face ruddy as a cowpoke, his brawny body cleverly slimmed in a black silk leisure suit. Sinclair Lewis might have modeled Elmer Gantry after him. Some people called him Dorrie's mentor, a father figure who loved her like a daughter. Others added incest to the mix, insisting they were lovers.

"And so it was, friends, that my wife and I invited Dora June into our home as our daughter so that she could finish her primary schooling—"

"Oh, sure—" The words had slipped from Jennie's lips.

"Shut up!" Lou hissed, a demand echoed by those around them. Andrew Van Kennan could be seen moving toward them. "Now you've done it, kid. They're going to throw us out."

Once started, Jennie Bliss Sternholdt couldn't stop. It was a form of whispering hysteria that more often seized her at friends' weddings or during love scenes at movies. "You see her?" She pointed to Foxy Fenton, the "baby" agent. "I've heard she's got two cars. A Matzoh and a Vulva."

"Please—!" A woman in front of them turned to scowl. She was wearing a black DORRIE LIVES button.

Andrew had reached the end of their row and gesticulated at knee level. The miscreants ignored him, staring intently at Tom Jennings as he traced Dora June's progress from Nashville to the "Whispers" column of *Newsmagazine* under the guidance of the outstanding woman publisher, Connie Michelin. A turning of heads near the lectern revealed the presence of Connie Michelin herself, shaded from the sun by a black sombrero and butterfly sunglasses.

"Thank you, Connie, for being with us today to share our grief." Jennings bowed in her direction.

Andrew Van Kennan whispered furiously across a dozen laps, "Come with me, Dexter!"

Lou saluted him, forgetting the medicine bottle in his hand.

Jennie pulled it away and clasped it in her folded hands as if in prayer.

"Dorrie knew what folks said about her," Jennings continued. "Why, someone sitting right here called her a wunderkind—said she was a combination of Barbara Walters, Rona Barrett, Walter Cronkite, and the Virgin Mary. And you know what, Jack Anderson and John Chancellor said they felt left out."

The levity over, he wound up for the big finish. "The way I will always remember Dorrie Bridges is serving chicken and biscuits to Mr. Sadat and Mr. Begin. And reciting Confucius in Chinese to Mr. Teng and talking that unfortunate woman off that hijacked plane.

"She considered herself first and foremost a reporter. She knew some people called her a gossip columnist and she didn't especially mind. 'Folks can call me anything they want—as long as they call me!' To my mind, gossip is history. History is composed of who said what *to* whom and behind whose back. History is about people who loved, hated, betrayed, lusted, conspired, won—and lost! History is greed, passion, revenge, patriotism, religion.

"Historians are gossip columnists. They report what their sources have told them. They follow leads and uncover scandals all the time. In the very best sense, Dorrie the investigative reporter, Dorrie the communicator, *was* a gossip columnist. And in her hands and her heart and her mind, gossip has become history!"

A flurry of applause was quieted down by those who knew it was improper to applaud a eulogy. Looking pleased nonetheless, Tom fanned his hands for silence, his fine head framed by the western sky. "Dorrie is gone." He gestured toward the vast expanse of ocean. "The legacy she leaves is more than devotion to truth, more than a brilliant international career and numberless awards and honors. Ladies and gentlemen, Dorrie Bridges has given me a scoop for you today." He paused for suspense. "As executor of her will, I have her instructions to devote all—and I repeat—all of her assets and future income to the funding of a chair for Contemporary Communications at a university to be decided—"

Now applause spontaneously broke out.

"—the plan to include scholarships in all aspects of journalism, print and electronic. Quite a legacy, ladies and gentlemen. And may I direct my final remarks to the members of the press covering this event. I hope this aspect of today's story won't get lost."

"Let's beat the rush hour." Lou Dexter rose. The gilt chair stuck to him before clattering to the ground. With Andrew Van Kennan glaring from one end of their row, they pushed through to the opposite side, jumped a topiary hedge, and fled through the Roman colonnade. Those on the podium sang the closing hymn *a cappella.*

> *Amazing grace*
> *How sweet the sound. . . .*

"How *dare* you?" Van Kennan had caught them.

Jennie rolled her eyes. "Is he gay? Or is he A?"

"I'm hungry, Jennie," Lou responded. "You hungry?"

"I'm hungry."

"You're not getting away with this!" Van Kennan persisted.

Lou wheeled on him. "Touch me and I'll have you on sexual assault."

The sweet words brought the roses to Andrew's cheeks. "You shit!" A shoving match began.

Andrew's necktie, a rarity in California and worn as a token of sartorial respect to Dorrie's memory, struck Lou as an ideal way to end the conversation.

"You'll kill him, schmuck!" Jennie pulled his hand off the Bijan silk.

"This is a *memorial* service!" Tom Jennings pushed the two men apart.

"He's here on false credentials—"

"I'm Lou Dexter, *Weekly Insider*—"

"*Formerly* of *The Weekly Insider*—you were fired, Dexter. You are no longer accredited even by that snot rag." The Fernet Branca had indeed cleared Lou's brain. "It only happened last night. Who told you? Or were you hiding under the desk?"

Van Kennan looked as if he had swallowed a cockroach. "It was on 'Good Morning America.' . . . Rona had it. . . . She said Marceau called you an embarrassment—"

"You mean something could embarrass Marceau?"

"—an embarrassment to the United States of America—"

"And what about you, you third-rate lox?" Jennie leapt to Lou's defense. "Just because you've inherited Dorrie's column, don't think you're man enough to fill her shoes!"

"Tom, darling—" People were crowding by. Fawn Roberts embraced the publisher, brushing Lou Dexter aside without a sign of recognition. She must have seen Rona, too.

Others joined the crush. Glitz Dreamburg, sallow and subdued in a black dress, a joint trembling between chapped lips, supported by a pale Sonny Syntagma in a business suit and a tense Foxy Fenton, who stroked her friend's arm. Viktor Varvanza, still wearing his dead ballerina wife's diamond teardrop on his lapel. Slick Doob on crutches. Sis and Brov in matching outfits. Veteran movie fashion designer Claudine. Jesus Man Suggs and Marjorie Ullman. Nicky Zinn and Hoagy Harris brushing against each other but not speaking.

"Where are the Burnsides?" Lou wondered aloud, loud enough, as it developed, to be overheard by Tom Jennings.

"In seclusion, I'm afraid," the publisher sighed. "It's all been too much for Marva. Dorrie was like a daughter to her."

"Speaking of mothers, isn't Dorrie's mother here?"

Andrew pushed in between them. "I told you to get out!"

"Come on, Lou." Jennie led him away.

Across the street at the Seafood Shanty, Lou ordered

Bloody Marys for them both. "Extra Worcestershire and white horseradish." They drank deeply and gratefully, allowing the nutritive benefits of the tomato juice and lemon to take effect.

"Have they no shame?" he asked.

"What do you mean?"

"They were her victims. What were they doing at her memorial service, making sure she's dead?"

"You know the story about Harry Cohn's funeral. 'Give the public what they want—' "

"The public doesn't want Dorrie Bridges dead. But somebody did. Somebody who was probably there today."

"Come *on.*"

"I'm telling you, it was either somebody seeking revenge— or somebody who wanted to stop her from finding something out." He downed the rest of his drink and banged the glass for a refill.

"Lou?" Jennie put her hand over his. He shrugged it aside.

"Lou?" she persisted.

He capitulated. "You—"

"We've got to talk."

"I know what you're going to say."

"You don't know what I'm going to say."

"I've known enough women to know what women are going to say."

"I'm not women. I'm not any woman you've ever known. I'm me."

"Okay."

"Okay, what?"

"Just okay. Forget it."

"Okay, you can tell me what you think I'm going to say."

"Okay. You're going to say I can stay with you with no obligation and no strings attached and that I shouldn't worry about money because it doesn't matter."

"Boy—"

"Was I right?"

"Well, only till you get another job."

"Money does matter, Jennie. And there's no such thing as no strings. I'm heading back east—"

"You won't find a job there."

"I appreciate your confidence."

"You wouldn't have taken this job if you could have found a job so don't tell me you'll find a job."

"Stop quoting me to myself. You sound like a parakeet."

"A parrot, you mean. Try getting your birds straight."

"The bird I better get straight is you. What the hell's wrong with you?"

"There's nothing wrong with me."

"Why are you begging me to wreck your life? Why don't you find someone your own age?"

"You're staying with me and that's settled. I've been thinking about this all day. You're going to write your book about Russia."

"Can't do that. Not yet."

"Why not?"

"*Becozzzzz*"—he put on his best Russian accent—"my *leeps arr silled!*"

"Can the jokes? You always make jokes. This is serious."

"You want serious? Who supports my kid?"

"And just how old is your kid?"

"Nineteen."

"Nineteen? Why can't she support herself?" The minute she said it, she knew she had stepped over the line.

His voice was wet chains on gravel. "Hear me, Jennie, and never forget. No cracks about my daughter. I'm a rotten father and I know it . . ." His eyes filled.

"Lou, please—I'm sorry. Please let me help you. You're not much, turkey, but you're the best thing that's happened to me in ages—"

"Jesus, Jennie, don't do this. Don't make me into some late-show hero. I know you think I'm some kind of romantic foreign correspondent. Russian prisons. Pulitzer prize. All that crap. Well, I'm not a glamour boy. I'm not romantic."

"You don't have to be romantic—"

"You're wrong. You want me to say 'I love you.' Women want that. I can't do it."

"You don't have to say 'I love you'—"

"And I don't want you saying it—"

"I'll never say it. I promise—"

"I don't know what the hell it means, anyway. 'I love you!' They've got jerks on TV saying it to their armpits. 'I love you' to their goddam deodorant. 'I love you' to their *toilet paper!*" He was grooving on the thought. " 'I love you because you're so squeezably soft! Now wipe my ass!' "

"I can assure you, Lou," she said quietly. "I will never wipe your ass."

His eyes squeezed shut in chagrin. He sighed deeply before opening them. "I didn't mean that, Jennie. Please forgive me. I may not be doing a Class A job on my life but I am not looking for a mother or a nurse or a floor rag."

"It's okay." Hot tears burst through her best efforts to keep them in. "I'm sorry. I can't drink."

He pulled her close and kissed her with a tenderness that astonished them both. "Neither can I."

"Oh, Lou—"

"I'm an ungrateful bastard. I haven't even thanked you for last night. God knows where I'd be now if you hadn't—"

"We'll make a deal. Stay with me for a while. Contribute whatever you can to the kitty. Send your daughter whatever she's expecting. Wash your own coffee cups. Take out the garbage—" She licked her finger and inserted it in the corner of his mouth. "—and make love to me every Saturday night."

This woman was offering him life. All he had to do was say something romantic. Loving. Be a *mensh*. "It's all wrong—"

"It's not wrong, Lou. We'll do fine—"

"Dorrie Bridges has been murdered. I know it. I can feel it. I can't just forget it and start playing house—"

"She's drowned. Lou—accept it. The investigation proved it. She tried to escape from the fire. She was cut off from the road. She probably tried to get to her boat, but by that time she was suffering from smoke inhalation. She fell into the water and was washed out to sea. You'll see. One of these days her body will float ashore somewhere up the coast."

"Somebody killed her and I'm going to find out who it is."

"Come *on,* Lou. People don't just go around killing people."

"Where've you been the last ten million years? Jack Kennedy did not slip on a banana peel."

"You're touchingly naive."

Jennie Bliss Sternholdt emptied her makeup case on the table and began to separate the lip gloss from the eyeshadows, humming under her breath.

"Okay, Jennie, spill it."

"Have you ever heard of Aimee Semple McPherson?"

"What's that got to do with it?"

"She disappeared, too."

"That was in the twenties."

"And everyone thought she drowned and they offered rewards and held memorial services, and later it turned out she was shacking up with some married man."

Lou finished his drink and signaled for the check. "As the actress said to the bishop, your point is well taken. But as Dr. Watson said, there's more to this than meets the eye. If Dorrie Bridges wanted a little romance, she wouldn't have to hide out. She's had lovers, hasn't she?"

"Only Sonny Syntagma, as far as I know—"

"Listen to me, Jennie. I may be down but I'm an experienced reporter. This thing doesn't add up. It's like Watergate. There's something very wrong. Very illogical. The whole thing about the fire and drowning without a trace. It's a cover-up, I tell you. She's been murdered and I intend to find out who did it."

In the privacy of the car, he continued, "This could be the biggest story of my career."

"I know."

"All I have coming in is my unemployment insurance."

"It's okay. You can send it to your daughter."

"If I pull this off, maybe I can be the man you want me to be."

"You're what I want right now. But, Lou—?"

"You—"

"There's something I've got to say—"

"If it's about making love on Saturday night, I'll—"

"Lou, I'm *jealous!*"

"Of what? You mean last night, that girl—"

"I can't help it, I'm jealous of Dorrie Bridges."

"But—she's dead!"

"I know—but you sound like you're falling in love with her."

At first light of morning, he slipped quietly from Jennie's arms, his entire being charged with energy. Bean sprouts, whole grains, and joyous sex might be factors, but more basic to his transformation was his new sense of purpose.

A man's got to do what a man's got to do, he confided silently in the ever-vigilant ficus. Jennie lay in a poem of carnal sprawl, her nakedness open to him and trustful. The expression on her face and the utterly relaxed attitude of her body confirmed what he knew to be true. He had loved her well. He had loved her to shrieks of laughter and cries of joy. He had loved her with lovingness he didn't know he possessed, and finally, he had loved her to sleep.

Her sweet belly begged to be kissed. To touch her now and make love again now would be gluttony. Always leave the party wanting one more drink. Always leave your woman wanting one more kiss. *Down, boy!*

Closing the bedroom door, he padded into the kitchen, started the coffee, drank down a cold beer in one gulp, and cut up some onions and potatoes. While they fried in deep safflower oil, he folded a sheaf of typing paper in half and in half again. Frying onions and strong coffee reminded him of his early days as a police reporter, hanging out in greasy spoons, waiting for a break in a story.

By the time he consumed the last crisp crumb of charred grease and put up a second pot of black death java, he had refined his list of those who had good reason to want Dorrie Bridges dead.

In alphabetical order, they were:

Lil Bingham   Secretary and later wife of
                               the Tennessee senator in-
                               volved in the orphan botulism
                               deaths scandal.

Claudine   Oscar-winning veteran film
                               fashion   designer   whose
                               adopted "son" turned out to
                               be more than that.

Mallomar Crane   Black activist candidate for
                               the United States presidency
                               who suddenly withdrew from
                               the primaries.

Toni Dean   Tennis champion who played
                               like a man.

Slick Doob   Movie producer whose finan-
                               cial shenanigans crippled his
                               studio and put him in a
                               wheelchair.

Glitz Dreamburg   Owner   of   the   infamous
                               Malibu Bitch House and cre-
                               ator of top-rated TV shows.

Ann Elving	"Ugly Duckling" who was with a famed political leader when he suffered a heart attack.
Foxy Fenton	Baby-faced talent agent with an emotional and irrational friendship.
Hoagy Harris	Actor whose macho image was publicly destroyed.
Richard Lord	Park Avenue pimp and real estate manipulator.
Pia Melanaiki	Greek heiress whose marriage plans ended abruptly.
Connie Michelin	Publisher of *Newsmagazine,* which is rumored to be on the brink of collapse.
Suzy Newcombe	Top model whose photogenic qualities were the result of *anorexia nervosa.*
Peachy Purdy Nichols	Her trademark, the knitting needle skewered through her hair.
Fawn Roberts	Mother of dead Dawnette and weather child Winnie.
Sidney Silver	Novelist with an obsessive fear of women.
Sis and Brov	Brother-and-sister act with a unique personal relationship.
Sonny Syntagma	Just another jock until Dorrie made him a star.

"Cholla" Torres	Wealthy organizer of California agricultural workers.
Marjorie Ullman	Ex-Broadway star who joined with Jesus Man Suggs in the Holy War against homosexuality.
Viktor Varvanza	Husband of the ballerina who performed her final "Dying Swan" off the top of the Empire State Building.
Burt Whitechapel	Cockney owner of the New York pub frequented by the IRA.
Nicky Zinn	The "St. Nick" who made every night Christmas Eve for sexually underprivileged women.

On a separate short list were the three men who figured prominently in Dorrie's life who did not seem likely suspects to Lou, but were nonetheless worth investigating: Jim Ed Loomis, Dorrie's childhood sweetheart; Tom Jennings, the Nashville publisher who discovered her; and Andrew Van Kennan, a congenital coward so far as Lou could determine.

He was drinking his fifth cup of coffee when the morning paper hit the door. Covering the entire front page was a portrait of Dorrie Bridges, her solemn eyes staring straight at him and challenging him to prove his case.

"Don't worry, kid. Sam Spade to the rescue. Old born-again Bogart will find out what really happened."

With infinite care, he wrote the names on the photograph, drawing lines to separate each from the other so that the final effect was that of a jigsaw puzzle. The list added up to twenty-eight names.

Instead of a twenty-ninth name, he inked a heavy question mark in the middle of Dorrie's forehead. The unknown subject of Dorrie's last investigation might be locked forever in her mind. Or might have been the cause of her abrupt disappearance.

And?

Number thirty was the name he might wish to avoid but which had to be considered. Dorrie Bridges, herself. The sadness of her last column haunted him. *"That I have just begun to live and that I have lived long enough"* revealed a touching ambivalence that could have taken her in either direction.

If, as she quoted from Ecclesiastes, "To every thing there is a season," he could not ignore the grim possibility that at the age of thirty Dorrie Bridges had deemed it her season to die.

That area of the North American continent now known as Tennessee was first visited by the Spanish explorer Hernando De Soto in 1541 and later by the French explorer Robert Cavelier La Salle, who built Fort Prud'homme in 1682. The name "Tennessee" is Cherokee for the collection of villages on the Little *Tanasi* River.

France claimed the territory until 1763, when Britain politely suggested they hand it over. In a minor footnote of cartology, Tennessee was part of North Carolina until 1790, and formally joined the new United States of America as a separate and slave state in 1796.

The first of Tom Jennings's ancestors to settle in Tennessee was David Jennings, a Welsh orphan kidnapped from the Cardiff slums and transported to the New World as an indentured servant in the mid-eighteenth century. After seven years laboring for a French grain merchant, he was given his freedom, a suit of homespun, a flintlock, ten acres of wilderness on the Natchez Trace, and a lecture on the merits of hard work. In an eleventh hour fit of bountitude, he also received M. Gaston's only child, Marie, who had responded to David's Celtic charms to the point of pregnancy.

By 1847, *Da* Jennings's grandson, Henry, named for the Tudor kings, had become rich enough in cotton, granaries, and railroads to acquire the fine Georgian mansion now occupied by Tom Jennings, his equally aristocratic wife, Nedra, and their sons, Thomas, Jr., and Charles Gaston, aged ten and eight respectively.

Belle Marie was one of the few old Nashville homes still in private hands. Much photographed and frequently borrowed for kind charity, it was famous for its Louis XIV ballroom, English rose garden, and seventeen bedroom suites furnished in authentic antebellum splendor.

Dora June's new quarters, for instance, took up the entire northeast corner of the third floor with a direct view of the oldest stand of boxwoods in the state of Tennessee.

"From here on in, consider this your home, Dora June," is what Tom Jennings had told her as they turned up the driveway and again at the front door, where Jackson the houseman took her belongings, including the portable Singer, and carried them inside. "You're part of the family now. Just you remember that."

So much had happened these last six months, she wasn't certain sure half the time which way was up. After mailing in her story about Senator Bingham's connection to the botulism deaths at the orphanage, she had heard nothing.

"Any calls for me?" she asked Loretta in Classifieds and Grandpa Jeb so many times, Loretta turned mean and wouldn't answer.

"*Loretta*—I'm expecting an important call. From Nashville."

"Now, who's calling you from Nashville? Is Roy Acuff calling you down to sing on the Opry? You been holding out on me, Dora June? With all your other talents, your writing and all, have you been holding out on me, Dora June?"

Grandpa Jeb wasn't feeling too good. "Quit fussin', darlin'. I wouldn't keep anything from you."

"Maybe it got lost in the mail," she ventured to Jim Ed.

"The United States Government doesn't lose mail."

"What could have happened? That's a big, important story. The kind of story Mr. Jennings said he was looking for."

"Face facts, Dorrie."

"What facts. I sent him the facts."

"Senator Bingham's one of the most important men in the state. You think the *Nashville Times* is going to run a story by a schoolgirl saying he killed helpless orphans?"

"Well, he did, didn't he? And I got Lil to tell the truth, didn't I?"

"And what about Lil?"

"What do you mean what about Lil?"

"What about ruining her life? What about her reputation? How is she going to hold her head up if you go around printing things about her and Bob Joe Bingham? You haven't thought about that, now, have you?"

"I've thought about it."

"And you think it's your God-given right to just go on in and expose people's privacy and tell their secrets?"

"Truth—it's truth that's the most important thing in life—"

"And people don't matter?"

"Jim Ed—!"

"I'm sorry, darlin'—you've got me turning every which way—"

"Those orphan children are dead!"

"I know—"

"Murdered same as if somebody crept up on them and smothered them in their sleep. Only worse than that. Those children suffered. They suffered pain and they suffered fear. Think of those sweet little bodies. Think of those pleading eyes, begging somebody to help them but nobody could help them. It was murder, Jim Ed. Murder for profit—"

"Well, Lil couldn't help that. She's just an innocent bystander!"

"Innocent bystanders are supposed to call the police. If you witness a crime, you're involved whether you like it or not. That's what I put in my story."

"And just who's going to believe what some little schoolgirl has to say?"

"Now stop that, Jim Ed. I'm a reporter—"

"A beautiful reporter—" His attempt to embrace her was repulsed.

"I happen to be a professional reporter and an official stringer for the *Nashville Times*—"

"That being the case, why hasn't the editor of the *Nashville Times* called you to thank you for your big story?"

Misery choked her. She had no answer. Evidently she had been too big for her britches, thinking what Lil had to say was important.

Jim Ed added, more kindly now, "And why haven't you called him to find out what happened?"

"I did call him—"

"Only once, Dora June. Admit it. You know in your heart what he'll say to you. He'll say thanks, we appreciate your fine effort but be a good girl and stick to covering the farm news like they're paying you for and leaving the scandals and such-like to others more experienced."

What with Grandpa Jeb feeling poorly and Momma trying to sit her down and talk when talking was the last thing Dorrie wanted to do and what with getting the following week's edition of the *Roper Valley Echo* on press and writing her term paper on *Madame Bovary* as well, she had more or less decided to forget about her big story when the early morning Sunday bus dropped off its usual bundles of the Nashville newspapers and magazines.

A banner headline across the front page of the *Nashville Times* demanded the resignation and arrest of Senator Bingham and his associates for the willful murder of orphan children and for conspiracy to defraud the State Education Commission through their dummy corporations and illegal contracts.

A tearful Lil, photographed at her mother's farm, confessed all that she had told Dorrie, and more. A News Brief, datelined Juarez, Mexico, confirmed her divorce and noted that it followed Senator Bingham's by a week. A glowering Bob Joe Bingham dismissed the story as a Communist conspiracy, his picture juxtaposed to the one taken at the orphans' funeral. An added element clearly calculated to destroy Sunday breakfast appetites was the Medical Editor's graphic explanation of what botulism does to the human body.

The by-line was Thomas B. Jennings.

Nowhere was there a mention of Dora June Bridges, their respected Roper correspondent.

This time when Dorrie telephoned through, Mr. Jennings was indeed in his office. "But I'm afraid he's in conference, ma'am."

"Please tell him—"

"Sorry, ma'am, but the television people are here and the governor's on the line and—yes, *sir!*" The harassed woman cut her off. The words of one of Grandpa Jeb's favorite songs came to mind. *I ain't gonna be treated thisaway!* Late Sunday night, after Jim Ed took her home and told her not to fret and that everything would be just fine, Dorrie packed a change of underwear and hose, her "good" black leather pumps, and white cotton gloves, and the scrapbook of her clippings. She left a note on the kitchen table and set off on foot for the interstate, making a short detour to the high school where she slipped her *Madame Bovary* term paper under the door. Her thesis was if Emma was so miserable, why didn't she leave home and get a job.

So determined was the figure of the young woman standing by the side of the highway that the first trucker that saw her stopped and carried her all the way down to Nashville.

"Mr. Jennings isn't in just now."

"I'll wait." Dora June sat herself down on the bench.

"You can't do that. How'd you get up here anyway?"

"I have an appointment with Mr. Jennings."

"I am in charge of Mr. Jennings's appointment book and I can tell you Mr. Jennings does not have an appointment with you."

"That may be, ma'am. I don't deny he has no appointment with me but I do have an appointment with him, an important appointment."

The secretary regarded her with fear. The young woman looked ordinary enough, a God-fearing Christian if she had to describe her, neat and tidy with her legs crossed at the ankles and her white gloves in her lap. Not one of those radical outside agitators making all that trouble with the *nigras* and all. Though you never could tell what was in that suitcase, a bomb maybe, those radicals blowing things up as a form of protest.

"Get me Security, quick!" Her voice was strident with terror.

"What's wrong? What's happening?" Dorrie jumped to her feet in sudden concern. Was the woman sick?

"Don't you come near me, hear?" The woman scrambled for her letter opener and thrust it toward Dorrie.

"What's wrong, ma'am? Is there anything I can do?" The only time she had ever seen a person in such a state was when the Roper Bank was robbed and Liz-Ann was warned not to speak for ten minutes or she would die.

"Stay away from me. You're not supposed to be here. They're supposed to stop you downstairs at the front desk. How'd you get up here?"

"Now, please, ma'am. All I did was tell them I had an appointment with Mr. Jennings and then they called you but you didn't answer—"

"Lies—I only went to the water fountain—you're lying—"

The door crashed open.

"She's one of those outside agitators!"

The two security guards seized Dorrie.

"Take your hands off me!"

"Come quietly, ma'am—"

In the scuffle, her clean white gloves fell to the floor. "You're stepping on my gloves—"

"Don't fuss, ma'am. Just come with us—"

A John Wayne of a man suddenly appeared in their midst. "Now, just what in the name of hell is going on here—!"

"Oh, Mr. Jennings, this girl forced her way in here without an appointment and I—"

His crew-cut head was well shaped and furry as a tennis ball, his face tan, his nose peeling, his blue eyes impatient. "This is not how we generally treat young ladies who don't have an appointment." He took Dorrie's hand as if leading her to her place in the cotillion. "We generally stand them up against the wall and execute them." His secretary burst into tears and fled to the corridor. The security men followed after her sheepishly. "Now don't go putting the water fountain under arrest!" Jennings called after them. "This whole Civil Rights movement has got them all nervous as hell. One little bitty old bomb scared them out of a year's growth."

Dorrie had forgotten about the White Supremacists' attack on the *Nashville Times*. In a signed editorial, Tom Jennings had denounced the Birmingham church bombing that killed four Negro girls as mentally deranged and subhuman. It had not occurred to her that the powerful forces behind Senator Bingham might also use violence to express their displeasure.

"Now, young lady, what exactly can I do for you? Is it a raffle? After all this fuss, the least I can do is take a book of tickets." He led her into his office, a clutter of leather, cherry wood, books, plaques, and mementoes going back to the War Between the States.

"I'm Dora June Bridges and you stole my story."

Thomas B. Jennings looked as if he'd swallowed a porcupine. Whole. "You're Dora June?"

"Yes, sir."

"But you're just a child."

"Seventeen next month. And grown-up enough to track down that story."

"I've been looking for you. Where in the name of hell have you been?"

"In Roper, same as always—" Despite the excitement of sitting in the private office of the publisher of the *Nashville Times*, she reminded herself that they had printed her story. On space rates alone, they owed her a small fortune. "My address and my grandpa's phone number were on my copy same as always."

"Not on this story!" He rummaged through the papers on his desk. "Here it is. 'By Dora June Bridges'! Period. Not even a postmark. We traced it through the RFD pickup. No town. Nothing."

She couldn't believe her eyes. Black and white, the evidence stronger than the deceits of memory. "You could have found me through the Farm News Editor."

"Farm News?" He was pressing buttons on his intercom.

"I'm your stringer in Roper Valley. I've got clippings to prove it." She brought out her scrapbook.

He bellowed into the phone. "Send a photographer to my office."

Dorrie waited for him to replace the phone before saying one of the things she had rehearsed during the long night's drive. "I added up the inches. There were close to a hundred, not counting the pictures, of course, and at my regular space rates—"

"A hundred inches is a big story—"

"Yes, sir."

"And it wasn't all yours. We had to track down Miss Lil at the Kinkaid Farm to confirm our source and then get Senator Bob Joe's statement, too, which was not included in your story—"

"Well—" she hesitated.

"You're not thinking that we should pay you for the part of the story we had to get ourselves, now are you?"

She was considering the justice of his reasoning, twisting her white gloves in her lap, when he burst into delighted laughter. "Dora June Bridges, you have broken the story of the year! You've given us the material to shake up the whole political machine. You've probably changed the history of the state of Tennessee, girl! And you're only sixteen years old. I can't believe it. There's more in this than space rates. There's —" He leaned across his desk. "How much do you think the story's worth?"

Grandpa Jeb had always cautioned her, "Never answer a hard question with an easy answer you might regret."

"Like you said, it's a mighty big story." She stalled for time to think.

"That it is. And there's more in today's paper."

The photographer rushed in looking like he'd chased a train after it left the station. Jennings waved him silent.

Grandpa had also said the only time to ask for something was when someone wanted something. Screwing up her courage, Dora June Bridges looked Thomas B. Jennings square in the eyes and said, "I want two hundred dollars cash money and—"

He scribbled a cashier's chit for the money and handed it to her. "And—?"

"And a staff job as a reporter!"

"But—"

"I want to be a reporter, Mr. Jennings."

"You are a reporter, Dora June. But what about your schooling? And your family? Where would you live? Do you have kin in these parts?"

She had worked the whole thing out. She had only one more term at high school to get her diploma and she was certain sure she could complete her course in Nashville. With Momma getting married and moving to Mississippi, she'd be on her own anyway. "The way I see it, I can live at the YWCA Residence, take my courses, and work for you."

"And you're not walking out or fixing to get married?"

As she had told Jim Ed, "Not until I do some of the things I'm mindin' to do."

He flipped through her clippings without appearing to read them. "We could start you on the Society Page—"

"No, sir—thank you, anyways."

"What's wrong with that? You'd cover weddings, church luncheons, fashion shows—"

"I'm interested in news and the truth. You don't find either one on the Society Page."

"Now what if Lil Kinkaid was to be marrying Senator Bingham? Now isn't that a wedding you'd like to cover?"

"That would be front-page news, Mr. Jennings."

"Take her picture," he instructed the photographer. "I want to look back on this day and remember what she looked like her first day at the *Nashville Times.*"

Jim Ed raised a mighty ruckus when she got back to Roper, driven home in style in a chauffeured Packard limousine. "Where've you been without telling me?"

"You can't go living on your lonesome in a city the size of Nashville!" Mallie objected when Dora June revealed her plans. "You'll get into bad company. That settles it. Jerry Lee'll just have to cool his heels. I'm staying right here in Roper till you finish your schooling. And anyway, what will

Grandpa do if you leave him? You know how much he depends on you."

It was Dorrie's first experience of those who loved her trying to talk her out of doing the things she most wanted to do, a situation that would be repeated many times in later years. Only Grandpa Jeb, whose age might be expected to make him most cautious, gave her a warm vote of confidence and encouragement. "You're going to do just fine, darlin'."

"You taught me everything I know, Grandpa."

"You'll learn more about newspapering than I could ever tell, but there's one thing you have that you mustn't let them take away."

"What's that, Grandpa?" she teased. "My sweet little ways?" She hugged him as she had from the time she was old enough to reach up. "I don't think the Nashville folk are going to favor me as much as you do."

"It's your heart I'm talking about."

"Oh, Grandpa—" How could she explain that she loved Jim Ed but that she didn't want to get married, not so soon.

"You are the only person I know who is pure of heart, Dora June. I've watched you grow. I know what I'm talking about. Always do what you know is right, no matter what anyone says. And you'll be a happy woman, mark my words."

Now, these six months later, she kept thinking about Grandpa's words and wondering if it really was the right thing for her to be moving into the Jennings house. The trouble was, Grandpa couldn't help her. He'd been taken sudden and gone to his rest, leaving Momma so nervous in addition to being nervous about getting married and moving to Mississippi, all the advice she could give her daughter was to be nice and pay attention and remember that she came from a Good Christian upbringing.

Dora June had known all along that the YWCA Residence had a strict six months' maximum stay. When it came to an end earlier this week, she would have had to move somewhere and could find no good reason to refuse her employer's Christian invitation. As he had pointed out, alternatives would be some rundown boardinghouse or a little bitty furnished apartment with only the bedbugs for company.

In her several visits to the Jennings home, she had never been invited above the first floor. On her arrival three days earlier, Nedra Jennings had kept to her rooms with a headache. Tom and the boys escorted the new guest upstairs. There were four clothes closets. Dorrie's few belongings fitted into half of one of them.

Tom shooed the boys out and sat her down in the tufted window seat. "I don't want any back talk. You're one of the family now. Like a daughter. You won't be paying out board so you can spend your wages on some clothes and things and—"

"Tom!" Nedra Jennings was the only woman Dora June had ever seen who looked more like a painted portrait than a flesh-and-blood woman.

"Just look at her, Nedra. Doesn't she look as if she belongs here?"

"I'm sure Miss Bridges would like to refresh herself."

"Not Miss Bridges, dear! And not Dora June anymore! It's Dorrie! That's what we're calling her at the paper."

"Dorrie—" Nedra tasted it like medicine, barely tolerating its presence in her mouth.

"Dorrie." Tom beamed. "Isn't she wonderful?"

Nedra echoed softly, "Wonderful—"

Tonight, Dorrie sat in the selfsame window seat watching the driveway with growing anxiety. Momma and Jerry Lee had tied the knot at last and were on their way to Mississippi. Tom had invited them to have supper and see Dorrie's new home. "I want your momma to see we're treating you right."

From the minute she heard Jerry Lee's twelve-wheeler grind up the driveway, Dorrie wished she were dead. Her eyes darted around the bedroom at the high four-poster and cut flowers and trellis wallpaper and polished wood and quilted chintz and felt the searing pain of the outsider. She did not belong here. Nor did she belong in the naked light-bulb ugliness of the YWCA. Her home in Roper, however humble, was no more. She did not belong anywhere.

The doorbell reminded her that it was her mother arriving at this sumptuous mansion and that Mallie and Jerry Lee would be shy and intimidated by its splendors. Tom was welcoming them as she hurried down the stairs.

"Jim Ed!"

Mallie Bridges looked about to crumple. Her eyes begged her daughter's forgiveness. Her mouth opened but gave forth no sound. Her new husband cowered behind her looking shorter than Dorrie remembered, red wrists protruding from French cuffs.

Jim Ed stepped forward with the grim dignity of Lochinvar in Frye boots. "Your mother said this was a family occasion and I consider myself kin." White knuckles belied his poise but it was clear he had stormed the castle and planned to stay.

Tom Jennings saved the situation with a hearty clap on Jim Ed's shoulder and an order to set another place at the dining room table.

"Momma, I'm so happy for you!" Dorrie kissed Mallie and sat beside her on the velvet settee in the living room, leaving Jim Ed to fend for himself.

"Do I look all right? I wouldn't want to embarrass you."

"You look beautiful, Momma." Both of them knew she didn't look beautiful and that she was ill at ease and ashamed for herself and her husband and her child. Both knew, even before Nedra Jennings made her entrance, that the worst was yet to come.

"I've got to talk to you, daughter. I've been trying to talk to you since before you moved to Nashville, back when Jerry Lee and I decided to make plans—"

"We'll have time later—"

"It's got to be tonight. We're leaving for Pass Christian and Lord knows when I'll be seeing you—"

"A toast!" Tom Jennings declared. A silver tray of champagne had been passed around by Jackson. "To the bride and groom!"

"The bride and groom!"

In a show of suavity, Jerry Lee clicked his glass against Mallie's with such force, it shattered.

"Momma!"

"Never mind. It's good luck!" Tom replaced the glass and the contents. "And now, another toast." He raised his glass to Dorrie. "To—"

"To my future wife!" Jim Ed shouted.

"How perfectly charming and romantic." Nedra Jennings skimmed across the Aubusson in a hostess gown of aggressive simplicity. "Shall we hold the wedding here? Oh, Tom, look at Dorrie blush." Without a pause, she embraced Mallie and Jerry Lee in turn. "I'm Nedra Jennings and I'm proud to meet you." To Jim Ed, she said, "And just when are you planning to carry off our darlin' Dorrie?"

"Jim Ed tends to dramatize, don't you, Jim Ed?" Dorrie said. "Ever since we were tadpoles, we've joked about getting married, haven't we, Jim Ed?"

"I've won a Fulbright and I want you to come with me to England."

"Supper is served." Jackson interrupted the discussion.

"Won't you join us, young man?" Nedra said gaily.

"I've already ordered a place set," Tom informed her.

"Thank you kindly but I've said what I came to say." The water he had used to slick down his hair had dried up and his cowlick sprouted in all directions. Dorrie ached to pat it back into place but the anger in both of them prevented it. "Dora June!" His lower lip trembled and his Adam's apple gulped. "I'm offering you my heart and my life. Marry me and come with me and share my life with me, darlin'."

She wanted to hold him and to kiss him and to lay with him and sleep with him and to sing songs and make jokes and watch the sun and moon and stars with him. But not to share his life, not unless he was willing to share her life.

"I'll walk you to the car, Jim Ed."

"Not unless you're getting into it with me."

No one moved. At last Dorrie sighed and kissed his cheek. "Good-bye, Jim Ed."

Nedra's menu was calculated to starve those lacking in gourmet sophistication. Mallie was so stymied by the mere sight of the artichokes that she was unable to serve herself and Jackson had to serve her.

"Don't you know how to eat artichoke?" Charles Jennings piped up with the smug exasperation of an eight-year-old.

"Now, Charles," Nedra chided her son. "Some people don't eat the same things as other people. Mind your manners. Don't you care for artichoke, Mr.—?"

"Perkins," Jerry Lee said. "No, ma'am, it ain't that I don't like it. It don't like me."

"He said 'ain't,' Momma!" Tom, Jr., sneered.

"Hush now," his father warned.

"But you said only niggers and hillbillies say 'ain't.'"

"Now, Tom, Jr. Children should be seen and not heard. Jerry Lee and me, we were just starting to have us a talk about the fishing business, now weren't we, Jerry Lee? So why don't you boys listen and maybe learn something."

Following the uneaten artichokes were squabs served whole and beyond the manual dexterity of the guests. "You don't seem to be very hungry," Nedra observed.

"I don't generally eat much," Mallie said feebly.

"Do try this. I ordered it specially."

With a game try, Mallie drove her fork into the tiny carcass and sent it skidding into her lap.

"Dora June!" she whimpered.

Dorrie led her mother upstairs to sponge off her skirt and calm her down. "It's all right, Momma. Don't fret."

"I'm mortified. I've shamed you."

"You've made me see that quality folks don't necessarily have quality."

"That woman. She doesn't want you here."

"Never mind about that now, Momma. Now we're alone, why don't we have that talk you've been wanting to have?"

"Well—" Mallie rummaged through her new mock alligator pocketbook for a worn envelope.

"What is it?"

"Your papers."

"What papers—?"

"You're just about grown now and I'm starting a new life and—"

"It's my birth certificate!"

"Oh, Dora June—"

"You said it was lost—in that robbery—"

"There wasn't no robbery—that was just a story—"

"It says here 'Date of Birth: May 19, 1949. Name of Child: Dora June. Sex: Female. Name of Mother: Malvina Rachel Bridges. Name of Father—' "

"I tried to tell you—"

"Oh, *Momma*—it says '*Unknown*'!"

"I kept thinking 'She'll ask me about her daddy. She's such a smart little rascal, she's going to climb up on my lap and she's going to ask me where's a picture of my daddy?' "

"But you said he was dead and everything got lost in the robbery and that's why you came back home to Roper because New York City was no place for a widow woman and a small child and no husband to take care of us. And Grandpa always told me 'Never ask about your daddy because it grieves your momma too much to talk about it.' "

"Grandpa said that?"

"He said that's why you took back your maiden name, so you could forget the past."

"Praise God—"

"What happened to my daddy, Momma?"

A calm suffused the older woman. "I don't know."

"You don't know?"

"Don't look at me like that. I was young and I was scared and I wanted all those nice things I saw in the picture show. *Weekend at the Waldorf. The Hucksters.* All the tall buildings and handsome men and big cars and nice clothes and doormen saying 'Good morning.' "

"Tell me what happened."

"I was voted the prettiest girl in Roper High and so I went to the Conover office but they said I was too short and too plump. And then—" Her composure began to crack with the memory. "I trusted men, darlin'. . . . There was this one who was going to manage my career. He took me to his friend, a photographer, and he took pictures of me—"

"And then—?"

"Then, I waited and waited for him to call me and I was running out of money. His hotel said he moved, no forwarding address. So I went to the photographer and he said I wasn't photogenic—leastways with my clothes on, but if I wanted to pose nude—so I just ran out of there and then—"

"Oh, Momma—"

"Then I went to an audition at the Radio City Music Hall and they said my legs weren't long enough and there was this press agent there and he offered to help me out. He said I was prettier than Rita Hayworth and Betty Grable both—and then—" She shrugged and burst into tears.

"Which one was my daddy?"

Mallie could not meet her gaze. "I don't know and that's the truth."

"How can you not know?"

"Maybe it was all three. Maybe that's why you're so smart and talented—"

"Mallie?" Jerry Lee called through the door. "You all right in there?"

Dorrie opened the door.

"Reckon it's time for us to go, girl. Got us a long drive ahead of us. Your momma's all worn out with all the goings-on. Be glad to get her home to Pass Christian." He put his arms around his weeping wife. "And Dora June, I want you to know you always have a home with your momma and me."

"Do you forgive me, Dora June?" Mallie whispered.

"I'm not *God,* Momma. You did the best you could and I'm going to do the best I can."

When they had gone, Tom Jennings drove her downtown to the plant. The building throbbed with activity as the first edition rolled off the presses and into the waiting fleet of delivery trucks. A far cry from the *Roper Valley Echo.*

Jennings had called a special editorial meeting to discuss the Bingham trial, slated to start the following morning. Having married the defendant, Lil Kinkaid could not be forced to testify against her senator husband. Background stories had been written and set. A photo summary of all that had led up to the trial was also ready to go. Three photographers would cover the Senator's house and the exterior of the courthouse. Inside would be the staff sketch artist and three reporters, including Dorrie. A copyboy was assigned to keep the direct phone line in the courthouse press room open for instant relay of a decision.

"Dorrie, this is a big night for us—"

The meeting over, they were alone in Tom's office, the hum of the presses vibrating around them. He took a bottle of French champagne from the ice chest.

The excitement of the Bingham trial could not erase her hurt and sadness. "No thanks," she said when he was about to pour the sparkling wine into a crystal goblet.

"Senator Bob Joe Bingham wouldn't be going on trial tomorrow if it weren't for you."

"I—I think I need some coffee—"

"Coffee it is!" He pressed a buzzer and ordered it from the executive kitchen. An emergency call sent him racing down to the press room. When he returned, Dorrie was sipping the strong black brew and playing with a handful of sugar cubes.

"Dorrie—"

Her thoughts had wandered back to the events of the evening. She stared blankly at him. He took the coffee from her and put it on his desk. "Pay me some mind."

Her thoughts remained on Jim Ed and the sweetness of his desire for her and the warmth of his body she had missed these many weeks and the quaver of his voice asking her to marry him and go to England.

The arms that embraced her were not his and the mouth kissing her was not his but she responded nonetheless.

"Dorrie—I'm crazy about you."

The sound of Tom's voice brought her to her senses.

"What are you doing?"

"So brave. So beautiful—"

"Let me go!"

"So talented—so sweet—"

"You mustn't—"

"Please don't push me away—"

"You're—you're *married*—"

"Trust me, darling. I wouldn't do anything to hurt you."

She pushed him away and made for the door. Tom Jennings followed her down the darkened corridors, pleading for her to listen. "Forgive me. I'm sorry."

"I'm leaving your house."

"I got carried away."

"I can't stay under your roof."

"I swear to you, Dorrie—"

"And I can't go on working here, either—"

"Don't be a fool. I'm grooming you for big things. Important things."

"I resign as of right *now*—"

"You're tired. I'm tired. We've both been under a strain. The Bingham case. Your mother. That boy wanting to marry you."

"He's a fine boy."

"Don't throw yourself away on a boy. You've got big fish to fry. Trust me—"

"The only one I trust is myself."

In the car, she sat as far from him as she could.

Tom Jennings made no move toward her. "We'll talk about this tomorrow. After the trial. You'll see. In the light of day you'll see things different."

He was right about one thing. She was tired. She did need a good night's sleep to give her the strength and clarity of mind to do what she had to do.

The house was dark. She ran up the stairs to her room and locked the door. Safe inside, she discovered a handful of sugar cubes in her pocket. Selecting two, she drew on the dots needed to convert them into dice. The first roll came up seven. Three more sevens followed.

Dora June, you'll have a better chance of winning if you roll your own dice. Cheered by the thought, she popped the sugar into her mouth. Defying all cautions of science and sense, she chomped them to syrup with her strong white teeth.

Lou Dexter was wondering whether it really was such a great idea to drop in on Hoagy Harris unannounced when Hoagy Harris himself stepped from behind a king palm tree, his trademark black Stetson low on his forehead, a sawed-off shotgun aimed at Lou's groin.

"Can't you read?"

"Is this the Harris residence?"

"It says 'No Trespassing.' "

"My name's Dexter—"

"You're on posted property, stranger. I could blow you away and not a court in the world would convict me."

"My mistake," Lou muttered as he backed toward the distant feeder road where his car was parked. "I'm writing this article, you see—" In defeat lie the seeds of victory.

"An article?"

Lou decided to take the plunge. "An article about the quixotic nature of fame and fortune. The synergistic contradictions inherent in mass culture."

"Talk English." The shotgun relaxed.

"I'm talking about gossip. I'm talking about stardom. I'm talking about Dorrie Bridges—"

Hoagy Harris considered this, picked up his shotgun, and aimed it at the topmost frond of the palm tree. The blast shook him more than the tree. "That's one way to shoot your load without knocking anyone up."

He turned his back on Lou and crashed noisily through the palm grove. Lou hesitated and then followed. He had come here to find out if Hoagy Harris had killed Dorrie Bridges. It occurred to him that, in the best crime caper tradition, nobody including Jennie Bliss Sternholdt knew where he was and that he, too, could disappear with no one the wiser.

According to a 1976 picture story in *People* magazine, the Brooklyn Cowboy called his vast San Fernando Valley spread the Coney Island Ranch, his mansion a replica of the Neptune Turkish Baths where the young Heshy Hershkowitz had first encountered tits and ass as a towel boy. Rather than green lawn or flagstone terrace, a vast stretch of authentic boardwalk led to an Atlantic Ocean of a swimming pool replete with artificial waves and a "pollution" of foam rubber orange peels, banana skins, bagel halves, and Trojans, "to make me feel at home."

The guest cabana was an actual IRT subway car of the Brighton Beach line, its destination roller turned to CONEY ISLAND. Hoagy had bought it through Mafia connections and had it shipped on a freighter via the Panama Canal, a testament to wealth and imagination more amazing to him than the Moon Walk.

Visitors were given the familiar locker room wristlets with dangling key, the difference here being that Hoagy's were made of sterling silver on special order from Tiffany's. To complete the Brooklyn Cowboy Makes Good picture, a Nathan's Famous stand dispensed hot dogs, specials, pastrami, corned beef, and real rye bread with the Pechter's paper tag baked into the heel, all of it shipped west weekly and supplemented by local offerings of celery tonic, black cherry soda, and the inescapable if incongruous Perrier.

Ironically, Hoagy's screen persona was not that of the urban ethnic but of the basic roughneck cowboy of American myth, his rugged features and Zapata mustache as much Tex as Mex, his wayward mane of black curls as thrilling a sex symbol for men as Farrah Fawcett-Majors's hair was to women the following year.

In each of his top-grossing movies, his trademark black Stetson would be knocked off, shot off, or passionately removed by a hot-fingered woman. The sight of his wild shag of hair brought screams of excitement from his fans, especially the women who longed to be clutching it while abandoning themselves to his embrace. Like Samson of old, he was famous for his hair, and like Samson, the instrument of his public humiliation was a woman.

People had killed for less. So far as Lou's research could reveal, Hoagy Harris had disappeared from public view since that terrible Sunday night nearly two years before. His fans had exploded in anger at Dorrie. Wires, threats, letters to newspapers, had followed. TV humorists and the Las Vegas comic network had a field day of Hoagy jokes. Questions of legal action and denials of retirement were followed by the months of silence, until the present.

His appearance at Dorrie's birthday party had stirred little more than passing embarrassment among those former sycophants who didn't know what to say. His appearance at the memorial service had in retrospect struck Lou as sinister. The murderer reassuring himself that the crime had been done.

It didn't take more than a first glance for Lou to see that the Coney Island Ranch had gone to seed. The white stucco was stained and flaking. The boardwalk was littered with debris, as was the gigantic swimming pool, which looked more like a festering lake. The Nathan's stand had been battered by a storm and never repaired.

"You want a drink?" Hoagy asked.

"Got some black cherry soda?"

His host nodded his acknowledgment of the ploy. "What are you, some kind of wise guy?"

"Okay, I'll have a beer."

"I've got enough black cherry soda for the State of Israel. Come on inside." Lou hesitated. "It's okay. They all left. My wife. The kids. My mother-in-law. My dog. They needed a better *environment*. They didn't want to be identified with a scandal; it was bad for the children's ego, my wife said. Was it bad for the dog's ego? Her lawyer took care of that. The scandal made her so emotionally upset, she needs all my money to calm her down. I get my balls cut off and she's bleeding all over the place."

"The same thing happened to me, pal—"

Hoagy was not interested in Lou. "The hell with her. She can go fuck herself." He made a broad sweeping gesture. "The hell with all of them. All my good and dear friends, coming here every Sunday, eating me out of house and home. Where were they when I needed them? They can all fuck themselves."

"Including Dorrie Bridges?"

The two men were seated on opposite sides of the huge kitchen table. Hoagy slid low in his chair and put his feet up on the table. The Stetson tipped forward and hid his face. "You won't let go." His voice came through soft and muffled.

"You've never told your version of the story."

"She's dead now."

"I know."

"So what's the difference?"

"The truth is the difference."

Hoagy Harris pushed the brim of his Stetson up far enough to peer at his challenger. "That's what Dorrie said."

The truth about Hoagy Harris began with a fluke. Like many an overnight success, he had been snatching at the gold ring for over ten years, spurring the flanks of the carousel horse until it stopped going round in circles and became the snorting stallion that galloped him to stardom.

He had played thugs, he had played creeps, he had played cops with and without hearts. In a World War II prisoner-of-the-Japs movie, he had shaved his head for the part. It had grown back thicker and curlier than ever. "It broke my comb!" he bragged. He had married his Brooklyn sweetheart but a Texas girl he was *schtupping* on the side went crazy over his hair. " 'It's so strong. It's so sexy. I just want to roll around in it naked.' That's what she said. What could I do?" The Afro was coming into fashion. The wilder he let his hair grow, the crazier the broads. "Except Bernice, of course. She said I looked like a *shvartzeh*. I said it was a Jewfro and I liked it. The bitch cut me off. 'No haircut, no nookie.' She did me a favor. Believe me, I didn't have enough to go around."

Instant overnight stardom came with a low-budget spaghetti western made in Italy. The American producer had promised a Major Star for the lead and had gone so far as to announce negotiations under way in *Variety* in the naive belief that this would stimulate interest from said star. When said star's agents and lawyers responded with stiff cease-and-desists, Hoagy Harris dolled himself up in a Nudie's rodeo suit and presented himself at the producer's Beverly Wilshire suite.

The man's secretary was so turned on by Hoagy's machismo, she fell over the coffee table and nearly fractured her hipbone bumping into the doorknob leading to the bedroom.

That very night Hoagy was airbound to Milano. The money

men balked but the production was set to go; their mistresses all had parts; the locations and horses were arranged; there was nothing to do but go ahead *senza* Major Star.

Hoagy had never ridden a horse before. The cowboy who checked out his western saddle and adjusted the stirrups to hang low gave him a succinct lesson. "Just screw the saddle, *pardner*. Just wrap your legs around the lady's belly and pretend she's a two-dollar whore!"

In the scene between the good guys and the bad guys, Hoagy in his bad guy black Stetson was shot down by an ostensible good guy who turned out really to be a bad guy. When the good girl was impelled by compassion to remove his Stetson in order to treat his wounds, she improvised a moment of torment, torn between Christian charity and sudden sexual arousal. When her fingers sank into the thick black hair and twisted themselves into the curly tendrils, all the while pressing his bruised and sweating face to her ample swelling bosom, the entire set crackled with electricity.

When, at the climax of the movie, he proved that good guys sometimes wear black Stetsons and took his ministering angel leading lady to the riverbank for the obligatory final love scene, her fingers raking his hair sent an orgasmic shiver through all those watching. As the scene progressed, the young woman lost all control, her shrieks and bites getting wilder and wilder as she tore at his hair, her skirt flung up higher than required for simulation. *"Che gioila!"* she moaned even as they dragged her away.

I Capelli, they called him in Italy. Mr. Hair. In the States, he became Hoagy "The Head" Harris. In each successive film, the Stetson came off and the black curly head had its way with waves of wanton women. In Indianapolis during the sneak preview of his last movie, the sight of his curly head grazing the bare breast of the heroine and moving slowly down her midriff past her navel and off camera resulted in the almost total destruction of the theater. Frail young women ripped the seats out by the roots, pounded soda cans into the floor, threw popcorn into the air, thrust matches under their finger-nails and waved blazing five-finger candelabras in the darkness while sparks flew and set myriad small fires.

"That's when I made a mistake." Hoagy smiled benignly.

It was during a publicity tour back east. Bernice had come along, of course, with her four wig cases and five fur coats even in the summer just in case any of her old girl friends from Erasmus High should come around. Hoagy wanted to get laid and his friends arranged an evening of Ass and Grass in the East Village. "Formerly called the Lower East Side."

The party had everything. Held in a crumbling loft, it had incense, dope, quim of every color and description, a freak scene in which he was encouraged to star and, as it turned out, an itinerant army of crabs and lice who marched in and made camp in the two hairiest regions of his body, his groin and his head.

"My crotch they shaved so close, I looked like Kilroy was there, with a sunburn. Then that bastard dermatologist wants to shave my head. 'What are you talking? I start my next movie in ten days. It'll never grow back in time.' My hair is like steel wool, he says. Those nits can live in there to an old age. Nothing can get rid of them unless I shave my hair. So—"

"So—?"

"You won't believe this. I can hardly believe it myself."

He remembered having nits as a child and how his grand-mother had washed his hair in kerosene and patiently combed out the dead vermin with a fine-tooth comb.

"I got some kerosene, poured it over my head, and wrapped some paper towels on it to sop up the excess. You know what I mean?"

Lou nodded.

"And then you know what I did?" Hoagy's head bobbed up and down in mournful reminiscence.

"Jesus—"

"That's right—"

"You lit a cigarette—"

"That's right. The whole fucking place went up in flames. There I was alone in the fucking Hilton Hotel with my whole head on fire. Screaming. Trying to pull the fire off with my bare hands. Trying to remember that you're supposed to roll yourself in a blanket. Yanking at the bedspread. Trying to put my head down. Thank God, the maid heard me scream, I'd be dead. We paid her off good and got me to the dermatologist."

All of his hair and the entire epidermal layer of his head had been burned away, including the follicles from which new hair grew. "I was covered with a brown scab bathing cap. I looked like something from outer space." The vested interests around him conspired to keep the disaster a secret. His asking price for films had jumped to two million dollars. There had to be a solution.

"Didn't you have a million-dollar policy with Lloyd's?"

"Yeah—but who wanted to collect?"

Fortunately his face had escaped unmarked. The shooting date for the next film was postponed "because of production problems." Ramon Gow, the hair expert who did the wigs for *The Great Gatsby, Julia,* and *Death on the Nile*, was called in to create a facsimile of Hoagy's famous head of hair.

The new movie had gone into production. A special adhesive kept the wig tight to his scalp during the obligatory frantic love scenes and his co-star none the wiser. Hoagy was uncomfortable but all seemed to be under control when Dorrie Bridges invited him to be a guest on her live Sunday night TV show. Against all sound instinct to avoid public appearances until further scalp treatment or painful transplants, he agreed to appear.

In retrospect, how could he have refused? The theme of that night's program was a provocative "Are Men the New Sex Kittens?" Usually, it was Andrew Van Kennan's job to round up the guests. In this instance, Dorrie herself had phoned Hoagy personally.

"I understand you've got Robert Redford worried" was how

she started out. "You're getting more fan mail than Travolta and Eastwood combined." How does an ordinary mortal, conceited bighead deal with that kind of pitch, Hoagy asked Lou. "You are a superstar, Hoagy, and on your way to becoming a mega-star, the biggest of the big. What I want to discuss with you—frankly—on my TV show, is whether it's your talent as an actor *or* your sexy head of hair that's making you a star—and whether you care which one it is," is how Dorrie clinched it.

Lou had been in Russia at the time, destroying his own stardom, but he had seen the tape before driving out to the Coney Island Ranch. Putting himself in Hoagy's place, live in Dorrie's TV studio, he had felt the cold dread of apprehension as the program began with a film montage of female stars and the sexual appeal of their hair. Sex kittens maybe, but the narration clearly emphasized the impact of Jean Harlow's platinum locks, Veronica Lake's peek-a-boo, Audrey Hepburn's gamine, Brigitte Bardot's tousled, through to the current preoccupation with Farrah, Jaclyn, and others of the A*ctresses*, as Dorrie punned.

Without so much as asking Hoagy to comment, the film montage next whirled through the various appealing factors of Clark Gable's ears, Cary Grant's chin, Paul Newman's eyes, Robert Redford's teeth, Clint Eastwood's squint, Sly Stallone's shoulders—and Hoagy Harris's hair. Dorrie had spliced all of his best love scenes together. The results were an electrifying succession of torrid kisses, gropes, and frantic carnal focus on his hair.

From the film clip, the live studio camera had switched to Hoagy himself, the black Stetson tipped forward on the multimillion-dollar black curls as usual, the only thing different being the expression of sheer terror on his face. The poor bastard had been set up; he knew it, and there wasn't a thing he could do except walk out, a spot decision he was too stunned to make because there was the faint possibility he might be overreacting, that maybe he was simply being paranoid about his hair, and also the program was live and there were God-knows-how-many million people watching.

"So which is it, now, Hoagy?" Dorrie had smiled her quiet smile and put the question to him, silky soft. "While the women of America are recovering their equilibrium after seeing your best love scenes at one time, how do you as an actor feel about all this attention to your *hair*?"

Hoagy had recovered sufficiently to grin. "As long as they pay attention, Dorrie. That's all any serious artist wants." He made an enormous effort to be brash. "That and a few million dollars, of course."

"They call you Hoagy 'The Head' Harris."

"I've heard that."

"I've also been told that you receive two thousand letters a week asking for a lock of your hair."

"I believe it's up to four thousand."

"Do you send them a lock of your hair? There wouldn't be much left if you did, now would there?"

"I send my fans a picture of myself, including my hair—" He leaned into the TV camera at that point, making seductive eye contact with the television viewers. "Keep those cards and letters coming. Only please, no more panties. My wife, she doesn't understand."

"Now, Hoagy," Dorrie admonished. "My correspondents around the country tell me that thousands of men are copying your hair style. Men with straight hair are getting permanent waves so they can have thick curls like yours. Doesn't that strike you as strange?"

"I'm highly complimented."

"What about personal values? Does a mop of curly hair make a man a better person? What kind of a people are we becoming when the shape of a girl's behind or the thickness of a man's hair is more important than what's inside the person's heart and soul and mind?"

Hoagy Harris had no response.

"I'm putting you on the spot, Hoagy, and I know it, but I want to make a serious point to my audiences." With the camera close up on her earnest face, Dorrie had asked her viewers, "Would you love Hoagy Harris if he didn't have a hair on his head?" Just seeing the tape had made Lou squirm. "Would you line up for hours and lay down your hard-earned money if the famous curly hair was gone and he looked like this?"

A man's bald head, shot from behind, slowly turned sideways. The profile was unmistakably Hoagy's. A palm tree intervened as the hand-held camera jerked into a frontal position, a zoom lens suddenly filling the frame with his face.

That's when Hoagy had enough. The next shot was back in the studio. The live camera had flashed on Hoagy's chair as it overturned until the evidently rattled director switched to the number two camera to capture the final seconds of his hasty departure.

Back to an incredibly poised Dorrie Bridges, who, without missing a beat, said, "To answer the question for myself, I personally don't care what Hoagy Harris has on his head—a Stetson, beret, or grandmother's nightcap. He's a fine actor and I'd pay my money down to see him anytime.

"I'm sorry that he chose to leave before I made this point. Maybe this is too strong a point, but it's a point that I think needs to be made, and since I'm privileged to have the nation's top-rated TV show, I feel like as how it's my responsibility to make it."

The camera then switched back to Hoagy's bald head with Dorrie's mellifluous and hypnotic voice-over. "I had not expected tonight's program to end on quite such a melodramatic note. Perhaps I was overzealous in my desire to make a point about truth and human value, two subjects which are not often dramatic enough to hold our attention. All I have been trying to say is that truth is substance, not form. Truth is the intelligence inside the head, not the hair on top of it. Truth is also trust. Hoagy Harris suffered a terrible accident and dreadful loss. Millions of fans love him, yet he did not trust their love enough to tell them the truth."

"And then your wife left?" Lou prompted.

"She said I embarrassed her in front of her relatives. A very classy family. Her mother still puts newspapers down on the kitchen floor."

"And that last movie was withdrawn?"

"Some citizens' group filed a suit. Fraud, they said. Deceptive advertising. The distributor got chickenshit."

Lou attempted humor. "I hear some promoter tried to tour you in *The King and I*."

"Very funny. But you want to know the worst of it? The women! Sending me back my pictures! I must have got back a hundred thousand pictures, some of them torn up, some with the face crossed out. One woman painted out my hat and hair and drew on a Humpty Dumpty head."

"Jesus."

"Yeah—"

"You over it?"

"I'll never get over it. It's the kind of thing you never get over."

It was getting to the delicate part of the conversation. Lou knew he must tread carefully. "Did you ever speak to Dorrie Bridges again?"

"No comment."

"You were at her birthday party, weren't you?"

"I was invited."

Lou phrased his next question very carefully. "It's a kind of coincidence that you lost your hair in flames and Dorrie died in a fire?"

"Why is that a coincidence?"

"Well, it's almost like a poetic justice. I mean, like you couldn't have planned it another way."

"Planned what. What the hell are you driving at?"

"Like if, for instance, if you wanted to get even with her for what she did, I mean—what I'm really trying to say is you hate her so much, you'd—"

"Hate her?" Hoagy Harris walked briskly out of the kitchen, beckoning Lou to follow. "Let me show you something."

The private cinema in the basement was a miniature homage to the Loew's Pitkin Avenue of Hoagy's childhood, with a star-studded dome, gilt statuary, green plush and red velvet draperies. "Make yourself comfortable. No putting gum under the seats."

Lou wondered if Hoagy had turned into Norma Desmond, playing his old movies over and over, living in the past in order to forget the present and ignore the future.

"You're a nosy bastard, aren't you?"

"Just a reporter doing a job."

"That's what Dorrie said. Look—I'm going to show you something that nobody else has seen—except for the few people involved, of course."

"What is it?" Maybe he'd murdered Dorrie and filmed it. Very Hollywood.

"After my wife left, I cut out of here myself. I just got into my car and drove until I ran out of gas. Then I got out of the car—it was in the High Desert past Palm Springs—and I just kept walking until I couldn't walk any farther, until I collapsed. I must have been out in that desert two, three days when they found me. A family in a camper. From Lodi. They didn't know who the hell I was or whether I had a dime. They took care of me—treated me like some mental retard hipster or something, I don't know, I was half out of my mind anyway. Finally, when I was up and around, they bought me a bus ticket back to L.A. and when they put me on the bus, the daughter—eighteen years old, Phyllis her name was —she gave me the fifty bucks I knew she had saved up for Disneyland." His voice cracked. "I sent them a thousand dollars when I got back and then I began to think of what had happened and I wrote a script about a fugitive—a fugitive from truth—and I sent it to Alain LeGrand. You know, the French *cinéma vérité* guy. This was my *Four Hundred Blows*, my personal cavalcade. I told him I would finance it myself if he would agree to total secrecy."

He darkened the room. The screen lit up. Hoagy Harris continued. "We spent the last six months making this movie. LeGrand says it's his finest film and I have given the performance of all time. He says I'm like Sinatra's Maggio when Sinatra was all washed up. He says he's proud to call me an actor."

Lou watched the film and felt like the man who peered through the hole in King Tut's tomb and reported seeing wonderful things. Here was a raging panther of a man, bald, weather-beaten, menacing, terrifying, and heartbreaking at the same time, with nary a touch of Savalas cutes or Brynner suaves. This was a wounded American, an urban animal who has been hurt and banished by the tribe. In order to live he must face his own mortality. In order to survive humiliation, he must learn to love himself for the man he is.

"You'll win the Academy Award for this."

Hoagy busied himself with the film and the projector before replying. "So, you were asking me if I hated Dorrie Bridges? How could I hate her? She's given me my life. If I'm a whole person now, if I'm a fine actor, it's because of her and what she says about the truth. That's what I wanted to tell her that night at her birthday party."

With an abrupt gesture, he took off his Stetson and whirled it across the room. "And I wanted her to see this!"

The hair on his head looked uncannily real.

"Looks good—"

"Pull it."

"I'm—I'm not into personal violence."

"Come on—" Hoagy grinned encouragement.

Lou took a handful of curls and tugged.

"Harder, man."

Lou pulled harder. "Amazing. It feels real."

"It should. It is real. The goddam stuff grew back."

"Congratulations—"

"What's to congratulate?"

"I don't understand you. Aren't you glad it grew back?"

"Sure I'm glad. I like having my hair. But I know something now I didn't know before. I don't need the hair. It's just something I wear. I can shave it off any time and still be me! You understand?"

"You should have seen him!" Lou said to Jennie Bliss Sternholdt in the Polo Lounge a few hours later.

"Where've you been? I've been going crazy!" Jennie hissed.

He kissed her cheek. "Please. Not in front of all these people."

"You nearly missed her—"

"Missed who?"

"That woman over there. Finishing her drink." She indicated a heavyset woman in a drab shirtwaist dress, her gray hair in a sagging bun, her tired features bare of cosmetics.

"Who is it?"

"She was paged. It's Pia Melanaiki. I recognized the name. One of your Hot Thirty!"

"The Greek heiress?" It couldn't be. The file photographs showed her slim and sultry with the lush mouth and harem eyes of the eastern Mediterranean aristocracy. True, Dorrie's story about her had been eleven years before, but no woman could change that much. She would be in her early thirties now. This woman appeared to be on the wrong side of fifty.

"It can't be."

"Why are you so stubborn? Waiter?" Jennie asked the waiter the woman's identity, jogging his memory with a five-dollar bill.

"Melanaiki. Greek family. Maintains a suite year round."

Lou scribbled a hasty note introducing himself and asking if he might have a word with her. Her response was an abrupt and speedy departure.

"Miss Melanaiki, *please*—" Lou caught up with her in the lobby.

"I don't know you."

"All I want is to ask you one or two questions—"

"What about?"

She was walking fast. "Dorrie Bridges."

"How dare you!" They had reached the elevator. The door opened. She stepped inside and was gone.

"Did she do it?" Jennie had paid the bill and joined him.

"I wouldn't be surprised. After all these years, she's still mad."

"I can't imagine any woman running away from you."

When Jennie looked at him like that, he had to admit there were worse things than being an unemployed love object. "Okay, angel, what do you want to do tonight?"

"Well—" She moved very close so that their toes touched.

"Well, indeed—"

"I thought you might like to come with me."

"You mean you're taking me home without buying me dinner?"

"I had something better in mind. I'm going out to Malibu to see Glitz Dreamburg—"

"The infamous Glitz Dreamburg at the notorious Malibu Bitch House?"

"The same. I thought it would make a great location for a new Japanese beer commercial."

"Doesn't Foxy Fenton live there, too? What a coincidence."

"Yeah—isn't it? I can't imagine what made me call Glitz to see if she'd let us shoot there."

He felt like a jackass. "Jennie. I don't know what I'd do without you."

"Keep that thought."

They crossed the lobby and joined those waiting in the porte cochere for their cars.

"I may get a commercial to direct," she confided. "They

wanted Joan Tewkesbury but they're waiting to hear from her agent."

"You're better than Joan Tewkesbury."

"Maybe not better. But I'm good."

"I'll say you're good. I'll take a billboard on the Strip to testify to that. 'Jennie Bliss Sternholdt is good!' "

Her face crumpled. "Goddam you, I'm talking about my work. Not sex. Why do you make everything a joke? Why can't you be serious?"

"Okay, I'll be serious. Let me ask you something very serious."

"What?"

"To get what you want—would you commit murder?"

At that precise moment a golden Venus swathed in gauze arose from the crimson shell of a Ferrari 308. "Hi, handsome!" Raising her eyebrows at Lou with provocative impudence, she pushed him playfully aside on her way into the hotel.

The spaniel hurt in Jennie's eyes reminded him of the girl he took to his high school prom and then abandoned to the hag line when the princess he later married crooked her little finger at him. Wounded or not, Jennie Bliss Sternholdt was made of stronger stuff. She took a small piece of his skin from the tender place at his wrist and pinched it as hard as she could between two fingernails. "I might."

"New York City!" The bus driver smiled at her through his mirror as the Greyhound Bus dipped into the Lincoln Tunnel and roared across the belly of the Hudson River. It was just before eight of a fine summer morning. After twenty-two hours on the road including stops at Knoxville and Washington, D.C., Dora June Bridges was about to arrive at the city of her birth.

All she could remember of her infancy was the sound of

crying, her own and Momma's mingled together. In her mind were faded snapshots of surfaces with cracks in them: broken sidewalks, stained and dripping bathtub and sink, a drinking mug with a Mickey Mouse face that had a jagged line between the ears.

Mallie had brought her home to Roper before she was two. She had no notion where she and her mother had lived in New York and had lacked the nerve to ask. If she had any actual memories of the city, they were long since absorbed in the subsequent lifetime of impressions provided by movie shows, TV, and magazines. She wanted to see it all, the skyscrapers she had glimpsed in the Nineveh distance from the Jersey flatlands, the Statue of Liberty in the harbor, the Metropolitan Museum, Bloomingdale's emporium, Times Square, Central Park, Fifth Avenue, all of it, every inch of it and including the Atlantic Ocean. She had never seen an ocean, though Mallie had once told her about a Sunday picnic at Coney Island where Dora June meandered away and was found playing in the surf, naked as a jaybird, laughing as the waves crashed over her.

"Watch your step, girlie." The driver gave his final benediction as the passengers disembarked in the gloomy lower level of the Port Authority Terminal on Eighth Avenue and Forty-first Street near Times Square. It being the height of the morning rush hour, there were more people than she had ever seen in one place before, running, shoving, shouting past her. Everywhere were signs, arrows, warnings. This Way Out. Watch Your Bag. No Spitting. No Soliciting. Pickpockets Will Be Prosecuted. No loitering. No littering. No *nothing,* someone had scrawled in spray paint.

Her money belted to her skin, Dorrie staggered under the weight of her oversize suitcase and portable sewing machine. In movie shows about New York, smiling colored redcaps tapdanced attention and always said, "Carry your bags, lady?" There were none to be seen. Maybe they had all moved to Hollywood to be in the movie shows.

The crowd carried her to the street where the noise roared up to smite her like a runaway freight train. Cars, trucks, buses, and pedestrians fought vocally for every advantage to inch them closer to their destinations. Sirens screamed for the privileged passage of an ambulance and squad car. Youth on bicycles and pushing hand carts teased the traffic by moving against it, snaking through the stalled vehicles in sneering triumph.

"Taxi!" she called out feebly. An old woman knocked her aside and scrambled into the cab.

"I believe I was ahead of you, ma'am!"

"Git outta here!" The sweet old grandmother brushed the back of her hand to her chin in the traditional Italian gesture of dismissal.

"You just arrive in the big city, sugar?" The colored man beside her looked like Sidney Poitier. He was all dressed in purple and he was smiling at her.

"I'm sorry, sir. I don't speak to strangers." While she believed in Civil Rights with all her heart, she felt uneasy conversing with a man she did not know whether he was colored or white.

"I'm not a stranger. My name's Duke. Like, you know, Duke Ellington? Now, little lady, you look lost and hungry. How would you like to have a nice breakfast. I know a nice place just around the corner."

"Thank you kindly, I'm sure, but—" A taxi had deposited a passenger in the middle of the avenue. "Taxi!" she called.

"I'll getcha taxi, lady!" A boy of about ten in torn sneakers seized her suitcase and darted out into the traffic, shouting "Taxi!—taxi!"

"Stop! Come back here!" she called.

"The little bastard!" Duke started into the traffic after him.

In her fatigue and agitation, she failed to notice another street urchin creep up behind her and snatch up her sewing machine, fleeing into the terminal. "Sweet Jesus!" Not knowing which way to go, she stopped dead in her tracks. *Oh,*

Tom— Maybe he was right. Maybe she was too young and inexperienced for the big city.

"Please don't go," Tom had begged her up to and including the very last minute the previous morning before the bus pulled out of Nashville. "I've kept my promise, haven't I?"

He had.

"I told you I lost my head and I apologize and it will never happen again."

"I've got to go to New York."

"Wait a year. There are big things for you here. There's so much more I can teach you. Then you can go to New York."

He had played her coverage of Senator Bingham's trial front-page, her by-line a bold 24-point type. The day after the verdict, the *Nashville Times* entire front page was given over to a picture of Bingham knocking her down on the court-house steps with poor Lil howling like a stuck pig in a barn-yard. Because of her, Bob Joe and his cronies were convicted and sentenced to three years' suspended sentence. Never one to miss an opportunity, Old Belle Kinkaid had rushed to Dorrie's side and kicked her. "Your ma's a bad one and so are you, Dora June. Jesus Man Suggs says you are the instrument of the Devil!"

Jesus Man himself had then stepped forward into the direct line of the television cameras and pointed a dramatic finger at Tom Jennings. "And that man *is* the Devil. 'Be not deceived. Whatsoever man soweth, so shall he reap!' "

After the first edition went to press, Tom and Dorrie returned to the Jennings house. "We just put the paper to bed!" Tom told his wife with pride.

"I presume that's not all you put to bed," Nedra Jennings said, pursing her lips out of shape.

"Now what kind of a damned remark is that in front of our houseguest?"

"It's the kind of remark I've been hearing at the club and at the beauty shop and from my very best friends."

"I know your very best friends."

"And today, young Tom asked me a question."

"Maybe I'd better go—"

"Stay right where you are, this concerns you," Nedra commanded, striving to control her feelings. "My own son asked me, 'Momma, can a man have two wives?' And I said, 'Sugar, what do you mean?' And that child, the child that carries your name, he said to me, 'A boy at school, he says Daddy's going to marry Dora June.' It looks like to me the whole world knows you're carrying on with this *hillbilly!*"

"That's a lie, Mrs. Jennings. I've never—"

"Don't never me no nevers, you little bitch, moving into my house trying to take my husband and the father of my children—"

"But I *never*—I'm—I'm a *virgin!*" Dorrie blurted.

"How dare you use vulgar language in my home!" Nedra slapped her across the face. "This is a clean Christian home and I won't have foul language here—"

"The child is trying to tell you—" Tom attempted to be heard.

"Don't tell me. I know what's been going on. And virgin she may very well be, praise *God,* but there are ways and there are ways to be an abomination in the eyes of the Lord. We all know that—"

Tom's angry flush turned puce with rage. His wife was alluding to a sexual practice she denied him as perverted and now accused him of enjoying with Dora June. "You're right, Dorrie. You can't stay here. I'll find you an apartment."

"I'm going to New York."

"Just like that? Where will you live? What will you do?"

"I'll be fine."

"Don't be foolish. I got you into this mess and I'm going to see to it you get a good start in New York." A good friend of his was a woman named Connie Michelin, publisher of *Newsmagazine,* the weekly magazine that presented the lighter, livelier, glossier side of world and national events that *Time* and

Newsweek missed. "I'll fix up an interview for you. No guarantees, of course. But she owes me one."

Dorrie's face fell. "I don't want a favor."

"Don't be silly. I'm doing her a favor."

"But I want to make it by myself," she had insisted. A fine independent woman she had turned out to be. Within five minutes of arriving in New York, both her suitcase and her sewing machine had been stolen. A colored man had tried to pick her up. There wasn't a police officer in sight. She could not seem to raise her voice loudly enough to penetrate the noise.

"Hey, lady—" The police officer emerged from the terminal, her sewing machine in one hand and the small culprit twisting and turning in the other. "This yours?"

"I was minding it for her. Wasn't I minding it for you, lady?" the child begged.

"You ready, sugar?" Duke had pulled up in a long purple Cadillac matching his attire. He pointed to her suitcase on the front seat beside him. "Ready for a nice hot breakfast?" He tipped his hat at the policeman.

"Do you know him?" the police officer asked Dorrie.

"This is her luggage, ain't it? Of course she knows me," Duke purred. "Tell the nice policeman you know me. After all, we're both from the South, ain't we, sugar?"

"Do you?" the officer persisted.

Dorrie opened the Cadillac door and eased out her suitcase. "Thank you, Duke. I surely do appreciate it."

The police officer hailed a taxi and stowed her and her belongings into it. "Do you have a hotel reservation?"

"I most certainly do. The Times Square Hotel!" she proclaimed proudly.

"You're kidding!"

Tom Jennings had made a reservation for her at the renowned Barbizon Hotel for Women, but she had seen an advertisement for this little hotel in the heart of the entertainment and cultural center of the city that took transients. Since she was a transient, she had thought it would be more exciting to make her own arrangements.

The boy who had stolen her sewing machine saw a chance to escape and took off down Eighth Avenue. "Stop! Or I'll shoot!" the officer shouted. *Sweet Jesus!* Dorrie held her breath. The officer had not pulled his gun. "Hope that scared the shit out of him. Now, Miss, did you say the Times Square Hotel?"

"Yes, sir. I made a reservation."

"On Forty-fourth Street?"

" 'West of Times Square!' " she quoted.

"Oh, lady. No *way*."

"I assure you, I do have a reservation."

The hotel sign hung from a broken hinge. On the crumbling front step lay an old woman wearing several layers of clothes despite the summer heat, surrounded by laden paper shopping bags. Standing in the doorway was the biggest man she had ever seen, pasty-skinned behind mirror sunglasses. He was cleaning his fingernails with a switchblade knife. When he ducked his head to peer in at her and stepped forward as if to open the cab door, she reckoned she had had about enough independent adventure for one day. "Take me to the Barbizon Hotel for Women. Lexington Avenue and Sixty-third Street," she instructed the cabbie. Taking a cue from New York movies, she added, "And step on it!"

"Make up your mind! What do you think, I'm a mind reader? First one place, then another place. I'm telling you. Today, I should have stood in bed. A mind reader."

There was a message from Tom Jennings waiting with a dozen American Beauty roses. Her appointment with Connie Michelin was for four o'clock that afternoon at *Newsmagazine.*

"That will give you time to unpack and rest," the hotel receptionist assured her. "Your roommate is out, so just go on upstairs and make yourself at home."

"My roommate?"

"Yes. Most of our rooms are double occupancy and most of our girls love it. It's like still being in college." She consulted a file card. "Ah, yes. Another newcomer. Gloria Greenberg, Roslyn Heights, Long Island. Another newcomer. Just been here a week. She wants to be a model. So many of our girls want to be models. What about you?"

"A reporter."

"Well, if that's what you want. But you're pretty enough to be a model."

The room contained two beds, one four-drawer dresser, two chairs, one closet, a corner sink, and a window facing an airshaft. Everything was covered with Gloria Greenberg's things, the beds and chairs a jumble of skirts, jeans, jackets, dresses, sweaters, most half inside out as if peevishly discarded as insufficient during the act of being tried on. On the floor were more boots in one place than Dorrie had seen at the Sears, Roebuck store, shoes of all colors, bedroom slippers, sneakers, hose, panties, bras.

From the open closet and the dresser drawers spilled more riches. On the dresser top was a bazaar of bracelets, chains, scarves, sunglasses, open lipsticks, spilled powder, creams, pencils, rollers, used tissues, cotton balls, tweezers, and the dried remains of spilled nail polish. In the midst of it all stood a wig stand with a painted face supporting a flowing lion's mane of golden tresses. Where the eyes stared vacantly were several pairs of false lashes caked with mascara.

"Oh, shit! You're here."

Gloria Greenberg's sigh expressed the martyrdom of centuries of abuse. Rather than a symphony, her appearance was a dissonance of textures, shapes, and shrieking colors. Green vinyl boots. Mondrian checked mini-dress. Kabuki white face. Mink-lashed eyes framed in tiny penciled twigs. Gleaming plum lips puckered to produce a pink gum bubble. The entire living sculpture topped with a shag of raven curls.

Kicking aside the mess on the floor, she scooped up armfuls

of clothes from one bed and dumped them on the other. "Okay?"

"Thank you, kindly." Dorrie set her suitcase and sewing machine on the empty bed. "I'm Dora June Bridges."

"Gloria Greenberg. Glo. So where's the rest of your stuff?"

"That's all I have."

"You're kidding. One suitcase?" The Kabuki mask smiled with ghetto eyes. "So—you won't need much room, right? I'm sorry I'm all over the place. But this place is strictly for midgets. At home, my dressing room alone is twice the size of this hole. Tell you what I'll do—" She made a finger calculation of writing numbers on a grocery bag. "One drawer ought to be enough for you. Okay?"

"Whatever you say."

She chose the top dresser drawer, shallower than the others, and emptied it onto her bed. "There. Plenty of room. Okay?"

"Real fine."

"Now, about makeup and stuff." She used her forearm to clear a few inches of space on the dresser top. "Okay?"

All Dorrie had was a jar of Pond's cold cream to help dry skin lines caused by sun and wind and an as yet untried tube of Erace which was guaranteed to hide the dark circles certain to result in the high life of New York.

"That's it?" Glo exclaimed. "That's the whole shmeer?"

"Wha-at?"

"What do you use? The pill?"

"I—I feel fine."

"Come on, tell me. I know about those hot southern dudes. Emko? Enovid? The Dalkon Shield? You know what happened to me, I lost my Dialpack, could you die?"

Dorrie had been taught it was polite to be polite. She couldn't understand a word Glo was saying.

"Here, try this!" Glo held out a tube called Cupid's Quiver.

"What is it?"

"Taste it!" Glo insisted gleefully, squeezing some on Dorrie's finger.

"It tastes like—candy syrup—kind of sweet—"

"You don't know what it's for?" Glo doubled up in hysterics.

The laughter got Dorrie's goat. If this was what New York people were going to act like, then maybe she'd have another think about living here.

"Hey, listen, I'm sorry. Listen, it's—it's—" Hysteria cracked her up again. "Okay, I'll tell you. It's a new kind of hair cream. You know, conditions your hair—" So saying, she removed her wig and hung it on the doorknob. Her own hair was a mass of short brown ringlets. "What do you think?"

"About what?"

"My hair. You think it's too curly? My brother says I should change my name to Shirley Synagogue."

"Change your name?"

Glo shook her curls and pressed the tip of her finger into her cheek. "Shirley Synagogue is a Jewish Shirley Temple! Get it? 'On the goo-ood ship, loll-i-pop—' " The stunned look on Dorrie's face brought her up short. Without asking permission, she scooped up most of Dorrie's Pond's cream and began to work it into her face. "Let's get one thing straight." She glared at Dorrie in the mirror. "I'm Jewish. If that's a problem, let me know."

The only Jewish people she'd ever known were Irv and Becky Levy, who kept the fine jewelry store down home. Not that she hadn't heard things about Jews, and Catholics, too, and New York being overrun with both. "Well, I'm a lapsed Baptist. If that's a problem, be sure and let me know."

"I mean, you're not—"

"Not what?"

"—a member of the Ku Klux Klan or anything like that?"

"Now what the hell kind of an idea is that?"

"Don't get sore. It's just—you know— Listen, I'm sorry."

"The only time I ever wore a sheet was last Hallowe'en. Scared Jim Ed Loomis out of a year's growth!"

"You want to go eat?"

"I'd like to but I think maybe I'd better settle in and get myself ready for my job interview. This afternoon."

"You're in town five minutes, you've already got an interview? Where?"

"Newsmagazine."

"What are you, a secretary?"

"Reporter."

Glo was impressed. "What are you going to wear?"

Dorrie showed her the neat seersucker suit, black leather pumps, and white cotton shorties she had planned in her mind.

Glo was incredulous. "You're going to wear *that?*"

"What's wrong?"

"Where've you been, the moon?"

Undaunted, Dorrie explained, "It's important for a young lady to look responsible as well as refined."

"What do you want to look like, a prison matron? I'll have to loan you something of mine. Here!" She thrust a navy blue gym slip at her. "The latest from Mary Quant." Blue patterned pantyhose and red vinyl boots completed the outfit. "Got them in the King's Road in London."

Dorrie saw herself in the mirror but had grave doubts. "I can't go out on a job interview looking like this."

"Believe me, kid. British is in. You want to succeed in New York, you got one motto, 'Dress Briddish, think Yiddish!'" She tapped the side of her temple. "Trust me."

Dora June Bridges's first meal in New York City was at the Dee-Lish Coffee Shop where Gloria Greenberg insisted on ordering a typical dish, cream cheese and lox on toasted bagel. "Put hair on your chest! Isn't it great?"

"Real fine." Dorrie managed to grin while choking down the strange slimy pink substance.

"Who's your friend?" A darkly handsome man of about Tom's age slid into the booth beside Glo.

"Dorrie, this is Nicky Zinn. Rhymes with 'sin.' Keep your legs crossed."

When it was time for Dorrie to leave for her appointment at *Newsmagazine,* Nicky Zinn insisted on accompanying her. He ran a travel agency downtown but lived near the Barbizon and had come home to walk the dog. "I'm divorced," he pointed out, "living all alone and hungry for love."

"Watch out for him," Glo warned. "He's cocksure."

Outside the offices of *Newsmagazine,* Nicky said, "Don't worry if they turn you down. You can always be a model. I'll send you around to a couple of photographers I know—"

"I don't care to be a fashion model. I happen to be a reporter and that's what I intend to remain, Mr. Zinn."

"Okay, okay." He waved his fingers as if they'd been burned. "Call me Nicky, huh? I'll be by for you at eight."

Her head whirling from all that had occurred in the few hours since her bus arrived, she gave her name to the *Newsmagazine* receptionist.

At the sight of Connie Michelin, Dorrie thanked her stars she had let Glo dress her for the occasion. The woman could have won a Twiggy look-alike contest—her hair blunt-cut by Vidal Sassoon himself, her narrow frame housed in a Tuffin and Foale mini-dress—except for one thing. She was twice Twiggy's age and despite good intentions, good connections, and considerable stamina, the extra years showed, though those who depended on her, especially Andrew Van Kennan, assured her they did not.

"Have a pew, angel puss! I'm on the phone."

The phone was a microphone kind of contraption in the center of her glass and chrome desk. "Go on, Quin."

Quin's voice sounded tired. "I say dump Twiggy. Save her for next week. I say go with Svetlana."

"And I say who wants to see a Russian fat lady on the cover of a newsmagazine, right, Drew?" The man standing beside a wall-size aquarium simply nodded. "Drew says 'right'!"

"It's Stalin's daughter, for God's sake," Quin persisted. "She's defected. *Time* will have it. *Newsweek* will have it."

"Exactly!" Connie slapped the table. "Let them run with the Russian fat lady. Let them tell the people who the Russian fat lady is. We'll go with Twiggy—outsell them all—then next week, we come out with a Svetlana exclusive, right? Andrew here knows everyone, don't you, angel puss?"

"But, Chief, this is a *news*magazine—"

"And Drew here is going to get us an exclusive news angle on Svetlana. Maybe her favorite borscht receipe or Secrets of Soviet Sex, right, Drew?"

If Connie was enjoying herself, Drew and the unseen Quin were not. Dorrie wondered if she should be pretending not to listen, like sitting next to a family argument in a bus station.

"Whatever you think best, Chief." Quin's spirit had gone.

"Glad you agree. Do it like this." She included her visitor in the conversation with an ingratiating smile. "Twiggy and Justin on the cover. Small head of Svetlana with blurb, 'Stalin killed my mother but he was my father and I tried to love him,' shorter and punchier but you know what I mean. Then 'Ralph Nader: Saint or Con Man?' And the editorial page, remember what we discussed this morning?"

"I remember." Quin's lack of enthusiasm faded into a grunt.

With a wink at Dorrie, the publisher said, "Just do it. Mick Jagger's mouth, that's all, the entire page, and the cut lines, 'Can't get no satisfaction from local, state, or Federal Government agencies? Send them this picture with your complaint.' Okay, everything else as discussed. Antiwar UN. Florence Art Treasures and starving Italian children, which to save? Go, everybody, go!"

Connie switched off the phone and did a mock collapse on the table. Drew applauded languidly. "You should be on the cover."

"Dorrie? May I call you Dorrie? That's what Tom called you. *Dorrie Bridges.* I like the name. Dorrie, Drew here is the best-looking man in New York and he knows it."

Drew didn't bother to deny the allegation. "How do you do?"

"Modest, isn't he?" Connie laughed.

Drew preened himself. "You know as well as I do that the only truly modest people truly have something to be modest about." The summer heat did not appear to affect him. His three-piece white linen suit worn with a pink shirt and tie showed not a sign of wrinkling or damp. "Must go."

Her face smiled but her voice hardened. "Must stay while I talk to Dorrie Bridges."

"I've got Serge Obolensky waiting."

"Maybe he'll marry Svetlana. Make a White Russian princess out of her. That would really show the old man."

"Connie, really."

"Look, Drew, it's turkey-talk time. Your connections are great, you're great. You're young, not much older than Dorrie here, are you?"

"I'm twenty-three."

"She's—how old are you, Dorrie?"

"Eighteen."

"Drew, you may be young, but your column sounds old. Newport. Palm Beach. Tuxedo Park. Who the hell cares? We need to get the young readers. The war babies. The new postwar generation that doesn't care about the Old Guard. Now, Dorrie here—"

"Can we continue this later? I'm late—"

Connie simply stared at him. He sat down.

"Dorrie, here, broke the Bingham story in Tennessee. Biggest story from the South since Grant took Richmond." Dorrie laughed involuntarily. "Where you from? Nashville?"

"No, a little town named Roper."

"Where the hell is that?"

"Just a little ways down the road from 'Resume Speed,'" Dorrie replied with Minnie Pearl's famous line.

Connie laughed more than was rightly necessary while Drew cooled his heels like a naughty schoolboy waiting to be released from detention.

"No college?"

"No, ma'am, but I intend to keep on studying while I work."

"*Pas un problème*, believe me. I've been to three colleges, including Radcliffe—" Dorrie nodded. "That's part of Harvard, you know. Famous. Some call it Radcliffe Hall—"

Andrew snorted.

"Ever heard of Radcliffe Hall, Dorrie?"

"No, ma'am—but it does sound interesting." She wondered when the job interview would begin.

"Well, Andrew, what do you think of her?"

"Charming. Utterly charming—"

"I'm glad you approve. She's your new assistant."

"Now, just one minute—"

To Dorrie she explained, "Drew writes our 'Whispers' column—gossip, rumors, scandal, all the news that's not fit to be said out loud. It's always been the first thing people turn to, but lately—"

"Oh, for God's sake—"

"Lately, it's been slipping. Not much but definitely slipping. And Mr. Van Kennan here has been complaining of overwork. So here she is, Drew, your new assistant. Tom Jennings says she's not afraid of any*one* or any*thing*. So I'm sure she won't be afraid of you!"

"Connie—" Drew made a desperate appeal.

"Serge Obolensky is waiting, Drew. I suggest you hurry along, and for God's sake get some dirt on someone born after the storming of the Winter Palace. I want to talk to Dorrie. She'll report to you Monday morning."

Connie waited until he left before opening Dorrie's scrapbook. She read slowly and carefully, skipping nothing, nodding and making notes. "You're good. You've got an eye for the pertinent detail."

"Thank you, ma'am."

"Connie."

"Connie."

"How's two hundred a week?"

"Two hundred what? Words?"

"Dollars. Two hundred dollars a week salary."

"I— Well—" Nicky Zinn had told her not to take the first offer and to say she had something higher in mind. How could she say that to two hundred dollars?

"Okay, two and a quarter. You'll earn every cent, don't worry." She scribbled a note. "Give this in to Personnel."

Connie shook the girl's hand and held on to it. "Dorrie, you've got it all over that dumb schmuck. You've got it where it counts." She pressed Dorrie's hand to her own forehead. "Up here." Her hand moved Dorrie's hand to her breast. "And here, too." Her eyes met Dorrie's. The younger woman held her gaze, unflinching, steady. "You see this office, Dorrie? In a few years, it will be yours. I can feel it in my bones. In the next few years I'm going to build a communications empire, everything geared to the next generation, your generation, and I'll be looking to groom someone young and smart as hell to run *Newsmagazine!*"

Her face all but touching Dorrie's, her eyes held Dorrie's in a silence that seemed endless. Her lips parted. Her hands reached up and gently pushed Dorrie's head forward so that she could kiss her softly on the forehead. "Make me proud of you."

Things in New York moved faster than a hound dog on fire. Here she was in New York City less than one whole day and she'd been robbed clean as a whistle and rescued by a policeman and she had all but been drugged and taken against her will to a house of ill fame. What's more, she was sharing a room with a girl of the Jewish persuasion who, against all stereotype of stinginess and sharp practice, had lent her the right clothes to wear for her interview with Connie Michelin, and, most amazing of all, she had a job on *Newsmagazine* paying two hundred and twenty-five dollars each and every week. Furthermore, she appeared to have a social date for the evening with Nicky Zinn, whose parting words had been, "I'm going to show you some things you've never seen before."

Scooting up Madison Avenue, dodging cars nimble as a mare in a bull pasture, she wondered if he would take her to the top of the Empire State Building or on the Staten Island ferry, two things she had mentioned in the coffee shop. She had always thought she would see these things with Jim Ed but there was no use crying over spilled milk. Nicky Zinn certainly had a funny name and he was certainly old enough to have more important things on his mind than showing her the sights, but then again he did allow as how he was divorced and living alone with his dog so maybe he just wanted some company.

So did she, if the truth be known, except that if the truth really be known, the company she wanted was Jim Ed and Mallie, too, and maybe Tom, but mostly Jim Ed so she could tell him each and every detail of each and every blessed thing that had happened to her today.

Instead, there was Gloria Greenberg. With a high sense of anticipation, she turned her key in the lock and pushed. The door of their room was bolted from the inside. "Gloria!" She could hear movement. "Gloria, it's me. Dorrie!"

"Shut up!" Glo opened the door a few inches. The room was dark. "Oh, shit, I didn't expect you back so soon."

"You taking a nap? Sorry, I'll just tiptoe around."

"No!" Glo barred the way. "Look, I'm sorry, I've got somebody here."

It took a few seconds for Dorrie to understand. "But—the rules. No male visitors—"

"I sneaked him in. For God's sake, go down to the lounge. I'll be right down."

"Miss Greenberg!" The manager had materialized like a genie. The door slammed shut. He rapped firmly. "Miss Bridges. Kindly advise Miss Greenberg to present herself at my office. If she is not there in a quarter of an hour, I'll be forced to call the authorities to remove her."

Nicky Zinn emerged smiling as if this was an ordinary occurrence and disappeared down the fire exit stairs. A tearful Glo blubbered like a haggard twelve-year-old, her ruined mascara like two black eyes. "My parents are going to kill me! Oh, Dorrie, why don't we find an apartment and share it?"

The manager gave Glo twenty-four hours to vacate the premises. Thanks to *The New York Times,* they found a one-bedroom apartment tenement on East Fifty-third Street featuring a broken toilet and exposed wires. "My parents are going to kill me!" Glo predicted happily.

Over the weekend, the entire Greenberg family moved in discarded furniture from the family garage plus a year's supply of stewed fruit. "You look like a very fine person," Mrs. Greenberg told Dorrie. "Please take care of my little girl."

On Monday morning at precisely ten o'clock Dorrie Bridges reported for work at *Newsmagazine.* The "Whispers" office was locked. Andrew Van Kennan was not in, the receptionist said. Nor had he left any instructions for her. Nor made any provision for a desk or place to sit.

"Would you please try him at home?" Dorrie asked, feeling as if she were taking up room.

"Mr. Van Kennan is not to be disturbed at home unless it's an emergency," the receptionist informed her.

"I do believe this is an emergency. I believe Mr. Van Kennan would like me to be covering some important assignment for him."

Andrew Van Kennan did not answer. Dorrie had two choices. To go running in to Miss Connie Michelin, telling tales and complaining, or to solve this problem on her ownsome. She sat in the reception area, reading old *Life* magazines, until Andrew Van Kennan arrived a few minutes past noon. "Well, if it isn't Miss Cornpone."

"Good morning." Never show a snake your true feelings.

Uninvited, she followed him to the "Whispers" office. Inside, there was only one desk. He sat down and dialed the phone, leaving her to stand in awkward neglect.

She could outstare a snake and outwait a badger if it came to that. When he finished his call, which consisted of a lengthy review of the weekend's drinking, she said, "Shall I order a desk moved in here with you or would you prefer me to sit outside?"

"Connie says you're a whiz. Any ideas for next week's column?"

"Well, as a matter of fact, there's a rumor that Guevara was smuggled in from South America and is hiding in Brooklyn—"

"And—"

"Yoko Ono is pregnant. Why don't I speak to her doctor—?"

"Uh huh—"

"Jack Ruby's diaries?" she said to test his reaction.

"I think you should learn a little bit about the city first." Her first day as Andrew Van Kennan's assistant, he sent her to Tiffany's to have his cigarette case repaired. She spotted Paul Newman and overheard his inscription on a silver pendant for Joanne Woodward's birthday. After which, she collected some fabric swatches from Jimmy Amster for Andrew's summer cottage, picked up his concert seats for the summer Pops, and then went all the way up to 156th Street to the Museum of the American Indian to check out a tip on a lost treasure only to find it was closed on Mondays.

"Sorry. I meant go up there tomorrow. A good reporter always checks."

"Never you mind, I enjoyed the experience."

The following days were a contest of wills. Andrew probing the Augean stables of his mind for dirty tasks. Dorrie frisky as a pup and just as tireless in chasing anything that moved.

"Pia Melanaiki's wedding is this afternoon at five. Plaza Hotel," Dorrie informed him one morning.

"Those Greeks! They're worse than the Jews. So ostentatious. The wire services will cover. We'll pick up on it if we have to."

"Maybe something will happen or someone will be there, like Onassis, and we can get an exclusive."

"Sorry, sweetie. Gloria Vanderbilt is doing a poetry reading. For the Heart Fund."

"Well," she said as casually as pie on a windowsill, "why don't you do Gloria Vanderbilt and let me do the wedding?"

"Why the hell not? It's about time you earned your keep."

Olympia "Pia" Melanaiki, nineteen, was to marry Johnny Capedis, twenty-eight. Both were the children of tycoons. The families knew each other and approved. What's more, the couple were known to be madly in love and planning a year's honeymoon. Romantic, yes, but as Drew pointed out, the wire services would cover it. There would have to be a special angle for "Whispers."

Dorrie stopped in the Plaza florist and bought the largest bunch of the cheapest flowers, daisies and jonquils, packed in a long box. Carrying these into the elevator, she asked for the Melanaiki suite. "Hurry. I've got the wedding bouquets."

Security guards patrolled the corridors. She walked right by the guards and knocked at the door. "Florist," she said.

"Maybe you can do something!" Costa Melanaiki stormed. "She's locked herself in."

"Who are you?" Lina Melanaiki, the bride's mother, greeted her with suspicion.

"I'm—I'm in her art class, ma'am. Dora June Bridges?" If the guards searched her, she had identification.

"Say something to her. Make her come out."

Dorrie tapped on the locked door. "Pia?" Pause. "Pia, darlin'. I have a message for you. A special message? A very important message." A long pause and then a thin voice pressed to the door quavered, "Who from?"

"From someone who loves you a great deal."

"Tell me who it's *from?*" the voice sobbed.

"Let me in and I'll tell you."

"Oh, no you don't!"

"Pia? It's *personal*. I can't go announcing something personal in front of all these people now, can I?"

"Tell them to go away. Tell them I can see through the keyhole and I want them far away from the door!"

The parents and retainers obeyed. Dorrie stood in close view of the keyhole. After another pause, the door opened wide enough for Dorrie to spring against it and into the bedroom before the distraught heiress slammed it shut again and locked it. The first thing to catch Dorrie's eye was a large steak and French fries congealed in grease on a coffee table.

"Who are you? A cop?" The bride looked too young to be getting married, as if she were playing actress in the pearl-encrusted Dior wedding gown. Her face drawn from crying, she seized a pointed, serrated steak knife from the tray. "I told them I'm not getting married. I told them I'd kill myself first."

"Now, Pia. Just let's us have a little talk about all this." It reminded her of the time Rainey Stone birthed a dead boy child and ran up on the roof threatening to join him in the arms of Jesus.

"Stay away from me."

Dorrie stayed where she was.

"It's a real Greek tragedy. They just don't believe me. Why won't they believe me?"

"Pia—"

"You don't believe me, either. Well, believe this!" She extended her arm, wrist up, and brought the cutting edge of the knife down as hard as she could on the pulsing blue vein.

Men talked about the Malibu Bitch House with awe and longing. *Playboy* had written it up as the ultimate sorority house for the most beautiful and insatiable women, the fortress of ferocious warriors known for their arrogance and cruel rituals.

Men who had actually been there spoke of their experiences with the smug aplomb of the survivor. Naked women oiling themselves and each other on the sheltered sun deck. Sex games of infinite variety and imagination, the most infamous being Harem Kidnap, in which a lone male was used and abused until he no longer amused. The indoor-outdoor Jacuzzi was surrounded by tropical plants and incense candles, the scented water pulsing through jets cleverly placed to provide sensuous contentment.

Much of what was said was true. The Malibu Bitch House first earned its name and notoriety in the mid-seventies. Nobody could remember who first called it that in print. Suddenly it became a California landmark, part of the Coast Mythology. It was where the floating population of International Beauties fled to hang out, hide out, dry out, and otherwise work out their problems, tensions, and future strategies regarding men, money, and careers.

Glitz Dreamburg had bought the beach house in 1973 when she arrived in California with the modest intention of becoming a major star of motion pictures and television. Since major movie stars lived in Malibu, that's where she would live. To help defray expenses and to attract attention, including a better class of men, she invited the prettiest girls she could find to share the house and use it as a kind of exclusive club.

Glitz Dreamburg was not her real name. At the urging of her numerologist, Gloria Greenberg became Glorious Dreamburg, a major movie star name clearly destined to go above the title except for one problem. Glorious Dreamburg could not act. Furthermore, the camera resisted her charms. When forced to photograph her, the camera turned nasty, distorting her features and adding lumpish pounds to what was actually a fine, voluptuous body.

After a year of heartbreak worse than psoriasis, she switched professions. The producer of a daytime humiliation TV show, "Boob Town," needed a zany production assistant to glitz things up.

"It was like leading a dog to watermelon," she later said in a *TV Guide* interview, committing her first Goldwynesque glitz to the English language. "You can't change the spots on a leper!" she dismissed one actor's attempt to change his image. Every TV show she was hired to glitz instantly climbed the charts until the job became her name and Glitz quotes became a form of sub-humor just below Polish jokes.

Her greatest gift was an instinct for finding people who would debase themselves on television. Fat men in bikinis learning to dance the Hustle. A young couple agreeing to marry on camera while being assaulted with cream pies, water hoses, and a *piñata* of garbage. One of her earliest triumphs was a cleanup contest between a team of young mothers changing their babies' diapers and dog owners following their pets with pooper-scoopers.

When several producers clamored for her services, she set up her own independent agency, Glitz Dreamburg Ltd. The entire world was her casting couch. Who was immune to the question, "How'd you like to be on television?" It was, as Glitz frequently noted, "a great way to get laid."

Though she could easily afford the upkeep, the Malibu Bitch House continued to function as before. Most of the women came and went. Some used it intermittently as a place to meet married lovers. Foxy Fenton had moved in after a sterling three-day marriage to a man she'd met on the Red Eye who did strange and wonderful things to her in the dead of night.

A leader of the Young Hollywood Brats, Foxy was the daughter of a Paterson, New Jersey, mortician. She had learned from her father all the undertaker's tricks of emotional blackmail and guilt. This basic training made her, at twenty-four, one of Hollywood's hottest agents. And youngest. A famous cartoon showed her going to work on roller skates. Another had her in the backseat of a limo done up as a playpen.

Between Glitz and Foxy was a symbiotic relationship that could only flourish in southern California. They hated and feared each other while vowing to be best friends. They borrowed each other's clothes, hairdressers, and studs. In collusion as packager and agent, they were responsible for eight of the Top Twenty shows on television.

They enjoyed the power games of dangling jobs and smashing hopes. They held frequent "auditions" for naive and trusting men. When the games bored them, they would fall into bed together and give each other the sexual gratification that men could neither understand nor provide.

"Lou?" Jennie Bliss Sternholdt interrupted his reverie.

"You!" he replied automatically, his eyes on the road. He didn't want to miss the turnoff.

"Before we get there," she said with an exaggerated slowness she evidently thought was cute but drove him bananas, "there's something I've got to tell you."

"You're married and have three kids."

"Please, Lou—"

"You're pregnant, God forbid."

"Come *on!*"

"You're not pregnant!"

"Pull over. We've got to talk."

"I'm pregnant."

"Lou, for God's sake, please cut it out and pull over."

"The force is with you?" He couldn't stop.

"This is serious."

"The Los Angeles Police Force?"

"One more word and I'm—"

"Okay, I'm sorry. It's not the toilet paper, I trust. I thought we settled the toilet paper." This morning they had had a fight about toilet paper. The roll had run out while he was in the bathroom and she had demanded to know why he didn't replace it with a new roll from the cabinet under the sink. He had made the chauvinist observation that it was her job, not his. The ensuing brawl concluded with his apology and their joint agreement that they were great lovers and great lovers did not fight about toilet paper and they would simply kiss and make up and forget the whole thing.

In Lou's experience, women did not forget. Since he also

had the bad habit of leaving the toilet seat up and Jennie had fallen in, it might well be that the Great Toilet Wars were about to start up again.

"Lou, I did something. Please don't hate me."

"Who is it? Warren Beatty? I'll kill him."

Jennie Bliss Sternholdt slumped against the car seat in tears. "You keep doing it."

Instantly he was contrite. "I'm sorry."

"What are you, a Neil Simon doll? I'm tired of wisecracks."

"It's fear, kiddo. I've heard about Glitz and Foxy. Saber-toothed piranhas. They're going to tear me to shreds. Now tell Papa what you did."

"You promise you won't get mad."

"Promise."

"Well"—she snuggled against him—"when I was telling Glitz I wanted to talk to her about using her place for the commercial and she was asking me what was happening in my life and I said I was getting it together with this great and really sincere person—"

"Da-*daaaaa!*" He twirled his mustachios.

"And she said what were you like and I said you were this brilliant reporter just like Robert Redford and Dustin Hoffman doing Watergate and that you were doing this big article on Dorrie Bridges—"

"Jesus H. Christ!"

"But don't worry, I didn't say you thought somebody killed her or anything. I just said you were looking to talk to people who'd known Dorrie personally and it was all going to be very exciting like a documentary and then before I could say anything else, she said of course I probably knew that Dorrie Bridges was one of her closest and dearest and oldest friends and of course you couldn't do the story without speaking to her and then I said would it be neat to get some of Dorrie's other friends around for some, you know, like reminiscing about old times, you know, like anecdotes and of course everybody would get their name in your article and—"

"—And?"

"Don't worry, Lou—it's all mellow. She said, are you ready? She said were you bringing a photographer and I was real cool and I said no this was just an exploratory visit and she said leave it to her and she'd get a gang of people together. I was going to surprise you but I changed my mind. I don't know how many of the Hot Thirty are going to be there but I thought you should know so you could have your wits about you."

"How could you do this? They won't tell me a thing."

"That shows how much you know."

"I want their innermost secrets."

"People out here love to reveal their innermost secrets. Except to Internal Revenue."

At this bleak moment of his life, Internal Revenue had no power to intimidate. He had no revenue, internal or otherwise.

Glitz Dreamburg stood high above them on the deck of the Bitch House when they pulled in. "What happened to you? You shag off for a Triple F?" It was her latest line, meaning Freeze Frame Fuck, and was being quoted all over town.

"We got lost," he sallied with an idiot laugh.

"Well, wax my Porsche, what in hell's *that*?" Their hostess pointed to his car. "It looks like a Japanese rowboat."

"It's a Putz!" he cried, knowing he sounded like a jerk but unable to stop himself.

"Fun-neeeee—" she gushed as they climbed the stairs. "Say hello to the people."

The people were lounging in and around the famous indoor-outdoor Jacuzzi. The sun had set. Clusters of red, pink, and purple candles were shimmering amid cacti, stunted palms, and carnation plants. Bodies were casually but perfectly arranged as if by a photographer. In the half-darkness, some appeared totally naked while others were in bikinis or towels. Classical guitar oozed from speakers. The sweet smell of grass mingled with the cloy of the carnations.

Nobody acknowledged the newcomers.

"Hello to the people." Lou could hear in his own voice a jauntiness that marked him asshole, schmuck, nerd, wimp, turkey, or all of the above.

"Get comfortable!" Glitz commanded, dropping her sarong. Her body looked as if it were made of caramel candy poured into a mold, smooth and flawlessly colored. Her breasts plump as beanbags, her pubic bush trimmed into a heart-shaped hedge, her sole adornments a pair of seven-inch Italian scuffs and triple-pierced earrings. "There's no cover charge. Strip down."

He was about to say that Jennie Bliss Sternholdt and he were en route to a religious church service and had only stopped in for a minute to say hello to the people and therefore there really wasn't much point stripping down because they really wouldn't be staying, when he noticed that Jennie had unbuttoned her wraparound dress and was standing there for all to see like a goddam statue of Venus de Milo. With arms.

"My—my mother warned me there'd be moments like this." Insane laughter slimed out of his mouth despite best efforts to the contrary. Pulling his T-shirt over his head, he discovered too late that he had forgotten to remove his driving glasses. More slime laughter as he fought to extricate himself from the embarrassment of his exposed white belly and hairy armpits. "Just call me the Lean Machine!" More insane laughter as he flung the T-shirt aside. By now, his asscrusher jeans had slid to half-mast. A slip of the zip, a Larry Csonka kick, and he was as bare as an El Greco Christ and feeling just about as attractive.

"Mind if I slide in here?" he asked Glitz, who lay in the Jacuzzi eyeing him with candor. Pauline Kael had once written that the ruthless have weapons the righteous don't have. In less than five minutes Glitz had him naked, helpless, and utterly in her power.

The water whirled around him, warm and scented. His buttocks found a contoured seat where a pulsing jet of bubbles forced his thighs apart and frothed against what his ex-wife the princess called his parts. Now that he was in the water, the others smiled and nodded, including Jennie, who quite suddenly seemed to be with them instead of him.

Them, he realized, were all women. He was the only man there, naked and helpless in their midst. He had heard the group sex stories, the gang despoilment of a poor, defenseless male. Was he tonight's human sacrifice? Was this what Jennie really wanted to tell him?

Laid back in a Fassbinder trance, his body soothed by the warm water while his genitals seemed separate and highly excited by the precision jets, he considered the women whose eyes were all on him. Except for Jennie Bliss Sternholdt, each and every one was on his Hot 30 list.

Ann Elving, the "Ugly Duckling" who saved President Spears's life. Peachy Purdy Nichols, her red hair skewered into a fetching knot as usual with her trademark knitting needle. Sis Logan seemingly lopsided without the omnipresent Brov of their sister/brother act. "Cholla" Torres naked like the others except for her turquoise earrings and black fedora. Claudine, who was older than Lou himself, looking young and peppy, as compared to Suzy Newcombe, less than half her age, looking like a skeleton with a poor appetite. Foxy Fenton, of course, and Glitz, of course.

All of them had cause and therefore in theory reason to hate Dorrie Bridges and to be involved in her disappearance. This was Manson country. This was high stakes and raw ambition. If each of them had a grudge against Dorrie, it was possible they had banded together and held a kangaroo court of her female peers. Maybe they had invited her to just such a Jacuzzi party as this and drowned her and buried her in the shrubbery.

"We started without you," Glitz said.

"What?"

"You catch up." She offered him a small crystal bowl edged in silver and filled with a fine white powder. A small curved silver spoon looked like a shovel in a miniature beachscape. This was not the time to confess he did not snort. He smoked J but he did not do the hard stuff. He had eaten sheep's eyes in Dubai and sipped hot goat's blood in Addis and smoked dried llama chips in the Andes on the way to Machu Picchu. Recently Jennie had brought home some northern California Sinsimilla that looked like a female mandrake root, voluptuous pods that sighed orgastically when chopped to pieces.

They were all watching him. He had no choice. He dipped a spoon and raised it to his left nostril, the side with the deviated septum, praying he would not cough, gag, spit, or otherwise embarrass himself. Sherlock Holmes did cocaine. He was Sherlock Holmes hot on the trail of Dorrie Bridges, wasn't he? *Alimentary,* my dear Manson.

"No!" Foxy Fenton restrained his hand. "Not like that. Open your mouth."

Lou Dexter opened his mouth.

"Now hold the spoon between your lips. Keep your mouth open." She leaned close and blew the powdery snow right up into his mucous membranes. "Have a toot, brute!"

The rush jolted him through the sound barrier riding the outside of the plane like those girls in *Flying Down to Rio.* His lungs were in his balls. He took a deep breath and tossed himself off. From the inside. Without touching himself. Or moving. The jets of water had eyes and lips and hands.

"Now, try this!" Glitz Dreamburg held a cupped hand to his mouth. "Open up."

He shook his head, wondering if they could all see the tremors shaking him out of his seat.

"Trust me!" she shrieked, forcing his lips apart. Sweet crystals exploded against the roof of his mouth. "Pop Rocks!" she howled.

The women slithered closer, oddly distorted in the candlelight as if separated from him by a fish-eye lens. "I guess Dorrie Bridges used to hang out here," he observed.

"Whenever she was looking for a story," Cholla Torres

sniggered. "But she would never strip off. So modest. Wouldn't even wear a bikini." Her strong Castilian face and black fedora were famous to all who read the United Farmworkers leaflets. She was eating a papaya with her finger with a movement so onanistic that Lou's cock shot to the surface of the water like a periscope. As Jonah said to the whale, you can't keep a good man down.

"What'll we do now?" Claudine growled in her leather voice.

"Nine against one. That's no fun," Peachy Purdy Nichols objected.

"Oh, I don't know about *that!*" a voice purred. Whose, he could not tell. Someone had snuffed out the candles. He was alone in the dark, zonked on coke and Pop Rocks, naked and helpless in a Jacuzzi with nine women including one he, in another context, loved. *If,* as Kipling said, *you can keep your head* while all about you hands were grabbing at you as if you were some kind of bargain counter. And *if you can meet with triumph and disaster* and *if* you can close your eyes and pretend you're really Humphrey Bogart and program your mind to remember every detail, *you'll be a man, my son!*

In ancient Rome, according to Suetonius, the Emperor Tiberius spent his dotage frolicking in a marble pool with schools of tiny boys darting and frisking in the water. Tiberius called them his minnows. These women were sharks and sea lions and porpoises.

They tossed him around like a beach ball. Teeth nibbled and gnawed. Fingernails raked his thighs and traced concentric circles from his navel. Breasts battered him. Hands and chins and knees and elbows smashed and bruised his fragile flesh as his assailants fought over his carcass like hungry dogs, shrieking and howling beasts of prey at the old waterhole.

Slammed against the far side of the Jacuzzi, he found himself in one of the contour seats, panting for breath. The guys at the press club would never believe this. The way things were going, he would not live to tell them. A thrashing body, definitely not Jennie, scrambled onto his lap and straddled him, breaking something under his nose that almost beheaded him and expertly guiding his distended eel into her snapping turtle.

"You're always doing that! It's not fair!" Strong hands pulled her away. Ripped untimely from the womb like poor old MacDuff, he had but a moment's respite for literary contemplation. His rescuer dove headfirst into his lap and sucked him in like an aquatic vacuum cleaner.

This enraged the other kids in the playground.

"She always does that."

"Not fair."

"My turn."

"Get her off him."

"Pull him out. He'll drown."

Terror, pain, and intense sexual excitement create a body chemical more powerful than adrenaline. A tongue found his armpit, a snub-nosed thumb his anus, a voice like Jennie Bliss Sternholdt's growled, "Ever get an Indian burn on your cock?" and proceeded to demonstrate.

"Okay, campers, everyone out of the pool!" Glitz and Foxy were lighting the candles like ushers getting the place ready for the next orgy.

Languidly, as in an Esther Williams water ballet seen through cherry Jell-O, the glistening bodies rose from the roiling water and into waiting floor-length T-shirts emblazoned MALIBU BITCH HOUSE, provided by their thoughtful hostesses.

"Here's a man-size one for you."

The glass doors slid open. The house blazed with lights. The women skirted the Jacuzzi to the indoor room and arranged themselves on the oversize pillows which formed the circular conversation pit. Jennie sat among them as if she had no personal connection with him at all. She was too busy munching from the huge platters of fruit and vegetables that awaited them along with the inevitable Perriers, Tabs, and fresh squoze.

"You sit here. Right in the middle." Foxy Fenton led him stage center to a canvas ottoman. What were they going to do to him now, stone him to death with pineapples? "Okay, turkey, the night is young, what do we do now?"

"Let's play a game!" Jennie said.

"Oh, shit—"

"Stick a pin in her airbag—"

"Sorry, I left my jacks at home—"

Jennie moved to Lou's side. "I say we play a game of Truth. The subject is somebody who was famous for telling the truth. For finding out the truth and revealing the truth and let the shits fall where they may! I'm talking about Dorrie Bridges."

"She's dead and gone."

"Ain't that the truth."

"You all knew her. Now you can dump all your feelings about her." Her eyes traveled rapidly from face to face. "Starting with—" They all leaned forward involuntarily. "Me! I personally say good riddance. Miss Goody Two Shoes. Holier than thou. Poking her nose into other people's affairs. Who appointed her? God? Memorial services. Rewards. Investigations. Who the hell was she? A gossip columnist. Peeking in windows. Picking through garbage—"

Her tirade struck Lou Dexter dumb. It was Jennie's body and Jennie's voice but someone else talking. With sudden recognition he realized she was reciting his words.

"Truth . . . truth . . ." the women began to chant.

"You want the truth?" Jennie's voice quavered. "I'm in love with this geriatric scumbag you see before you and all he's interested in is Dorrie Bridges. He's obsessed with Dorrie Bridges. He's never met the woman but the son of a bitch is in love with Dorrie Bridges. The truth is I'm jealous as hell. The truth is I hate her guts. And I can't even wish she were dead.

Because she is dead. And I can't even wish she were alive because then I'd lose Lou and he's the best thing that ever happened to me. Damn Dorrie Bridges!"

Jennie fell back into the cushions, sobbing. Claudine patted the shaking girl's shoulders before addressing the group. "I'm the oldest. Let's start with me."

Claudine was the name she had chosen back home in Kansas City when she decided to be a costume designer for motion pictures, a single name in the tradition of Adrian, Karinska, Irene, and other movie greats. Raised as Clara Schaumburg, she had come to Hollywood just as the era of extravagant costumes was coming to an end.

Producers soon discovered her genius for making clothes that photographed well for both men and women. She had a camera's eye for line, color, and texture that instantly made the wearer taller, slimmer, and better proportioned.

A winner of four Oscars and innumerable industry and fashion awards, she ranked just below Edith Head in the Hollywood hierarchy. Though hardly a media darling, she had enjoyed a modest visibility for years, giving interviews, appearing at charity events, being invited to the White House, until Dorrie's revelations drove her underground three years earlier.

Lou had read the clipping of the column that broke the story. "In a town where women outnumber men and even the beautiful women play solitaire instead of wearing one, veteran designer Claudine seems to have found a solution in her adopted son, Gar. The two were seen doing a golden credit card sweep of Rodeo Drive buying toys for them both, giggling over sand dabs at Robert's, and having late night drinkies on the top deck of the Queen Mary in Long Beach.

"How obscene, some say, to adopt a handsome young man. Well, the truth is better than that. Young Gar is not Claudine's adopted son. He is her real son, the fruit of a brief love affair with Clark Gable!"

Dorrie's column had concluded on a preachy note, saying now the rumors could cease once and for all. In this case, Dorrie was wrong. The rumors turned even nastier. Claudine was no longer an older woman robbing the cradle. She was a party to incest. Letters to the newspaper denounced her for denying her son's birthright. Ministers used the story as an example of perverted values in Hollywood. Tourists with cameras gathered outside the house to get Gar's autograph.

"The truth . . . the truth . . ."

Claudine still had her flat midwestern accent. "You all remember when the story broke. Dorrie Bridges shamed me and embarrassed me. She made me see myself as others saw me. A middle-aged woman obsessed with a boy. Pretending it was mother love and knowing it had become much more than that."

La Gioconda would have paid a fortune for her smile at that moment. "The truth is—yes, I did have an affair with Clark Gable on location in Europe. It was brief and it was secret and it gave me a happiness I can still draw upon today. I was never a beauty, you know. Most men looked through me or past me. Clark—" She had to stop and swallow hard before she could go on. "—he was still in mourning for Carole Lombard even though several years had passed since her death. He said that I—that I was kind and gentle and that I had beautiful hands, which I do, and that he wanted to spend some time with me.

"For me, it was the love affair of my life, the only moments of great physical passion I have ever known. But—"

You could hear a carrot crunch in the expectant silence.

Claudine dimpled and looked a vixenish decade younger. "—Dorrie Bridges will rise up from the dead when she hears this. Much as I may have wished it, I did not become pregnant. What really happened was the last day on location, the script girl came to me. She'd been with the production four months, a mousy kid, a pushover for the King. She didn't know about my relationship with him. She said I reminded her of her mother—I was only twenty-five—"

Sighs of sympathy.

"She was pregnant, she said, Gable was the father and could I help her. She didn't want him or her parents to know. She didn't want an abortion. I arranged everything including her agreement that I could adopt the child. Then I would have something of him forever."

"So he was adopted after all," Lou said, feeling instantly stupid for stating the obvious.

"I raised him as my son and treated him as a son. Until Dorrie's column drove us into each other's arms. I was forty-five and he was nineteen. At first he was frightened by the story and grateful to me and then he told me he was passion-ately in love with me. I resisted the whole idea. It was ludi-crous. I was forty-five and I looked forty-five. Chic, maybe, but definitely mature. But he pleaded with me and I gave in—"

Sighs of rapture.

"Gar and I are lovers. We live a quiet life on our ranch in Mendocino. Gar loves horses just like his father did. In my heart, he is my one true love. In the dark, he is my first true love.

"Dorrie's story brought me ridicule, but I don't hate her for it. I thank her with all my heart."

"Truth . . . truth . . ."

Carlotta Torres stood up. "Hate to eat and run. I'm meeting some people."

"They'll wait, *muchacha.*" Foxy Fenton waggled her thumbs western bad *hombre* style. "We're playing Truth. You can't leave till you talk." The implication being if she left now, she would forfeit her privileged inner-circle status at the Malibu Bitch House.

"Truth . . . truth . . ." Lou chanted. He stopped abruptly when he found himself chanting alone. Jennie rolled her eyeballs high and pursed her lips in the special way she had that provoked fantasies of ritual decapitation.

"You have good reason to hate Dorrie Bridges," Sis Logan said.

Suzy Newcombe joined in, a little the worse for dope and white wine. "Yeah. She really fixed your wagon. What'd you do, huh? Dump her in some arroyo in the Imperial Valley? Truth! Tell us the truth, Cholla."

Cholla is a spiny cactus that looks harmless until you brush against it. Then its protective mechanism releases hundreds of needle-sharp pricks. Even before she became the Jane Fonda of the Farm Workers, it was her nickname. That and *Boca Peligrosa,* which means "dangerous mouth." She was a child of wealth. Her ancestors had settled in California in the eighteenth century when it belonged to Spain and had enormous land holdings in Mexico. She was named for a grandmother with distant connections to the Empress Carlotta, the consort of Maximilian.

Educated in Europe, trained in labor law with Saul Alinsky at Cornell, she had served with the Peace Corps in Guatemala and become active in the Farm Workers Movement when an inheritance on her twenty-fifth birthday gave her economic freedom. She had traded in her Mercedes for a Ford pickup and her Holly Harps for boots, bibs, and the famous fedora. Her sole indulgence was a flamboyant squash blossom necklace in heavy silver and turquoise with matching rings and bracelets, worth close to twenty thousand dollars.

Critics accused her of using the Movement to salve her Rich Kid guilt and of letting the media blitz go to her head. As a cultural footnote the sudden popularity of spinach salad among liberal trend-setters was attributed to her lettuce boycott.

Until Dorrie Bridges did the investigating that her media cohorts were too lazy to do.

Carlotta Torres's family were the major stockholders in Western Brands, a vast holding company that in turn controlled ten of the largest growers in the Imperial and Salinas Valleys. Furthermore, Torres agents traveled the small villages of Baja and Sonora signing illiterate peasants to wetback contracts and arranged their illegal transportation across the border to "slave labor camps."

Dorrie discovered links between Western Brands and the Teamsters organizers who were trying to sign up the migrants and make sweetheart deals with the growers. She also unearthed a position paper signed by Cholla's very own father confirming the purchase of sophisticated mechanical harvesting systems designed to displace farm workers entirely. It was signed with a sarcastic, *"Viva la huelga!"*

With tears and curses, Cholla had made her famous impassioned *Brazos, Cabeza, Corazón* speech, swearing she had pledged her hands, head, and heart to the Movement and knew nothing of her family's involvements. She was booed off the platform and hit with rotten vegetables. Angry workers set fire to her pickup and took away her boots.

"I understand you're working for your family now," Lou Dexter said gently.

"Fuck you."

"Por favor." From someone else, his plea may have sounded like a knock. Lou Dexter's sincerity was obvious.

She wavered. "I have to get home and pound out some tortillas. On a rock."

"You've been through a lot. I've heard there've been death threats and someone sent you a disemboweled chicken."

"I had the cook prepare *arroz con pollo.*"

"You certainly have good reason to hate Dorrie Bridges. You were doing good. How could you help what your family does."

"They called me a fink. They said my family sent me to join the organization and sell the workers out! I would never do anything like that!"

Carlotta Torres, Lou had discovered, was a championship swimmer and owned a cabin cruiser. She quite easily could have learned Dorrie's whereabouts, gone to the beach house, and confronted her.

"We're playing Truth, Cholla," Lou reminded her, except how do you come right out and ask if you're a murderer! "Do you hate Dorrie Bridges for ruining your life?"

The young woman drew herself up proudly, her strong Castilian features straight out of Goya, her incandescence from Diego Rivera. *"No odiar; no vengar.* No hatred; no revenge. The Movement taught me that. At first I wanted to kill my entire family. They knew the truth would come out one day. They let me go on being a combination of Mother Jones and Appasionara. They didn't take me seriously. They thought it was something for me to do, working with the poor as women in our family always have, until I got married."

"But you're working for them. You've got a job with Western Brands."

"I'm the termite. I'm boring from within and I'm going to bring the house down. They think blood is thicker than water. Not always. I own a lot of stock and I'm buying up more. My family has committed injustice and it's up to me to right the wrongs. I guess you can say Dorrie Bridges did me a favor.

"She made me see the whole migrant trip was ego. *Señorita* Bountiful getting her hands dirty. Kissing undernourished babies. Throwing myself at a tractor in full view of the cameras. In a way, I was kidding myself."

"How is that?"

"I believe in the capitalist system. America is strong and is still the land of opportunity because of capitalism. But if we're going to make it to 2001, the workers have to have a fair share of the wealth and I intend to see that's exactly what happens.

"Sure, I miss the rallies and the songs and the companionship but I must not deny my roots, either. I come from a family that was born to rule. You can't be a peasant because you want to. I believe in divine right and my divine right—

and responsibility—is to see that justice is done. And if Dorrie Bridges was here right now, I guess I'd have to thank her for what she did. I wouldn't like it but I'd do it."

"Carrrrrramba!" Glitz said when the sound of Cholla's new Mercedes assured them she was out of earshot.

"Have some grapes!" Glitz brought them out. "I didn't want any hassles."

"My turn!" Peachy Purdy Nichols plopped herself at Lou Dexter's feet and looked up at him beseechingly, her best angle, photographers said, a fact which inspired frequent collapses in the vicinity of startled heroes.

A veritable picture of innocence, Lou thought. A cereal-box baby gazing at him with goo-goos of rapt expectation. Gazing back at this flawless skin and clear eyes and damp demanding pout, he wondered what she had done to him in the dark. Was she an armpit freak? A neck nuzzler? Or a Watership Down ever seeking surrender to the ecstasy of the deep?

He wondered and he could see that Jennie wondered, too. Peachy Purdy Nichols was on his Hot 30 list, to be sure, yet he could not seriously believe this child capable of foul play. He would take her number and investigate her story another time. Perhaps tomorrow when Jennie was setting up her commercial.

"Ann. I think Ann Elving should be next." He beckoned the shy young academic whom Dorrie Bridges exposed to the world as the "Ugly Duckling."

"What about me?" Peachy implored.

"I'll call you tomorrow," he whispered. "We'll talk privately." He patted her benevolently on the head for Jennie's benefit. Damn her, she had him acting married.

When Gregson Hale Spears, the former President of the United States, suffered a heart attack in his Washington, D.C., carriage house, a mystery woman performed expert cardio-pulmonary resuscitation, called an ambulance, kept him breathing until the mobile life-support unit arrived, and disappeared into the crowds as the ambulance pulled away.

President Spears insisted he was alone when felled and that his elderly housekeeper must have returned from her evening out and phoned for help.

Dorrie Bridges was dining at the White House that night when the story began to circulate. She drove straight to J Street. "White House," she said, flashing her press credentials at the police officer on duty. Let others describe the wallpaper, she wanted a clue. She found it on Greg Spears's appointment pad. A scribbled notation, *Ugly Duckling,* beneath a rakish s-m-i-l-e face.

"You were engaged to marry Felix Tull when all this happened, weren't you?" Lou began.

"Felix broke it off. He said he didn't believe in scandal. It was bad for his career."

"What about your career? You had a responsible post at the Smithsonian. Didn't you take an indefinite leave of absence?"

"Yes."

"That couldn't have been very nice for you. Pictures of you everywhere. 'The Ugly Duckling Who Saved Prince Charming.' "

Ann adjusted her glasses and ran nicotined fingers through the damp strands of dull, stringy hair before twisting them into a rubber band. Ugly was far too harsh a description for a face that was less plain than undefined. Her skin tone was sallow, her nose putty, her mouth chapped. Her cheekbones concave. She may once have radiated the bloom of youth. At the advanced age of twenty-eight, it was gone.

"I'm not what you'd call photogenic."

"They had a field day with you. That tacky joke about the Ann Elving doll—"

"I know," she sighed. "It comes wearing a nightgown with a bag over its head."

"But you knew President Spears called you the 'Ugly Duckling'?"

"Yes, it was our little joke. You see, his grandmother's Danish and 'The Ugly Duckling' was one of his sister's favorite stories and it was one of mine, too."

"How did Dorrie track you down?"

"She was extremely clever. She figured if there was a woman, the President would be sending her flowers. It was simple to find out where he had an account. She called the Potomac Florists and said, 'Good morning, I just received some flowers from President Spears but the note is hard to read. It looks like it says "To My Ugly Duckling." Maybe I've got the wrong flowers.'

"And the florist was back in a flash to say to Dorrie Bridges 'Aren't you Ann Elving?' and gave her my address just as simple as that."

"And then the shit hit the fan."

"In a manner of speaking."

The woman had presence of mind. A cool one. She could save a man's life and disappear into the crowd. Maybe she had taken Dorrie's life with the same degree of self-possession. The first for love, the second for revenge.

"Because of Dorrie Bridges, you've lost everything. Your fiancé. Your job. Your dignity. Your good name. Do you hate her?"

"I wanted to kill her," Ann Elving said in a monotone. "You see, I *was* the ugly duckling. No boy ever threw a snowball at me. I went through school without a date or a kiss. I got my master's in American history and went to the Smithsonian to do a research report on the domestic arrangements of American presidents based on their archives."

"That's where you met your future fiancé?"

"Felix was the first man to ever ask me on a date. He proposed two weeks later, so we got engaged."

"When did you meet the President?"

"About that time. He had donated a collection of memorabilia having to do with children in the White House. I asked his help on my research report."

"Were you lovers?"

Ann hesitated.

"Truth . . . truth . . ." the mesmerized listeners prompted.

"No—I admired him. I felt his love for children was genuine—and that—" Her nose had turned into a leaking red plum. She blew it several times to little avail. "Excuse me, I've got allergies."

Lou would not let go. "So there you were, the Ugly Duckling, a figure of fun and dirty jokes, hounded by the press. Didn't the President thank you for saving his life?"

"He called me as soon as he was released from the hospital."

"Did you agree to see him?"

"Yes."

"What did he say?"

"He apologized on behalf of what he called the civilized world for what he called the barbaric behavior of the press."

"Was that before or after Dorrie ran his wife's comments?"

"That was a few weeks later."

The former First Lady and Philadelphia Main Liner had been quoted as berating her husband for being caught with such an unattractive girl. "How do you think that makes me look? At least if she were a raving beauty, everyone would understand!" Dorrie had concluded her column with a cry for legislation limiting mouth-to-mouth resuscitation to winners of beauty contests.

"And what did the President say?"

"The President asked me if I would have dinner with him. He sent a car and we slipped away to a quiet little place in Virginia. He said he had asked his wife why she had said such cruel and hurtful things to Dorrie Bridges. She said she felt cruel and hurtful. He then said he asked her if she would rather have had him in bed with a raving beauty who let him die or an ugly duckling who saved his life and she said yes, if he wanted her honest answer, that was exactly how she felt."

Even his ex-wife the princess was never as bad as that. "I know this is hard on you, Ann. If you want to stop right here, it's okay with me."

"No. We want to know what happened next!" Glitz insisted. The others agreed. "Don't leave us hanging. What happened? Did he buy you an apartment house or something to show his gratitude?"

"Well—"

"*Well—?*"

"He kissed me." She swallowed the words and folded her arms in a stand of defiance. "I mean, it was the first time he ever kissed me. Honest. He took me in his arms and he said, 'Ann, dear. You're the only honorable woman I've ever met. You've given me a second chance to live. I'm nearly twice your age but I'd like to live it with you. I'm happy just being with you and I'd like to spend the rest of my life making you happy.'"

"Could you die?" Glitz shouted. "Could you just die?"

Ann Elving addressed herself to Lou Dexter. "You're doing an article on Dorrie Bridges. Well, let me tell you something. I'm happy for the first time in my life because of her."

"You speak of her in the present tense, like she's still alive."

"If she's alive, I hope she reads the papers."

"Why?"

"Greg Spears is in Mexico today, getting his divorce. I'm flying down to meet him tomorrow. The Ugly Duckling is going to live happily ever after."

The denizens of the Malibu Bitch House cheered. All except Foxy Fenton, who reached behind her cushion for a radio headset and put it on. "Happily ever after. Bull*shit!*"

"She's shutting us out. She always does that. Look at her. Mental masturbation." Glitz talked directly into Foxy's face.

Foxy bopped to the music coming through the earphones, ignoring her.

"Dorrie Bridges did a worse thing to Foxy than she did to anyone else."

"And what was that?" Lou asked.

Glitz laughed and did a sassy belly-dancer bump in Foxy's direction. "She ignored her!"

"Up yours!" Foxy evidently could hear through the headset. She shoved her fuck finger upward for emphasis.

"She tried everything. Remember when she dyed her hair in brown and purple stripes—the peanut butter and jelly look as worn by L.A.'s hottest young agent? Dorrie ignored it."

"You don't know anything."

"Who doesn't know anything? I know everything about you, Foxy the Doxy. What about calling Dorrie to say you've packaged Streisand and Stallone for a remake of *Streetcar*? She checked it out and found it was all in your head!"

"It was a concept. A breakthrough concept."

"It was a lie and you know it and Dorrie knew it and that's why she wouldn't take your calls."

"You're crazy!"

"Listen to who's crazy? Could you die? You forget. I was here, remember? Remember the day you made that Dorrie doll and stuck pins in it? You said you'd get even with her. You said your father taught you all about dead bodies and embalming—"

"I was stoned!" Foxy defended herself. "What about you? You were Dorrie's roommate in New York—"

There were gasps all around.

"I never said I wasn't," Glitz mumbled.

"You never said you were because you pretend to be younger than you are. You're thirty-five if you're a day—"

"I'm thirty-one and I can show you my passport!"

"And furthermore—you hated her because she took Sonny Syntagma away from you."

"She did me a favor. I'd have paid her to take him off my hands."

"That ain't the way I heerd it. She was always taking your men. Nicky Zinn was after her, too. Not that she wanted Sonny or Nicky—"

"Well"—Glitz included everyone in her triumph—"I've got Sonny now. I've cast him for the starring role in 'The Love Game' and I've signed him to a personal management contract, so I've literally got him coming and going! As for Nicky Zinn—"

"Don't you say a word against Nicky Zinn!" Foxy threw her wine at Glitz. "He's a better man—a better lover than—"

"Any eunuch in southern California!" Glitz shrieked, dumping the platter of cold vegetables on her opponent.

"Here they go. I'm leaving." Sis Logan attempted to leave.

"Sit down or I'll burn a new tattoo on your ass," her gracious hostess demurred.

"Tattoo?" Lou's head felt like an electric light bulb that was half-screwed into the socket, turning on and off and in danger of losing contact completely and crashing to the floor. He was a beer-and-bourbon belter in a sniff-and-snort town. The coke had fried his brains and made him horny as a bull in a porno shop. Jennie explained. "Sis and her brother. Don't you know anything? Dorrie exposed the whole sordid story. Where the hell were you?"

Sis Logan strong-armed her way past Glitz. "Just any of you cows try to stop me." Glitz grabbed her. A karate chop. An exchange of shoves. And Sis was gone.

"I thought you had stuff on her," Jennie said.

"The incest story—?" He was groggy and fighting to keep his mental tape recorder working. He would need every ounce of will to remember all that he had learned tonight.

"I'll fill you in later," she promised just as Peachy Purdy resumed her earlier grovel at Lou's knee. Jennie pulled her upright and pushed her away. "She's too dumb to have done anything to Dorrie. She gives dumb redheads a bad name."

Peachy pulled the knitting needle out of her hair, releasing a shimmering red tribute to nature and Clairol the onlookers had no time to admire, since she lunged at Jennie with the knitting needle, missed, and drove the weapon into a pillow.

Glitz wrestled the knitting needle out of her hand. "I'll sue you. This is going to be in a commercial, right, Jennie? You're destroying valuable property."

"Gee, I'm sorry." Peachy examined the hole in the fabric, Jennie sharing her concern.

Suzy Newcombe was emptying a jar of macadamia nuts into her mouth. "I thought you had *anorexia nervosa,*" Lou said.

"My husband made me take it back."

"Didn't I hear you were suing Dorrie Bridges for eight million bucks?" A good question, he thought. Not a subtle question, but in the circumstances a good direct question.

"Seven. It was his idea."

"You were only fifteen when you married him."

"Sixteen. And fat! Or at least I saw myself as fat. I weighed a hundred and ten."

"That's really fat."

"Well, it was. I was up to a size five. Bulges all over. What a mess. I couldn't stand myself."

"Didn't I read somewhere that he picked you up?"

"On Fifth Avenue. Said he was a photographer. A lot of dudes use that line, but he really was a photographer."

"And he took your pictures."

"Great pictures, man."

"He made you into a hundred-dollar-an-hour model. He married you. So why did you destroy his studio?" The burglar alarm had gone off when she broke through the door. When the police arrived, they found smashed cameras and darkroom equipment torn apart, chemicals poured over hundreds of negatives, print files scattered, and Suzy herself looking like an Auschwitz cadaver. Her face like a skull, the bones of her body jutting through the tight parchment of her skin.

"Speed," the police noted in their report.

"Anorexia nervosa," Bellevue Hospital noted in their report.

"Matrimonial homicide," Dorrie Bridges noted in her report, as Lou discovered in his research. Nor had Dorrie stopped there. For weeks afterward, Dorrie demanded action from the New York District Attorney's office.

"Where, sir, is your responsibility to helpless victims?" she asked in an Open Letter. "You arrest Suzy Newcombe for committing a senseless crime while under the influence of drugs supplied by a greedy, exploiting husband and gallantly drop the case when the gallant husband himself gallantly declines to press charges.

"What I would respectfully inquire to know, sir, is why you have not arrested the real criminal, the husband who has maliciously addicted his wife to diet pills and seduced her to starvation. Clearly, Ken Newcombe has endangered Suzy Newcombe's physical well-being and mental health. What do you plan to do about that, sir?"

The D.A. did not respond too well to this advice on how to do his job. To show Dorrie Bridges who indeed was District Attorney, he had Suzy Newcombe picked up and committed to psychiatric custody on Roosevelt Island. Although she was married, she was under eighteen. When a cooperative judge declared Ken an irresponsible spouse by virtue of mischievous acts, Suzy was made a ward of the court.

Lou Dexter had seen some TV news footage made at Roosevelt Island. "It shows you throwing that note out the window. The one that warns Dorrie Bridges to start running. . . ."

"That was just before they let me out."

"You said you were a certified nutball so they could never give you the chair."

Suzy shrugged. "I was bored cooped up in that place. I must have gained twenty pounds. Potatoes. Macaroni. Beans."

"You said you were going to kill her and make it look like an accident."

Another shrug. "Everybody says stuff like that. My generation learned how to talk from watching television."

"Dorrie Bridges is dead."

"Not necessarily. She's missing."

"Don't you think this casts suspicion on you and Ken?"

"Wrong. Roy Cohn said we had a strong case against her and her newspaper syndicate and the TV network, everybody who let her say those rotten things about us. Why should we want her dead? You can't sue a dead woman."

"Had enough Truth?" Jennie asked.

His head felt like a steel helmet filled with hot custard. Something was lolling. Either his head was lolling or the room and all the people in it were lolling. The word "lolling" was beginning to soothe him. *Lo-llling.* Traces of Humbert Humbert. *Lo-lo-looooo-ling!*

"Got to talk to Glitz and Foxy and about Sonny Syntagma. Nicky. Gotta find out about Nicky—"

"They'll keep."

Across the room, Glitz had collapsed in the harem of pillows, snoring faintly. Foxy sat on the floor with a bottle of red nail polish, painting Glitz's toenails.

"Air." Lou Dexter took a shortcut through the Jacuzzi to the deck and climbed the fence rail. The beach lay some twenty feet below. The calm Pacific beckoned. It still bothered him to be living where the sun set in the ocean instead of rising from it. It still bothered him to see dinky little waves instead of the churning undertow of Coney Island and the Hamptons.

"You'll fall!" Jennie warned. Nag. Nag. Just like his ex-wife the princess. All that granola and lecithin were not helping her disposition.

"Say g'bye to Norman Main!" He'd show her. The old legs could still hack it. The Lean Machine leapt into space and made a soft landing on the sand.

"Darling . . . *please* . . ." Jennie leaned over the railing, using her hands as a megaphone. He heard Jennie shout but kept going. In the first two versions of *A Star Is Born* Fredric March and James Mason had worn bathrobes. In the last version Kris Kristofferson had worn a beard. Here he was in a Malibu Bitch House T-shirt racing toward the surf like Groucho Marx in a nightgown.

He looked back to see Jennie Bliss Sternholdt poised like an Olympic high diver. "Don't!"

She fell like a rock. "Oh, God—" He started toward her. She rose to her feet cursing and spitting sand. "Jesus!" The pivot-and-reverse that had won him a letter for basketball was still in smooth working order. Norman Main needed a nice refreshing dunk in the ocean. Dorrie Bridges was dead but it was his private conviction that Norman Main lived. He had disappeared in order to escape the insufferable martyrdom of Vicky Lester.

God save him from the tear-filled eyes of understanding women. It wasn't that they really understood but that they kept *saying* they understood, a form of mind control perfected by organized religion. All you had to do was exactly what they said and they would understand all your weaknesses and failures.

He hit the water. The water hit him. Cool rather than cold like the Atlantic. Cooler than the Mediterranean or the Caribbean or the Aegean. Nice names those, reminders that he had peed and mingled his water with most of the major bodies of water in the world. A nice thought that.

Strong arms grappled him. *Sonya Boris in the Black Sea before the journey to Ekaterinburg.* All motives suspect. All acts of love and kindness suspect. All women suspect. *Get your hands off me, I'm trying to have a swim.* All those women at the Malibu Bitch House. Were they telling the truth? "Rather than love, than money, than fame, give me *truth!*" is what the wise man of Walden Pond said. A high school English teacher had forced him to commit it to memory. He thought Thoreau was a jerk then and had not changed his mind. Truth was not comparable to anything. It was its own amorphous quicksilver. Now you *seize* it, now you don't.

Dorrie Bridges mocked him. She knew what had happened and he wouldn't stop until he found out. Pia Melanaiki had ducked him, but he would track her down tomorrow. Nicky Zinn. Sonny. All the rest of the Hot 30. One of them had the answers, he was sure.

His ex-wife the princess had called him this morning from New York. Maybe he should have asked her. She always knew everything. She had all the answers and most of the questions. He had saved up a zinger for her. He told her she was like one of those special savings accounts that imposes substantial penalties for premature withdrawal. That's when she hung up.

Then there was his daughter, the literary genius. She had written him a letter that accused him of having the selectivity of a slotted spoon. "Daddy, you think you're getting the best of life by picking out only succulent bits and leaving the broth. Well, Daddy dear, the broth is the healthier part. To get all of life's nourishment, you've got to consume both."

A-plus claptrap. Picking on poor old Dad. An easy target at best. Another woman who was out to bust chops. The righteous had weapons, too. A Vicky Lester Certificate of Understanding to you, too, my daughter.

"Lou—" Jennie's voice dropped like sweet rain on his face.

"You!" he croaked.

She was on top of him, kissing him, stroking his hair. "Lou—"

"What the hell's going on?"

"We're—we're doing a scene from a famous movie."

"Not *A Star Is Born*. Norman Main was a jerk. You don't die for love. That's a cop-out."

"I am directing and starring in this movie." She had him flat on his back on the sand. "I am Fred Zinnemann, the film is *From Here to Eternity*, only I'm reversing the roles. I am Burt Lancaster and you are Deborah Kerr, waiting to be wakened by my animal lust."

"You—"

"Lou!"

All those hours in front of the mirror were paying off. He was a love object at last. *Fornicalia, here I come.*

"Blood!"

It oozed from Pia's wrist and fell in sullen puddles on her pearl-encrusted gown. "The bride wore red."

"Come on, darlin', give me the knife," Dorrie whispered.

"Stay back!" Pia slashed out wildly, glaring at Dorrie in triumph, her breath a series of whimpers.

Dorrie had never seen one person so full of hurt. Pia's thin little shape shook like the first day of school. With her mascara all damp and smeared around her sad and sorrowing eyes, the Greek heiress looked for all the world like a stray calf caught in barbed wire.

That damned little fool would bleed to death if she didn't do something. "Pia—let me tell you something—"

"Who sent you, my shrink?"

"I'm a reporter."

"Oh, sure—" The weight of Pia's wounded arm was suddenly too much for her. She let it fall. The pull of gravity caused the blood to flow more quickly.

"For *Newsmagazine,*" Dorrie inched in. "Just trying to get a story."

"I'll give you a story!" She held the blade against the torn and ragged wrist.

Dorrie sighed with annoyance. "That's not the way to do it."

"What do you mean?"

"You call that slashing your wrist? That's not worth a paragraph in the back of the magazine."

"Are you nuts? Look at this blood. Look at my dress. It costs my father twelve thousand dollars!"

Dorrie shrugged. "You missed the vein."

By now Pia Melanaiki was growing faint. "I—listen—"

"Here, let me show you." Moving faster than a fox in a henhouse, Dorrie knocked the knife clear across the room.

"No! No! No!" Pia shrieked as Dorrie pushed her down on the rumpled bed.

"Pia? *Chérie?*" Lina Melanaiki called through the locked door. "It's *Maman,* darling—"

Dorrie wrenched Pia's torn arm into an upright position so that the pull of gravity could stop the flow of blood. "Tell her you're real fine." A pitcher of ice water gave her an idea. She dipped a linen napkin into it.

"I'm real fine, Mother. We're talking—"

Dorrie wrapped the cold wet cloth around the girl's wrist and used a fork to make the tourniquet as tight as possible.

"You want me to get you out of here?" she whispered.

Pia nodded.

"Just answer me two questions. Do you love Johnny Capedis?"

"We've known each other since we were children. We played together at my grandmother's villa in Glyfada."

"Do you want to marry him?"

"I—*can't!*" Sobs shook her.

"Why can't you?"

"I can't!" Pia stamped her foot. She was feeling better.

"If you don't tell me the truth, I'm going to leave you here. If you do, I'll find a way to get you out."

"Please—"

"The truth, Pia!"

"I'm—I'm so ashamed!" Pia Melanaiki, born at Olympia, two hundred miles west of Athens where the first Olympic Games were held in 776 B.C., educated in Switzerland, related to the world's leading Greek families, who were at this moment sipping champagne in advance of her wedding, could not take her vows before God.

"Why?"

"I'm not a virgin."

In respect to Dorrie's own condition, the confession elicited a pang of personal envy in addition to journalistic curiosity. "Is that what all the fuss and thunder's about? Oh, darlin'. So you had a little flirt with another boy—"

"Not just another boy—"

"Well, now, New York is an exciting metropolis. You must have had lots of beaus hanging around you like chickens around a June bug—"

"I was a hooker!"

"Oh, Pia, darlin', don't say such things. You were susceptible—"

"A call girl. I got paid fifty bucks a trick. I met this man. Richard Lord. He's in real estate. Lives on Park Avenue and

Seventy-third. He took me out and introduced me to all his friends." Once started, the whole story poured out. It was an old story with a new twist. Richard Lord had the looks, charm, and social standing of old-money aristocracy. Unfortunately most of the old money was gone. He was in the midst of several multimillion-dollar real estate deals but was hard pressed for ready cash.

Knowing the sexual tastes of a wide circle of married friends, he arranged discreet "dates" at his luxurious apartment. What the men paid for these interludes was supposed to be between them and their newfound playmates, who in turn kicked back half to their cash-poor host.

"But why did you do it? You didn't need the money."

"It was—thrilling. Exciting. I don't know how to explain it. All of my upbringing was to keep my body pure, to save it for my marriage bed, and I believe in that. And that's why I can't marry Johnny. I'm no good. I'm a harlot. I loved it. I loved the different men. The excitement of not knowing who it would be. What would he be like? What would he do to me and make me do to him! And—"

Dorrie's heart was pounding, afraid to ask but asking anyway. "And—?"

"And to get paid for it. Why, let me tell you something. There's a certain football hero who said I was the best thing since sliced bread and stuck hundred-dollar bills—" She blushed and finished lamely "all over me!"

"How's your arm?"

Pia tested it. "Okay, I guess."

Dorrie looked out the window. They were too high to jump and there was nothing to climb. A connecting door opened to reveal another connecting door, which was locked.

"Better change into something else." The wedding gown looked as if it had witnessed a pagan sacrifice. Pia exchanged it for a blue knit mini and brushed her hair into a neat mane. "Now what? My whole family is out there."

"If I let you hold that knife again, will you do what I say?"

The girl nodded.

"Put your arm around me and hold the knife to my throat. And for Lord's sake, be careful!"

Dorrie opened the bedroom door a crack and called out, "Mrs. Melanaiki?"

"Thank God—"

"I'm afraid I'm a hostage—" Dorrie said as she and Pia moved slowly into the living room of the suite. "Pia wants to leave."

"Pia—" Constantin Dmitri Melanaiki looked as green as the olives that were the basis of his wealth.

"Don't try to stop me, Daddy."

"Phone downstairs and tell the chauffeur we're on our way down," Dorrie said.

"Young woman, do you know who I am?"

"Do what she says, Costa!" his wife implored.

They slammed the double doors of the suite and ran down the hotel corridor. "We made it. We made it!" Pia bounced into the air, clicking her heels.

"Not the elevator!" Dorrie decided. They danced down eight flights of marble stairs and across the lobby to the Cadillac waiting on the Central Park South side of the hotel.

"Bloomingdale's and step on it!" Dorrie ordered.

The shiny black monster inched and clawed through the rush-hour traffic. Stuck halfway across Fifth Avenue, Dorrie looked through the back window in time to see Costa Melanaiki run down the Plaza steps, looking wildly in all directions.

"He sees us," Pia moaned.

"We're getting out of here."

With Dorrie leading the way, the two young women sprinted across Fifty-ninth Street, across Park Avenue against the lights, ducking between two Lexington Avenue buses and into the crowded depths of Bloomingdale's.

"Oh, look. Purple eyeliner. Just what I need." Pia stopped at the Revlon counter like there was all the time in the world.

Dorrie was in no mood for small talk. She was nervous and touchy and wracking her brains trying to figure out where she was going to hide Pia. The apartment was no good. Glo would put her two cents in and tell three people. A forced march through Cosmetics and Toiletries, an oblique turn through Notions to Men's Wear, and they were out the Third Avenue exit and standing on Sixtieth Street.

"I'm *tired!*" Pia announced in the manner of one who expects instant coddling.

Dorrie was tired, too. She had half a mind to leave her there when inspiration struck. A five-minute walk and they were signing Pia in at the Barbizon Hotel for Women under a false name. "This is my cousin, Mary Jo Bridges," she explained to her friend the receptionist. "The airlines lost all her luggage so I'll pay her first night's rent."

Over cheeseburgers and fries and through endless cups of coffee and Boston cream pie, Dorrie culled the details of Pia's secret life. The shame. The excitement. The guilt. The basic decency that stopped her from wrecking the life of the innocent young man she had left at the altar.

It was very late when Dorrie tucked Pia into bed in a borrowed baby-doll. "Aphrodite in her nightie!" It was later still when she returned to the deserted offices of *Newsmagazine* and sat down to write her first big story for "Whispers." She was just finishing it when Connie Michelin materialized.

"Are you working late or starting early?"

"What time is it?" Dorrie yawned.

"Seven o'clock. I always get in early. I read eight newspapers, talk to all my European bureaus and stringers, and get a day's work done before everyone else gets in. What happened at the wedding? I hear the bride did a flit."

"Here's my story."

Connie grinned. "Good work. I hope you got plenty of snappy quotes from Onassis and Niarchos. 'Greeks bearing gifts,' right? 'But the bride chose freedom instead!' right? Can't wait to read it. What did Ari say? Did he make a grab for you?"

"I didn't meet him."

"You didn't?" Connie continued to smile like someone who bites into a chocolate cream and cracks a tooth. "Well, then, I'm sure you have your reasons. Any news on Pia's whereabouts? Let's turn on the radio for an update."

"No need to do that."

"What about the groom? Did you get him?"

"I got Pia."

Connie couldn't believe her ears. "You saw her leave? Did you get a quote?"

"I've got her in a hotel room and I've got her whole story here."

What happened next happened so fast, it was all Dorrie Bridges could do to keep up with it and to pinch herself to prove she was real. Connie returned with her to the Barbizon and moved Pia into her own apartment. When Van Kennan sailed into the "Whispers" office at noon, Dorrie's piece was in type galleys on his desk.

"How dare you send this down for type without my okay!" His head was throbbing. After the Gloria Vanderbilt do, he'd gone on a pub crawl with some people. He mistook Dorrie's exhaustion for chagrin. "I told you I was already in overset for this week's column. If you got me a good quote—an exclusive quote, not something picked out of the dailies— maybe I could fit it in. Depending on ads."

Dorrie watched in silence as he read her copy.

"I don't believe this," he said. "I do *not* believe this!" He ripped it to confetti and threw it at her. "How dare you write such unmitigated claptrap. What do you think this is, *Confidential*? Concocting a story like this. Richard Lord's a friend of mine. We play cribbage together. Calling him a pimp! I have had about as much of your south-in-the-mouth bullshit as I can take. You're fired."

"Correction." Connie Michelin entered softly on his last words. "The column runs as is. With Dorrie's name on it."

"Goddammit, Connie. *You can't.*"

"Shit, Drew, if there's one thing I hate it's a man who uses profanity."

He laughed with glass teeth. "Richard Lord is a very important V.I.P.—"

"That's redundant."

"He'll sue."

"I checked the story out myself."

"But—what about my Lady Bird Johnson story—and my Gloria Vanderbilt and my Mary Martin—"

"You'll have to find another way to freeload. You're out."

"Out?" He echoed the word as if it were Urdu.

"O-U-T. This is the 1960s, remember? We're going through a revolution, right? Revolutionary tactics pertain. You made a bad tactical error. You fired Dorrie Bridges. You have no authority to do that. I alone have that authority and I hereby fire you. Please be off the premises by five o'clock this afternoon."

The following week's issue of *Newsmagazine* hit the stands in a flurry of excitement. TV and radio commercials hailed the appointment of Dorrie Bridges as America's youngest columnist in a national magazine. "Dorrie Bridges asks the questions you want to ask and gets the answers you want to know."

The first day of sale, Mallie sent a telegram from Mississippi saying she was proud. Tom called from Nashville to say the same thing in words. Pia Melanaiki showed up weeping, with two lawyers. "I thought you wanted to help me. I didn't know you were going to print it."

"I did help you. I saved you from marriage, suicide, and your parents. I wrote only the truth."

"I'll never forgive you for this."

Richard Lord left the country on an extended business trip. Andrew Van Kennan dropped into the office to pick up his vintage Burberry. "I'll get even with you if it's the last thing I do. Count on it," he told Dorrie in a conversational tone.

She had not heard from Jim Ed. That night, Connie Michelin took her to Sun Luck East to celebrate. Her fortune cookie said, "Your long lost friend will be coming soon."

The next day, Jim Ed phoned from LaGuardia Airport. "I gave back the Fulbright. I got a scholarship to Columbia Journalism. I took it to be with you."

"I'll take him. You can have Nicky Zinn," Glo whispered to her in the bedroom with poor old Jim Ed sitting not more than three feet away on the living room davenport.

Glo's behavior had become mighty peculiar. Like she was attempting to go against her own nature. The day after the Pia escapade, when Dorrie told her about the column and all, why Gloria Greenberg took it all in and smiled and ducked her head like Uriah Heep in a girl's school. That night she had washed the dishes instead of letting them sit and collect bugs and straightened out the bedroom closet. "Now that you're going to be famous, I thought you'd need room for all the scrumptious clothes you're going to buy. Isn't it neat, we're both the same size?"

Glo's saintliness was a sight to behold. She scrubbed out the bathtub after herself, bought food for the first time since they had moved into the apartment, and gave Dorrie back the ten dollars she had borrowed.

Even before the first column appeared, the word had spread through the publicity world. Dorrie Bridges was a new and important contact. Messenger boys crowded each other at the *Newsmagazine* reception desk delivering new books; records; cosmetics; tickets to previews, galleries, and fashion shows; and telegrams of congratulations.

"You're a celebrity!" Glo exulted, arranging the invitations in chronological order on the narrow mantelpiece. "And I'm your best friend!"

"I'm not a celebrity. I'm a reporter, pure and simple." Her solemn expression softened. She gave Glo an affectionate shove. "Stop grinning at me. I've got to wash my hair. Jim Ed's coming by."

Jim Ed Loomis did look good enough to wrap and set under the Christmas tree for some deserving girl. He had let his hair grow some and his shoulders and chest had filled out. He seemed taller than she remembered. The deep blue turtleneck brought out the vivid color of his eyes. "Jim Ed, you look like a movie star."

It was clear from his expression he had expected to find Dorrie alone.

"I thought we'd double tonight. Nicky Zinn's coming over. We can go eat chinks and hit Arthur's." Glo bustled and chirped like a hen with a tack in her tail. She made Jim Ed a bourbon and water that was so strong, he damn near choked.

"You're my date tonight." She greeted Nick with a possessive hug. "Dorrie's boyfriend's here. All the way from the hills of Tenn-o-seeeeee! So you're stuck with me."

"Congratulations, Dorrie. I wish you every success." It had taken a "Late Show" movie to show Dorrie who Nick reminded her of. Gilbert Roland in *The Bad and the Beautiful*. Suave, dark, sophisticated. Deeply tanned, he too had a villain's mustache and gleaming teeth. His shirt opened to reveal chains, medallions, and a hairy chest, the sleeves rolled high on his arms to show off hard and muscular arms. Glo thought he must be over forty, the same age as her father. "But Daddy don't look like that!"

"Where'll we go?" Nick asked.

Jim Ed closed his eyes as if to shut out the agony of making social chitchat for the next several hours.

"Jim Ed's been doing some hard traveling," Dorrie apologized. "Why don't you two go along?"

"You can talk later! Come on. A couple of drinks, you'll feel fine!" Glo persisted.

Jim Ed yawned to demonstrate his fatigue.

"Come on, Gloria. Let's split." Nick finished his drink.

Glo had envisioned the four of them entering the restaurant

and being fawned over and bowed to the best table. She did not enjoy being thwarted. She stamped her foot. "It's not fair."

"It never is." Nick glanced at Dorrie and sighed. "Come on, Glo. You're making me insecure. Is it so terrible to have dinner with me alone?" He cupped her face in his massive suntanned hand.

Her cheeks flamed. She slipped her arm in his. "Don't do anything I wouldn't do!" She wagged a meaningful finger in farewell.

By mutual consent they let the sweet ensuing silence roll over them until by mutual recognition it was time to kiss and catch up. "I missed you, Jim Ed darlin'."

"I missed you, too, Dora June."

"How are things in Roper?"

"Different. Belle Kinkaid took the fever and died. Lil Bingham came home to bury her. Asked me had I seen you."

"Jesus Man Suggs?"

"That man! Calling more heed to himself than the dearly departed. Worked himself up something fierce, let me tell you. Got so carried away with his grief, he started foaming at the mouth and speaking in tongues and then when that calmed down, he hollered for six strong men to hold him down, keep him from jumping in the open grave."

Dorrie grinned at the thought. "Wished I'd have been there. She liked him, though."

"You can say that again. She left him her farm and all her savings certificates. Next thing you know, he's all dressed up in white satin like the Grand Ole Opry. Got himself a white guitar. A white Cadillac car. Spangles all over everything. Going around the tent shows playing and singing the Gospel for the Lord."

"What about Lil?"

"She was going to fight the will but it looked to be more time and trouble than she cared to spend. She got the furnishings inside. The spinet piano. The cherrywood bedstead and sideboard and the string of Japanese pearls her daddy brought back from the First War."

"Looks like to me all the big news is happening in Roper, Tennessee. Tell me, Jim Ed, is there anything happened to the *Echo?* Mama left it in the lawyers' hands. Is it closed down?"

"You didn't know?"

"Tell me. Did somebody buy it?"

He took her hands in his. "I did."

"Jim Ed! But who's going to run it?"

"I will. Some day. When I finish my wandering and my education and go back to Roper to live out my life. Meantime, I hired a fellow, a retired editor from Knoxville, to keep things going."

"I'm that proud of you, darlin'."

"And I'm proud of you. And I'm proud to be here in New York. Oh, darlin'—" He gathered her to him. "I knew my heart would break in half if I didn't see you."

In a U.S. Government report on malnutrition, Dorrie had read that a human body could die of starvation without knowing it. The human heart and soul could also die for lack of true affection. She had starved her heart and soul and body since leaving Roper. This man holding her in his arms was the man she truly loved. She would not give herself to another. Let them make sport of her. Let them keep their diaphragms and spray foams and pills. That wasn't the point. She would not make love with Tom Jennings or Nicky Zinn or any of the men she had met, no matter what they or Gloria or anybody else had to say about it. Until or unless she found someone she could love as much or more than Jim Ed.

"Kiss me, Jim Ed."

At first they kissed softly and sweetly and then they bit gently and then harder and more savagely until the sweet mixed with salt and they were laughing and crying together.

"I love you more than ever, Dora June." His body trembled so hard, she feared for him.

"I love you, too, darlin', and I've missed you so much, I can't hardly stand it." She put his hand on the buttons of her blouse. "Undress me, dear."

The look on his face was plain. "Remember that night in the meadow? With the honeysuckle vines? I said you were going to be like one of those stars in heaven. Shining bright and out of reach. It's all happened, hasn't it?"

"I'm not out of reach, Jim Ed. I'm right here." If he wouldn't undo her blouse, she would. In a moment her breasts were bare against his cotton turtleneck. She worked the fabric up until her nipples made connection with his quaking chest. "I love you, Jim Ed. Take me, darlin'."

He slumped against her, kissing her breasts and belly, sliding to his knees, his face buried in her thighs like a weeping child. "I wanted to die without you, sweetheart. I almost signed up for Vietnam. I was going to get myself blown to pieces and make you sorry."

"I'm glad you didn't get blown to pieces." She snarled her fingers in his hair and twisted hard. He rocked back on his heels.

"I'm on my knees to you, woman. I love you and want to marry you."

She sank to the floor. "I'm on my knees to you, Jim Ed. Begging you to love me. Pleading with you." She threw her arms around his neck. Their two bodies toppled over, wrestling for supremacy, grunting and cursing with exertion until Jim Ed yanked her to her feet and held her at arm's distance.

"I don't just want to have my ashes hauled! I want to marry you. Don't you understand? I want to make an honest woman of you."

"Jim Ed, I am an honest woman."

"Dear Lord, I didn't mean—"

"I know you mean to honor me and I appreciate your feelings. But I am eighteen years old and I've got a lucky break in my career. It's too soon to get married. Too soon for you, too. You've got your studying to do. What would you want with a wife hanging around?"

Desire got the better of him. His arms clasped her like a life raft. "Marry me, darlin'!" His mouth savaged hers, sending hot chocolate through her veins, melting her into hot marshmallow sauce. Her few remaining garments were choking her. She pulled them off while tearing at his as well until they stood together, naked in each other's sight for the very first time.

"We are Adam and Eve in the Garden of Eden, the very first man and the very first woman," she said.

He turned his back on her. "It's wrong."

"It's wrong if you think it's wrong."

"I think it's wrong."

Suddenly it was all too much. Suddenly she had lost patience with him, with love, with all the foolishness of sex and men. She had a full and busy day tomorrow. She had gotten a lead on a juicy scandal in the fashion industry. Connie had invited her to lunch with Nelson Rockefeller. There was a nudist camp in New Jersey where expatriate Cubans were said to be training for a new Bay of Pigs. Suddenly impatience vanquished lust. She wanted nothing more than to take a good New York shower without worrying about the hot water running out and to get a good night's sleep.

"I don't think we should see each other," she said when he was ready to leave.

"Let me know if you change your mind."

In the weeks that followed, Jim Ed moved to the back burner of her mind. The column had caught on. Hundreds of letters poured in. Strangers stopped her on the street.

Her little spare time was spent bargain hunting with Glo, who considered paying the list price for anything a crime against nature, or having a quiet dinner with Connie Michelin. In a city the size of a New York, she and Jim Ed could live out their lives without ever seeing each other again. They ran into each other only once, at a Bob Dylan concert. He was with an extremely pretty and clinging girl who called him Jamie, she with Nicky Zinn, who seemed content to be her friend.

"Don't think it matters to me because it doesn't!" Gloria Greenberg assured her. "But watch out for that *momzer,* I'm warning you. He's a snake!"

One of the things she liked about Nicky was his sense of humor. One August day when the temperature hit 105, he said, "It's hot enough to fry an egg on the sidewalk." So saying, he took her and an egg from her refrigerator to the street.

"Here's a nice clean spot." He brushed clear an area of cement caked with chewing gum and dog shit. New York pedestrians have an innate sense of events in the making. An instant crowd gathered to see what this squatting man with the egg was about to do.

"Sunny-side up?" He broke the egg onto the sidewalk. The yolk wobbled but held firm. The white spread and bubbled as if on a griddle.

A woman got all excited. "What's this? 'Candid Camera'?"

"Salt and pepper, anyone?" Nicky asked.

"What's going on here!" A police car had pulled up. One of New York's Finest, sweating profusely and in no mood for protesters, peace marchers, or anything else, got out to investigate.

"I'm frying an egg, Officer." A wise guy. The crowd pressed in, heat wave and destinations forgotten.

The cop sipped from a cardboard container. "Looks to me like you're committing a nuisance. What if somebody slips in that mess? Break a leg. Sue the city."

The egg had cooked to perfection, a Dali painting. A small French poodle in a pink bow solved the problem by swallowing it in a single gulp. "There goes the evidence!" Dorrie said. The crowd laughed. The defender of public safety reached for his book, changed his mind, and got back into his air-conditioned car.

"Let's go to the beach," Nicky said. "I know a place we can swim nude," he teased. It was a reference to Dorrie's modesty. A few days earlier, she and Glo had gone up to Tar Beach on the roof of the building, Dorrie in a one-piece bathing suit, refusing the offer of one of Glo's bikinis.

"Can't. I'm working." The Forest Hills Tennis Championships were in a couple of weeks. In June a girl named Toni Dean had come out of nowhere and nearly won the Women's Singles at Wimbledon. Nothing was known about her except she came from someplace in Texas. She had refused to give interviews. "I'm here to play tennis. Period." Dorrie's information was that she was hiding out somewhere in Queens or Long Island while training for Forest Hills.

"What about tonight? A nice cool movie?"

"Sorry. Connie asked me over for supper. Something important, her secretary said."

"You owe a lot to Connie," he said with a strange look.

"She gave me my big chance."

"Remember one thing, Dorrie. All you owe her is to do your job. That's all. She doesn't own you."

Dorrie thought of his words that night on Connie Michelin's terrace. The 21 Club had sent over Connie's favorite cold Senegalese soup, a creamy puree of potatoes spiced with curry. She had just finished describing how she had tracked Toni Dean down to a small private tennis club in Queens where the champion was working out incognito.

"How's your apartment working out?" Connie changed the subject.

"Hot. The air conditioning sweats and stomps but it doesn't do too much good. It's an old building."

"And Gloria?"

Dorrie laughed. "Glo is Glo! She keeps buying wigs and changing her makeup, trying to get jobs. It's a losing battle. Like she says, they all want Twiggy and she's Sophia Loren! I feel for her. She wants it so bad."

"I'm sure she must resent your success."

"No. She's happy for me." Which wasn't exactly true. Glo had become increasingly sloppy and argumentative. When this month's rent and utility bills arrived, she had said, "You pay them. You're the big star. I'm broke."

"I've had an idea I've been wanting to discuss with you, Dorrie," Connie said, not quite looking at her. "This is a triplex apartment, as you know. Fourteen rooms and just little old me. I thought you might want to move in here. Plenty of space. Peace and quiet. Someone to cook your meals, take care of your laundry."

Dorrie was taken by surprise. "Well, I don't know—"

Now Connie looked at her earnestly. "I'm extremely fond of you, you know. You're more like—a daughter to me than an employee. Your column is a smash. By the time you're twenty-one, you can be the most important journalist in America."

"How would Walter Cronkite feel about that?" Connie had taken her hand across the dinner table and was holding it so tightly her rings were crushing Dorrie's fingers. The night was hot and murky, the massive Manhattan skyline strangely one-dimensional, like a giant cardboard cutout on a panoramic stage. Maybe it was the heat, maybe it was like New Yorkers always said, the humidity, and maybe it was Connie Michelin's face looming large in the candlelight. She wanted to run for her life.

"It's mighty kind of you, Connie, but I couldn't afford living in a place like this." She extracted her hand and pushed back her chair. Connie sprang to her feet and maneuvered her to the terrace wall.

"You see this city? It's a cliché but it's true. It's yours, Dorrie, if you know how to take it. And I can show you how." She slipped her arm around Dorrie's waist. "I feel close to you, Dorrie. Proud of your achievements. You're just start-ing, there's no limit to what you can do. Together"—her hand trembled, her voice became husky with emotion—"we can be the most powerful women in America."

Blind panic sent her racing out of the triplex apartment and into a taxicab. Unable to deal with Gloria, she gave the driver Nicky Zinn's address. "What happened? You look like you were hit by a truck."

"She—asked me to live in her apartment."

Nicky Zinn was wearing a thin red silk robe and nothing else. He had been lying nude under his sunlamp refreshing his tan when she rang the bell. "I'm not surprised. Come on in. I think it's time I contributed to your limited sexual education."

Connie Michelin was a notorious closet lesbian, he explained. Usually, she contented herself with a live-in "social secretary" or a comely young student hired to do "research" on a pet project.

"You really can't blame her for making a move on you."

Dorrie was indignant. "What do you mean?"

"Well, it's common knowledge you don't make it with the boys, so she probably thought you like girls."

"What business is it to anybody?"

"Sex is everybody's business. Take me, for instance. I'm probably the best stud in town."

"You stop that kind of talk."

"Seriously. Women have offered to pay me for my services."

"Come *on*. You're embarrassing me."

"Seriously. It's because I love women. I truly do. All kinds of women. Short. Fat. Tall. Skinny. Old. Young. I love making love to them. I love breaking down all fears and guilts and self-doubts and making them shriek and moan in my arms. Women are much more complicated than men. Much more subtle. Much more erotic. Let me tell you, if I were a woman, I'd probably be a lesbian."

"How can you say such things."

"Dorrie—"

He had his arms around her and she could feel his naked body through the thin red silk. "Please, don't—"

"I've been patient. I've wanted you to trust me and know

that I'm your friend. Now I want to love you. You've been a girl, now it's time to become a woman."

"Please—"

"Trust me. I'm not a callow boy. I know what I'm doing and I'm going to do it all for you. Slowly and tenderly. I'm going to make you come like you've never come before."

She had had orgasms but only by herself and they had frightened her. "But I'm not in love with you!"

"Dorrie, Dorrie—you're too much!" He picked her up by the buttocks and pulled her legs around his hips. "You're wet!" he whispered. "Your breasts are so swollen, they'll burst if I don't kiss them—"

"But—sweet Jesus, I'm—I've never—"

"It's all right. Don't worry. If it's your precious virginity you're worried about, it doesn't matter." His fingers skated gently up her arm sending tremors to her neck and shoulders. Her back arched. Her thighs parted. Her mouth opened and gulped for air.

At that moment, the phone rang. "Don't move, Dorrie. It's just a friend of mine. I'll tell her not to come over."

Literally saved by the bell from her own abominable weakness, she crept past his closed bedroom door and fled once again into the night streets. There was only one place she truly belonged.

"Jim Ed—"

He was in ragged cutoffs and eating a peach, his books and papers on the table behind him in the glow of a single lamp. At the sight of her, he threw the peach up in the air with an exultant shout—"Dora June!"—and swung her up in the air over his head. "Do you love me?"

"Put me down, you crazy fool."

"I'll drop you on your head if you don't say you love me. Say you love me."

"I love you. I love you." Restored to her feet and breathless from the exertion, she added, "And if you still want me, I'll be proud to marry you, James Edward Loomis."

It took a moment for her words to sink in and then he opened his mouth wide as an Arkansas mule. "*Hooooo-eeeeee!*" he howled, and danced her around his small room, kicking over stacks of books, scattering clothes, magazines, empty beer cans, and take-out pizza boxes until they fell together onto the lumpy mattress on the floor.

"*If you don't want me, mama, you sure don't have to stall!*" he sang to her in the voice of an old Jimmie Rodgers 78. "*If you don't want me, mama, you sure don't have to stall. 'Cause I can get more women than a passenger train can haul!*"

Picking up on the song favorite, Dorrie sang, "*T for Texas, T for Tennessee—*"

"You won't be sorry. I promise to make you happy!"

She slept the night with him in his bed, in his arms, happy in his closeness and strangely content to respect his wish to wait until they were married.

After the next day's editorial conference, Dorrie stayed behind in Connie's office. "I'd like to share some news with you, Connie. Jim Ed and I are getting married."

"You sure you know what you're doing?"

"I'm sure. And I wanted to thank you for offering to take me into your home—"

Connie cut her off. "Excuse me. I've got a call to make."

That afternoon Dorrie found Toni Dean at a municipal tennis court in Nassau County and discovered the secret of her thunderbolt serve and jet-speed backhand. Feigning sleep on a locker room bench, she watched the Wimbledon women's champion change and saw at eye level that Toni Dean was a man. From there on, it was a matter of good reporting, pure and simple, the relentless and painstaking pursuit of facts. Toni Dean had given March 5, 1947, as date of birth. Dorrie's hunch was that not only was this correct but that the imposter's name was probably Dean. Starting with the major Texas cities, she checked the Board of Health records for that day and a few days before and after.

The Amarillo registrar reported an Anthony Laurence Dean born on that day, giving a home address and phone number. The number now belonged to someone else. The Amarillo phone company said the Dean phone had been disconnected in 1959 with no forwarding address.

Working night and day on the story, she nonetheless found time to go with Jim Ed for blood tests and to get their marriage license. They were to be married in a week's time. On her day off.

It was one thing to find out Toni Dean was a man, it was another to find out which man, who exactly he was. The most important thing was to get the story and keep it quiet until her column appeared in *Newsmagazine*. A disadvantage of a weekly was the lead time before the magazine appeared, during which time a daily paper or a TV news show could jump the gun.

The day before *Newsmagazine* went to press, she was watching the "Today Show" coverage of some American troops leaving for Vietnam. "That's it!" A check of the United States Army files in Washington, D.C., disclosed a Private A. L. Dean of Amarillo, Texas, released after two years' compulsory services with an honorable discharge.

Whatever Connie Michelin's private disappointment in Dorrie, she was the total professional when it came to her magazine. "This story is a son of a bitch! I'm going to print an extra hundred thousand copies."

Dorrie's days off varied. The day the magazine hit the newsstands was generally the slowest, with the staff members resting and getting ready to work up their energies for the next week's deadlines. This week's pub date was not only her day off but her wedding day. Whatever the ruckus caused by her revelations, she had spent the morning at Bloomingdale's buying a groom's gift for Jim Ed and a bridal nightgown for herself, the plan being to meet Jim Ed and Glo at City Hall at two o'clock.

Jim Ed had given her his grandmother's lavalier fashioned of ruby-and-diamond lover's knots. Together, they had chosen plain gold bands at the Forty-seventh Street Jewelers Exchange.

Back at her apartment, she wondered if she was doing the right thing. At this moment she would even have asked Glo's advice, but her maid of honor had gone to an important go-see at J. Walter Thompson for a Ford commercial. "We love each other," she assured herself. "I've always known Jim Ed was the man I was going to marry. So why not now?"

She had no heart for the one-night stand. She could see sexual warfare escalating all around her faster than the Vietnam War. She had battles aplenty to fight without fretting about sex. She truly loved Jim Ed. With him she would have a home and a husband as a firm foundation to her life. As Glo often said, all a woman needs is emotional security and she can do anything.

In simple contrast to Pia Melanaiki's rich lace, Dora June Bridges made her own wedding ensemble on her portable Singer, a three-piece cream silk suit copied from a picture in *Glamour* of a Tuffin and Foale. For "borrowed," she wore one of Glo's half-slips, for "blue" a frilly lace garter also provided by her resourceful maid of honor. An apricot velvet wide-brimmed hat and matching sling-back Chanel knockoff shoes completed the outfit. No illusion veil, no princess train with inset panels. She was a disgrace to society page editors everywhere.

She had loaded up her Instamatic and checked the champagne on the ice and was about to leave when the phone rang. Connie's voice was crisp and skipped the preliminaries. "Get your ass over here. The shit's hit the fan."

Connie hung up before she could explain it was her day off and she was on her way to get married. She couldn't simply not show up at the office. She would have to tell Connie why. Hastily, she dialed the older woman's direct line. Busy. Several tries, it was still busy. The main switchboard was equally swamped. At last she got through to the operator. "Sorry, Dorrie, there are a dozen calls waiting. What the hell's going on? Paul Newman?"

Her watch said one fifteen. She would hop a cab over to *Newsmagazine,* keep it waiting while she rushed upstairs to explain, and still get to City Hall by two. She called Jim Ed to say she might be late. No answer. *Damn* Connie. Even the Lord God in heaven got himself a day off.

"Look who's here, Lois Lane herself. You're going to need Superman himself to get you out of this one!"

The four men sitting there with twenty-dollar haircuts and tassels on their shoes were lawyers, two of whom she knew. They represented *Newsmagazine.* Their able staff had checked out her story, verified her sources, and accepted her notarized deposition as an eyewitness to the male status of the women's championship tennis star. The other two were legal counsel for Toni Dean's interests.

"Every word of my column is true," Dorrie said. This, it appeared, was not in dispute. The problem was an infringement *on* and co-opting *of* Toni Dean's private and personally registered property, namely himself! His invasion of the women's ranks was actually a plot to draw attention to himself and a recent move to pit men and women against each other in open competition, regardless of gender.

"Dean's point was to show that an ordinary average male tennis player like himself could beat the world's top-seeded women players."

Not only had Dorrie killed his story but a book deal the lawyers had made with a Major Publisher for exclusive rights. Now the Major Publisher had canceled the book because the story was out and wanted back their fifty-thousand-dollar advance.

Dorrie's files and records were strewn on Connie's table. "Those are mine," she said.

"Wrong. They are the property of *Newsmagazine.*"

By now, it was past two o'clock. The lawyers insisted on reviewing every scrap of paper Dorrie had scribbled plus the tapes of all her phone calls to Texas and Washington.

"Please—" she excused herself.

"Where the hell are you going?"

"I—I've got to make a phone call."

In the outer office, she called City Hall and begged to have Jim Ed paged. The operator said that was not possible.

"Give me the press office." Mayor Lindsay's people would help her, she was sure.

"Sorry, we're having a problem with the phones. Call back later." It was hard to argue with a click. Poor Jim Ed, she could just see him standing there, twisting those two wedding bands in his pocket, wearing a suit and tie and leather shoes and, Lord give him the patience, having to listen to Gloria Greenberg complaining nonstop and making a spectacle of both of them.

She was caught between the rock and the hard place. There wasn't anything she could do. Those lawyers and Connie needed her here. Even if she jumped into that elevator and into another cab, it would still take her a half an hour or more to get down to City Hall and find Jim Ed sure enough gone anyways.

"This is serious stuff, Dorrie," Connie snapped when she returned to the office.

"Is it against the law to write the truth?"

"These gentlemen here have managed to get an injunction against us. All copies of this week's *Newsmagazine* are to be withdrawn from circulation."

"But they're already in circulation!" Grandpa Jeb always said lawyers was like wagon wheels. You had to keep them greased. She wondered how much these shoe tassels were paid for sitting around offices getting out injunctions.

"True, but what the law is ordering me to do is go through

the enormously expensive and certainly futile exercise of sending trucks and couriers to every newsstand—or be subject to an enormous fine and possible imprisonment."

"I have done my job," Dorrie said. As Gloria Greenberg might have added, there was something not too kosher going on here.

"You have jeopardized the very existence of this magazine with your below-the-belt yellow journalism!"

"I have told the truth. Does anyone deny that?"

Connie was wearing the same expression she had when she fired Andrew Van Kennan, vindictive and almost gleeful. "I have no choice but to put you on suspension without pay until all of this is straightened out."

The hot line buzzer beeped. "Sorry, Mrs. Michelin, but there's an urgent call from Chuck Keaton of the L.A. *News* for—"

"Put him on! That bastard front-paged us this morning without so much as a credit. 'According to a *national weekly,*' it said, not *Newsmagazine,* 'a national weekly, it has been revealed that women's tennis champion Toni Dean is—' " She switched on the conference phone. "Let's hear what the bastard has to say."

"Is that Dorrie Bridges?" Keaton's voice echoed through the open speaker. Connie ssshhed the others and motioned Dorrie to reply.

"This is Dorrie."

"Congratulations. That's quite a job of investigative reporting."

"Thank you."

"I'll come right to the point. Are you under any contractual obligation to Connie Michelin or *Newsmagazine?*"

Connie crossed her arms and smugly nodded in the affirmative.

"No, sir, I am not." The Personnel Department had sent her something to sign after a discussion with Connie, but she couldn't make head nor tail of all the whereases and where-fors. It was still in her In Box.

"Here's my idea. I'll pay you twice what you're getting and I'll give you your own front-page column, upper left-hand, above the fold, in the L.A. *News*. Plus international syndication. What do you think?"

All eyes were on her, especially the dumbstruck Connie's. Dorrie's mind was going faster than a runaway freight train with fleeting thoughts of Grandpa Jeb in his grave and Momma in Pass Christian and Tom in Nashville and poor Jim Ed the Lord knew where and she realized with the full certainty of her fate and deep feelings that it was time to move on. She had stayed around this old town long enough to know that summer was almost gone, winter coming on in fact as in symbol.

Momma had once told her she had an itching heel. "Sounds fine to me."

"When can you leave?"

Connie glared at her, disbelieving.

"How about sunup tomorrow?"

"I'll be at the airport to meet you myself. And, Dorrie—?"

"Sir?"

"Tell Connie to close her mouth. I can hear her breathing."

Gloria Greenberg railed at her while she packed. "How could you do this? You act like a fucking saint, so holier than thou!"

"This is yours." She gave back the half-slip and the blue garter.

Gloria threw them aside. "That man loves you to pieces. He was in tears."

Dorrie had been dialing Jim Ed's number every few minutes since her return to the apartment. "It's none of your worry. It's between him and me."

"Between *he* and *I* if you're so smart!"

There was no sense arguing. Her head felt like she'd been

kicked by a mule. The fresh chicken salad and sweet potato pie she had made herself for them to have with the champagne lay in the refrigerator untouched.

"Dorrie—" Jim Ed was drunk and shrunk to half his weight and size.

"I'm sorry, Jim Ed!" Seeing him in his condition, she pitied and scorned him both. She didn't want a man falling apart so easily. It would take more than a postponed wedding to tear her to pieces, loving him as truly as she did. "I didn't mean to cause you pain. Get yourself some coffee and stop all this carry-on."

"You're packing—"

"I told you, Jim Ed. Getting married was a bad idea for now."

"She's going to California. To be a Beverly Hillbilly!" Glo managed a metallic laugh. "You think you'll last five minutes out here? They'll make chopped liver out of you!"

"Gloria, do me a favor and—would you please make us a cup of coffee."

Gloria would not be silenced. "How can you do this to him? And what about Connie, after all she did for you? And what about me? I'm your best friend. You owe me half of next month's rent. Don't try to weasel out of that—"

Jim Ed found his voice. "Please don't leave me, Dora June. I'll do anything to make you happy. Anything."

Anything but let her be herself. Anything but let her spread her wings and fly as fast and as high as they would take her. Why was it that the people who said they loved you were all the while trying to stop you?

Maybe it was the changing times. In the past it was the men who went away to seek their fortune, leaving the women behind to wave and weep and wish them God's blessings. Now she was the one leaving on a jet plane while her sweetheart stayed back to watch her dust.

A few hours later she lay back in her first-class seat on American Airlines Flight 9 nonstop to Los Angeles International Airport. For the time being, she could not be the wife Jim Ed wanted or the woman Nicky Zinn insisted she could be. For the time being she would concentrate all her energies on being a fine reporter.

Instead of seeking love, she'd search for truth.

"Lou, baby?"

Glitz Dreamburg's voice shot from the phone like a poisoned blow dart, piercing his eardrum and landing in the jellied remains of his brain. He was too weak to hold the phone. It lay on the pillow beside his head.

"You there?" she persisted, digging the blow dart deeper.

He was not there. He was long ago and far away in the basement of the N. N. Ipatiev house in Sverdlovsk, formerly

Ekaterinburg, where the last Tsar of all the Russias and the Imperial Family including pre–Ingrid Bergman Anastasia had been slaughtered by the Bolsheviks some sixty years before. Called the House of Special Purpose in one of Soviet communism's first triumphs of euphemism, it had become a museum and regional archives. Some eight hundred miles east of Moscow, the small Ural city had grown since the Revolution into a coal and steel center comparable to Pittsburgh. If you'd never seen Pittsburgh.

Here is where the KGB had kept him and Sonya Boris for questioning for more than a week, within sight of each other but permitted neither to speak nor touch. They had been ambushed a few kilometers from town near an abandoned mine shaft, the final repository of the Imperial Family after being chopped into stroganoff by the Cheka on July 16, 1918.

"The Romanovs did not perish that day," Sonya Boris had assured him a week before during a briefing. A simple wood-cutter who lived in the forest near the village of Koptyaki, where the atrocity supposedly occurred, had kept silent all these years. On his deathbed, he now wanted to relieve his conscience before meeting his Maker.

In Lou Dexter the Russians had found the perfect American patsy. They had quite correctly counted on his romantic nature. In their security check on him before approving his assignment to Moscow, they had undoubtedly seen the series he had written early in his career about Anna Anderson, the German woman who insisted she was the Grand Duchess Anastasia.

At the time he had been young and vainglorious enough to intrude his first-person opinion that she was the Tsar's daughter. Knowing this predilection, they had trapped him in a breach of national security.

With the Geneva talks at a standstill, what better way to embarrass the United States Government than to accuse an award-winning correspondent of being a spy?

"Lou, baby?" Glitz Dreamburg was the kind of person the

U.S. Spy Department should send to places like the Soviet Union. Within five minutes she would *noodgy* them crazy, demanding a Jacuzzi, complaining about the gristle on the lamb chops. Glitz and his ex-wife the princess. The two of them would be more lethal than threats of nuclear sabotage. Neither of these women knew the meaning of fear or diplomacy. By divine right, the world was theirs to command. "Answer me this minute."

All he could manage was a groan. He did not like being called Lou, baby, any more than Charlie Dickens would have liked being called Chuckie, baby. Jennie Bliss Sternholdt materialized at his bedside, dressed and bustling like a prison matron. God save him from strong, efficient women. "Who's this?" She picked up the phone.

"Glitz."

"Drink this!" She held out a jelly glass. Just like his mom, as if she didn't know.

"What is it?" His mouth was like stale white bread.

"Morning-after for coke snorters. A tablespoon of powdered yeast in a glass of watermelon juice."

"Don't tell me you have an electric watermelon squeezer?" Sarcasm triggered his salivary glands. He could speak.

Jennie crooned into the phone. "Hi, Glitz. Wonderful party last night."

Lou's energy level may have dipped and he was surely on the emotional ropes and battling negative space, but this did not stop his seeing an instant savage jealousy transform Jennie's face.

"Is everything okay? I'm on my way. The camera crew and agency people are meeting me there." Today, they would set up the props and lighting for the commercial and actually start shooting the following day.

"If you break anything, I'll sue your ass off. Let me speak to Lou."

"He's sleeping."

"He left his clothes here."

Jennie's proprietary tone was almost convincing. "I know. He's like a child. I had to drive him home naked and sneak him up from the garage."

"She's after your bod," Jennie told him after hanging up.

"You didn't mind last night. Sharing me, that is."

"That wasn't sharing you. That was eat-your-heart-out time. The sin of pride. Showing off. Shoving it to them. I've got something they don't got. Oh, Lou—" She sank down beside him, kissing his eyelids and parched lips. "Please don't leave me for Glitz!"

He would have trouble leaving if the bed caught fire. He knew what she wanted to hear. "I love you, Jennie."

"See you later, *switthott*—"

The door closed. He drifted back to the Urals. Ever since Francis Gary Powers and his U-2 were shot down over Sverdlovsk in 1960, the Russians had been sensitive about nosy Americans. A French correspondent had nicknamed the episode the *Moi, Aussi* or *Me, Too*. In a natural progression, his capture was privately tagged the *Lou, Too*.

The phone rang again. "Lou, baby?"

If they had sent Glitz Dreamburg to Yalta, Russia would be the fifty-first state. "She just left."

"I know."

In the Woodward-Bernstein recess of his failing mind, it occurred to him that this might be his Deep Throat. Who other than Glitz Dreamburg knew everything about everybody? If she didn't know exactly what happened to Dorrie Bridges, she might know who it was that Dorrie was closing in on just before the birthday party. The more Lou examined his Hot 30 list, the more convinced he was that the answer lay with the rumored victim of Dorrie's last investigation.

"Look—" he protested. Jennie's tonic had caused some faint stirrings in his limbs. In time he would sit up, he was sure. The thought of any further assault, verbal or physical, filled him with terror.

"Don't worry, turkey. I won't jump on your bones."

He raised his head. A mistake. An invisible bat knocked him flat. His hair hurt. He hallucinated a joint funeral for Ed Murrow and Homer Bigart and Ernest Hemingway and Charlie Mingus and Bob Capa and Lou Gehrig. All heroes. His heroes. All dead. His skin hurt. It was too tight for his body. He should have died, too. At the crest. There were no more heroes for him, and no more heroines, either.

Except for Rita Hayworth in her black satin Gilda dress. He had only to think of her gyrating in that dress to get horny. *If I were a ranch,* Gilda had said, *they'd call me the Bar Nothing!* Let Jennie the film buff top that one!

"Lou?"

"Go away."

"You still there?" Glitz wanted to know.

"Where would I be?"

"Listen. I like you. You know what I'm saying?"

"Great."

"Listen, you can't do a series on Dorrie Bridges without talking to Sonny Syntagma, right?"

"Right."

"Well, I'm on my way to the 'Love Game' taping. I'll introduce you. Pick you up in twenty minutes."

The way he was feeling, it would take a ten-ton derrick to pick him up. A ten-ton earth mother with two-ton tits to cradle him and nurture him.

There was thirty-seven dollars in cash on the dresser. Good old Jennie, trying to be subtle. He was too old to be a gigolo. The money on the dresser was the last straw on his camel ride to oblivion. So what if someone had knocked off Dorrie Bridges. It wasn't Richard Nixon. Or was it? The thought gave him his first laugh of the day. At this point in time, it didn't seem likely.

And at this point in time, he had to get a job. He could not live off Jennie Bliss Sternholdt. He could not forever ignore his parental duties. He could not go on losing his head while those around him were keeping theirs.

Glitz Dreamburg, dressed in electric green satin, did not give him the chance to explain his change of mind. Before he knew it, he was folded into her Gucci-lined Cadillac Seville, clinging for dear life to the red-and-green-striped straps.

"You look sick!"

They were flying low on Sunset Boulevard.

"I feel sick." The asscrusher jeans were cutting him in half. He felt like a plastic bag of garbage about to burst.

"Not on my new upholstery! I don't *believe* this!"

The Beverly Hills Hotel loomed ahead. The mobile Gucci loafer swerved crazily between a 1956 T-bird and a Lagonda Rapide to reach the hotel driveway.

Stagger and retch. A Dickensian law firm. *Stagger and Retch, good morning!* Do not heave your guts or commit other vile acts of emission in the lobby of the Beverly Hills Hotel. It was against the law. The law-abiding citizens who would never cheat, lie, steal, or double bookkeep, got out of his way. *If you see me coming, you better step aside.* One Baby Mogul, two Major Money Men in business suits, and a Young Hopeful dressed in Cute Kink stopped in mid-choreography to stare.

It was like the time he snitched the box of bing cherries from in front of Bernie's Grocery Store and ate them all before the nine o'clock assembly. He had prayed to God then as he did now, his insides playing *The 1812 Overture. Please God, I'll be good from now on—just don't let me shit my pants—*

He made the men's room just in time. *I found you just in time.* Bent and spent, he found himself in direct eye contact with a pair of black-and-white wingtips pointed at him. "You okay?" a voice asked.

"Fine."

The shoes retreated. With a Hitchcock flash of the old déjà view, he knew he had seen these rather singular shoes before. Several times, in fact, which was why he now remembered it. On a man of David Niven grandeur. Several times in the past week, Lou had felt someone's eyes and looked across a crowded restaurant or bar to find this man idly nodding as if they had gone to polo school together.

The shoes were waiting when at last he emerged. Lou washed his hands and stared morosely into the mirror. The David Niven clone smiled back encouragingly. "Happened to me once with a bad oyster. Had to pump me out, as a matter of fact."

The man was standing very close. *Jesus Horatio Christ.* Was he being cruised? An exciting new career node for Big Lou. He could stop typing his poor little fingers to the bone. Even here in Youthburg, opportunity smirked. His battered Bogart charms might yet bring in a dollar or two.

"Got to watch what you eat," Lou mumbled. Wrong. Flirtatious in the circumstance. Big Lou, honey, your big mouth always gets you in dutch.

"I hear you're doing an interesting article on Dorrie Bridges."

He had heard that this particular men's room was Howard Hughes's favorite place for secret meetings. Could Dorrie have had a Hughes connection and was this the Hughes Mafia on a fishing expedition? "I've been talking to a few people."

"Come across anything interesting?"

"Oh—a little of this, a little of that."

The man smiled genially but Lou could sense a contained desperation. "Well, good luck to you." He was gone before Lou realized he should have gotten his name.

Glitz was waiting for him in the Polo Lounge. Convinced that it was Jennie's yeast and watermelon juice that did him in, he decided to take charge of his own medical care. A double Fernet-Branca shocked his insides into working order, like banging a stopped watch on a table. Following that, a Bloody Mary heavily laced with white horseradish shrank his mucous membranes like an antihistamine. In a matter of minutes he was functioning and almost friendly.

"So fill me in on Sonny Syntagma," he asked.

"What about him?"

"Last night, I got the impression that you and Dorrie had a falling-out over Sonny—and Nicky Zinn, for that matter."

Glitz was wearing her emerald green contacts today. She glared at him like the world's most vicious mountain lion. "I don't remember that."

"You know—Sis Logan got sore because somebody mentioned a tattoo and incest—"

"You mean you really never heard of the Tattoo Lovers? That's the story that put Sis and Brov into retirement for a year. Where the hell were you, anyway?"

"In Russia."

"Yeah?" Why anyone would be in Russia instead of southern California was clearly beyond her understanding. "Well, Sis and Brov were this cute-as-a-button, five-hundred-percent, squeaky-clean middle-America brother and sister act, you know what I mean? Like Donny and Marie. All teeth and health. Barbie and Ken in the flesh. Not a mark on them. Personally I think they're from Mars. The whole family, not a mark on them. Perfect bodies. Perfect teeth. Hair. Skin. All singing. All dancing. If you unzipped their chests, you'd find wires. Anyway—"

She palm-kissed several people before continuing. "You ever hear of Rasputin?"

She was serious. He heeded Jennie's advice to quit making wisecracks. "Some Russian—"

"Right! Only this Rasputin was, you know, like a hypnotist, and also he was into tattoos. He had learned how to do it in the Orient. So, what happens? He meets Sis and Brov and he lures them away from the Logans for an afternoon at his place in the High Desert."

"Your family does not know where you are?" the man had asked the two visitors who had arrived in matching white jeans and T-shirts.

"We're free. Free! At least for a few hours," Sis had giggled excitedly. She and Brov stripped down to tiny bikinis and dove into the pool to cool off before arranging themselves like wet puppies at their host's feet.

"Over there." He pointed to a vast terry cloth-covered waterbed. Obedient to his command, they had arranged themselves side by side, the hot sun beating down on them. The man, heavily bearded and wearing a flowing white caftan, sat cross-legged before them, swaying and chanting and pouring them small silver cups of honey-sweet liquor.

Soon they were chanting quietly with him, rolling their heads in slow circles as the waterbed rippled and swelled beneath them. "Hap-pi-ness" had begun to surface from the gibberish. "Hap-pin-nessssss," they sighed, holding hands and breathing more deeply as the sun and the elixir and their own soothing voices relaxed their bodies and minds.

From where they lay, the man sitting cross-legged at their feet was in dramatic silhouette against a blinding blue sky. A biblical Moses bringing them the word. "Happiness is love," he said. "Love is man's miracle," he intoned. "The love between man and woman is the most beautiful." His voice rose passionately. "But the love between flesh of the same flesh is the most sacred of all!"

Sis and Brov had clasped hands in ardent agreement.

"You love each other very much, don't you, my children?" the man had whispered.

"Yes—" The single word in perfect harmony.

"Here are sacred love oils. Anoint each other in the holy spirit of this harmonious love."

Once more obedient, they coated each other's warm, smooth flesh with the musk oil given them, laughing self-consciously at first.

"Let there be no impediment!"

With reverence Brov untied his sister's bikini and gently put it aside. She smiled up at him serenely and then removed his, averting her eyes.

"If the civilized world is to have a future, it must come from the loins of perfect specimens. Families like yours are a genetic triumph of healthy bodies, physical beauty, and commercial cunning. The leaders of the next generation must have all these blessings. There must be no chance of alien genes destroying what chance and nature have achieved.

"Embrace each other!" he crooned. The slender glistening bodies turned slowly toward each other. "Families like yours must reject the intrusion of alien blood. You are gods and goddesses and you must reproduce yourselves unto the next generation."

Sis and Brov smiled lovingly at each other but did not touch.

"You love each other?"

"Yes." Both smiled beatifically.

"More than anyone else?"

"Yes—" Tears welled in Brov's eyes; Sis brushed them aside.

"Then kiss each other to seal this moment."

At the end of their weekly TV show, Brov always bussed his sister on the tip of her nose.

"A real kiss, my friends. On the lips," their mentor corrected.

The two perfect mouths met chastely, pursed and pressed together as if posing for the cameras, their bodies held rigid and separate.

"*Love* each other!" the sermonizer of the mount exulted. "Heart of your hearts. Flesh of your flesh. Become one and rule the earth!"

While their new guru sat and watched benevolently, a disciple inside the adobe hut videotaped the entire proceedings. Much, much later in the day, after many tears and confessions and pledges of fealty, the leader suggested they be tattooed as symbols of their new devotion.

"Love," Sis had sighed. "I want *love* written all over me."

"Think, my children. What are the instruments of love and why are they regarded as vile dirty words instead of the sacred means to a golden heaven on earth?"

Glitz Dreamburg paused for effect, her fluorescent T-shirt in spasm.

"What did he do, the Lord's Prayer?" Lou asked.

"He tattooed them right on their bikini line. Very small. On Sis, he did 'his cunt' with Brov's initials and on Brov, 'her cock' with her initials."

"Very touching. And Dorrie broke the story—the whole story?"

"As much of it as the papers would run."

"And then what happened? Did it destroy their career? They're still on the box, aren't they?"

"Are you kidding?"

"No, Glitz—" He was still not altogether well. "I am not kidding. I am trying to find out the whole truth about Dorrie Bridges."

"Okay, okay, I know what you're saying. Then you haven't heard? Sis and Brov have founded the International Incest League to do scientific research into the benefits of sexual relationships in families. If it all works out, they're planning to form an Incest Party and get some political clout."

Only in America. The possibilities were mind-boggling. Famous brothers and sisters getting it together for the common good. "In other words, Sis and Brov are not mad at Dorrie?"

"You weird? Why should they be? Apart from everything else, neither one of them ever had such good sex."

He knew he'd missed something by not having a sister.

"Call for Lou Dexter!" Buddy Page approached their table.

"What is this, a con?" Lou snapped.

"You Mr. Dexter? Call for you, sir." The miniature bellhop plugged in the pink telephone.

"This your idea of a joke?" Lou's voice rose. Glitz shook

her head. "Then who the hell knows I'm here!" Suddenly, not three feet away, Pia Melanaiki was again making her way out of the Polo Lounge. "Pia!" The woman glared at him but kept going.

"Your call, sir," Buddy pressed the phone at him.

"Glitz—go after that woman! I've got to talk to her! Hello? Who the fuck is this?"

"This is the long-distance operator and I'll thank you to shut the fuck up!"

Here was a woman after his own heart. "You married?"

"Long-distance call for Mr. Lou Dexter."

If this was a con, it was an elaborate one. "This is Mr. Lou Dexter. Who is calling him?"

"One moment, please. New York, I've got Mr. Dexter."

For a fearsome moment, he thought of his ex-wife and his daughter.

"Lou Dexter?" A woman's voice but not one he knew.

"Speaking."

"This is Connie Michelin. I publish a magazine."

"That's like saying Henry Ford makes cars."

Connie Michelin laughed appreciatively. "You're quick. I like a man to be quick."

"That makes you different from any woman I've ever met."

"I'm not like most women. I haven't the time. So let's not waste any more of it. This is my nickel so I'll do the talking. I understand you're doing an investigation of Dorrie Bridges."

"True."

"And that you're a totally free agent. Not under contract or option to anybody. Is my information correct?"

"Right on."

"*Newsmagazine* is about to launch its own book imprint. Nonfiction only. Hard-hitting exposés and investigative reporting. I'm prepared to offer you a fifty-thousand-dollar advance on this book, terms to be negotiated. How soon can you be in New York? I'll have my L.A. bureau make the travel arrangements."

"I charge five thousand dollars to make house calls."

The same laugh. "You're expensive to do business with."

"I wasn't so expensive when I came looking for a job."

She had the style to sound embarrassed. "Sorry I had to stand you up that day. My pals in the State Department said you were a no-no and I would start World War Three if I hired you." There was a pause. "I was wrong. Now I see there's something fishy about this Dorrie situation. She used to work for me, you know. I gave her her start. I've had a team of hotshots tracking down leads, but all they send me are expense chits from Le Bistro."

"Is Friday too soon?"

"Friday sounds fine."

Glitz had Pia trapped on the sofa near the phone booths.

"Thank you for waiting. It means a lot to be able to talk to you," Lou said.

"Tell this woman to let go of my arm. I really don't want to make a scene!" the Greek heiress complained.

"Glitz. Your eye makeup is running. Why don't you go fix it while we have our little talk."

"What is it you want of me?"

"Did you ever marry Johnny Capedis?"

"Of course not! He married one of the Georgopolous girls. That woman said you were a reporter. A reporter would know that."

He knew he should be a walking index, but he wasn't. He still thought Liz was married to Eddie Fisher. "And what about Richard Lord, the man who wrecked your life?"

She shrugged.

"He didn't wreck my life. Nobody wrecks your life. You wreck your own life." If that were so, there were no innocent people, and dictators, terrorists, and murderers were merely a grandiose form of self-service.

"He lived off your earnings, ma'am, and when Dorrie Bridges broke the story, he disappeared. Whatever happened to him?"

"You're some reporter. Richard Lord is in the federal penitentiary."

"What for?"

"Remember that big franchise swindle? A chain of Lone Ranger Barbecue Pits? Our friend sold over ten million dollars in franchises. Took people's life savings. Printed up magnificent brochures. Actually built one model Lone Ranger on a vacant lot in Eatontown, New Jersey, and flew people in to see it. Disappeared with all their money and filed for bankruptcy. Must have been three, four years ago."

"I was out of town. How'd they get him?"

An elfin smile lit up her face. "Who else?"

"Dorrie?"

"Of course, Dorrie! The police couldn't find him but Dorrie did."

"Is there any chance he's—you know, responsible for her disappearance?"

"I doubt it."

"Why not?"

"Well, she didn't mean to but he said himself that she did him a favor. He's serving four years and when he gets out, he'll have several million dollars to spend any way he likes and nobody can stop him. Anyway, he's too nice a man to hurt anyone."

"And what about you?"

She stared at him in amazement. "What *about* me?"

"To be blunt about it—well, look at yourself. You were a young and beautiful heiress when Dorrie blew the whistle on you—How long ago was it?—only eleven, twelve years ago? You can't be more than thirty-two. You look fifty! Did Dorrie Bridges ruin your life?"

Pia Melanaiki straightened her back and raised her chin. A deep and audible sigh sent shudders through her body. She fought for control of her emotions, clenching her eyes shut but unable to staunch the cascade of tears. "Ruin my life? Oh, my God, my God—" She reached into her bodice for an ornate crucifix and and pressed it to her lips. "Don't you know anything?"

He was past conceding his stupidity. He shook his head.

"Because of Dorrie Bridges, I did not marry Johnny Capedis. Nor anyone else who wanted my body or my money. I married the one I was always meant to marry. I married my Lord Jesus Christ. I'm a nun!"

She had joined the Teaching Order of St. Constantine, nuns who wore a modified habit that could be mistaken for civilian wear. Most of the year she lived on the island of Rhodes. Her current visit to California was for a series of educational seminars.

"May Jesus forgive me. I have always meant to see Dorrie Bridges and apologize for my threats and bad behavior. And now it's too late. Perhaps wherever she is, she knows what I feel."

"And what is that?"

"That because of her, I have found my life's work. You must forgive me now. I am late."

Lou slumped back on the couch to wait for Glitz and try to make mental file folders of all that had transpired. One of the phone booths opened to reveal the man with the David Niven wingtips, which walked rapidly away. It was then that he realized that, apart from Glitz Dreamburg, this man was the only person in the world who could have told Connie Michelin where he was.

"I just called Sonny. He's dying to meet you," Glitz announced on her return.

"I'll bet."

"You know something?" She draped her arm over his shoulder as they waited for her car. "I double dig you."

Ever the pushover, he replied, "I double dig you, too."

She swabbed his ear with her tongue. "Why don't we get it together, you know?"

Ever the coward, he failed to mention Jennie or the fact

that he was living with her and off her and maybe even loved her. "Sounds wild and crazy—"

"Doesn't it ever—"

"But—"

"But what, turkey? Hmmmmm? You were really something special last night. A genuine club selection—"

"Glitz!" A familiar figure in Sergio Tacchini tennis togs ran through the porte cochere waving his racket. Firm and supple, Nicky Zinn's was the kind of authoritative tan that coated him like a baloney skin. Past his ankles. Between his toes. Across his instep and over all the nooks and grabbies of his ageless body, including the dimple on his left buttock. "I heard you were in the hotel."

"Bub*bee,* darl-*ling!*" She thrust forward her glossed lips for a kiss-kiss.

"I also heard what you said about me and Dorrie last night." Using his famous backhand, he raised his customized $235 Tony Trabert C-6 graphite racket with the fourteen-carat-gold three-initial-monogram stick-on label by Daedalus and knocked her flat on her Fiorucci.

Twenty-seven floors above Doheny Boulevard, peering through the smog toward what that nice Beverly Hills realtor woman with the charm bracelets had called a panoramic view of the Pacific Ocean, Dorrie Bridges kicked off her shoes and sat herself out on the porch of her exclusive high-rise condominium apartment.

Back home in Tennessee high-rise meant biscuit flour. In

this instance it meant 2 bdrms, 2½ ba., an entertainment flow lvrm w/fpl leading to 30 ft. ter., and a gourmet kitch. that looked like a nuclear sub and had no place to sit down. Downstairs was 24 hr. monitored security, swim. pool, rec. room, gym, and a sauna she was too shy to use. Her one attempt was aborted by the sight of three unnaturally voluptuous neighbors stretched out smooth and tan as calves at the slaughterhouse.

The hum and damp of the air conditioning had driven her outside. Even after six years in southern California, she was not used to air conditioning. Not yet seven o'clock, the morning temperature was already moving up past ninety-five degrees Fahrenheit. Hot and sticky as a mare rode hard and put away wet, she was melting faster than a ten-cent cake of ice at a Fourth of July picnic. Even the poor old chinaberry trees Tom Jennings had sent her up from Nashville for shade were a sick yellow and not doing much but look homesick. Her satchel lay where she had thrown it, still packed, on the bedroom floor.

She rolled herself a Bull Durham and cozied herself on the porch swing with a sigh of gratitude to be home, though at the same time thinking that this was about the time when they used to put the *Roper Valley Echo* to press and how real nice it would be to be sitting in Min's Truck Stop Diner having eggs and grits and a glass of fresh buttermilk. She remembered how Jim Ed would gulp down a whole big glass of buttermilk and grin fiendishly at her through a dripping white mustache. *Now, Jim Ed, just you quit that! Hear?*

He remained in a special compartment of her mind with private walls separating him from the other people and events of her life. Like Sonny Syntagma, the first man to cause any damage to her nervous system since Jim Ed. Not that anything had happened. Yet. The trip to France had not worked out. She had been tipped about an Islamic Holy Man in exile near Paris who was plotting to overthrow the Shah. For five days she had sat in her suite at the Lancaster waiting for the call that never came. The Ayatollah, it turned out, did not approve of young, unmarried women.

The long hours had given her the chance to think about Sonny and whether to start something she might regret. She wondered if he had been thinking about her. A week's recorded messages oozed from her private answering machine. Press agents. Invitations. Hi-hellos. Two heavy breathers. One overt obscene. Tom calling from Nashville. Nicky Zinn from someone's yacht, showing off. Marva Burnside to remind her of next week's fund-raising. And yes, Sonny Syntagma, calling her five and six times each of the seven days she was away to remind her and inform her of the fact that he was thinking of her constantly.

A final message from Chuck Keaton welcomed her back and advised her to get some sleep and not to fret about the Ayatollah. It had cost the L.A. *News* at least five thousand dollars, and she had returned empty-handed.

"Don't worry," he had said when she telephoned from Paris to concede failure. "It's the first time you haven't brought home the bacon."

It was true, if she had to say so herself. She had talked herself into a job as a prison custodian and cleaned Charles Manson's cell, committing to memory the insane poetry he had scrawled on the walls. She had hunkered down with striking steel workers in Gary, Indiana. She had traveled personally with a shipment of food and medical supplies to Biafra and found out which few relief officials were diverting it to a separate warehouse, speaking of a couple of bad apples spoiling the barrel.

After Chappaquiddick, she traced a high school admirer of Mary Jo Kopechne's from some school photographs. Mary Jo had never dated him, but Dorrie had seen the adoring look on the adolescent boy's face in a group picture. "She was obsessed with the Kennedys. They were better than movie stars or football heroes. The Kennedys were gods and she didn't have time for ordinary mortals. She said she didn't care what she had to do, she was going to Washington and work for them and make herself so indispensable that she'd become part of the inner circle. How could some ordinary guy with acne and a second-hand car compete with all those teeth?"

Hardly stopping to change hose or catch her breath, Dorrie watched a legal abortion and the delivery of a baby on the same day, starred in an underground movie wearing a green wig, applied for a *Playboy* bunny job but failed, and telephoned Fidel Castro to suggest they meet for lunch in Mexico City. It was either he or one of his alleged doubles who arrived with two bodyguards at the discreet Zapata Club for chicken *mole* and margaritas. All she got from that was a signed photograph and a box of Romeo y Julieta cigars which U.S. Customs confiscated at the border.

Very much a chameleon, she had a way of blending with the scenery. Often when there were groups of people, they talked as if she weren't there. Then, when she turned the full demanding gaze of her eyes on them, they felt compelled to dig deep and speak truth.

Even now, after a year's exposure on television, she was not instantly recognized. In stores she would quietly wait her turn and often give way to the more aggressive Vuitton people. Her appearance—except for the eyes—remained ordinary well-scrubbed fresh-off-the-Greyhound-bus girl-next-door dime-a-dozen what's-her-name. Although she had no time to sew, the clothes she bought were exactly like the ones she always made.

Nobody looked at her twice when she took an assembly-line job with Inter-American Foods and discovered they put wood shavings instead of pips in the strawberry jam, added plaster to the frozen cream pies, and perfumed all their sanitized baked goods with chemical aromas they advertised as "Mom's in the Kitchen Bakin' Pan Fresh."

She knew she had reached a certain plateau when people tried to buy her. The small thank you of a bunch of flowers or a single bottle of champagne were, she felt, a courtesy, and when they were from people she knew, she accepted them and returned them in kind at appropriate moments. Books and records were shared with the L.A. *News* staff. Everything else went back. Her favorite attempted bribe was the press agent who pitched a story on the starlet of a new TV series whose previous claim to stardom was winning a Carol Doda topalike contest.

"Are you into portraits?" he had asked. "You know, like famous people's portraits?"

Nicky Zinn had been the first to take her to a portrait gallery, the Frick Museum in New York, where she had admired Lady Hamilton. More recently on a trip to London, she had stolen an hour to explore the National Portrait Gallery. "Yes, I am," she had replied, wondering what that had to do with the price of cornmeal.

She did not have long to wonder. The following day, a package arrived with a note reading, "I hope you enjoy these special portraits of William McKinley and Grover Cleveland." Inside the package, beautifully framed, were a crisp new five-hundred-dollar and thousand-dollar bill engraved with the portraits of each of the two presidents respectively.

"Sorry—they don't match my decor." She had sent them back.

Truth to tell, she was exhilarated but not satisfied. She would just complete one story when she would be digging around for the next. "You're doing great," Chuck Keaton praised her continually.

"Not great enough." What bothered her was that she was doing stories that were obvious, that anyone could do. What she wanted were the deep, dark secrets, the buried stories. Somewhere, she knew, were even bigger and more important stories, like the Lou Dexter affair in Russia. There was something very fishy about a Pulitzer prize winner in a jam and everybody from the State Department down warning hands off.

Sometimes she felt like a crusader in an eternal search for the Holy Grail. She would never stop looking. Meanwhile she herself had become news. "You're famous!" Glo Greenberg had trilled from New York when "Laugh-In" took a tip from *Women's Wear* and introduced a seven-foot news hen named Scarlett O'Horror.

At a time of cultural acceleration and instant fame, she was an instant overnight success in a city and a country that worshiped overnight success. Unlike some others, hers was grounded in basic journalistic value. It wasn't that she was doing anything new. Others had been fearless, tireless seekers of truth. It was an indefinable star you either have or don't have.

Dorrie Bridges had it double. What she wrote was now syndicated in newspapers across America and throughout the world. Her Sunday night television report had started out slow but was picking up ground speed in the ratings.

"Any regrets?" Chuck Keaton had asked her teasingly the last time they had gone to Musso and Frank's for lunch.

"Go whistle up a rope!" She blushed furiously in an overwhelming rush of gratitude. If there were any regrets, they couldn't be helped and she would rectify them if she could. In time.

Connie Michelin, for one, had coldly rejected all efforts to bury the hatchet. When an interviewer boyishly asked Dorrie if she were America's best newswoman, she had said, "No. That honor belongs to Connie Michelin." There had been no response, direct or indirect, from Connie's Manhattan fortress. At Tricia Nixon's wedding, Dorrie had gone up to her in the Rose Garden and said, "Hello, Connie." Her former employer stopped in midsentence and turned her back, leaving Dorrie holding out her half of a handshake.

Jim Ed, for the other, had taken his Fulbright after all and wrote impersonal travelogue letters from Oxford, reporting on his daily travails as if she were a distant cousin and not the woman he loved. Perhaps he had found a new fair maiden who was treating him better than she had. She missed him and often dreamed of him at night.

Momma wrote regular from Pass Christian, threatening to come visit but never quite setting a date. Tom Jennings was flourishing. He ran her column front-page with the slugline *Tennessee's own Dorrie Bridges*. . . . Still her self-appointed adviser, it was he who insisted she invest in this condominium when the money began to roll in. His first choice had been Bing Crosby's old North Hollywood estate, a twenty-bedroom mansion, two acres of landscape, and an electric gate. "Not on your life. It looks like a sanitarium for the criminally rich."

Apart from Tom, other people in her past kept popping up like corks. Nicky Zinn couldn't seem to walk through L.A. International Airport without calling her. "Hi, beautiful, I'm on my way to Taiwan. Just checking in." Or trying to see her. "Hi, babe. Just got in from Fun City."

Jesus Man Suggs had just plain showed up at the paper one day same as he'd done in Roper. "You've changed, Dora June. You're a fine growed-up woman now, Praise *God!*"

He had changed, too. From a fire-and-brimstone rural evangelist, he had transmogrified himself into the King of Gospel Rock. A walking, talking, and singing Tabernacle of the Lord, according to *People* magazine, which she had heard had had a hard time deciding whether to put him in "Entertainment" or "Religion."

On this particular occasion, the Walking Tabernacle was garbed in a peach suede performance suit of the kind worn by Porter Wagoner at the Grand Ole Opry, heavily encrusted with jeweled crosses, including the matching cowboy boots. His shirt front was a trompe l'oeil of Calvary drawing the eye upward to a sky blue neckerchief held in place with a silver tie ring in the shape of Christ crucified.

He was a rascal sure as hens lay eggs, but she was glad to see him. "Come to cleanse us of sin, Brother Suggs?"

"Let me tell you something, the smell of sin and abomination is so strong here, Beverly Hills especially, I have to take me an antihistamine pill every hour just so's I can breathe."

"Ever change your mind about the Beatles?"

"See what happened to them? Broke up. Tore apart. Scattered to the winds. The Devil won that one time. The good Lord and I fought to save those boys. Tried to show them their sins. But they were too far gone. Five years from now, you'll say Beatles and folks'll say 'Who?' "

"Who's going to take their place? The Stones? Simon and Garfunkel? Acid rock? Moog?"

He placed before her a copy of his first LP on his own Tuning Up for Jesus label. "I am. If the good Lord's willing and with a little help from my friends like you."

"Getting by with a little help from your friends is from a Beatles song."

He smacked his thigh like a farmhand caught backing up a milk cow. "You see? You see how the Lord works in special ways?"

The LP had already made some waves. More Gospel Porn than rock, the songs were jointly credited to J. Suggs and his collaborator, J. Christ. In "Succor Me, Mary," Jesus Man sang as a demented sinner crazed by his passion for Mary and torn apart by his carnal lust for a woman who was both the virgin Mother Mary and the evil Mary Magdalene.

> *Mary, hold me, Mary,*
> *Mary, help me, Mary,*
> *Mary, succor me, Mary. . . .*

Ignored at first by rock stations, it was now banned from air play although selling so well, *Billboard* and *Cashbox* were forced to list it in the Top Twenty.

"Will you help me, Dora June?"

"If I can."

"Hear me, sister woman, don't you know the Lord works, his wonders to perform? There's no such thing as chance meeting. The Lord expressly wanted me to meet up with you that long ago time in the mountains in Tennessee. The Lord has brought you to your high place to do His work and the Lord has brought me to you to help me in my work for the Lord.

"Billy Graham, Oral Roberts, Kathryn Kuhlman—all of the old-fashioned preachers, they're finished, through, not keeping up with the times. There's a new generation growing up in the land, conceived in rock music, weaned in rock music, doing their homework and driving their cars and getting married and starting new lives unto the next generation wearing headphones and turning dials. The only road to salvation is on the twelve-track stereophonic. The only way to bring high fidelity meaning to your life. Will you write about me, Dora June, and bring my ministry to your millions of readers?"

"If I do and when I do, it will be the truth as I find it."

"Praise *God!*"

The way that man was going, he'd either get himself shot stealing rabbits or become President of the United States. Or, if some of her recent digging hit pay dirt, go to prison.

Gloria Greenberg had joined the westward migration, too, with the explanation, "New York sucks. There are no jobs. All they want is Swedish cadavers or Japanese midgets. Even showroom jobs. Seventh Avenue! I tell you. They've flipped out. All the Bernies and Seymours have factories in Taiwan. They get a fagerini designer who had plastic surgery on his asshole to make a new, new, *newnie-newnie NEW* fashion statement. The buyers are wearing polyester double knits and queen-size support hose for their varicose. They order in volume. The American woman takes one look and wears last year's blue jeans and the Big Brains scream."

The New York men were even worse than before, if that

was possible. They, too, wanted Swedish cadavers and Japanese midgets. "They're spastics, I tell you. I'm a basket case. I looked around my encounter group and I didn't know whether to shit or go blind."

Dorrie didn't quite remember inviting her to stay, but suddenly there she was in the spare room. "Isn't it a trip being roommates again, Dorrie? Remember how I took you in and took care of you and almost supported you in New York? Aren't old friends the best friends?"

At first Dorrie had thought it might be a fine idea. Living alone, she was becoming too self-centered. It might do her character some good to do some sharing. The concept of sharing appeared to be beyond Glo Greenberg. If she wasn't using the phone, she was asking Dorrie to keep her calls short since she was expecting to hear from a very important casting agent. She was like a mosquito on a summer night. Wherever Dorrie was, she was. If Dorrie sat down to write, she pulled up a chair to talk. In some mysterious proof of Murphy's Law, she managed to squeeze Dorrie out of all nine closets and to be using all 2½ bas. at the same time.

After three weeks of interviews, go-sees, and auditions, Glo was discouraged. "All you get in this town are two promises. 'I won't come in your mouth' and 'I've got the perfect part for you in my next pilot.' "

An eight-hundred-dollar phone bill, a bowl of chili knocked over her new IBM Selectric, and a three-day Sex Olympics staged while Dorrie was away finally snapped all diplomatic relations.

"If that's how you feel. I don't see what all the fucking fuss is about."

"I think you'll feel more relaxed in your own pad," Dorrie said, trying to avoid a scene.

"You don't have to be sarcastic. After all I've done for you! I never thought you'd go big head on me."

It was several days before she realized that in Glo's haste to pack, she had included Dorrie's favorite white silk shirt and the Biba print she had bought in London on her way to Prince Charles's investiture as the Prince of Wales. As a thank-you gift, Glo sent her the current status item, the Cartier ivory-faced tank watch with the pigskin strap. It stopped dead the first time Dorrie wore it. When she got around to bringing it into Cartier's for repair, she was icily informed it was a knock-off.

The one person she never expected to hear from was Drew Van Kennan. A few days earlier, just before leaving for France, a basket of daisies arrived with a note. "Can you ever forgive me?" It was signed "A." The handwriting was familiar but she couldn't place it. The following day, Drew Van Kennan solved the mystery. "I wouldn't blame you if you hung up on me."

"That wouldn't be neighborly, now would it?"

"I was a bastard, Dorrie, and I'm sorry. Jealous as hell. I could see you running rings around me and I guess I OD'd on envy. I'd like to apologize with all my heart."

"Like we say down home, 'More fun, more people killed.' "

"Can't we forget the past and be friends?"

The man wanted something for certain sure.

Encouraged by her equanimity, he gushed, "I knew you'd go places and fast. Now you're a communicator—"

"That's not my word. That's hype. I'm just a little old hard-nosed reporter, doing my best."

"Lois Lane—only prettier."

Gratuitous flattery made her puke. The man was as full of horse manure as ever. Buttering her up like she was one of those vain society women with the face lifts. "I've got a call waiting, Drew, but thanks for the flowers."

"Call me Andrew. Didn't you notice I signed 'A'? My shrink says I've been suffering an identity crisis and I should use my entire name."

"Andrew—"

"I know you've got to go, but look—I know it's pushing things—but, well—can I take you to lunch?"

It would not have been southern ladylike to remind him that he had never once so much as taken her out for a lemon Coke when she was his lowly assistant. In the Elvira Madigan gardens of the Bel-Air Hotel, after a lunch of baked potato shells with sour cream and beluga, Andrew Van Kennan, looking like Robert Redford's weak-chinned second cousin, took her hand and asked her for a job.

"You can't do it all. You need someone like me. Someone you can trust professionally and personally. I saw you at the Stigwood party the other night." She had brought a civilian, an attractive lawyer whose major contribution was to keep saying, "You ready? Let's go."

"I finally told him to leave," she admitted. "He couldn't seem to understand that I was working."

"You need an escort who can socialize, who has good manners. I would never say, 'Let's go!' "

Oddly enough, the idea appealed to her. Not to lord it over him or for some petty revenge. She did need the kind of help and support he described. He was devious. He was vain. He was independently wealthy so he didn't need the money. He did need a special kind of job, one that gave him the status he so evidently craved.

She felt she could handle him because she understood his weaknesses and his needs. She would be able to control him because she was his ticket to ride. He was the kind of man who needed to answer to a strong woman. In New York it was Connie Michelin. In California, why not Dorrie Bridges. Being younger than Andrew didn't matter; being stronger was what really mattered.

Recently she had read a biography of Queen Elizabeth I and how the Virgin Queen had ruled men by keeping them off balance and dependent on her. Whether the English ruler remained virgin would never be known. The fact was that she attained her position of power young and spent the rest of her life protecting it.

At age twenty-five Dorrie could understand the dilemma.

Though hardly a reigning monarch with the power of life and death, she did have the power of the press—to affect if not change people's lives. She could praise an obscure book one week and see it bought for six figures for a movie the next. She could knock a congressman and start a snowball of revelations that could lead to defeat at the polls.

In direct proportion to her increased power was a deepening fear of men. This was based not so much on the sexual act but on shame and embarrassment at her inexperience. If not exactly untouched, she was in the most fundamental sense virginal. Because she had never been penetrated by a male organ, she could not in truth feel she had experienced sexual intercourse.

What made things even worse was living in the sex capital of the world. She knew all about the positions and mechanics of erotic bliss. The problem was, she was famous and presumed worldly. How could she take up with someone and risk his contempt? As Glo Greenberg had sneered at her way back in New York, what did she know from fancy fucking! Except for Nicky Zinn and, of course, Jim Ed, there was no man she could trust. She could not afford to be the butt of Saint Dorrie or Dorrie the Virgin jokes. It would be far better to stay aloof and mysterious about her private life.

Men like Sonny Syntagma unnerved her the most. She had never before been turned on by physical beauty alone. Just seeing him across a room made her feel weak. A situation, like cigarettes, that was dangerous to her health. His manager had *suggested* she might like to meet him. "Another time," she had gasped, and fled.

Sex and love aside, it was also hard to develop any real friendships. The few she had attempted had ended with them wanting to promote her. An introduction. A plug for a new project. A short-term loan. In fact, in six years the only new friends she had made were Marva and Norris Burnside. They were Old Money California Establishment. They didn't need her for anything but her company. They were too rich and too well-connected from the governor on down.

Marva formed committees to build museums and libraries and add wings to hospitals. She had no children except, as some wags said, for Norris, who had been born with a golden rattle in his hand and seemed content to do Marva's bidding and be polite to her friends.

They were a handsome and stylish couple. Marva, with her shock of thick white hair and trademark emerald earrings, wore no makeup on her tanned and unlined face. Norris styled himself elegantly in blazer and flannels with those two-tone wingtip shoes that reminded Dorrie of Fred Astaire.

The Burnsides would like Andrew Van Kennan. Marva would have him on one of her committees before he knew what hit him, and what's more, Andrew would be tickled pink. As for her own personal problem, he was right, she did need an escort who wouldn't keep saying "Let's go!"

Before leaving him she had promised, "We'll talk about it some more when I get back from France."

She stretched and yawned. It was still too early to call him. She would wait until she got back from Westwood Village Mortuary. Today was the anniversary of Marilyn Monroe's death. She wanted to be there and see if anyone showed up. Even if nobody showed up, there would be a story in that, too.

Dedicated in 1904, the Westwood Village Mortuary and Memorial Park, owned and operated by the original Pierce Mortuary Family and offering the only complete funeral facilities in the West Los Angeles area, occupies a modest hatchet-shaped tract of land on Glendon Avenue between Wilshire and Santa Monica Boulevards. Eye-high on a wall of white marble crypts, the inscription reads:

MARILYN
MONROE
1926–1962

To its right, a metal vase held the expected six red roses, said to be delivered daily on orders from Joe DiMaggio. The crypts to the left and above were vacant. To the right was someone named Bruce Fred Fisher, Jr., 1918–1954. Dorrie made a note and mentally kicked herself for not having thought of the angle sooner.

Who was this Bruce Fred Fisher who had died at the age of thirty-six, the exact same age as Marilyn when she died? It was unlikely they had ever met, yet there they were side by side in necrophilic cohabitude until the end of time or a nuclear war, whichever came first.

Bus Stop was one of the first movie shows little Dora June had ever seen. She couldn't have been more than nine or ten years old, kneehigh to a duck and clutching a paper sack of horehounds when Momma and Grandpa Jeb took her over to the old Bijou down Clarkstown Crossing.

Cherie was Marilyn's name, and even at Dora June's young age she had been smart enough to know Cherie's southern accent was playacting. Like the time she and Jim Ed had to playact Christopher Columbus and Queen Isabella and they had to do Spanish accents and all the kids giggled and carried on.

At the old Bijou nobody had giggled. They were sighing and sobbing when Cherie's prince charming took off his coat and wrapped it tenderly around her shoulders and you knew they were going to get on that bus and drive north on that interstate and live happily ever after.

In the movie show Cherie gave up her career as a glamorous nightclub singer for a true and lasting love. Standing pensive and alone at Marilyn's stark marble marker, Dorrie pondered the possibility of having both. The crux of the problem was confidence. She felt utterly self-confident about her work and equally lacking in confidence about herself as a sexual, loving woman. Like Marilyn, she didn't know who her papa was. Every man she'd ever taken a fancy to had tried to change her, like Joltin' Joe tried to make Marilyn into something else. Even Jim Ed, who knew her better than any living person, he couldn't let her be. He wanted to change her.

All she really wanted was a nice loving man. Down home at Roper High, the girls would whisper about boys wanting just one thing. She wanted to give that one thing with loving tenderness and she wanted to be loved tenderly in return. For her own self and not for her success.

"So you're the famous Dorrie Bridges?" Sonny Syntagma had said to her when they met. "How'd you like to make me famous?" Her face had shown her feelings. "Hey, I'm sorry. I was just kidding—" he had called after her.

If Marilyn Monroe, with her beauty and wit and intelligence, died alone in her bed on a Saturday night whether by desire or default while half the men in America were dreaming about her, what hope was there for her? Success was like getting an All-A report card. You wanted to share it with someone close.

Oh, Marilyn. She closed her eyes and whispered, "Was it worth it?" A feathery touch like an angel's kiss grazed her cheek. She shuddered and opened her eyes to find Sonny Syntagma at her side.

"I knew you'd be here."

"How did you know?"

"Last February—for Valentine's Day—you wrote in the paper that you were in mourning for romantic love, remember?"

She had complained that women were romantically deprived, that sex was not enough and that it was just as important for a man to give a woman a pretty compliment as an orgasm.

"You said Joe DiMaggio was a romantic throwback and that you were going to disguise yourself as a palm tree and see if he showed up on the anniversary of Marilyn's death." Sonny looked over her shoulder. "Look who's coming."

If it wasn't Joltin' Joe, it surely resembled him. "Quick— act like a tourist." Dorrie took Sonny's arm and walked him briskly along the wall, chattering and pointing like a visitor in an art gallery. At the far end of the vast lawn they turned and watched the solitary mourner. Was it Joe? She couldn't see his face. In her romantic heart of hearts she wanted it to be Joe, thinking about the times he and Marilyn had had together. Was he crying and telling Marilyn that he missed her and still loved her?

With the sudden graceful movement of the born athlete, the man pressed the whole of his body against the cool marble and kissed it lightly. A quick dissolve and he was gone. Call it jet lag, call it emotion, Dorrie's knees went weak. She was a reporter, wasn't she? Nothing should upset her. This was a private moment of grief she should not have witnessed. She would not write about it.

"You all right?"

Without realizing it, she had sagged against him. "I'm real fine."

"You look all washed out. What you need is a good hot breakfast."

"I've been up all night on a plane. What I really need is some sleep."

"I've got an idea."

The old come-on. She was too worn out for flirt games. "Excuse me, but I've got to get home." She stumbled, so tired now that her feet wouldn't behave.

"You can't drive like that. You'll get killed. We'll leave your car here."

"I'll get a cab."

"For God's sake, Dorrie, what do you think I'm going to do to you?"

She had to laugh at that. "It wouldn't much matter. I'm so tired, I'm numb."

He took her arm. "Trust me, babe."

"Should I?"

"What have you got to lose?"

She couldn't think of a clever reply because she fell asleep in his car. It was an old heavy Buick. The hum of the wheels and the soft leather seat lulled her mind and soothed her aching bones. Soon she was aware of the air getting cooler. They left the freeway for a secondary road leading northeast into the mountains. "Hang on!" Sonny warned as he turned into a rutted dirt track in a stand of pine trees.

A partially built A-frame stood in a small clearing.

"What's this? Yours?"

"Me and a friend. We're building it ourselves. Feeling better?"

"Still dragging." The clean mountain air reminded her of home. Let them sniff snuff and snort coke, this was her idea of fine breathing. It cleared her head and her lungs and untied all the knots in her neck and shoulders.

Beside the house was a small brook. "Let's just sit and stare for a while." The ground was damp. "Got a blanket in your car?"

"Better than that." He hauled out a huge double sleeping bag and opened it out on a blanket of pine needles beside the brook.

"Is that a mink lining?"

"Sable." She had heard that rich women gave presents like that. She was richer than she had ever been and getting richer. She wondered if soon she would be giving sable-lined sleeping bags as casually as a book or flowers.

"Down on your face," he said.

"What are you going to do?"

He scooped her up like a child and placed her on the soft fur. "What the hell do you think I'm going to do to you? Chop you up and feed you to the fishes?"

She had lain just this way, flat out in a farmer's meadow back home, feeling the earth and grass and wild flowers with every inch of her young and yearning flesh. The sable lining was even softer and more cherishing and smelled of rare perfume.

"You need someone to take care of you," he said from somewhere above her. Drifting to sleep, she thought of Jim Ed and the time they floated on the river in a borrowed inner tube. "Relax, babe. Leave everything to old Sonny here."

Strong, insistent hands kneaded her neck and shoulders and loosened her spine. *Don't spoil it,* she begged. As sleep descended on her in ever deeper concentric circles, her tiny message center at the spiral's core began to buzz. She felt him remove her shoes and rub the pain from her feet, pain she didn't know was there till it began to fade.

She could only dimly perceive him lying down quietly beside her. He folded the sleeping bag around them and slowly pulled up the zipper. Snug as a bug in sable fur rug, the thought came to her that she really could, if she took the notion, make him a star.

13

Nothing in his previous experience had prepared Lou Dexter for Connie Michelin. Not cattle prods to the genitals *a la Russe*. Not Harlem the night Martin King was killed. Not his ex-wife the princess on the occasion of his missing a dinner party. Not Sonny Syntagma's demonstrated offer to snap his windpipe with one hand. Nor Jennie Bliss Sternholdt's threat to cut out the crotch of all his trousers if he left California and went to New York.

Lou had heard about offices designed to intimidate the visitor in subtle and subliminal ways. This was his first time in one. In its way, it was more terrifying than a KGB detention room. The walls were thickly quilted like a padded cell, the ceiling low and swagged in matching floral fabric, the floor ankle-deep in tufted snarls. A heavy cloying perfume filled his sinuses and paralyzed his eyeballs.

Before entering the inner sanctum, he had been the battered born-again Bogart, world weary yet stylishly dressed according to Jennie's instructions, after she had calmed down, in gray flannels and the Saks Fifth Avenue blazer with a blue-and-white-striped Turnbull & Asser shirt and ruby silk tie for old-fashioned sincerity. Florsheims, Jennie had insisted. Not Guccis. Not to talk money and contracts in New York.

In a crazy way, he wished Jennie were with him, or even Glitz. A strong, noisy woman to do battle for him against the woman glaring at him. The women were the new warriors. Let the women fight it out. At this express moment his impulse was to take what was left of his five thousand dollars and hop a freighter.

Connie's high-priestess desk loomed imposingly on a raised platform, below it the chair she had indicated to him. Low to the floor and virtually backless, it forced him to hunch forward awkwardly with his knees like earmuffs. On a wobbly table beside him was a toy ashtray. When he reached for it, the whole thing toppled over.

"Clumsy!" He grinned rakishly. Connie's glare intensified. He felt as if he were made out of spare parts, a road company Frankenstein monster. Compared to him, Gerald Ford was Baryshnikov. And speaking of ballet reminded him of his appointment later in the day with Viktor Varvanza, whose beautiful ballerina wife had been driven, some said, by Dorrie Bridges to do a dying swan dive off the top of the Empire State Building.

"You've pulled a dirty on me, Lou!" The tone of Connie

Michelin's attack was exactly that of his ex-wife the princess, a whining laser beam aimed at his balls. He leaned back protectively to cross his legs only to find himself in an even more vulnerable position. The light fixture on the wall behind Connie's head now shone directly in his eyes, blinding him.

"Well, what have you got to say?" She swayed at him like a bleached-blonde cobra.

He had no idea what she meant. "What do you mean?"

"What do you mean what do I mean? What do you take me for, Rebecca of Sunnybrook Farm?"

After all the bleak months since his return from Russia, the book contract was his first realistic hope of saving his life and his career. There were only a half-dozen more of the Hot 30 to track down, including Connie Michelin herself. He was circling in closer and closer to the truth of what had happened to Dorrie Bridges. He had come today to talk of books and money, his book and Connie's money. Instead of contracts and champagne, he was in a parachute on a target range.

Attila the Cunt, meet mild-mannered Clark Kool. "Why don't you tell me what's bugging you?"

"Don't you read the papers? It's Dorrie Bridges—"

He had flown in last night and sallied forth this morning without, it was true, so much as a glance at the good gray *New York Times*. All he could think was that they had found the body. The movieola of his life slipped its sprockets and fell in a tangle. "What about her?"

"Somebody else is writing a book. Announced last night at Twenty-One." She read from the *Times*. " 'A trenchant analysis of the life of Dorrie Bridges, the most influential personality of contemporary mass culture in America. To be written by America's most trenchant intellectual—' "

"And who might that be?" And what did it matter, anyway? He was still ahead, he was sure.

"Care to guess?"

"It's hard to think of anyone that trenchant. Tatum O'Neal?

That kid's got a good head on her shoulders. Truman Capote? Not really his cup of tea. Rex Reed? David Halberstam? Gloria Steinem? I'd give all of them full marks for trenchant."

Connie folded her arms like Ilse Koch waiting for a lamp-shade to stop breathing so she could skin it. "Give up?"

Maybe he should have given up long ago. "Okay. Who?"

"Sidney Silver!"

"The poor man's Philip Roth?" Sidney Silver had created a literary persona based on a pathological fear and loathing of women. Let other men declare themselves feminists and give tight lip service to the rights of wronged women. Sidney said all men were liars and only said what they said to get laid without having to spring for dinner.

Shaped like a baked pear with a chronic pre-natal drip and Day-Glo sties on both lids, his reputation stemmed from a monograph which blamed the disintegration of major male creative talent on the women in their lives. He cited Scott Fitzgerald, Ernest Hemingway, and Thomas Wolfe among others as victims of emasculating, demanding women.

Dorrie's discovery that he had stolen the essay from a fifteen-year-old high school girl who handed it in to him dur-ing a writing seminar in the Catskills had caused a rash of Letters to the Editor of several literary journals, all read by the same favored few. While his coterie defended him, Sidney had sulked in seclusion. Now that she couldn't fight back, he would vindicate himself by zapping her posthumously.

"Don't worry. I can write onion rings around Sidney Sil-ver."

"That's not what worries me."

"What worries you?"

"That he might—get a beat on you."

So that was it. She was worried. By giving Lou a book contract, she would know if anything about her had leaked out. She had no control over Sidney Silver.

"Don't worry. Sidney's a stylist, a trenchant thinker. He

wouldn't know how to find a dead fly in a sugar bowl. Let's forget Sidney Silver." Charm the lady, Lou baby. "What I want to talk about is—you!" There wasn't a woman alive who could resist talking about herself.

Connie Michelin was the exception. "Save the banana oil."

"You're the publisher of my book but you're also part of the story."

"That's why I want it to be absolutely honest. You know, of course, Dorrie came to me barefoot from the hills of Tennessee. I taught her everything she knew. And how did she repay me? I made her a star and she walked out on me. Never once, not once in ten years did she drop me a note or call up to say hi, hello. Last year the American Women in Media gave me their 'Woman of the Century' award and asked her to be on the dais and she didn't even have the courtesy to reply. That Van Kennan—"

"Her associate—"

"My foot. Her secretary/body slave/ass licker. What a pair. The Two Nellies. She the Nice Nellie, he the Nasty Nellie. Imagine him going to work for her after what she did to him?"

"What did she do?"

Connie clutched her head in mock mourning. "Some reporter you are. Let me ask you, did you know Dorrie's first big success was running the 'Whispers' column in *Newsmagazine?*"

He nodded.

"And did you know who was writing 'Whispers' before she took it over?"

She had him there. "No—"

"Andrew Van Kennan! He was bad, she was good. I fired him and gave her his job. Law of good driving out bad."

"And then he went to work for *her?* Has the man no pride?"

"Like they say in the gay health clubs, he turned the other cheek."

"Do you think he had anything to do with her disappearance?"

"That, Mr. Woodstein, is what I wanted you to find out."

"Some people wait years for revenge."

An odd look crossed her face. "Patience is its own reward."

He personally was running out of patience. In all these weeks since the memorial service, he had explored nearly twenty-five of the original Hot 30. Like the White Queen in *Alice* he'd been moving fast but getting, on balance, nowhere. His contract with Connie was being drawn up. He had everything to lose by asking the next question. "I understand Dorrie was about to blow the whistle on *you,* Connie, and you were desperately trying to stop her."

She sighed with genteel exasperation. "You're whistling through your asshole."

That would get him on "The Gong Show." "Get one thing straight, Connie. This is my book. I have final control over the contents. Nothing deleted, nothing added, without my approval."

A low buzzing was followed by a quiet voice seeping from the speaker phone on her desk. "Tom Jennings for you, Ms. Michelin."

Clearly, Connie didn't want to take the call. "Tell him I'll get back to him—" A hearty voice broke in. "Connie? Has Lou Dexter agreed to—"

"He's here now, Tom," Connie cried out with the special not-in-front-of-the-kids falsetto women assume. "Let me get back to you, huh?" Before he could agree, she switched him off.

"What's Tom Jennings got to do with this?" There were rumors linking him and Dorrie Bridges, too. Maybe he and Connie together had bought her a concrete kimono for her thirtieth birthday.

"Tom Jennings discovered Dorrie. He brought her to Nashville to work for him and then sent her to me. He was her patron and I was her patroness. We were both extremely distressed by her—"

"Death?"

"—tragic disappearance. Tom and I have long thought about a joint book publishing venture. When we heard you were doing this book, it seemed ideal. A fitting monument to Dorrie and earn a few bucks besides."

"Whatever happened to Jim Ed Loomis?"

"You mean Li'l Abner? It was his fault Dorrie left New York."

"He's not exactly a hillbilly, Connie. He was a Fulbright scholar—"

"He wanted Dorrie to marry him!"

"That's really gross."

"She ran away from him to California and I lost fifty thousand readers."

"What happened to him?"

"Why don't you find him and ask him? What do you think we're paying you for?"

That was exactly what he planned to do. He wasn't sure where Jim Ed was, but he could find out. First, there were the remaining Hot 30 to find, most of them on the East Coast. Movie producer Slick Doob was on location at Ellis Island for his first project since the accident that put him in a wheelchair. Burt Whitechapel's cockney restaurant, Stodge, was packing them in despite Dorrie's disclosures.

Posters and billboards all over town were hyping a Madison Square Garden TRIBUTE TO GOD, MUSIC & MOTHERHOOD starring Jesus Man Suggs, the King of Gospel Rock, and with a Featured Added Attraction of Marjorie Ullman, the onetime Broadway musical-comedy star turned spokeswoman for the Anti-Homosexual League.

As Dorrie's disclosures had shown, the things zealots denounce most hysterically in others is what they secretly fear

236 ■ JEANNIE SAKOL

most in themselves. Where big egos were involved such as these, getting even might still be the best revenge.

When Mallomar Crane's plans to be the first black president of the United States hit a snag called Dorrie Bridges, he turned his considerable energies to young people. To prove that his views on integration were both practical and positive, he had opened a Youth Hustle in upper Manhattan where black and white neighborhoods overlap. "Hustle," he felt, was more expressive than "hostel" to the urban disadvantaged.

To Lou's amazement, Viktor Varvanza had agreed to see him and had himself suggested they meet on the Observation Deck of the Empire State Building at the very spot from which the tragic Verita Varvanza had jumped.

As for Dorrie's mother, several attempts to locate her in Pass Christian, Mississippi, had come to a big *rien*. There was no phone listing or a record of an address. Short of going there himself, he had asked a novelist friend who lived nearby on the Gulf Coast to do some sleuthing.

Much as he would have enjoyed connecting Dorrie's disappearance with either Sonny Syntagma or Nicky Zinn, Lou's last few days in California had effectively dispelled that possibility.

Glitz Dreamburg's response to Nicky Zinn's attack was instant-primitive-animal-vicious. She did not question his motives. She did not consider the state of his astrological chart. She did not attempt to reason with him or suggest he share his unhappiness. Knocked flat on the green carpet of the Beverly Hills Hotel porte cochere, she kicked out at his bare legs with her Ralph Lauren cowboy boots and wrestled his tennis racket out of his hand.

"Scumbag!" she screamed, turning his weapon against him in a series of chop shots that had him leaping in the air like a Hungarian sword dancer. "I'll kill you! I'll kill you!"

"She's crazy! Get her off me!" He ran through the hotel as if it were the first lap of the Beverly Hills marathon, Glitz hot behind him still screaming, until he reached the sanctuary of the men's room.

"Dorrie was too nice to you!" she bellowed through the door. "I know what you are! A eunuch pretending to be a superstud!"

A quick detour to phone Rona Barrett's office with details of the scuffle and she returned to the hotel entrance where the Great Wheeled Guccimobile was waiting.

"Did Dorrie actually say he was a eunuch?" Lou asked as they headed once more toward the "Love Game" taping and Sonny Syntagma.

"Worse than that." She patted Lou's crotch. "A eunuch at least, you know what I'm saying, there's something there. You know what I'm saying, it looks good but it doesn't work. With Nicky—" She switched to baby talk. "—it's *aw gohn*! Nothing there but a great big wide open space. Has to stuff his jock with a cucumber."

"I thought he was such a lover. What happened?"

"He picked on the wrong plastic surgeon."

She made a chopping motion.

"Come *on*—"

Nicky Zinn's genuine affection and compassion for the Female Race was what ultimately proved his undoing. Having moved to California five years earlier—rich, fit, and pushing sixty—he decided to devote himself to a minority group thus far ignored in the complex tapestry of social awareness.

In the wake of the sexual revolution of the sixties, a small and extremely deprived stratum of women was treading water merely to stay afloat. Nicky had appointed himself lifeguard and was teaching them to swim.

"Hundreds of them in Bel-Air alone. Women thirty-five, forty, forty-five. Married during the sixties. Had kids. Didn't fool around. Born a little too soon. Wired into the old-fashioned idea of one man, one cock, that's it. They knew the sexual revolution was going on but they were married and didn't want to rock the boat. So what happens?"

"The boat rocked them."

"Smart! Lou, baby, you're not just another pretty face. Hubbie gets an attack of mid-life crisis and leaves them for a young chick. Especially after *Shampoo.* When Julie Christie left Warren Beatty for an older man, half the marriages in Holmby Hills split. Leaving all the Lee Grants to fend for themselves."

"She didn't seem to do so badly."

"Most dumped wives aren't like the Lee Grant character. Most dumped wives of that age were virgins when they married and were faithful to their husbands all through their marriage. So what happens, there they are out on their own in a free swinging world."

Nicky Zinn had been deeply affected by the sad plight of these women. Not only were they in automatically losing competition to the perfect California beauties, they were utterly and totally lacking in sexual experience. Veritable virgins at the orgy, they were in the more pitiable position of looking old enough to be experienced veterans.

"Nicky told me. The whole thing started out like a hobby, you know what I'm saying? The ex-wife of an old business associate looked him up. He took her out and then he took her home and this forty-year-old woman locked herself in the closet and began to bawl. She was afraid to have sex because she didn't know what to do. She had read all the sex books and seen all the pictures but she'd never tried any of it. Nothing, Nicky said. Her ex-husband never even touched her. *Anywhere,* you know what I'm saying. She felt like a horse's ass. So that's when Nicky got the idea of giving sex training to deprived women."

"A noble enterprise. Getting nothing out of it for himself."

"Only the satisfaction of helping others, he said. And he did, believe me. This ex-wife of the plastic surgeon, for instance. Frieda Bamford. She told me herself, she didn't know what a clitoris was until she met Nicky. He taught her how to get satisfaction and give satisfaction and did she learn fast."

"If she was divorced from the plastic surgeon, what did it matter to him?"

"That's what was so crazy. Nicky and Beale Bamford played tennis together. There are rumors that Beale put a few tucks in Nicky's scalp. After all, he must be seventy if he's a day."

"He's fifty-nine, Glitz dear. I checked."

"Fifty-nine, seventy-one, what's the difference. He couldn't get it up. Some chick sent him an anonymous valentine that said 'If you can get it up, I can get it in.' A bummer, I tell you. So then, okay, meantime, Dr. Bamford is experimenting with this new kind of penis implant." She extended her bent index finger and straightened it out. "Works on a kind of push button with a little spring inside—"

"You look at me and suddenly, I spring—"

"—and so he says to Nick, why don't we try it on you? And so Nick says, 'What have I got to lose?' "

"*Jesus*—you mean the doctor set him up on purpose?"

"Not exactly. It was more a question of bad timing. Bamford didn't give a shit about Frieda until—"

"What? *Jesus*—"

"Until the day before the operation, Frieda showed up at her ex-husband's office and proceeded to show him all the cute little sexy tricks Nicky had taught her. Nobody really knows what happened. Bamford's nurse says he was acting like a lunatic all morning, popping pills and grunting to himself.

"Nicky had to sign a paper absolving him of any responsibility. And then—"

"The knife slipped."

"Please. Nothing as obvious as that. The implant worked okay but in a few days a virulent infection flared up. Nicky

went everywhere. Chicago. New York. Zurich. That sex clinic
in Bucharest. It was no use. If he wanted to save his life—"
She made the throat-slit gesture.

"And Dorrie wrote about it?"

"She could really be Miss Holier Than Thou, you know
what I'm saying? She did a series on people setting themselves
up as gods—not including herself, of course. She didn't name
names but everyone knew who it was. She called Nicky the
Sex God butting in on the sex lives of vulnerable women.
'Showing them the way—and the means!' she said. And plastic surgeons like Doctor X tampering with nature. She said—I
remember it word for word, I couldn't believe it, you know
what I'm saying?—she said, 'An erect organ is less important
than tenderness and sincere affection.' *Yccch.* Can you imagine anybody saying anything like that?"

Lou Dexter could and wished more than ever that he had
known Dorrie Bridges. Maybe Jennie was right. Maybe he
was a little bit in love with her. "Do you think Nicky was
involved in her disappearance?"

"Nicky? You mean, like"—her voice dropped an octave—
"getting even or something?"

"Well, she did—bare his secret to the world, didn't she?"

Glitz smiled pityingly. "You don't know much, do you?"

"Not much," he conceded.

"He's more in demand than ever. The women are lining up
pleading for sex lessons. You don't need a cock to teach
women about their bodies and how to have orgasms. And
lately, I've heard . . ." She let her voice drift off.

"What—for Christ's sake—tell me!" International intrigue,
torture, conspiracies—nothing in his past life could compare
to southern California.

"Well—Nick started having volunteer studs around—you
know, like life models for a painting class?—so he could teach
the women how to arouse a man and drive him crazy and all
like that. And all of a sudden, there's a rash of these middle-

aged rejects snagging the best men around. All Nicky Zinn graduates!"

They drove into the executive parking lot at the Radford Avenue studios. Several hundred women in basic shades of polyester stood steaming in the sun waiting to see Sonny Syntagma in "The Love Game."

"I've got the next Marlon Brando here!" Glitz said, pulling into Roger Gimbel's space. "Right now, Zanuck-Brown are after him for a remake of *Mutiny on the Bounty*."

"Weren't he and Dorrie shacked up?"

"Shacked up?" she sneered. "That sure dates you!"

"Sorry. I'm an old man. *Living* together? *Sharing* the same space? In fact, weren't they getting married? Until she found out he was just using her?"

"If that's what you're going to ask Sonny, we can stop right here. I'm not having my star upset."

"All I'd like to know is his reaction to Dorrie's disappearance."

"You can ask me. I was with him when it happened."

"You were?"

"I said I was."

"And how did you feel when you heard about the fire?"

"We were both very chagrined."

Not as chagrined as Lou himself felt in Connie Michelin's office recalling the frustration of his brief interview with Sonny Syntagma. Seeing him close up caused Lou to feel his age, his own physical deficiencies, and the absurdity of denying either. Clearly, the Golden Greek's much vaunted constitutional endowments were of classical proportions. Since he received his visitors without benefit of cover, Lou could only gasp at his beauty and conclude that whatever Dorrie's reason for ending their affair, Syntagma had no cause for resentment.

Connie Michelin snapped him back to the present. "When do I see manuscript, Lou?"

"When you sign the contract and the check for the advance."

"I'm not sure I can accept the clause about full editorial control."

"If I don't get that, you don't get a book."

"Okay—you win—I'll see you back here tomorrow morning."

At the door of her office, he turned back. "Connie—"

"Yes—"

"One question."

"Sorry, Lou. I never tell my age."

"Do you know what really happened to Dorrie Bridges?"

"What the hell kind of a question is that? Are you crazy? Do you really think if I knew something, I'd hide it—?"

"Sorry." It was all he could do to contain his sudden jubilation. A woman like Connie Michelin didn't blow her stack unless she did have something to hide. "Just one more thing. That day at the Polo Lounge, remember? You called me to offer the book contract?"

"So? You're here, aren't you?"

"How did you know I was in the Polo Lounge?"

She had the decency to smile. "You more than anyone should know a good reporter never reveals a source."

Moments later, he boarded the down elevator. As the doors closed, he saw the elevator doors on the opposite bank open and the man in the wingtip shoes step out. Riding to street level, Lou remained in the elevator and returned to Connie's floor. The man had disappeared.

"Excuse me, sweetheart." He did his battered Bogart number on the plump little postwar baby peering at him suspiciously from behind the reception desk. "Who was that distinguished looking gentleman who was just here? I think he was a professor of mine at Harvard."

"The one with the shoes?"

"Uh huh—"

She stared down at her sign-in book as if reading were a new and exotic skill. "Nor-ris Burn-side."

Marva Burnside's husband! The pair of them were Dorrie's

dearest friends and patrons. Pillars of society, they functioned in a stratum of wealth and power far above the petty envies and bickering of the entertainment world. The Burnsides were interrelated with other Old California stock, including the Hearsts. They and their friends controlled the banks, real estate, agriculture, and most of the automobile and fuel oil dealerships on the West Coast.

Thinking back, he realized Marva Burnside had not been seen in public for quite some time. Since before Dorrie's birthday, in point of fact. Lou had telephoned the Bel-Air estate hoping to get a few quotes from her about Dorrie's charitable activities. The maid had said Mrs. Burnside was away indefinitely.

Asking around, he had heard rumors of a mastectomy, a trip down the Amazon, a spiritual retreat to Nepal, a visit to Australia to see a sick childhood friend. So far as he could tell, the Burnsides had no grudge against Dorrie. With no reason to include them in his Hot 30, he had dismissed them from his mind. Until now. Norris Burnside had to be following him for a reason and the reason had to be Dorrie Bridges.

The door to Connie Michelin's private office opened. Lou ducked behind a partition. "I asked you not to come to New York," Connie scolded Norris Burnside. "You missed running into him by five seconds."

"Does he know anything?"

"Trust me. He hasn't a clue. Stop worrying and stay away from this office."

This was the lead he'd been after. The Burnsides were involved after all. Dorrie's last big story, the one she was supposed to be working on just before she disappeared, the really explosive biggie about someone in high places—who else could it be but Marva Burnside?

Back at the Algonquin, the hall porter called him aside. "This arrived for you." The package was taller than he was. "I don't believe it will fit into your room."

"What the hell is it, a tree?" He tore off the paper wrapping. It was an eight-foot suhuaro cactus. Some son of a bitch was taking one hell of a lot of trouble to call him a prick. Who else could it be, but Jennie Bliss Sternholdt! The card confirmed this conclusion, although the message was more romantic than expected. She did not call him the world's biggest prick, which he undoubtedly was. "I'm stuck on you," she wrote in the way of a woman who knows how to hurt a guy.

"Send it up. It can sleep with me."

"But—"

"But what—?" Were they going to charge double occupancy?

"Your wife is upstairs."

He had expressly said he would meet her in the little Blue Bar where Brendan Behan always got fractured, at precisely one fifteen for a ritual glass of Moët et Chandon to ease the pain of paying out alimony. He most certainly did not want her in his room poking through the few belongings that were still his.

The only good offensive was to be as offensive as possible before she could get a word out. He threw open the door of his room. "What the hell are you doing here?"

"Waiting for you," Jennie Bliss Sternholdt said sweetly. "After you left I got to thinking. Slick Doob's making his Ellis Island movie so I called him and asked him if he needed some New York streets that look like they did at the turn of the century. He said it was just what he needed and to come at once so here I am. Aren't you glad to see me?"

He was glad to see her. "What was I supposed to do with that cactus?"

"Shut up and kiss me."

"Bossy women! Do this. Do that."

"Lou!"

"You—" Without further instruction, he did a little of this and a little of that. No woman had ever crossed a continent for him. Or sent him an eight-foot cactus tied in a red ribbon.

"I'm stuck on you, too, Jennie," he whispered with a rush of tenderness at being the object of this young, talented, zany, adorable lunatic's affection.

"Do me a favor," she begged.

"Anything."

"Don't answer the phone."

"It's not ringing."

"It will."

It did.

"Mrs. Dexter is here, sir. Waiting for you in the Blue Bar."

Ten minutes later, Lou Dexter slouched through the literary Bethlehem of the Algonquin lobby. With one resentful woman upstairs in his bed and another waiting to eat him alive in the bar, he gazed with longing at the revolving door. All he had to do was keep walking into the fetid air of West Forty-fourth Street and never see either of them or Connie Michelin or Peter St. John or Glitz Dreamburg or any fucking one of the Hot 30 ever again.

The Hitchcock rustle of an open *Wall Street Journal* diverted his glance to the wingtip shoes of the man hidden behind it.

Marva called the meeting to order. Dorrie sat beside her on the French provincial couch, rehearsing her words and feeling skittish as a mare in a barn in a storm. She felt like she wanted to run. Try as she might to concentrate on the important business at hand, she had other things pressing on her mind.

Sonny, for one. She had begged him to turn down the role in Glitz Dreamburg's movie. It was Glitz's first project as a producer but Sonny's part was crude and debasing. "You don't own me!" had been Sonny's parting remarks. He had been away nearly a month now, on location, with nary a word. A few days ago one of the columns had run an item about Glitz jetting to North Carolina to check up on her production and her star.

Andrew, for another. That man was like a fly on a peach, nagging on and on at her to let him appear with her on camera. "I can add a new dimension to the show. Take some of the burden off you." It was reaching the point that if she had to look at his resentful face one more time, she would have to fire him. "You owe me this!" he had said. The only people she owed anything to were her audience and that was to tell them the truth.

And then, late last night, when she was home alone and brooding about the rift between herself and both men in her life, there was that anonymous phone call. If the woman was a crackpot, she was cunning enough to have found Dorrie's private number. If what she said was true, it could be the hottest story of Dorrie's entire career.

Among those gathered for the committee meeting in Marva Burnside's living room were some twenty Double-A List biggies, smiling and sending her kiss-kisses while Marva described the forthcoming leukemia dinner. Following tradition, the dinner was a tribute to a famous personality. Other famous personalities pitched in to prove their worthiness despite their wealth and fame and to make the subscribers feel they were getting more than indigestion for their two-hundred-dollar-a-head tickets.

Next year's guest of honor was to be Dorrie Bridges. "The most powerful woman in communications. And the most responsible," Marva was saying. "Like George Washington, she never tells lies. And she's a cute kid, besides!"

Dorrie's innards churned so loud she could swear they could hear it all the way to back of the room where Tom Jennings had just come in and waved at her. Pride cameth before the fall. She was just a little bitty country girl who'd worked hard and hit lucky. In all these years of living in California, Marva remained her best and truest friend. She just wished the woman would not embarrass her with praise. "I never know what to say," she had explained.

"Relax." The doyenne of California society overrode her objections. "You're not blowing your horn. I am. Enjoy it. You deserve it."

White knuckles clenched the advance copy of *People* magazine in her lap. On the cover was her portrait taken by Francesco Scavullo, the photographer who invented the *Cosmopolitan* magazine cleavage and had tried to achieve the same voluptuous effect for her. The top cover line: *THE DORRIE DECADE: TEN YEARS OF SCARLETT O'HORROR.*

It was strange to read about herself as others perceived her, even though they got most of the facts wrong. She was not a runaway orphan who assiduously hid the facts of her hillbilly roots. If anyone had had the courtesy to call her, she'd have told them all about Roper, Tennessee. The five pages of pictures included some she hadn't known existed. Senator Bingham thumbing his nose in her face at the Nashville courthouse. Sidney Silver refusing to shake her hand with the remark that brought the Anti-Defamation League down on him for reverse anti-Semitism. "It's against my religion to touch a shiksa!"

There was a shot of her with Jim Ed, captioned "Dorrie and fan" and one of Andrew Van Kennan handing her a phone that called him her "live-in amanuensis" that was sure going to make him spit tacks.

It detailed some of her eccentricities: rolling her own Bull Durham cigarettes, making dice out of sugar cubes, and using the white cardboards that came with pantyhose for reminder notes over her desk.

The closing spread celebrated romance with candid shots of her last five years with Sonny Syntagma. *She made him a star;*

he makes her happy. A helicopter shot of them sunbathing on her penthouse terrace. Outtakes from her TV valentine to him. Lovey-dovey arrivals at premieres and the inevitable silhouette fadeout at dusk beside their favorite mountain stream. She had thought they were alone. Some paparazzo grizzly bear must have snuck up and snapped their picture.

She wondered what Sonny would say when he saw it. Even a small Carolina college town had a newsstand. Glitz would surely notice her picture on the cover, now wouldn't she? The movie was not something Dorrie thought Sonny should do. A combination of *Animal House* and *Heaven Can Wait,* it had Sonny playing a real Greek god who comes to Earth, joins a Greek letter fraternity of a bankrupt college, and saves the bacon by winning the football championship single-wing and single-handed. The humor was crude and ugly. Sonny's character was a moronic simpleton. She wanted better things for him.

She was relieved at one major omission in *People.* Thankfully, they had not discovered the truth about her hot romance with Sonny Syntagma. He was impotent. Doctors had doctored without results. Hormones merely added muscle and strength to his limbs and not, as he quipped, his root.

After the initial sense of rejection, she had found it surprisingly simple to be celibate. Fundamentally a puritan about sex, she had steered clear of the group scenes, one-night stands, and situations like the Malibu Bitch House that were part and parcel of the California life-style. It wasn't a question of disapproval. It was shyness, and the old-fashioned notion that sex was an expression of love, or at least affection. With Sonny in her life, she was free of other sexual pressures. She styled herself as a one-man woman, a fact that was grudgingly and sometimes incredulously respected.

"Why should that mean you can't get it on with me?" a major Super Stud had persisted. She knew the answer but could not tell him: In her scramble for success, she had ignored her own sexual education. She had made her bed and was afraid to lie in it. How could America's top media darling get it together with a major Super Stud and not know what the hell she was doing!

"Sorry, darlin'. I'm a—well, sort of like a—a virgin."

She was smart enough to know that one story like that could make her a figure of contempt. One dirty joke could destroy a woman's career. Her strength and integrity would be better served by being sexually aloof and being known as Sonny's old lady.

Having adjusted to Sonny's problem, the absence of sexual intercourse had proved both practical and convenient. She sublimated, as the shrinks of Bedford Gulch would say. Her sexual energies were diverted to her career. If at day's end she had to provide her own orgasms, Sonny helped her, and she found herself contented with the physical presence and closeness of her sweet and beautiful man.

Until recently, that is.

Marva's beaming smile and the applause of those gathered snapped her back to the present. She was being introduced.

Her mouth felt like dry grits. It was a strange contradiction. On television she could look straight into the blinking red eye of the camera and talk easily to millions of invisible viewers. Yet in person, a roomful of flesh-and-blood people panicked her. It was as if they were expecting more from her than she could give, while at the same time inspecting her closely for hidden flaws and factory defects.

"Marva told me this wouldn't hurt a bit," she began. "I'm not sure about that. You're the toughest audience I've ever had to face. Because the aim isn't ratings or critical reviews. It's children and trying to find a way of keeping them safe from leukemia."

She thanked them all for the honor they were paying her. She thanked Tom Jennings for getting Jo Walker of the Country Music Association to send a Grand Ole Opry contingent to perform at the dinner. She thanked Sissy Spacek and

Loretta Lynn for providing a preview scene from *Coal Miner's Daughter.*

"But more than anything, I want to thank the anonymous volunteers who make all the phone calls and write out all the envelopes. And I ask all of you important and famous people here this evening to join me in a round of applause for them —and yourselves!" She concluded in triumph and a pool of perspiration.

"You feelin' okay, darlin'?" Tom Jennings pushed through the crowd to embrace her.

"A little poorly. Just a little tired, I guess."

She could not tell him about Sonny. He had long ago expressed his disapproval. Out of respect to her in recent years, he had limited himself to saying, "There's no man in all the world good enough for you—except maybe me!"

Marva did not approve of Sonny, either. In all the years of their friendship, it was the only sore point between them. "Actors are whores!" she had exploded when things began to look serious. "They are incapable of love or loyalty. They're only out for what they can get. If you treat them with respect, they'll walk all over you! If they find somebody who can do more for them than you can, they'll walk out on you without a backward glance."

Marva had never expressed herself on the subject again except to say, "I don't blame you for wanting him. He's the most delicious hunk of man I've ever seen and I've seen plenty. Be happy. If you need me, I'm here."

The friendship had continued to flourish. The age difference diminished with the passing years. In just another few weeks, Dorrie would be thirty years old. Though Marva was well past fifty, their relationship had developed into one of near contemporaries. She spent most Sunday afternoons at the Burnsides' and lunched with Marva at least once a week at La Scala.

Glitz had warned Dorrie that Marva was the worst kind of

bitch. "An aristocrat. She gives orders. Others take them."
Dorrie had never seen Marva commit an unkindness or pull
rank. Getting involved with this fund-raising made Dorrie feel
a little uneasy. She didn't feel entitled to such honors. But she
knew Marva's intentions were of the best and meant only to
bring credit to her.

Tom Jennings scrunched his eyes at her like a hanging
judge. "It's not just tired, darlin'. Don't go trying to fool me.
You look meaner than a bear backed into a beehive." His
mocking use of southernisms served to emphasize his deep
feelings.

She laughed and tried to answer in kind. "Just plumb tuck-
ered out, I reckon. All these fancy goin's-on and all these fine
upstanding people. Just a mite too much excitement for a
tater-eatin' country girl—"

"Seriously, Dorrie—"

"Seriously—?" Seriously, she was thinking how nice it
would be to curl herself up in a ball on Tom Jennings's lap
and hide her face in his chest and let him hold her and rock
her till she fell fast asleep just like Goldilocks in the fairy
story. She was more than bone weary. She was in misery over
Sonny. Pissed off with Glitz. Touchy as hell with Andrew.

What's more, the network wanted her to do a hemorrhoids
commercial which she refused to do; let them take her to the
Su-preme Court. "There's enough asshole on TV right now
without me contributing to it!" She had stormed out of a
shocked executive meeting. Nobody had ever heard Dorrie
Bridges talk like that.

"You're working too hard, girl. You've got more deadlines
and commitments than David Frost and everybody knows
he's twins."

"I just didn't sleep last night. Got a call around midnight."

"Sonny should know better than that—"

"A woman. On my private line. She said she had come into
possession of a certain document—"

"Let me guess—a nuclear conspiracy?"

"It's a diary—about Adolf Hitler—a sex diary—"

"Old hat."

"How can you say that?"

"Hitler's sexual perversions have been revealed. He was the original dirty old man—"

"She said the diary was in English and involved the young and beautiful daughter of an American businessman in Berlin circa 1937."

"And—?" She could feel his excitement.

"And that young girl is socially prominent today."

"Who is it?"

"She wouldn't tell me."

"Did you arrange to see her?"

"She told me to meet her outside the old Los Angeles railroad station. I sat there until six this morning. She never showed up. I'm a basket case."

"Nothing more? No further attempt at communication?"

"Not a word. It's like maybe I dreamed the whole thing."

He cupped her face in his hands. "Did you, darlin'? You sure it isn't time for a little vacation?"

"Oh, Tom, for God's sake. I'm not snapping out. I'm too tough for that." She gestured toward Marva's lavish buffet. "Let's us skip the rich folks food and got get us a bowl of Tex Mex, a Moon Pie, and a jeroboam of RC."

"Something *is* wrong—"

"What could be wrong?"

"You tell me—"

What *could* be wrong. Her column was in more papers than Bill Buckley and Jack Anderson combined. Her TV show averaged sixty percent of share and was beamed by satellite around the world. She was wearing patty nails and silk drawers and store-bought shoes.

She was riding around in fancy cars and in love with a handsome movie star, wasn't she? She didn't love Sonny the way she had loved Jim Ed. But then again, Jim Ed was her first love. If she and Sonny split, she could likely sure find a

254 • JEANNIE SAKOL

new Sonny and one who could love her better. There would never be another Jim Ed.

A woman wearing a diamond ring so big it had to be real handed her a pen and a paper napkin. "Would you mind signing this—"

Tom stepped in protectively. "Would you forgive us? Dorrie's not feeling too fine—"

"It's for my colored maid!" The woman bristled. A refusal would mean Dorrie Bridges had no time for poor people and blacks.

"My pleasure," Dorrie said.

"Of course I don't read you myself, but my Hattie was all excited about my meeting you. She says you're the world's best gossip columnist—"

Something snapped. Dorrie crumpled the napkin into a ball and tossed it over her shoulder. "I am not a gossip columnist, ma'am. I am a reporter."

The hubbub of munching guests diminished as if someone had turned down the volume control.

"Well, I'm sorry—" The woman backed away.

Dorrie pursued her. "Gossip is rumor. Gossip is hearsay. Gossip is speculation. Gossip is fiction. I do not traffic in gossip—"

"Look, I'm sorry. Forget it. All I wanted was a stinking little autograph—"

Dorrie had her by the arm. "Why don't you think about what you're saying before you say it? I never do gossip. I write *facts*. Facts that I check out, carefully and exhaustively. Never once—not *once*—have I ever had to print a retraction or an apology. People have threatened to sue me, sure—but not because I didn't tell the *truth*—"

Shaking with rage, she allowed Tom to steer her through the throng.

"You're leaving? You can't leave!" Marva had been showing some of the committee her new horse ring and had missed the excitement.

"She'll call you in the morning," Tom assured her.

Once outside, Dorrie slumped against him. "Oh, Tom. I shouldn't have jumped on that poor stupid woman like that!"

"She deserved it."

"That doesn't make it right."

Tom insisted on riding home with her. "Is this the new land buggy?" Harrington, the English chauffeur, opened the door of the stretch Cadillac Andrew had fitted out with all the comforts of a multimedia environment. An eight-inch Sony TV. A Betamax for recording shows she might miss and need to see. A miniature tape recorder with a two-hour cassette. A baby Hermès typewriter powered by batteries. A fridge with splits of Moët et Chandon Imperial belly to belly with RC cola and a bowl of carrot and celery sticks with onion dip.

"Now this is what I call southern comfort!"

"Beats all, doesn't it?" she sighed. "Andrew's idea. Never thought I'd live to see the day that I would *need* a chauffeur-driven car! Maybe that's what's wrong with my life. I *do* need a chauffeur-driven car. With all I have to do, every minute counts. I'm like a machine. I can't waste time parking my own car, now can I?"

She pressed a lever. A small writing desk popped up beside her like a piece of toast and clicked into position across her knee. "Only thing I don't have is a bathtub."

"Or a commode," Tom laughed.

"Don't laugh. Andrew was considering it. 'For long trips,' he said. Can't you just see me riding along, wiping my ass on the San Diego Freeway?"

Now she was laughing, too. They stopped at Adobe Heaven for chili and frijoles, which they ate picnic-style in the back of the car. Harrington's silent disapproval only added to their hilarity.

It did her good to be with Tom. In the dozen years since she broke the Bingham story, he had become her closest adviser. His early passion had matured into a tender regard and guidance. Leaving *Newsmagazine* was one of the few decisions she had made without consulting him. It was one he wholeheartedly approved.

"It took guts to walk out on Connie Michelin. She's my friend but she can get mighty high. You gave that woman a real shock. I don't think she's over it yet."

She and Tom were in continual touch by phone and got together whenever he hit the West Coast, which was frequent. There were only two things she declined to discuss. Her refusal to return to Tennessee. Her relationship with Sonny Syntagma.

By the time Tom dropped her home, she was feeling easier in her mind. These feelings of doubt and despair were only natural in a pressure cooker society. It wasn't as if she needed lithium or a psychiatrist. Nor did she drink hard spirits or do drugs.

Work was her addiction and her high. She and Sonny had agreed not to live together. When the apartment beneath her penthouse was put up for sale, Andrew had suggested she buy it and install an inside staircase like the one in *The Seven Year Itch*.

The lower floor was gutted and reconstructed at incredible expense as an office for Dorrie, a guest suite, and a self-contained apartment for Andrew Van Kennan. Marva compared him to *All About Eve*, warning her as Thelma Ritter had warned Bette Davis that he was memorizing her. "He's the Fifth Column. The enemy within!"

Enemy or not, he was an enemy she knew. She could control him. She needed him as both an assistant and a personable escort when Sonny was unavailable. Sometimes Sonny just didn't feel like going. As every successful woman learns, men don't like being appendages.

That's where Marva was blessed. Norris Burnside clearly adored her. Whatever the occasion, however boring, he was there, gazing at her with pride, holding her wrap and handbag as if it were an honor. That man would kill for her, Dorrie was sure.

Tired Dorrie might be, but sleepy she was not. Out on her porch high above Doheny, she kicked off her stiletto sandals. The Greek tiles felt good under her bare feet. She wished Sonny were here to massage them and to share the night aromas of the honeysuckles, carnations, and dwarf lemon trees growing among the jacarandas and the venerable chinaberries.

She settled into the porch glider cushions and picked up the phone. It was after midnight in Carolina but she didn't think Sonny would mind. All she wanted to do was say good night.

The sleepy desk clerk at the Magnolia Arms said there was no answer in Mr. Syntagma's room. She did not ask to be connected to Glitz Dreamburg.

Tennessee was an hour earlier than Carolina. It would do her good to hear Jim Ed's voice. Soon after she left New York, he had taken the Fulbright scholarship and lived in Europe the next few years. She had just met Sonny Syntagma when Jim Ed returned to the States and flew to California to see her.

His clothes were all wrong but he had grown handsome and self-assured enough to turn heads at the various parties she had insisted they attend. If she had thought he would be impressed by the gush and grab chorus of "darling . . . you look gorgeous tonight . . ." and the like, she was mistaken.

When finally they were alone, right where she was now, on the upstairs porch, he looked like a mattress left out in the rain. "Are all those people your friends?"

"Most of them."

"Don't their tongues hurt?"

"What do you mean?"

He shook her by the shoulders like a rag doll. "From licking your backside!"

"Just what do you mean by that? Those people are movers and shakers, very important people in entertainment, communications, politics, fashions. They were proud and happy to see me and they'd have been proud and happy to sit and talk to you, too, if you didn't have your nose stuck up in the air.

"You're not the only person that ever lived in Europe, you know."

"You've changed, Dora June."

"I sure as hell hope so. Staying the same is not a virtue. It's an excuse. You've changed, too."

"Not inside. I still want the same things I've always wanted. A home. A wife— Oh, Dora June—" He kissed her and the years disappeared. She was in his arms again on the old car seat in a Tennessee meadow. She was in his arms again in his small student's room at Columbia University. She was in his arms as if she had never left them and never would.

"Jim Ed—"

"I read about you and this actor."

"Sonny Syntagma. We're— It's like they say in the fan magazines. We're just good friends. You're the only man I've ever loved, darlin'. I still love you, Jim Ed." Her mind had raced ahead of possibility. "Now we can get married, don't you see? It was too soon back in New York. Now we're grown up. I'll see about getting you a job. You'll love it here. Sunshine. Avocados. Tennis. All the good things of life."

"I don't know how to play tennis."

"We can live here to start. Plenty of room. And see these chinaberry trees? A touch of down home. We'll be happy—"

"I—I've got to be going."

"But—" She couldn't believe it. "Why? We still love each other, don't we?"

"I once told you I'd love you till the day I die."

"I'm a power in this town. I can open doors. What's wrong with that?"

"It's Dora June I love. I can't get a hold on Dorrie Bridges. She's glittering stranger and she frightens me. I'm going back home to Tennessee."

A few months later he had written her a letter saying he

had taken over personal management of the *Roper Valley Echo* and that an English girl he had met at Cambridge was coming over to visit with him for a while. Through all the years and miles, she had carried with her the bar of headline type that said I LOVE YOU DARLING. She had thrown it in the trash and fished it out again an hour later.

A woman with a British accent answered the Loomis phone. Jim Ed was at the plant, she said. "Who is speaking?"

Dorrie should have remembered. It was the night before the weekly paper went to press when they all worked through to dawn. She could smell the ink and feel the rumbling of the old flatbed press.

"How are you?" Jim Ed inquired stiffly when she got through to him.

"Real fine. How are you?" Was the woman at home his wife? She lacked the courage to ask.

"Fine." Couldn't he see she was not fine, not fine at all? She could think of nothing more to say. She was reaching out to him, wanting him, needing to know he was there, hoping he would say something important though she didn't know what.

"Well, I guess you're mighty busy, putting the paper to bed and all," she said after a pause.

"How are things going in California?" Why couldn't he say he loved her and missed her and would be on the first plane out of Nashville to tell her so in person?

"Real fine, like I said."

Another pause and she put a bullet in the heart of her agony. "Well, Jim Ed, I was just thinking about you and thought I'd just call you up and see how you're making out."

"I watched you on the TV last week."

"You did? How was I?"

"What you had to say was real fine. Honest. True."

"Proud to hear that."

"Only one thing—"

"What was that?" Who was he to be criticizing her? Pub-

lisher of a one-horse country weekly? She reached more people on a Sunday night than he'd ever get to in a million
years!

"Too many camera tricks."

"You mean opticals? That's to add drama to the story. We
got this new director. He wanted to lively things up."

"Well, the way I see it, the truth is plenty dramatic."

He was right. That's why she was so mad. "Can't argue
that."

"You have a reputation for truth. Don't spoil it. Keep on
truckin' with the truth."

Was he making fun of her? What was the *matter* with her?
How could she be suspicioning Jim Ed like this when what
she wanted him to do was drop everything and come to her?
Tom was right. She was tired. "Well—it was sure nice talking
to you. Take care of yourself now, hear?"

There was only one more person in this entire world of
strangers she could call. "What's wrong? You been in an
accident?" Her mother's voice wrestled with sleep.

"Tell her it's one o'clock in the morning and we're working
people!" a man's voice barked.

"Sorry, Momma." It was not the best moment to pour out
her heart. "I'll call you back real soon, hear?"

Swaying gently in the glider, she did not see the intruder
until a throaty female voice whispered, "Dorrie—"

Dorrie froze, her mind racing. She was alone with no
weapon and no training to use it if she had one, and only the
telephone at hand. While wondering how she could signal
her plight to the operator, she exerted every effort to keep her
voice calm. "Who are you?"

"Sorry I stood you up last night." The figure was hidden by
a shapeless coat, wide-brimmed hat, and large dark glasses.

"What's this about Hitler and a prominent American
woman? Don't tell me he's alive and well and living in beautiful southern California?"

"I won't tell you anything if you're not careful."

"I'm sorry. Won't you—sit down?"

"I'll stand and don't move from where you are."

"Okay."

"Adolf Hitler is not alive and well and living, as you say, in beautiful southern California. But the American teen-ager he seduced and secretly married in 1937 *is* and I've got the document to prove it."

"How much do you want?"

"This is not a matter of checkbook journalism."

"If you don't want money, what do you want?"

A silence. A sharp intake of breath. "Justice. The story must be told and you're the only one I would trust to tell it."

"When can I see this document?"

"I'll let you know where and when."

"Can you tell me the name of this socially prominent woman?"

"Why not?" The shrouded figure moved briskly to the sliding glass doors and disappeared into the darkness of Dorrie's apartment. In the night silence her husky voice floated back to Dorrie with chilling clarity. "It's Marva Burnside."

Lou Dexter was assessing the significance of Norris Burnside's shoes in the Algonquin Hotel lobby when the desk clerk called out to him. "This just arrived for you, sir. By messenger."

The envelope contained a letter agreement between Newsmagazine Books, Inc., and himself formally establishing their mutual agreement to negotiate a mutually acceptable contract in the immediate future plus a certified check for twenty-five thousand dollars, advanced as a gesture of goodwill and confidence against the actual and still-to-be determined amount.

He knew a little bit about book publishers. The advance for his first book had spent three months in the computer pipeline and was a thousand dollars short of what it was supposed to be when it finally did arrive. Newsmagazine Books was really hot to trot. Twenty-five big ones was a lot of cash on the barrelhead, especially when they didn't know what was inside the barrel.

It was nice to be wanted. He wondered what old wingtips would say if he set fire to the check and lit a cigarette with it. Or what his good friend the desk clerk would say if he asked the hotel to give him twenty-five thousand dollars in singles. And he set each of those aflame and lit cigarettes with them.

As Jennie Bliss Sternholdt endlessly complained, he made bad jokes when he was anxious. After all, what was there to be anxious about? Jennie was upstairs in a naked pout merely because he was meeting his ex-wife the princess for a drink. Connie Michelin was giving him a twenty-five-grand rush act. Norris Burnside was following him with the subtlety of a B movie. The truth about Dorrie Bridges was growing into an obsession of near psychopathic proportions. While kissing Jennie Bliss Sternholdt, he had envisioned Dorrie's earnest little face and had almost whispered her name out loud.

"*Lou?* I've been waiting for you!" The constant anxiety in his life, his ex-wife the princess, made a citizen's arrest and force-marched him into the Blue Bar. "You look good," she said with the tone of mild surprise she had always used on the rare occasions when he met her rigid standards, sexual and otherwise.

"You look pretty damn good yourself." The difference between Jennie and the princess was this: Jennie made him want to tear her clothes off and frolic with her in a state of erotic euphoria. The princess made him feel worthy only of covering her with expensive clothes and furs and jewels and be grateful for a dry hump.

Pleased with herself as always, she selected a large Brazil

from the bowl of nuts on their table and bit it coquettishly in half. As his old buddy George Santayana said, those who do not remember the past are condemned to repeat it. "I called your room. A woman answered."

"It was probably the chambermaid."

"Hot and cold running chambermaids?"

"What did you want to see me about?"

"I thought we could have a little talk. It's been too long."

She was one of those women with an extrasensory gland. She could sniff money. "I'm running late. Got an interview. On top of the Empire State Building."

"Be serious. This is important."

"Okay. I'm serious." She had taken everything. The bank accounts. The piece of property in Putnam County. The books and records including his collection of jazz 78s. The car. The cameras. The daughter.

"You know how much I've always loved you—" she began, averting her eyes demurely as always before lowering the boom. The sudden entrance of Norris Burnside diverted Lou's attention. With the suave aplomb of a David Niven stand-in, the older man peered amiably around the intimate Blue Bar as if expecting to find friends. He smiled pleasantly at Lou and with a philosophical shrug seated himself at an empty table. "Well—?" The princess smiled at him provocatively.

"Well—?" He had not heard a word.

"Well, what do you think?"

Norris Burnside was doing nothing more sinister than signaling the waiter. Yet Lou felt a distinct sense of jeopardy. "I'm—sorry. I must be jet-lagging. What were you saying?"

"I—was—saying—" She paused between words the way Mrs. Canner at P.S. 93 had always paused to get his attention. "Damn you, I was saying that I think I've punished you long enough. I've made you miserably unhappy and I'm sorry. I think it's time to bury the hatchet and stop acting like children and"—Jennie chose exactly that moment to enter the Blue Bar—"get back together again!"

"Lou Dexter! Imagine running into you! I haven't seen you since the International Bastards Festival in Blue Balls, Pennsylvania!" She sat herself down and introduced herself. "Hi, I'm Jennie Bliss Sternholdt."

"I—am—*Mrs.* Dexter."

"Lou's *mother?* This is really a pleasure—"

"Lou!" the princess snarled.

"Lou!" Jennie mimicked.

He travels best who travels alone. Women! They were all the same, Jennie included. He didn't need or want any one of them. There was room for only one woman in his life and that was Dorrie Bridges. "See you all!" He dropped a fistful of green on the table and sprinted to the street. As he flagged a cab, a New York pube, near Victorian in contrast to her California counterparts, shoved an Instamatic up his nose. "You anybody?"

Jennie spun the girl around and sent her flying up the street. "Empire State Building!" she told the driver, pushing Lou into the cab ahead of her.

"You're mighty handy with your hands," he said.

" 'I coulda been a contender,' " she Marloned.

"Blow your nose."

"Don't tell me what to do."

"Look here—"

"Don't tell me where to look."

He would have to be more judicious in his lovemaking. Obviously he had driven the poor girl mad. "I can't take you with me, you know."

"Who wants to go on some dumb interview? You seem to forget, I'm working for Slick Doob. On a major feature, remember? I'm on my way to the Battery. You're getting out at Thirty-fourth Street."

"No need to stop. Just slow down—"

At the Fifth Avenue side of the Empire State Building, Jennie bade him farewell. "Watch out for low-flying planes, Mr. Kong."

"I told you I'm too old for you. I saw the movie the first time around."

"Go fry a kite, turkey."

He got out of the cab.

"Lou? Will I see you later?"

He kept walking.

"Lou? Don't do this to me!'

"Lady, I can't sit here. Where to?" the cabbie barked.

"Lou—come back here!"

"Lou!" the cabbie joined in.

"Hey, mac—somebody's calling you!" The policeman at the building entrance blocked his way. "You stiff the driver or something?"

"See you back at the hotel!" Lou bellowed across the crowded pavement. "Can't stand to be away from me for a minute," he explained.

Fun was fun, but he could not go on this way. He would have to tell it to her gently. Over dinner. In a nice dark Bogart restaurant. With flowers and candles on the table if there were such things anymore. "Bogie and Baby were good for each other!" she had whispered to him in a moment of quiet. Much as he enjoyed the Bogart label, he would have to remind her again that he was not Bogart, that he was too goddam old for her and too goddam selfish to change his evil ways.

She had her entire life, including a great career as a movie director, ahead of her. He felt certain she would understand. They would have a lovely evening, perhaps an old-times'-sake roll in the hay, and part friends. Cheered by the thought, he headed for the Observation Tower elevator and his rendezvous with Viktor Varvanza. Waiting on line, alone in the crowd, he reflected on all that had happened since arriving in New York the previous night.

He didn't have to be Einstein's kid brother to know something fishy was going on. Or a certified paranoid to smell a cover-up. Clearly there was something Tom Jennings, Connie

Michelin, and Norris Burnside didn't want him to know. Or if he already knew it, he didn't know he knew it. By publishing his book, they would find out whether he did know even if he still didn't know he knew.

It struck him as more than coincidence that the remaining Hot 30 people were all somehow connected with Tom or Connie or Norris. The Burnsides were generous ballet patrons and close friends of Viktor and Verita Varvanza. Tom Jennings had known Jesus Man Suggs from his early days in Tennessee when he reviled the Beatles, and Dora June Bridges took him to task in the *Roper Valley Echo*.

Connie Michelin had contributed heavily to Mallomar Crane's presidential campaign. Not because she wanted a black president in the White House but because it gave her editorial access to him. Slick Doob had been an A-list regular at Marva Burnside's sit-downs and Connie Michelin's Tuesday Nights until Dorrie's column and the freak accident removed him from the social mainstream.

As for Burt Whitechapel, he was the cockney equivalent of a Jewish Mother, minding everybody's business, kiting checks, telling lies for husbands and wives without discrimination as to sex, status, or country of origin. He called his place "Stodge." A Major Food Critic described his Bubble 'n' Squeak as the quintessence of oral fixation. The midtown publishing crowd held informal editorial raps there. The clenchjaws and Sloane Rangers of the British Consulate and the good gray Beeb (or BBC) congregated daily for the expensive privilege of feeling superior while enjoying a good nosh-up.

"Does it bother you to stand on the very spot where the tragedy occurred?" Viktor Varvanza stood beside the telescope. It was a glorious day. Visibility, twelve miles. Wearing his dead wife's diamond teardrop on his lapel, he was a portly and dapper man with the continental charm of a Carlo Ponti. A wealthy industrialist of a respected Milanese family, he had forsaken his first wife and six children for the Spanish-born Verita and spent millions to create the world's finest ballet company around her incandescent beauty and ethereal talent.

"Not a tragedy. A triumph. A celebration of her immortality. Look down there at the greatest city in all the world."

Lou peered through the iron grille erected to prevent impulsive acts. He could see in the glistening distance the tiny figure of Lady Liberty in the harbor and beside it Ellis Island, where Jennie must just be arriving for her assignment with Slick Doob. "Really something."

Varvanza spoke in a trance of remembrance. "Hers was the most heartbreaking Dying Swan of all time. Danilova. Markova. Fonteyn. Ulanova. Beriosova. Hers was the most lyrical, the most passionate, the most—noble—" He paused in order to control his emotions.

"You've never felt bitterness toward Dorrie Bridges for revealing the truth?"

"My dear sir. Dorrie Bridges did not give Madame Verita cancer."

"But she told the story to the world. She said that this beautiful, artistic, disciplined body at the height of its physical perfection was riddled with cancer."

ODE TO A DYING SWAN

Cancer is a dirty word. Dirty because it kills. It is a shameful word because its victims feel that cancer is their own fault, that they have done something shameful and are being punished.

It is a shameful disease because it is a shaming thing to suffer. It is a crying shame to die before your time. Cancer is cruel and thoughtless in its selection of victims. Psychopathic hit men, rapists, and other subhumans of the species may die of cancer. If they do, we don't hear about it.

When someone with the gifts and virtues and beauty of Verita Varvanza is stricken at the height of her powers to give excellence and wonder to the world, we are all of us stricken and diminished.

Madame Varvanza may not like this column. Her adoring husband and manager may remove it from the breakfast tray in an attempt to shield her from the public protest at such an outrage.

He has announced her "temporary retirement," saying she needs a rest and spreading the rumors of a pregnancy, a story carried in this space two weeks ago. In checking further, I learned that it is not a living child growing in her womb but a cannibal tumor ravaging her firm and disciplined flesh.

It becomes clear that her plan is to hang up her red shoes and slip quietly into her grave.

Verita, I say to you, share your sorrow and your pain. We have loved you for the sheer perfection and joyful artistry you have given us. We do not love you less for your affliction. Allow us to express our love and appreciation in this dark time of trouble.

I call on the entire world of ballet to rise up on your toes and tell Verita we love her and honor her and are with her every day and every night of her ordeal.

All of us must face a final curtain. Only the worst of sinners and chosen saints may know when it will fall. When it falls for Verita Varvanza, let her final bow be to the wild ovation of stage center.

"What did your wife say when Dorrie's column appeared?"

"At first?" He smiled sadly. "She cried. Her first tears since we got the news. Uncontrollable sobs as if her chest would burst. At last she grew quiet. She kissed me and said, 'Torio, I feel better. Thank God I no longer need to pretend.' "

It was the first time she had cried in all the months of secret treatments and tests. "It's good to be able to talk about it. I'm dying. It's never happened to me before. I *want* to talk about it. I want to see my friends and talk to them about it."

In the following months the world of music and ballet paid living tribute to the dying ballerina. The special concerts, recitals, and festivals culminated in an International Gala of the Musical Arts in Lincoln Center, presenting the world's outstanding musical talent from Baryshnikov to Nureyev to Balanchine to Bernstein and including a guest pas de deux of Agnes De Mille and Fred Astaire. The event was filmed for PBS and the Ballet Archives. The proceeds went to cancer research.

Some weeks later, on a crystalline winter's night when the sky was black velvet strewn with diamonds, Verita said she wanted to look out at the vastness of New York from her favorite perch, the top of the Empire State Building. "She parted her black satin hair in the middle and pulled it taut in the traditional style, framed in egrets. She had wrapped herself in the floor-length Russian sable cape I had given her the first night she danced *Swan Lake*. I had the feeling of what she was planning to do and pretended not to see her tutu under the fur.

"We rode the elevator in silence, holding hands. She looked more beautiful than I had ever seen her. The gauntness of her face emphasized the dark beauty of her eyes. We stood where you and I are standing now. She pinned the teardrop on me and gave me a piece of paper. 'Read this to me, darling one.' "

Viktor Varvanza closed his eyes and recited from memory. " 'To take the air. To challenge space. To be at once stronger and freer than any time in life. To lift up the hearts of those who watch. To be carried on their response. An ancient glory breathes around us and the spirit of the dedicated dead. The veils tear. It is enough.' "*

* Agnes De Mille in *The Book of the Dance.*

Without a word she shed the sable cloak and shinnied effort-
lessly up the iron grille. A twist of the torso and she was free
of gravity. Her long legs pushed upward from the tower in an
exultant entrechat. For a moment she was dancing on air,
soaring on the night sky like a shimmering silver bird until
finally, she floated to earth, all gauze and feathers, her arms
fluttering wings in the most spectacular dying swan dive of all
time.

The sentimentalist in Lou Dexter sniffed back the tears.
The cynic in him rebelled. The man had allowed his wife to
jump off the top of the Empire State Building. Why the hell
hadn't he stopped her?

"I know what you're thinking," Varvanza said gently.
"How could I do it? I ask you to think of her dying in a
hospital room with tubes in her mouth attached to a machine.
How could I stop her?"

Sentimentality threatened to clog Lou's throat.

"Sorry I'm late—" A slender young woman with a long
braid down her back and the unmistakable dancer's posture
hurried to Viktor's side.

Cynicism shrank Lou's membranes. His tear ducts dried. It
hadn't taken the randy old impresario long to find a newer
and younger replacement.

Varvanza kissed the girl on the cheek and caressed her arm.
"This is Mariamne. Isn't she lovely?"

Just lovely. Really lovely. "Lovely."

"Herbert Ross did such a lovely job with *Turning Point,*
I've been trying to interest him in a film of Verita's early years
and I thought Mariamne would be ideal—"

Wily old fox. Even in ballet, it was the same old story set to
music. *Stick wit' me, keed, I'll make youse a star.*

"Won't you, darling one?" The older man pulled the girl to
him in a rush of affection.

"I'll try, Papa—" Verita's daughter blushed.

"Forgive her, Mr. Dexter. She's embarrassed."

She wasn't the only one. Lou got away before he compounded his embarrassment by asking the Varvanzas to forgive him for his dirty, low, suspicious mind.

Jennie Bliss Sternholdt was right. He didn't know the first thing about real, honest love. The thought being the father of the act, it seemed to be a good moment to visit Ellis Island and discuss the matter. She was always horning in on his act. Now it was his turn. He was certain Slick Doob wouldn't mind.

In the Kinky Sex Underground, there are those of special refinement who prize physical deformity. What may be weird, unappealing, grotesque, or clinically incomprehensible to most people has an intrinsic erotic appeal for these exclusive few. Obesity, hairiness, the absence of limbs, and humpbacks rank high. After Dorrie Bridges's exposé of Slick Doob, and the freak accident that left him paraplegic in a wheelchair, an apocryphal two-liner circulated:

Slick Doob: Dorrie Bridges made me a cripple.
Envious Sex Kink: If I gave her the money, would she make me one, too?

T. C. Maria was Slick's first production since Dorrie's revelations caused more havoc in the film industry than the Begelman scandals. As a top creative executive at the Carillon Studios, S. Licht Doob had brought new meaning to the field of creative accounting.

Dorrie named it the Chiseller Syndrome and revealed how certain Percentage Meltdowns were cheating actors, writers, production people, as well as the stockholders and ultimately the entertainment-hungry public. The fallout of this "accident" would affect the film industry for years.

His method of cross-collateralization added a byzantine flavor to computer gymnastics. What this meant was that Carillon would group successful movies with duds, charging off the expenses of the losers to the earnings of the hits. If, therefore, you were a writer such as Mario Puzo with ten percent of the net on *Godfather II,* you might read in *Variety* that the film grossed fifty-two million and discover that your part of the net got lost in a cross-collateralization with a lesser picture.

Once Dorrie got victims to talk, Slick was accused of paying out large amounts of Carillon's development money to independent producers and packagers and taking cash kickbacks. Cross-collateralization could be construed as legal. Kickbacks were not.

While conducting her investigation, Dorrie unearthed some unsavory personal facts. Doob was a notorious laxative freak who produced a private series of Scat Movies, the scat being for scatalogical, and there was one rumor about the basic ingredients of an infamous Boeuf Bourgignon which Andrew Van Kennan thought hilarious. Dorrie did not print it.

What really aroused her sense of fair play were the tricks that were legal but immoral. *T. C. Maria* was just such a case. Written by Bianca Tinti, it was an autobiographical novel about her grandmother's arrival at Ellis Island as a young Italian immigrant before the Great War. The novel told how the twelve-year-old Maria was rejected by the doctors for trachoma and placed in quarantine to be deported, a chalked *T.C.* on her sleeve.

Young Maria's mother was dead, her father had died on the voyage from Naples. She was alone and determined to stay in America. In the dead of night she slipped from her dormitory and swam from Ellis Island to the Jersey shore, eventually becoming the matriarch of the author's family.

Five years before, Slick Doob had bought the novel outright for three thousand dollars from the author's inexperienced literary agent. Slick then sold the novel to Carillon for fifty thousand dollars.

Impervious to industry opinion, Slick had waited for the uproar to die down and another scandal figure to take his place. Upon commencing principal photography a few weeks earlier, he had replied to a *New York Times* reporter, "No, I don't feel I took advantage of the novelist. Her book sold two thousand copies and most of those to relatives. Now that I'm making the movie, she got a quarter of a million for the paperback rights and ten foreign sales. Anyway, I think I've paid my dues to morality," he said, referring to the accident that confined him to a wheelchair.

He had designed the chair himself, a custom hybrid of a canvas director's chair on an electric wheelchair chassis. Stenciled on the back was TOP CRIPPLE. He was wearing his familiar green derby hat, *Soccit Tuum* T-shirt, and the frayed "lucky" jeans he wore on every picture, as the small ferry brought Lou across the harbor from the Battery.

Ellis Island looked like a vast chocolate cake built in the shape of a Victorian fortress a mere Coke bottle's throw from the Statue of Liberty. It was built as an immigration reception center in 1890 to receive the huddled masses yearning to breathe free, processing more than twelve million of them during the next quarter century, including Lou's own grandfather from Kovno.

Watching him amid the hubbub of people, lights, cameras, and other equipment, Lou wondered if the story he'd heard about the accident was true. At the height of the scandal when he was under indictment, Slick had driven home from a party drunk, crashed through the patio wall and into his own swimming pool.

The noise had awakened his wife and several neighbors who managed to pull him out of the submerged Mercedes 350-S. His injured spinal cord enhanced his lawyer's plea for leniency. "Fate has punished him sufficiently for excessive zeal," the presiding judge had agreed, putting him on probation. Since then, his den was lined with blowups of Jon Voight in *Coming Home* and Marlon Brando in *The Men*.

Special exercises had built up his chest and arms. He had insisted on leaving the car at the bottom of the pool and delighted in diving down to the "wreck" for the amusement of his friends.

Lou saw Jennie the precise moment she saw him. Crew members were moving the heavy lights and rolling out cables, actors in costume were huddled on makeshift benches, Slick was giving orders and also listening to Jennie. She stopped talking in midsentence, enabling Lou to fill the lull. "Hi, I'm Lou Dexter—"

"This is a closed set."

"—actually, I'm with *Newsmagazine.*"

"I have a subscription—"

"I'm sorry about this, Slick." Jennie Bliss Sternholdt had found her voice. "He's a friend of mine. Follows me every-where." She batted her eyes at Slick for understanding. "I'll just let Lou go over to the commissary and have come coffee while we finish up, okay?" She consulted her notebook as if Lou were not there. " 'A slum street circa 1913,' right? 'Some old Italian immigrant family photographs.' I know just where to get them—"

"I'm writing a book—" Lou said, ignoring her attempt to get him the hell away from Slick.

"Yeah? Who isn't? My canary is writing a book." The director raised a Mickey Mouse megaphone. "Okay, people. Take ten but keep close, while I work with Bess here—" He indicated a young girl dressed in a pathetically fetching im-migrant outfit with a T.C. chalk mark on the sleeve.

"My book is about Dorrie Bridges."

Slick Doob wore two watches, one California, one New York time. He checked them against each other and both against the Birns and Sawyer Super 8/16 mm footage dial stopwatch. "Ever see one of these little fuckers?" he asked. "It's dust resistant and water resistant but not bullshit resis-tant. The jeweled movement records elapsed and accumulated time which you are wasting. The shockproof antimagnetic units are self-compensating and contain unbreakable mainsprings. The Velcro wristband and rubber tick suppressor were optional. I took them because I am rich and powerful and can have anything I want. I don't give a French fag's fart what you're writing. Get off my set. Bess, dear? Come give Uncle Slick a blow job." He beckoned benevolently.

The child fashion model and ex-Pablum baby was out of earshot. She handed her bubblegum to her mother and ran to him.

"Now, Bess, we're going to rehearse your escape from Ellis Island. You are going to slip into the water right here and start to swim toward New Jersey."

Bess gulped. "I thought we were going to do that in a tank at the studio."

"Authenticity is best, pumpkin. I got the harbor permit. The water is warm. This is one of the most important scenes in the script."

"But the sun is shining. I thought I was escaping in the middle of the night."

"Leave that to us, dear. We'll do a day for night. Just you listen to me and you'll be a big star," he cajoled. The magic incantation of "star" settled it. "Doctor!" he bellowed through his Mickey Mouse. The actor playing the Ellis Island health inspector hurried over. "Do that thing again with the button-hook!"

"No—please!" the child gasped. "Ycccch. It's disgusting."

An A.D. brought a basin of disinfectant and what looked like the buttonhook Lou's grandmother kept on her chifforobe in the old Bronx apartment. Bess stood quivering while her mother grinned encouragement. This was the child's chance to get out of commercials and into the big time with Tatum and Brooke.

"Okay, okay, okay—it didn't hurt you before, Bess. It's the idea that scares you and that's good for the role. You're Maria, right? You're twelve years old. You're in America but they want to send you back." He put his arm around her and held out the buttonhook. "The doctor has dipped this into the disinfectant and—flipped up your eyelid."

"Ycccchhhhh." She recoiled.

"He's found trachoma—a contagious disease of the eyes. He's marked you with chalk—a big white *T.C.* and you're scared. A steamship is in the harbor waiting to take you back to Italy. It's now or never—"

Some fifty feet away at the water's edge, the crew had set up arc lights and camera positions atop twenty-foot parallels. A dollying track had been laid down so that the close-up camera could first precede and then follow the refugee into the river.

"Let's go," Jennie whispered to Lou.

"Please. I've never watched a movie being made."

Circling above was a helicopter camera waiting for a cue and a police helicopter watching him. A few yards offshore was an Evinrude outboard for covering shots and a certified lifeguard to assure the girl's safety.

"Fish pole!" Slick shouted.

A boom mike on a long handle was made ready.

"Okay, Bess—you're scared—lonely—desperate—you don't even know how to swim—"

"But I do know how to swim—"

"Maria can't swim—they didn't have swimming pools where she came from. When you hit the water, you're going to panic—thrash around—swallow water— Don't worry, we're not going to let you drown, but we're playing for realism—this is not an Esther Williams movie—"

"Esther Williams?"

"Forget it— Now, you're crouching—running—go on—"

Bess did as he told her. "Into the water—shoes and all—"

"Jesus Christ," Lou muttered.

The child eased her way into the water, her fear real as the strong undertow grabbed at her dress and shoes.

"That's it!" the director cried. "Struggle. Great. But look as if you're trying not to splash. You don't want them to hear you. Right— Now, start swimming—fine—"

The wheelchair had reached the top of the ramp improvised for the dolly. Lou saw what was going to happen just as it began to happen. The wheels of the chair clicked into the dolly tracks and began to move down the steep incline. "What the fuck is this?" The sudden movement jerked the director backward. His green derby sailed off. In the split second it took people to see what was happening, the wheelchair picked up speed like a rollercoaster on the final downhill plunge.

Bess looked up from the water and screamed. Crew members whose job was to watch her turned abruptly to Slick. An A.D. threw himself at the wheelchair but it slipped from his grip. The scene veered from stop action to slow motion as figures jumped, gestured, and used body language to try and repeal the law of gravity.

Inches from the water, Slick Doob pushed himself upright and jumped from the runaway chariot. "Swim out! Out of the way!" he shouted to the struggling figure in the water. The chair hit hard, followed by its owner, who pushed it angrily aside and retrieved his star.

"It kept me out of jail," was all he would say to Lou on the short ferry ride to Manhattan.

"That was an act of spontaneous courage, Slick. Do you think Dorrie Bridges made you a better person?"

"Only a more careful one. But not careful enough. I should have seen that dolly track."

"You mean what I have just witnessed is not a miraculous recovery?"

Slick Doob tapped the thigh of his lucky jeans and flexed his calf muscles. "Well—Jesus Man Suggs is in town. Dorrie did a number on him, too, didn't she? You could say he's getting back at her by healing me."

Maybe he had got back at her more directly. While Slick Doob had managed to avoid jail, Jesus Man Suggs had served sixteen months for using the mails to defraud. A pilgrimage to the Holy Land had inspired him to create the *Jesus Man Knock-on-Wood Holy Medallion*. A piece of wood in the shape of a cross and set in an electroplate disc offered the superstitious a religious opportunity to knock wood for luck and praise God at one and the same time. Offering the medallion for sale was not fraudulent. Suggesting the wood fragments were from the same grove of trees as the True Cross, was.

"Dorrie sent him to the slammer?" Jennie asked Lou on their way uptown to Madison Square Garden.

"No. A Hawkeye postal inspector did that. What Dorrie did was to save him from making another error in judgment and all it cost him was a half a million dollars—a small price to avoid going back to prison."

The confinement further stimulated Jesus Man's imagination. Through a spokesman, he announced total forgiveness to all those who had conspired to put him in durance vile. By pulling a few purse strings, he arranged for his release on Good Friday and announced a massive free outdoor meeting on Easter Sunday at Griffith Park.

There the self-crowned King of Gospel Rock blamed his transgressions on ignorance. "My own ignorance for not understanding the law and not knowing I was breaking the law. Ignorance is no excuse. I know that. Neither is the fact that I did not have the advantages of a formal education."

Men of evil had good education. It was time for men of God to have an education, too. To remedy this gap, he announced one hundred free scholarships for deserving men and women. "Now where are we going to get the funds for these scholarships? The Lord Jesus has told me the scholarship funds are right here in this vast crowd today and we're going to gather this scholarship fund for one hundred deserving men and women *right now*."

Attendants passed giant-size Hefty bags through the crowd. "Folding money please. No loose change; it rips the bag."

Estimates varied between four and five hundred thousand

dollars raised during the next few weeks for the scholarships. About six months later Dorrie called Jesus Man's office for a list of the scholarship winners. She was told selections were still being made. Another few months went by, another call, and the answer was the same.

"There must be at least a hundred worthy young men and women in the United States," Dorrie had told his administrative assistant.

"We are still in the process of processing them," she was told.

Being old friends, Dorrie had decided to help the Reverend Suggs out. By telephone, telegram, and telex, she had queried the top educators of all fifty states and asked them to recommend a boy and girl deserving of a scholarship. A short time later her column praised Jesus Man for generous and noble devotion and sympathized with his problem of choosing the recipients.

To help him in his good works, she offered the hundred names. "Two from every state in the Union, boys, girls, all races and religions, unified in the single ambition of education." She knew he would want to distribute the half-million-dollar fund as quickly as possible. "Nobody likes that much cash laying around the house."

Jesus Man's response had been to give the cash awards of five thousand dollars each to the hundred winners on prime-time television. As a finale he had them wave the greenbacks at the camera while shouting in unison, "Thank you, Dorrie Bridges."

"Brother Jesus is resting." Marjorie Ullman viewed Lou and Jennie with fretful suspicion as they entered the dressing area of Madison Square Garden.

"We're from the press."

The King of Gospel Rock was astride an electric bicycle, the sweat pouring down from his cascade of blond hair into the neck of his "Eight Track Jesus" sweat suit. "Welcome, friends. Praise *God!*" A buzzer sounded. Jesus Man sprang from the saddle. "Ten minutes a day keeps the Devil away. A sound body giveth a sound mind into the service of the Lord."

"Some of the best bodies I've ever seen belong to homo-sexual men!" Lou decided to strike while the irony was hot.

"They are vile creatures of sin. They are filth and corrup-tion!" Marjorie Ullman looked like a Macy's balloon with some of the air leaked out. Twice the size of the Marjorie Ullman who had starred in Broadway musicals for twenty years, her once famous features had been applied as with a palette knife in the soft collapsed face, the hair carrot red in a mockery of 1940s glamour.

"What we are talking about is God's warnings," Jesus Man intoned. "God is losing patience with us for our sins. You think Three Mile Island was human error? It was God's warn-ing. You think the San Andreas earthquakes are *gee*-ology? No, sir. They are *thee*-ology and they are the result of too much *me*-ology."

"Do you mean to say homosexuality is going to cause Armageddon?" Lou's aim was to anger him and then bring up the subject of Dorrie Bridges.

"Now, Brother—?"

"Dexter. Lou Dexter."

"Now, Brother Dexter—Jesus loves *all* of His children. *In-cluding* sinners and homosexuals."

"He just doesn't want them teaching in the schools," Jennie said.

"Jennie!" This was Lou's interview. Why couldn't she keep her trap shut!

Marjorie Ullman popped a Fireside marshmallow into her mouth. The white powder stuck to her deep purple lips. "They should be castrated!"

"Sister Marjorie is upset by the recent court decisions," Jesus Man soothed. "I trust that you will respect this outburst as off the record?"

"Sure. But I would like to know how you feel about the separation of Church and State. Education is the responsibility of the State, wouldn't you agree?"

"There is no separation between Church and State. We are one, united in the service of God and man. Reach into your pocket. Show me a dollar bill!"

Lou did as instructed.

"Now turn it over. What does it say? 'In God we trust!' The Lord is America's partner! The Lord is your partner! The Lord is part of everything on earth from the smallest blade of grass to the biggest spaceship that leaves the Earth and soars into the outer space of heaven. And the Lord does not want homosexuals destroying His work. Tonight I am going to introduce my new eight-track gospel rock hit *'Save Your S and M for Jesus!'* Not sadism, not masochism. *S* for your *soul, M* for your *mind* and if you're going to be *queer*, make it for salvation and if you're going to be *gay,* the only *way* is in the joy of loving God.

"Forgive me now, I have to change into more suitable attire." Marjorie Ullman held up the jeweled white performance suit for his inspection.

"What's your reaction to the disappearance of Dorrie Bridges? I understand you knew each other back in Tennessee!"

"That lesbian!" Marjorie Ullman spat. "As soon as she defended Gay Lib, I knew what she was. Making up those statistics about heterosexual teachers seducing girls! Let me tell you, that woman made more mischief—"

"Now, Marjorie. The Lord Jesus *forgiveth* the sinner. If the Lord can forgive Dorrie Bridges, how can we hold back our prayers? I pray for Dorrie Bridges. I pray that she has found the light. I *know* the Lord has forgiven her for all the pain and sorrow she caused with her writing and her TV talks."

"I hope she is burning in *Hell!*" The woman would not be soothed.

"Tell me, Mrs. Ullman, have *you* ever had a lesbian experience?" Jennie Bliss Sternholdt asked in the same tone of voice she would ask for a Kleenex.

The enraged bull of a woman charged at them with the steam iron. Jesus Man hung onto the electric cord like it was the tail of a bucking bronco.

"Race you to the street!" Jennie cried.

"How could you do such a thing?" He was panting hard. Jennie had not only beat him to the street but flagged down a cab.

"I was a track star. I know women aren't supposed to beat men at sports but I thought you were more liberated than all that shit and—"

"You know what I'm talking about. How could you accuse Marjorie Ullman of being a dyke?"

"It is human nature to attack in others what you fear most in yourself. Marjorie Ullman must have either had a lesbian experience or wanted to—and maybe Dorrie knew about it."

"Do you think Marjorie or Jesus Man were responsible for her disappearance?"

"What do you think, Lou?" She snuggled against him.

"Don't tell me you're asking my opinion?" He kissed her nose. "What I think is—" He kissed her left eye. "—those two are capable of anything." He kissed her right eye.

"Would you like a road map?"

"For what?"

"So you can find my mouth."

"You've got one hell of a fresh mouth."

She did her breathless-hiccup Jackie Onassis little-girl voice. "That's 'cos I—gargle—twice a day—with Lysol—"

He found her mouth. The cab driver, too intent on watching to ask their destination, did so now. "Where to?"

Jennie's hand was between Lou's legs. "Where to?" she echoed huskily.

Lou looked out at the passing scenery. They were approaching Times Square. "West Forty-third Street. *The New York Times.*"

"I thought we were going to Burt Whitechapel's."

"Later. I just remembered an old buddy of mine—we both started out as copyboys on the *Daily News*—he's the night man at the *Times* morgue."

"Dead bodies at the *Times*?"

"It's been said. No—the morgue is where they keep clippings and pictures and background material going back maybe a century. Every newspaper has one. The *Times*'s is the best, the most thorough in the world. If Mickey is on, I'm sure he'll let us use it."

The entrance to the *Times* building looks like a hospital. In the heart of the Times Square theatrical district, the street was dark and deserted because curtain time had passed and the first intermission was still to come.

"How do you feel about aggressive women?" Jennie asked when they reached the building vestibule.

"Dominate me—"

She raised her face to his and put her arms around his neck. "Lou—"

"You—"

"You know what Audrey Hepburn said to Cary Grant in *Charade*?"

"No, what did Audrey Hepburn say to Cary Grant?"

"She said, 'You know what's wrong with you?' And Cary Grant said, 'No, what?' And you know what Audrey Hepburn said?"

"No, what?"

" 'Nothing,' you idiot!" she howled. "Absolutely *nothing*!"

Lou's body was facing the good glass front doors of the Good Gray *Times*. As his eyes fluttered and closed in erotic submission to the carnal greed of this sex-crazed barracuda, he glimpsed the ever-popular figure of Norris Burnside getting out of a car.

Upstairs, his old friend Mickey brought them the Burnside files. Among the early clippings were the engagement and wedding of New York debutante Marva Von Schmidt to

California heir Norris Burnside. "Can you get me the Von Schmidt file?"

It was dusty. It was musty. The newsprint crumpled and made him sneeze. Among the photographs was one of American industrialist Eric Von Schmidt and his sixteen-year-old daughter Marva in the Obsersalzberg area of the Bavarian Alps. The year was 1937. A third person in the photograph was German Chancellor Adolf Hitler. According to the caption, *der Führer* was inviting the Von Schmidts to return for another visit and bidding them safe journey on their homeward journey aboard the first spring voyage of the zeppelin *Hindenburg.*

The rich red leather was embossed in gold.

DEAR DIARY
1937

There was no key. Dorrie squeezed the gold lock. It clicked open in her hand. The paper was thick and smooth, the handwriting schoolgirl clear in green ink. The opening page gave the owner's credentials.

THIS IS MY DIARY

MY NAME IS: Marva Von Schmidt
MY BIRTHDAY IS: April 9, 1921
MY ADDRESS IS: 723 Fifth Avenue, New York, New York,
United States of America,
The Earth,
The Universe

The opening pages were datelined *New York*. In a dot-and-dash diary style, they referred to hasty preparations for a trip to Germany with Father. That Mother had decided to remain behind. That this was Marva's first time abroad and her excitement knew no bounds.

Her clothes, her German lessons, and the ocean voyage (mostly blank pages because of heavy seas) brought the diary to Berlin by the end of January. A shopping spree on the Kurfürstendamm included a red leather shoulder bag at the famous Lederer's, a small incidental fact, but one that chilled Dorrie to the bone.

Marva adored red leather. She would have had a red leather diary and a red leather bag. Barely able to sleep, Dorrie had convinced herself her previous night's intruder was either a loony or a blackmailer and that the diary, if it ever materialized, was a hoax. If she heard no more, she had decided to forget the whole thing and not even mention it to Marva.

The package had arrived first thing this morning.

The handwriting! Just the other day Marva had written one of her frequent little notes. She found it and compared it. There was no doubt about it: there were marked similarities in the circles for dots over the *i*'s and the triple dashes between phrases as well as the general configurations of penmanship.

Fascinated, she continued to read. By early February the Von Schmidts were in Munich. Father's business meetings going well. Concerts. Opera. Museums. Handsome and extremely polite soldiers in Nazi uniforms.

On February 6 someone pointed out a luxurious building on the Prinzregentenstrasse where Adolf Hitler has an apartment. His niece, Geli, committed suicide there. Someone jokingly said Marva was the image of Geli.

Great excitement over the next few days. Father about to make a deal with the German government. Hints about "you know who." Scribbles in German. On February 18, "We are going to the Berghof for the weekend!"

Her mouth dry, her fingers sweaty, Dorrie read the following pages with a growing sense of panic and revulsion. This could not be Marva Burnside thrilling to the attentions of *der Führer*, making fun of Eva Braun's jealousy and calling her an old hag.

Yet there it was, the description of the Obersalzberg area, the view from the living room of the Untersberg peak, the Wagner recordings, the Titian reclining nude. The guest rules prohibiting smoking, whistling, and makeup struck Marva as hilarious. Also the prohibition against guests keeping a diary!

As Hitler's personal interest increased, he insisted she must sit beside him and share his vegetarian meals. She must walk with him in the woods. She must pose for him while he makes pencil sketches for relaxation.

By the opening days of March, Mr. Von Schmidt was telling his daughter that Hitler's attentions were an honor. That he was a genius and much misunderstood by the Jewish-dominated American newspapers. Eva Braun was sent back to her villa in Munich. The Von Schmidts were asked to stay on. There were a few blank days in the diary until March 11 and a breathless description of a large iron-framed bed covered by a brown quilt embroidered with a huge swastika.

"I thought I'd be scared but I wasn't. He says I am the perfection of Aryan womanhood. I am his niece brought back to life. His eyes are hypnotic. I cannot resist them. He undressed me and made me lay down on the swastika. He gave me a gun. A Walther 6.35 pistol, he said. Geli killed herself with it.

"I started to cry. He said babies cried, women did not cry. He asked me if I would do anything he told me to do. I said yes. He told me to put the gun between my legs. 'Would you pull the trigger if I command it?' I have never known such happiness. I would do anything he said. Anything. Anything. . . ."

The entry ended abruptly and the next few pages were blank. On March 18 there was a new tone to the handwriting. Arrogant. Haughty. "He says I am the woman he has been searching for all his life—Eva, Geli, Unity Mitford, all of them are nothing to him—"

A separate entry the same day was headed LOVE IS HUMILIA-TION. "He fell on the floor and told me to kick him. Hard. I was crying but I did it and then I hit him with a cane. Thrilling. So thrilling. He loved me he said. He would make me the most envied woman in the world. His wife, ruling the world side by side with him.

"Oh, Diary—I don't know how to tell you what happened next. It may seem terrible to you but it wasn't. It was a religious experience. I took off my panties and sat on top of him— Oh, Diary, I can't go on. Even you might not understand—"

The following pages were chaotic scrawls of explicit sex that made Dorrie sick, Hitler's growing insistence that they marry, her father's assurance that *der Führer* was a great leader and that marrying him would be wonderful for her and the family. "Germany and America have close ties," Von Schmidt enthused.

The wedding took place on April 7 at Berchtesgaden with all present sworn to secrecy. The wedding night was more of the sadomasochism the new bride evidently enjoyed describing with some new and even more repellent variations.

"*Mein Führer* is letting me return home with Father on the *Hindenburg* to tell Mother. I will come back to him in July and we will announce our union."

There was nothing until May 2. "Surprise, dear diary. We are in London. Adolf will be so mad. He thinks we are on the *Hindenburg* flying over the ocean. But Father wanted to see his tailor so we took the train here. Lots of excitement with the Coronation. The Savoy Hotel is so nice. They sent up a gramophone so I can play the Gershwin recording Hitler gave me as a farewell present. G. was a Jew but he was dead and if I like him, he would forgive him."

The last entry was May 7, 1937. A long erotic outpouring of her passion for her absent lover interrupted by a large ink blot and the words, "*Hindenburg*—crash— Did he try to kill me?"

"What is it, Dorrie? You got a bug? You didn't look so hot last night—" Marva's voice bubbled as always from the other end of the phone.

"I've got to see you. Right way."

"I've got meetings. Massage. Lunch. Want to come here?"

"I must see you alone. It's urgent."

"Is it Sonny?"

"No—"

"See you here two o'clock."

"Can you make it sooner? Like now—"

"Oh, angel. It'll take me the whole morning to rearrange my morning. It'll keep till this afternoon. It can't be that bad."

It was worse than bad. It was catastrophic. If it were true, it could be the biggest story of her career and the destruction of a beautiful friendship and a beautiful person. If it were fake, it would be front-page big, too, because it meant someone with more time than fine feelings had put in a whole lot of trouble to get Marva Burnside. Last night's visitor must know who that someone was.

The phone rang. She prayed it was the woman with the husky voice. "Hello?"

"Dorrie?"

"Hello, Sonny."

"I'm sorry you found it necessary to check up on me."

"I—" She had to think for a moment. "What do you mean? I thought you were on location."

"I heard that you called me last night. Well, it just so happens they closed down production for a week. I'm back here."

"In L.A.?" It was as if one part of her brain wasn't working.

"I'll be right there." He hung up.

"But—" That made twice in as many calls that a phone slammed down without final good-bye. She did not want to see Sonny Syntagma at this precise moment. She needed time to reexamine the diary and consider all the angles before confronting Marva.

Marva was her dearest friend and a good and generous woman. If the diary were authentic, it need not be true. A young woman with a vivid imagination could certainly fantasize a love story. But such a hideous love story and containing details of sexual aberration that were not within the experience of a sheltered young heiress of 1937.

How in *hell* was she going to broach the subject. "Marva, darlin'. I've got me a diary here says you had a mite of trouble in your early life."

Andrew Van Kennan buzzed through from his office on the floor below. "Want to check the day's schedule?"

"Do what you have to do, Andrew, and check back with me later. I've got Sonny coming by this morning." Andrew would break down in tears if he knew about that diary. He would rush it into the headlines and check it for truth afterward. It didn't matter much with stories like the one he broke the one time she was away and left him in charge. The one about Jackie Onassis eloping with Jerry Brown. Everybody got a big laugh out of that one except the more conservative newspapers who syndicated Dorrie and relied on her integrity.

"Love in the morning? Well, ex*cuse* me! I'll hold all calls. Some people have all the luck."

If only she could trust Andrew. If only she could say, "Drop everything, I've got something hot." In this town, in this business, loyalty was like a hoopskirt. Old-fashioned and utterly suspect. Andrew was ambitious and alert to the main chance. He may have forgotten what happened twelve years earlier at *Newsmagazine* but she doubted if he had completely forgiven. Recently when rumors appeared about *Newsmagazine* suffering heavy losses in circulation and advertising revenue, his reaction was, "Serves Connie Michelin right. If that magazine dies, I'll sing all the way to the cemetery."

When Connie cover-profiled Sonny in a roundup in "The New M&Ms. Mind and Muscle Make Money and Movies," the article called him the protégé of a leading gossip monger whose motto was "The word is mightier than the sword." Dorrie had laughed it off. Sonny had raged at her like it was her fault, looking a lot like he did right now, breaking through the door like a bull with a corncob up its ass.

"You're looking mighty handsome this morning, sir," she said, trying to establish the gentle ritual they had for too long used as a substitute for talk. Sonny Syntagma did look handsome. All in blue—jeans, shirt, and a skipper's cap with the visor pulled forward at a cocky angle.

He made no move to embrace her. "I've got a story for you, an exclusive."

Praise God, what did he have? Her head swam with the possibilities. A flying saucer? A man conceiving a baby? Oil discovered in the Carolinas? "Tell me."

His gaze faltered. "I'm—I'm getting married."

"Married?" They had of course discussed marriage but not recently. With her thirtieth birthday up the pike a piece, maybe it was the right time to take the plunge. "Well, I don't know what to say, I'm sure—"

"Don't worry. It's not to you."

"Well, now—" She felt like a turtle turned on its back.

"Well, now—"

"I don't suppose you'll tell me who the lucky girl is."

"There you go, patronizing me. I knew you'd do that. I told her you'd do that. But she said I had an unhealthy relationship with you—"

"Seems pretty healthy to me. I certainly didn't get any venereal disease—"

"See? Sexual blackmail! Exactly what she said you've been doing. Well, it's all over now. I'm cutting free and cutting out. She said it was your fault I'm not taken seriously in the industry—"

"Sweet Jesus, you're not marrying Glitz?"

He flushed inside his tan. "No, but she introduced me to Jill."

"And what does Jill do for a living?" Besides set traps for pea-brained movie stars?

"She's a sex therapist."

"Oh, Sonny darlin'—" She had come to terms with his impotence. They never discussed it anymore. Her heart went out to him. Leave it to Glitz to meddle in her affairs.

"Don't 'Sonny, darlin' ' me. I'm through with you. I'm tired of being owned by you. I'm a real actor. I'm tired of people saying you made me a star. Tired of pretending to be superstud. How do you think I feel when all those women tell you how lucky you are having me. All those stupid little girls sending me naked pictures of themselves, offering themselves to me, saying they'd do anything I asked. How do you think I feel?"

"That's the price of being a movie star. You mustn't feel responsible about bringing out the worst in people."

"Fuck them. What about me? How do you think I feel when the hardest thing I can show them is an eclair. Well, it's different now. Jill has changed everything. She's unblocked me. She's helped me to work my feelings of anger and hostility through. She helped me find out what was wrong with me."

"What was wrong with you?"

He stepped closer to her and growled into her face. "I once raped a girl. Nearly killed her. She was like you. Smart. The smartest girl in the school. President of the class. Captain of the debating squad. Head of this. Leader of that. Only thing she couldn't do was sports and I could do that. She loved me, she said. We were the King and Queen of the Senior Dance and afterward she teased me and let me go so far and then stopped me like she was some kind of traffic cop or something.

"That whole last year of high school, I was jumping on every girl in school, every girl in town, except for her. She said the Senior Dance was the night, that's when we would consummate our great love. She went too far, pushing me away. She didn't know what that does to a seventeen-year-old boy. I went crazy. I nearly tore that woman in half. I didn't give her a chance to yell. I clamped my hand over her mouth and I drove my pecker into her so hard I could hear it rip. 'I'll never forgive you!' That's the last thing she said to me. 'I'll never forgive you.'

"And Jill says that's why I've never been able to perform. When I'm with a woman all I can hear in my mind is 'I'll never forgive you.' Jill says it's time to forgive myself."

"Why didn't you ever tell me this?"

"You? I know all about you. You were glad I couldn't fuck. It gave you power over me. Jill explained it all to me. You hate all men because you never knew your father. Your father didn't even love your mother enough to know you were conceived or born. You weren't even rejected. The man who gave you life doesn't even know you exist!"

"When did you meet her?"

"About a month ago. The first thing she made me do was watch you on television while she talked to me."

"That must have been quite a turn-on."

"It was, lady, it was. She explained to me how I was afraid of castration. Afraid of vaginas. A classic case, she said. And that it was my bad luck to be tied up with you."

"That was kind of her."

"She said you were keeping me in this condition. You were like the United States giving handouts to underdeveloped nations. I was supposed to be grateful for everything you did for me. Well, I'm not. I *hate* you—"

"Jill sounds like quite a girl. How old is she?"

"Twenty-four!" he shouted triumphantly. "Young. Her body is young. Not soft and flabby like you. She couldn't believe it when I told her you were a virgin. A thirty-year-old born-again virgin—"

"Now, just one little old minute—"

"You shut up. This is the last time I'm going to see you and I'm going to make it a time to remember!"

He picked her up and carried her into the bedroom they had often shared in the most companionable of terms. She did not struggle. It seemed silly, like a satire of a Marlon Brando movie. "We've had this date from the beginning!" Sonny had played Stanley Kowalski in UCLA workshop. That being the case, couldn't he see she was not Blanche, she was Stella. She loved him, or had.

By habit, she began to undress.

"Oh, no. Not this time. I'm not going to make love to you. I am going to fuck you. To prove that I can do it. For the first and last time."

He unzipped his jeans and pulled out the long, hard cause of his grief and pain.

"Do I get to take off my pants? Or would you prefer I take your picture?" Technically virgin she might be but she certainly knew how to deal with what his sex therapist would doubtless call this new development of their relationship. She reached out her arms to him. "I've loved you, Sonny. I've waited for you. I agree. Let's love each other this once."

"Oh, no! You don't get me like that. I'm going to fuck you to prove I can fuck you but not the way you'd like me to fuck you."

He flipped her over and ripped off her pants. "Up on your knees, bitch. I'll show you what a man I am without stealing that precious virginity of yours."

Pain was not the word. "Invasion" was more like it. Invasion by force. A cruel and savage attack by an enemy she had thought was her friend and who must always have hated her to be this angry. When it was over, he collapsed on top of her and wept. "I had to do it. I had to prove myself. I had to—I had to find a way to live with myself—"

She lay inert, somehow detached from the flesh that covered her like a landslide. She had to find a way to live with herself, too. Maybe she was getting too old for this town. Maybe the pace was getting too fast and the action too heavy. Maybe she was getting worn down by scandals and deceptions and conspiracies. Maybe she had been naive to think that exposing evil would lead to good. It was twelve years since the Senator Bingham disclosures. Things hadn't changed much in Tennessee. Or anywhere else, for that matter.

It was not her job to save the world. She might have a high opinion of herself, but not that high. It was her job to find the truth and tell it as best and honorably as she could.

When at last Sonny got up, she ignored him. He covered her with the quilt Mallie had made for her and sent up from Pass Christian. "I'm sorry!" he said.

"I know," she said. He no longer mattered. It was Marva who was in jeopardy, Marva she would be confronting with the vile contents of the little red diary.

A nap, a hot bath, some judiciously applied baby oil, and two aspirin and she was ready to keep her appointment. The waiting limousine suddenly repelled her. Why had she let

Andrew talk her into this ridiculous show of affluence! On the way to Marva's, she had Harrington stop at the first automobile showroom they saw. As it happened, it was Toyota. She wrote out a check for a Corona liftback and had them switch her LURAY license plate from the Cadillac.

As Thornton Wilder wrote in *The Bridge of San Luis Rey,* there was a land of the living and a land of the dead "and the bridge is love."

"Does this mean I am no longer employed?" Harrington inquired.

"No. You can take care of Mr. Van Kennan."

"Actually, miss, I was rather hoping you would dismiss me. That way, I can apply for unemployment insurance. You see, I'm working on an idea for a screenplay and I can use the time."

"Okay, you're fired!"

Give the people what they want! The thought of Andrew's reaction gave her dutch courage as she drove her new car through Marva Burnside's Spanish gates. Marva was waiting for her in the patio.

"What is it, Dorrie? You look like hell! You sick? Tell me. Is it Sonny?"

"No, Marva." She took a deep breath. "It's—you!"

Smiling and gracious as always, Marva insisted on pouring the iced tea and settling themselves into facing wicker chairs. "Now, what have you got there?"

"A diary—" Dorrie held out the red leather book.

" 'DEAR DIARY 1937'? Sounds too delicious for words. Whose is it? Jean Harlow? Katharine Hepburn?"

"Look inside."

"Such excitement—" Marva's jaw literally dropped to her chest. "But—I don't get it. Is this some kind of a joke?"

"It's no joke. Is this your diary, Marva?"

"I—it's got my name in it! And that's where we lived all right, seven twenty-three Fifth, and I sure as hell was born in 1921 but—"

"The handwriting looks like yours—"

Marva was shaking her head wonderingly. "It sure as hell does but I don't remember having a diary like this."

"Did you have a diary?"

"Sure. All the girls had diaries. We got them for Christmas and wrote in them religiously every night for at least a week. But I don't remember this one at all." She turned the page.

"Did your father take you to Germany in 1937?"

"Yes, he did. He was German, you know. Von Schmidt. We dropped the Von in '41. Would have got rid of it sooner but my mother liked it. Her biggest complaint was there was no aristocracy in America. She'd have given her eyeteeth for a title. Anyway, my father had several business enterprises with connections in Germany and President Roosevelt sent him on an unofficial fact-finding mission in 1937 to get some idea of what was really going on. I was seventeen and the apple of my father's eye and I begged him to take me."

"Did you meet Hitler?"

Marva's face darkened. "That posturing little bastard! Shrieking and waving his arms. They should have put him in a straitjacket. He looked nuts. He acted nuts. To this day I can't understand the hold he had on the people. We were invited to the Berghof. What a dump. Not what I expected. Lousy food. *Der Führer* was a vegetarian."

"Did you speak to him?"

"He patted me on the head and complimented my father on my good manners. He asked me how old I was and what I was studying and if I enjoyed being in the new Germany. Then he and Father and the others had a meeting. We all had dinner together. Eva Braun was there, wearing a black dress with fur around the hem. She didn't speak to anyone but Hitler. After dinner there was an accordion player.

"We all went to bed early. The next morning my father and I left. In fact—" She grimaced.

"What—?"

"The official photographer took a picture of Hitler bidding us farewell. That damned picture came back to haunt us during the war, especially with a name like Von Schmidt. It made us look pro-Nazi until Roosevelt issued an official certificate of gratitude to my father for valuable and patriotic service to the United States Government. Now for God's sake, let me read my diary—" She sank back into the cushions with the leather book on her knee.

"Marva, please—"

The older woman waved her to silence. "This is spooky. It sounds just like me. Where did this come from, some new kind of boutique?"

Dorrie watched with mounting tension as Marva's face contorted with shock. "What is this? What is this filth? Where did this come from?"

"Please, Marva—" Dorrie tried to take it away from her.

"No, goddammit, let me finish this. It's grotesque. Who could write this—"

When she finished, her hands were shaking; her face and body seemed to have aged ten years. She had to clear her throat several times before she could speak. "Where did you get this?"

Dorrie told her about the mysterious woman visiting her the previous night and the delivery of the diary that morning.

"Have you shown it to anyone else?"

"Of course not."

"Tom Jennings?"

"Of course not!"

"Who could do such a thing, Dorrie?"

"You tell me."

"You—my God, Dorrie, you don't think this is authentic, do you?"

"My opinion doesn't matter. Marva—"

"I'm asking you! You don't think I wrote this—this obscene—this hideous, disgusting—"

"What I think doesn't matter. Is it your diary, Marva? Maybe somebody found it and doctored it up."

"I don't believe you're asking me this, Dorrie."

"Is it—or was it—your diary?"

The two women stared at each other in silence. "You're not going to—say anything about it, are you?"

"No—"

"Don't scare me that way—"

"I have to check it out further."

"You mean—you don't believe me?"

"I didn't say that, Marva. I'm saying I have to check it out. I happen to be a very good reporter, you know. I have to find out who our mysterious woman is and where she got this and—"

"What if it were true? Doesn't our friendship mean anything? What good would it do to reveal something as sordid as this? We're close friends, Dorrie. How could you even consider running it? For God's sake, let's burn it and forget it—"

"There's that woman. If it's a fake, she can always do it again, assuming she's out to get you—"

"And if it's authentic—what if it's *authentic* and you're sitting here with a woman who— It's so loathsome, I can't say it. Would you run it?"

Dorrie met her friend's anguished gaze without flinching. "I—I would have to run it. If it's the truth, it would be my duty to run it."

"Your duty? What about loyalty? What about friendship? What about wrecking my life? What about all the charities and things I'm involved in? All my foundations and educational services. Would you discredit those? What about the people dependent on them?"

Dorrie stood up. "I've got to go."

"Go where? What are you going to do?"

"Find the truth. I swear to you, Marva. I won't print a word about this unless I've got proof it's real."

"Thanks for nothing. If they're clever enough to do a forgery this good, they're clever enough to convince you it's not a forgery."

"At least credit me with knowing how to check out a story."

"You insufferable little cow. You self-righteous bitch! You've gone power-mad. It's all gone to your head. My life is in your hands—"

Without warning, Marva made a grab for Dorrie's tote bag, which held the diary. Dorrie snatched the bag back and ran to her car, locking the doors as Marva pounded on the window.

"Why are you doing this?"

Dorrie put the car in gear. "I've got to find out the truth!"

Marva ran down the driveway after her, punching the car with her fists. "Why, for God's sake? Why is it so important?"

Dorrie Bridges couldn't say why it was so important in so many words. It just was.

One of the easiest things to do in New York is get killed. By design, by default, or by degree, it is the city of indiscriminate opportunity for people of all genders, pigments, income, literacy, and countries of origin. Its streets paved with ghouls, its marketplaces a vast Samarra sprawl where Death keeps daily appointments with the unsuspecting, New York also offers fallen objects from high buildings, random bullets, bad clams, poor brakes, and the baroque possibilities of the Interborough

Rapid Transit System, more familiarly known as the IRT or Seventh Avenue Subway, as means to one's sudden end.

"Why can't we take a cab?" Jennie Bliss Sternholdt wanted to know for the eighty-seventh time since leaving the *Times* morgue and the picture of teen-age Marva *mit* kind and cuddly Uncle Adolf. They stood on the Uptown platform of the Times Square subway station waiting for the Seventh Avenue Express. The rush-hour stampede had ceased. Now there was the early-evening crush of those seeking pleasure and excitement one way or another.

"It's quicker by subway."

"But, Lou—"

"Look, you don't have to come with me." The charging steel bison with the cyclops eye roared into the station. "Stand back. What's the matter with you? Want to fall between the cars?"

"Hey!—" The doors had opened and the rush of people separated them.

"Seventh Avenue Express. Next stop Seventy-second Street!" the voice on the loudspeaker announced.

Lou held the door open just as he had as a schoolboy. "For God's sake, Jennie, move your ass."

She stood beside him refusing to step into the car. "I-want-to-take-a-taxi! I'll pay!"

Three young black men with Alvin Ailey grace lounged on their seats watching. With his pasty white face and lily-white liver, Lou felt a tribal necessity to express dominance or at least control over this noisy woman. If he did not, he would look chickenshit and risk getting his shoes cuffed and other indignities.

"Get your fucking ass in here!" Hemingway time but with a twist. Courage was disgrace under pressure. The door closed. They found seats. She opened her mouth. "Shut up!" he whispered. "Kindly shut up."

They sat in grim silence until the train screeched into Seventy-second Street. The three black musketeers bopped to the platform with buddy smiles for Lou and a throwaway "Right on."

"Why didn't you leave with your chauvinist pig friends?" Jennie hissed.

"I told you. I didn't ask you to come."

"And I told you white people don't take the subway to Harlem. We can still get out and hop a cab."

"We can't take a cab because Mallomar Crane said he would meet us at the Hundred Thirty-seventh Street Station. If we took a cab, we'd be saying we're afraid to ride with black people."

If their particular subway car were taken to the Museum of Modern Art, it could have been shown as a fine example of Urban Grotesque. The advertising cards were torn and defaced, the walls and windows caked with grime and graffiti, the seats and floor a sticky carpet of food, newspapers, and soda cans. Half the lights were out.

"That's racist and you know it."

"I know it—but I'm still afraid."

At Ninety-sixth they changed to the local, the condition of the train, if anything, worse. "The Transit Authority ought to be horsewhipped."

"I'll bet the Moscow subway's a palace compared to this."

He thought of the magnificent tiles and lights and murals. "Sure is."

"Well—"

"Well, what—"

"Well, I guess this is the price we pay for a democracy."

"You said it, I didn't. I don't really see filth and vandalism as an expression of the democratic spirit."

"Okay, okay. Don't be so touchy. I was just making conversation. God! I'm sorry."

He was about to tell her he was sorry, too, when the train pulled into 137th Street. He would have to remember how young she was and that she could not possibly understand the political subtleties of comparing the Moscow and New York subway systems.

Mallomar Crane was an O. J. Simpson clone with a Paul Robeson background of Princeton, Shakespeare, football, and the concert stage. His baptismal name was Milton, for the great English poet. At the time of his growing up in the early fifties, his half-white mother and "white" ambitions had inspired his playground friends to call him Mallomar after the snack cake that was brown on the outside and white in the middle.

The name stuck and became something of a cross-racial emblem as he became active in the Civil Rights movement, completed his law degree, became a media personality, and seemed certain to be the first serious black candidate for the presidency in 1976.

In late 1975 the Democrats had no surefire winner. A nobody from Plains, Georgia, named Jimmy Carter was appearing in various primaries but seemed a regional dullard with a bunch of red-necks running his campaign. Mallomar Crane was the equivalent of a black prince, handsome, elegant, educated, a black Jack Kennedy. The talk was going around that if an Irish Catholic could win in 1960, then the year of the Bicentennial was a patriotic and sentimental occasion for the first black president. The fact that he was a mulatto made it even more one hundred percent American, one of the early position papers noted. Intermarriage was what made America great.

The great political machinery began to roll. Rallies. Speeches. Banquets. Press conferences. Meet the press. Meet the churches. Meet the precincts. Meet the people.

The leaders were oozing with self-congratulations at their audacity of putting their money where their ideals were when the candidate issued a simple announcement withdrawing his name from all consideration. No explanation was offered. Crane dropped from sight.

A Teddy Kennedy spokesman was later quoted as saying that the party could be grateful to Dorrie Bridges for preventing a "difficult situation," a comment he denied. Asked if he knew the reason Mallomar Crane bowed out, he said it was Crane's decision and Crane's option to explain or keep silent and he, for one, would refrain from making a judgment.

He had made of his old brownstone house a biracial "hustle," as opposed to "hostel," for bright but poor prelaw students. "My wife and I do believe in separating the sexes," he said, indicating the boys' dormitory on one floor and the girls' on another.

His point was that the working classes needed lawyers and that the black and white factions of the working class needed to work together for the benefit of society instead of being pitted against each other. He saw a new generation of white and black law students learning together and making friendships that would deepen as they moved into their profession.

"What did you want to ask me?" He came right to the point. His workroom was small and comfortable. Pictures on the wall included Fannie Lou Hamer, Martin Luther King, George Washington Carver, and Jesse Jackson. There were none of himself, nor any of his athletic or civic awards.

"It's about Dorrie Bridges."

"Yes?"

"There was a rumor that she was responsible for your withdrawal from the 1976 presidential race."

"Was there, now?"

"Yes—and the rumor persists to this day."

"And—?" He leaned back in his swivel chair with his hands behind his head.

"Dorrie Bridges is dead."

"Missing—and *presumed* dead."

"And I'm wondering if by some coincidence you may be reconsidering your position." Clumsy! Lou could have kicked himself. He was out of practice. He was all but accusing this man of gething rid of Dorrie Bridges so he could run for

President! Which was what he had in mind but not so blatantly.

Mallomar Crane favored him with a smile. "You certainly come straight to the point, Mr. Dexter."

"Well—you did say you haven't much time—"

Mallomar Crane considered the issue for a long moment and rose abruptly. "Now is as good a time as any." His smile broadened. "And you do deserve a reward for surviving the IRT."

He moved Fannie Lou Hamer's portrait and opened the small wall safe behind it. He removed a folded document. "I told a lie and Dorrie Bridges found me out. Any good reporter could have done the same, but she was the only one who did. It was foolish and vain of me to think I could get away with it.

"When she called me to verify, I met her and we discussed it. I explained to her that my lie would boomerang on all blacks. 'Black men are liars,' they'd say. 'Can't trust these niggers nohow!' "

He opened the document and handed it to Lou. "She was a good and responsible woman. She was a southerner and she knew how far we had come in race relations and how easy it would be to slip back because of my ambition and stupidity."

Lou examined the document. "It—it's a birth certificate!"

"That's what it is."

"But—'Date of Birth December first, 1939'?—" He knew he was looking at the answer but he couldn't see it.

"Tortola!" Jennie exclaimed. "A British colony. You're not a native-born American. You can't be President."

"Exactly, my friends."

"But I thought you were born in Puerto Rico."

"That's what I thought. My father had a job there in the boatyards. My mother died. We moved to Miami during the war. My father died. I had come in on his papers and simply assumed I was born in Puerto Rico."

"How did Dorrie find out?"

"She was doing what she called an ordinary job of checking for facts. She wanted to do a story on my birth, find the hospital or the midwife or someone to remember the little black baby who might be the President. She hit a blank wall. No records. My mother was half-English, you know. Her family had a small guesthouse on Tortola. Dorrie found that out and checked the records there—and there I was."

"And here you are!" Lou said, returning the birth certificate.

"Will you use it?"

"I'm doing a retrospective on Dorrie Bridges. Do you think this is important to the story?"

"In New York the best way to answer a question is with a question. Why do you think I invited you all the way up to Harlem?"

"He'd have made a great President," Jennie enthused in the cab going Downtown.

"He's probably training a future President right now."

"Lou, I'm sorry I was such a pain in the ass on the subway."

"Those black dudes thought I was one lucky fellow. I'm sorry I hollered on you."

"And I'm sorry I hollered on you about Marva Burnside. It's just— Well, I don't see what's so terrible about getting your picture taken with Hitler."

"You don't, huh?" These were the times that fried men's soles. He reminded himself she was born after World War II and the Third Reich was probably in the same historical perspective for her as the French Revolution. Question: If Hitler had a Napoleonic complex, what kind of a complex did the Little Corsican have? Like his old friend Casey Stengel would say, look it up.

"It's guilt by association. I once had my picture taken with George Wallace. He was coming out of the Waldorf and I was going in and he bowed and let me by. Does that make me a bad person?"

He wasn't listening.

"Lou-oooooo!"

"Driver—start heading east."

"I thought we were going back to the hotel to *rest*—"

The cab continued toward the West Side, the driver leaden. Lou bellowed through the thick partition that prevented riders from boring drivers with suggestions. "Take us to Madison and Fifty-first—*Newsmagazine!*"

"The office? Why don't we go back to the hotel first—and then go by the office."

He pressed his fingers to her mouth. "Later, love. Best for last. Right now, I've got this feeling about Marva Burnside. Where the hell is Marva? Why the hell isn't she with her husband? And why the hell is he pussyfooting around Connie Michelin's office and following me around?"

"It's your aftershave," she purred. " '*Louuuuuuuu*—makes your skin tingle! *Louuuuuuuu*—makes you feel so good all over—' "

He laughed with delight and gathered her into his arms. "You're too much."

"I'd say I'm just right."

He kissed her with the sweet seriousness that cynics call banal. In that most banal of settings, the backseat of a New York taxi. "Remember what Bogie says to Ilsa?"

Jennie swooned against him. "When?"

"Upstairs in his apartment when she comes to him, he says, 'I'll do the thinking for both of us!' "

He could feel her body stiffen. She pushed him away. "Why are you doing this?"

The cab lurched to a stop in front of *Newsmagazine*. "To try to show you how things really are." He had been digging through his pockets. "I must have left my wallet at the hotel. Got any cash on you?"

There was a skeleton staff in the newsroom. Lou dialed Marva Burnside's Los Angeles number. "Marva Burnside, please."

"She's not here!" The maid's voice trembled.

"Is she out?"

"Not here."

"Out of town? Can you tell me where I can reach her?"

"Not here! Not here!"

"Is *Mr.* Burnside there?"

He could hear a murmur in the background. "Not here!" The phone went dead.

"I should have started looking for Marva Burnside sooner. Do you realize she hasn't been seen in public since before Dorrie's birthday party?"

The research files of *Newsmagazine* contained little on the Burnsides and nothing Lou did not know. Since Connie had started the magazine in 1962, the clippings and photographs only went back that far.

"Something's happened to Marva Burnside. Tom Jennings and Connie Michelin are somehow involved. Otherwise, why is Old Wingtips jumping out of the woodwork every time I look up? That's why they're putting up all that bread. To find out what I know. And to keep me from finding out what I don't know. Let's get back to the Algonquin."

"Oh, sure—" Jennie's mouth turned to prune.

"Not *that*. Don't worry, I'm not going to jump on your bones. I just have the feeling Old Wingtips may still be skulking around the lobby."

On their way to the night elevator, they passed Connie's private office. The door was open, the lights on. "She's here! Let's see what she has to say for herself."

The cleaning woman dropped her can of Lemon Pledge. "You scared me half to death!"

"Oh—you mean we're the first? Well, Jennie, why don't we just sit down and make ourselves comfortable till Ms. Michelin gets here."

"You didn't have to do that chipmunk talk!" Jennie said when the woman left. "She could care less. Her job is to clean the offices. She probably doesn't know who Connie Michelin is."

"That's where you're wrong," he said, locking the door. "That's how Deep Throat got started, disguised as a cleaning woman."

"You're cute."

"I know."

She raised her face to his and closed her eyes. "Kiss."

"No time."

"Always time. Kiss."

"Let me ask you something."

"Kiss first."

"You drive a hard bargain."

When he had complied with her request, she said, "Okay—"

"Just okay?"

"Okay, what did you want to ask me?"

"Oh—it's back to business, is it?"

"I thought that's why we're here."

"Okay. You're a woman. If you were going to hide something, where would you put it?"

"In your ear!"

"Jennie!"

"Okay. I'm sorry. You know where I always hide stuff when I travel?"

"You mean—"

"Money?—an emergency jay?"

"Where—no, don't tell me—"

"Where do you think—?"

"Oh, Jennie, please—not the old joke about hiding the covered wagon—"

"I'm serious! If you're going to be like that, I won't tell you."

"Please—tell me."

"In a Tampax box."

He made a face.

"See? Men are squeamish about Tampax. That includes customs inspectors—wouldn't touch it—afraid of a little cardboard and cotton—"

A mirrored door led to a private bathroom. "We'll give it a try." The lady apparently used a competing popular brand tampon. Her supply, however, did not share shelf space with any secrets.

"Look at this!" Jennie Bliss Sternholdt held out a heavily appliquéd lace Kleenex holder, the base of which was a distinctly uneven bulge. "This is either cardboard or she's got something here. Maybe stolen government bonds."

The sheaf of papers were Xerox copies of Marva Von Schmidt's 1937 diary. "Jennie, I love you. Let's get out of here."

"What does it say?"

"We're getting out of here before someone comes in."

"This is very exciting!" Jennie exulted.

She changed her mind back at the Algonquin when Lou refused to let her read the stolen pages. "It's a death warrant. That's why they killed her. They couldn't take a chance."

"Killed who? What are you talking about? Who wants to look at a dumb diary anyway?"

"Dorrie. She got the diary and that's why they killed her."

"Dorrie, Dorrie, *Dorrie*. I'm sick of her. Don't let me read it. What do I care." Before he could stop her, she snatched it from him and ripped it in half and in half again, leaping across the bed and evading his grasp. "I'm a human shredder. Now nobody can read it."

He caught her by the hair, twisted it in his fist, and then abruptly let go, shaking his head. "That's life—"

"Life is chance meetings and bad timing and waiting on the wrong corner and being in the shower when the phone rings —and being in love with a—necrophiliac!"

"Jennie—I'm a tired old man. Just leave me alone."

"I'm the best thing that ever happened to you. Remember how I found you that night at your hotel?"

"Nag, nag, nag, you're a fucking Mary Lincoln. All the way on the train to Gettysburg. 'Sit up straight, Abe. . . . Quit picking your nose, Abe. . . . Stop scribbling on that envelope while I'm talking to you, Abe. . . .' "

"Okay—you win. I give up." She set about repairing her makeup and hair. "I'll go quietly."

He lay on the bed and watched her. "It's for the best, you know."

"Are you going back to the princess?"

"Hell, no. Do I look like a moron? Don't answer that question."

"Is she a southern belle, too?"

"Who, the princess? No, strong New York stock once removed from the ghetto."

"I thought you had a thing for southern girls."

"You can't let it alone, can you? I told you, I never met Dorrie Bridges—"

"You mean you never got it together with one of those sugar-and-spice-everything-nice little-bitty old southern chicks?"

"Well—when I was younger— As a matter of fact, there was one girl. . . Can't even remember her name . . . Looked like Daisy Mae with clothes on. Came from somewhere in Kentucky, I think. Just as sweet as she could be—"

"And what happened to her?"

"How do I know? Hell, I must have been all of eighteen years old, working for a metropolitan newspaper, a real wisenheimer, freebies to movies and shows. Walter Winchell's baby brother! I had chicks coming out of the woodwork."

Her face crumpled.

"Jennie, Jennie—" He rocked her in his arms. "Don't go being jealous of girls I knew before you were born. I'm a tired old man. I'm the past, dying out like the dinosaur—" He ruffled her hair. "I learned to type on an Underwood upright. You are the future. Movies. Film. Electronics. Find yourself a nice—"

"Don't tell me what to find. I'll see you around."

"What are you going to do?" he called after her as she marched briskly down the hall.

"None of your fucking business."

When she'd gone, he stared at the empty space trying to figure out what to do next. He *was* a tired old man. The only sensible thing to do was go out and get drunk. He was sure to find some old chums at Burt Whitechapel's and maybe pick up some new leads on Dorrie Bridges. Jennie was right. He was obsessed. It was too late tonight to do anything more on Marva's diary. In any case, he'd have to be careful or he might wind up in a concrete overcoat himself.

This time when he crossed the Algonquin lobby, he did not see the wingtip shoes. That's because Norris Burnside had secluded himself in a corner armchair where he could keep his eye on the elevator. So intent was he on watching for Lou, he did not notice Jennie Bliss Sternholdt order herself a straight Campari no rocks at a nearby table.

A half hour and two drinks had gone by and she was still trying to figure out a way to pick up Norris Burnside without getting busted for soliciting when Tom Jennings dashed in. "Where is he?"

"He left a little while ago."

"Why didn't you follow him?"

"You told me to wait here."

"He's got the copies. We've got to find him!"

Not, Jennie decided, if she found him first. The obvious place was the home of his ex-wife the princess. Sure enough, she was listed. "Mr. Lou Dexter, please. Long distance is calling."

The sleepy female voice made her heart shrink. The bastard. There he was, back in Bitch Momma's bed. "He's not here."

"Are you sure?"

Movement, murmurs, and a male voice in a clear pique of *sexualis interruptus* said with curt precision, "Call back tomorrow." It was not Lou.

If not the boudoir of the princess, then where? Burt White-chapel's Third Avenue pub, Stodge, was the logical answer. Not only was Burt on Lou's Hot 30 list but Lou often talked with nostalgic affection about Stodge as the last authentic watering hole for the serious drinking newspaper crowd.

In contrast to Elaine's and Clarke's, Stodge was dim and musty, the long bar mirror blotched with age and yellowed clippings, the air sour with spilled beer and the wafts of disinfectant from the Gentlemen's. There was no jukebox, no TV, no tablecloths, no fancy food. And no Perrier.

Women were admitted by law but their status was defined by the absence of toilet paper and the broken lock in the Ladies'. Nor were there stools at the bar or convenient hooks to hang their coats. Here, women were the natural enemy, wives with dinners waiting on the table, girl friends needing abortions or fancy dentistry, "grasping creatures demanding to be fed or fucked or both," as one of the denizens had complained.

Burt Whitechapel himself, a transplanted cockney of Irish descent, liked to answer the phone. "Stodge. Whitechapel speaking."

"Is Lou Dexter there?"

The gentleman of that name stood a sparse three feet distant, playing the Match Game. *A woman!* Burt mouthed to him, indicating the phone. Lou was well on his way to a historic drunk. By happy chance, he had come upon old friends, real friends who had proved themselves friends when he was at his lowest. Lending him money. Putting free-lance assignments his way.

"I'm not here," he whispered with the martyred grin of all men on the run.

"Sorry, lovely. The lad doesn't seem to be here. Want to try back later, like a good girl?" A sharp outburst caused him to hold the phone away from his ear. "Dexter, lad," he laughed when he hung up, "you've got a rare bit of crumpet there. She told me to fuck myself."

All agreed that men were an endangered species. The women were getting smarter and stronger. "To all the beautiful birds!" Lou made the toast for the next round of drinks. "Drink up, you bastards!" he urged them affectionately.

Although they all surely knew about his brief sojourn with the *Insider,* it was against the rules to mention it unless he did.

"All the beautiful birds!"

"And a special toast to Dorrie Bridges!" Lou added, his eyes welling with bereavement. They were all looking at him but he couldn't help himself. His head hurt. He could feel himself swaying. A limited drinker at best, the weeks of California health had grossly affected his ability to store alcohol. "Come on, Burt. A toast to Dorrie Bridges." So saying, he tripped over his own foot and fell heavily against the bar.

"Friend, you've had a touch too much sun." The publican took him by the arm.

"I'm all right, perfectly all right." He grinned at all of them. "Ever see a one-eared elephant?" He emptied out his right pants pocket and placed the contents carefully on the bar before pulling out the pocket itself. "That's the elephant's ear!"

They were all watching intently.

"And this"—he unzipped his fly—"is the elephant's trunk!"

"Shit, mate, you'll give the joint a bad name!" Burt reassembled him.

"I thought Dorrie Bridges did that." Lou's voice was thick but impossible for Burt to ignore. At the height of terrorist activity in Belfast, Dorrie had revealed that Stodge was the New York depot for gun-running to the IRA.

"Easy now—"

Lou attempted to pull himself upright by grabbing Burt Whitechapel's lapels. "You—didn't—"

"That's a good lad—"

"You didn't—*hurt* her—"

"*Hurt* her?" He finally understood Lou's meaning. "You mean, because of that story? If she walked in here this minute, I'd stand her a bottle of French champagne. Those bastards were cheating me. Paying me half what they were getting instead of the deal we had made. Not gentlemen. Not gentlemen at all."

"Well, somebody got her. She was good. Honest." Lou lashed out at his amazed companions. "She wasn't a bird. She had more guts than all of us put together." He was being maudlin and he was fast losing his audience. "Don't you guys understand? We've got to find out what happened to her— Listen to me— It's not just another story. It's a precious human being—"

"Lou Dexter, of all people!" A hearty newcomer seized Lou in a bear hug. "Haven't seen this ole boy in a month of Sundays." Tom Jennings exaggerated his Nashville drawl. "Doesn't look too good to me," he told Burt. "I've got my car outside. Maybe I'd just better take him on home before he gets himself into real trouble."

Lou's eyes focused on the newcomer like a five-dollar camera. "T-Tom Jennings—?" He tried to ward him off.

"Come on, Lou. Time to go on home."

"See you, Lou!" His peers closed ranks for the next round of the Match Game.

"Wait—just a minute—"

"It's all right, ole buddy. Just a mite too much white lightning."

"Where—where we going?"

The black richmobile waited at the curb, the chauffeur at the ready. Norris Burnside held the back door open. "You found him."

"What's left of him. Help me get him in."

A taxi lumbered to a halt. "Lou—wait up—! Where you going?" Jennie Bliss Sternholdt shrieked across the pavement, shrewish and unattractive, she knew. By this time she didn't care. She pushed Tom Jennings aside and leaned into the cavernous backseat. "Get out of there this instant. You're coming with me!"

A slight shove and she was inside the car. The door slammed behind her. "I'm afraid it's you who must come with us."

Lou made a valiant attempt to grin. "Don't worry, Kid. Nobody gets the best of Fred C. Dobbs."

On this, her thirtieth birthday, Dorrie Bridges lay out on her porch swing staring at the western sky and trying to make the most important decision of her life. The phone call she had dreaded had just come through from Berlin. All the facts in the diary had checked out. Her heart was so heavy she could not move.

Since the terrible meeting with Marva, Dorrie had flown secretly to Germany, England, and Washington, D.C., look-

■ JEANNIE SAKOL

ing at records and comparing them to the dates and places in the diary. The passenger list of the final fatal journey of the *Hindenburg* did not include the Von Schmidts. Unfortunately, this morning's call from a Berlin stringer confirmed that they were on a preliminary list, now deep in the microfilmed file, and had apparently been dropped from the final list when they canceled their reservation.

As for the diary itself, it was printed by Frank Smythson in London. A personal visit to their New Bond Street offices confirmed its authenticity as a popular pre-War style. The handwriting checked out as being written with an old-fashioned nibbed fountain pen in ordinary Sheaffer Script ink. The date was something else. As in the Howard Hughes case, the experts did not agree. One judged the writing as recent as last month; another that it was definitely between 1935 and 1940.

Sweet Jesus, what in *hell* was she going to do? She was between the rock and the hard place. Much as she loved and trusted Tom Jennings, she couldn't bring herself to confide in him. Andrew could only be trusted to a point and this was well beyond it. Jim Ed was too far away and in the clutches of that English girl. She didn't know if they had tied the knot and didn't want to know either.

What she really needed was the sound and reasoned advice of an experienced reporter. Someone like Mike Wallace. Or Lou Dexter. Dexter, if she had the choice. Dexter seemed to be a man whose heart ruled his head, if that whole Russian incident was an example. She could still see the obstinate set of his jaw in the official Soviet photos of the trial. The absurdity of the affair was matched only by the viciousness of his captivity and subsequent expulsion. Caught in the woods near the village of Koptyaki with a sack of bones, jewelry, and scraps of clothing, he had been accused of conspiring with Sonya Boris to discredit the revolutionary honor of the Soviet Union.

Dexter's plot, they contended, was sponsored by international fascists and Jewry. The bones would be revealed as those of the Romanovs, Czar Nicholas II and the entire family, including the evanescent Anastasia with proof that they had been brutally incarcerated for twenty years in a foul and secret dungeon near where they had supposedly been thrown down a mine shaft in the summer of 1918.

At the trial Dexter had stubbornly denied everything but his name and professional credentials. In a superb example of throwing their own brand of double-think back at them, he steadfastly insisted he had never been to Sverdlovsk, that he had never met Sonya Boris, and that the photographs of them in bed and emerging from her car in the heart of the Urals were Soviet deceptions using impersonators and trick photography.

She had always wanted to meet the man. Her gut instinct was that she could trust him not to spill the beans. What would he do in her situation? she wondered. He had sounded real nice on the phone the other day, the poor thing, pretending like it was a big assignment to be getting a birthday quote for *The Weekly Insider*.

And that was another thing that was bothering her, allowing herself to be given a birthday party like she was the Queen of Rumania or something. It wasn't fitting to have a birthday party this size at the age of thirty. If she ever reached sixty was more like it, or better yet, a hundred and forty-seven.

It had been her intention to keep the festivities small but the diary had occupied her every waking moment and a lot of restless dreams besides. Now everything was coming to a head at the same time. Her birthday party was tonight, Lord help her, with her hair a mess and nothing to wear. The proofs about Marva Burnside's diary lay before her, demanding she take some action.

If she were really the ruthless barracuda everyone said she was, the time to break the story was right now, in time for the morning edition of the paper that would be delivered to Ma Raison at the height of the birthday fun.

It was a life-and-death operation. She desperately needed a second opinion. Marva? Since the terrible day Dorrie showed her the diary, Marva had dropped from sight. She refused to take Dorrie's calls and canceled out of all social and cultural events at which she might run into Dorrie.

Evidently Marva was keeping her own counsel, too. From what Dorrie could gather, Norris knew nothing. "What's happened to you, Dorrie? Why haven't you come over for Sunday afternoon?" he chided her one day when she phoned and he answered.

"I've been—out of the country—busy-busy—"

"You coming this Sunday?"

"Well—" she had said. Excuses did not come easily.

"What's happened between you two? Have a little tiff or something?"

"Now, Norris, don't be silly—"

"Listen, I'm going to get the two of you in a room and knock your heads together if you won't kiss and make up. I don't care what happened. It can't be as bad as all that."

It was. It was worse than bad. The mysterious woman with the husky voice had called again, demanding to know when Dorrie was going to break the story. "What's holding you back, Dorrie? Scared?"

"Not scared, ma'am. Careful."

Late last night, the woman said, "This is the last time I'm calling. I'm giving you fair warning. You have forty-eight hours to release the story. After that, I'll give it to someone else."

Absurdly, life went on. It was her birthday, after all. Gifts and messages of congratulations were pouring in. Momma had sent her up a hand-embroidered tablecloth-and-napkin set and an angel food cake. Tom, a bouquet of thirty-one yellow roses and a slender gold bangle. Jim Ed, a noncommittal card "To Someone Special" and signed "with affection."

From Glitz there was a purple scarf, a pass-along that she had received from someone else. Glitz had forgotten that she had shown it to Dorrie. One of these days, Dorrie planned to rewrap one of Glitz's gifts and give it back to her.

The thought cheered her, but not much. She rolled herself a cigarette from the Tiffany box and tried to concentrate on the alternatives. If she broke the story, she would kill Marva Burnside as surely as if she stuck a knife in her heart. If she didn't, somebody else would. She turned on the radio. Gershwin's "American in Paris" made her think of the Champs Elysees and the way it looked at dusk walking from the Tuileries all the way to the Étoile. She had never had time to wander aimlessly through Paris, never the luxury to simply let things happen. In truth, she had never in all her thirty years had a real vacation with no deadlines and no demands.

The announcer's voice penetrated her thoughts. ". . . really big news for all you Gershwin fans . . ." She thought of Marva. " . . . a Gershwin retrospective . . . six hours of Gershwin genius coming your way including the original-cast recording of *Porgy and Bess* . . ." Marva had that in her collection. ". . . Considering the scope of his creativity and the enormity of his output, it's hard to believe he was only thirty-eight years old when he died on July eleventh, 1937 . . ."

July 11, 1937.

The date did a pirouette before her eyes, demanding her attention. There was something about it that wasn't right. July 11, 1937? She leapt to her feet with a cry of excitement. It was strangely, crazily *kickass wrong!* "Thank you, Jeee-sus!" she shouted at the morning sky. It had been there all along, the single error, the time-honored goof that traditionally—culturally—saved the good guys from the schemes of the bad guys.

According to the diary, Adolf Hitler mentioned the death of said George Gershwin in May of 1937, a good two months before it happened! She opened her mouth and whooped a joyful sound unto the Lord. She capered and strutted up and down the length of the porch, patting whatever came to hand, lounge chairs, the glass table, gardenia plants, and lemons and the old chinaberry trees.

The breath she had been holding tight inside her chest since her first encounter with the mystery woman was now released in long and vocal sighs. "Ahhhhhhhhhhhhh . . . oh, Marva, we'll find out who did it . . . ahhhhhhhhhhhhhh . . . who'd want to hurt you like that. . . ."

With a sudden voracious hunger, she fixed herself a peanut butter and mayonnaise sandwich on white toast and dialed the Burnsides' number. It was early but she couldn't wait a moment longer. What a birthday this was going to be, after all. *Marva, you'll have to come to the phone, darlin'!* There was no answer. Could she have misdialed? She tried again. *Answer the phone!* Her impatience was unbearable. At last she heard the receiver being picked up. Nobody said hello.

"Hello, hello, Marva?" She was laughing and crying at the same time. "Norris? It's me, Dorrie—I've got to talk to you."

A dead pause, a click, and the dial tone. Whoever it was had hung up. "Marva! Oh, God—" She had to see her friend at once, see her and figure out how to trap the mystery woman and find out what she had against Marva.

Tailgating and lane-switching through the rush hour, Dorrie couldn't remember taking the elevator to the garage or getting into her car. She looked down at her feet. She was barefoot. She looked at herself in the mirror. Uncombed. A scarecrow with a California tan and a glob of peanut butter stuck to the roof of her mouth. Fear gripped her hands to the wheel. *Marva!* If anything happened to Marva, it was Dorrie's fault.

"Marva!" She ran barefoot up the sharp gravel path and up

the tiled steps to the carved Spanish door. "Marva!" The door was locked. She rang and pounded as if the house were on fire. "Let me in! Marva, please!"

She ran around to the kitchen door, peering in windows as she went. "Marva! Where are you? I've got to see you. To explain."

The back of the house was as quiet as the rest. The house was empty and locked up. Something was wrong. She was about to turn away when she saw the kitchen curtains flutter. "Let me in or I'll break the door down!"

A pervasive silence, the sound of a bolt being pulled, and the door opened a crack. "Nobody home," Maria said.

"Where is Mrs. Burnside? I've got to see her. Where is she?"

Maria burst into tears. "Not home."

"Please. For God's sake. Where is she?"

"Dead." The door slammed shut, the bolt restored.

It couldn't be. "Please—what happened—when—tell me, please—where are they? Sweet Jesus—"

She could think of nothing to do but return home. She called every hospital in the Greater Los Angeles area. If Marva Burnside were in one of them, it was under an assumed name. Next, she checked all the best mortuaries, Protestant and nondenominational, without satisfaction, before calling the Coroner's Office, where all deaths in Los Angeles County, natural and otherwise, were reported.

There was no hint of a corpse answering to the name of either Burnside or Von Schmidt, or even the pedestrian Schmidt. While it was possible to stay at a hospital under an assumed name, death certificates required honesty.

If Marva was dead, it was Dorrie's fault. Whatever the cause—a heart attack, pills, or outright suicide—it was Dorrie who killed her friend. The memory of their last meeting scalded her eyes with hot tears. How could she have said those things to Marva? Big head was right. Truth above personal considerations? Truth more important than love or friendship? Thinking of what Marva must have gone through these last few weeks, expecting the ax to fall any minute, made Dorrie physically ill.

While she was trying to figure out what to do next, more birthday gifts arrived. A chocolate Monopoly set which cost six hundred dollars sent by Neiman-Marcus. A sterling-silver fortune cookie containing a paper fortune that read "The next thirty years will be better yet" from the New China Trade Association.

"Flowers. Cables. Mailgrams. Champagne. What do you want me to do with it all?" Andrew Van Kennan had come upstairs from his office. She could tell from his expression that he was startled by her appearance but was too polite to say so.

"Later, Andrew."

"But, Dorrie. We've got a million things to do before tonight. Next week's taping schedule. The lecture dates. Chuck Keaton wants you to call—"

"Later! Don't you understand English? I said *later!*"

She was sorry. She hated to be rude. Courteous behavior was the linchpin of civilized society. But sometimes the man drove her bananas. That condescending look on his face. The snide disapproval of her personal tastes. She could still laugh at the thought of his embarrassment when she dished up the fried chicken dinner for Begin and Sadat. "It's insulting to them!" he had objected. The two Middle Eastern leaders had swallowed the insults and followed her lead by wiping up the gravy with their biscuits.

She had to be alone. She had to think. Something terrible had happened to Marva Burnside. She had done all she could to find out what it was. Now all she could do was wait.

She would spend the day at her beach house. Little more than a shack, it stood in stark isolation on a tiny spit of land up the coast past Trancas. What she liked best about the house was it could not be reached by car. People couldn't use the excuse of just being in the neighborhood to drop in. They had to know precisely where to turn off the Pacific Highway and how to find the hidden footpath through the tangled scrub.

Once she had come there with Sonny, but he didn't feel comfortable. It was too primitive for him. No electricity. No phone. No indoor plumbing except for a single water line. Mostly she liked being there alone with the panoramic sight of the sea to soothe her eyes and the sound of the surf to calm her mind.

"Don't forget. Your party starts at eight," Andrew reminded her when she told him she was taking the day off.

"Don't worry. I'll get a little sun, a little sleep. By the way—"

"What can I do you for?" Andrew was being charming again.

"Has Marva phoned? Or Norris? I couldn't get an answer when I phoned."

"They sent champagne, same as last year."

Dorrie had to fight to keep her voice casual. "Well, if Marva should call, tell her I can't wait to see her. Tell her I've got something very important to tell her."

"Something important?" Andrew was dying to know what it was.

"Never you mind. She'll know what I mean."

It was midafternoon and Dorrie Bridges was sitting in the sun, counting her toes, and wishing she could play the harmonica and that she had one with her. She needed the mournful sound of pain and loss as she thought about her life and tried to work out where she had gone wrong.

Oh, Grandpa! A big gray seabird had come to rest on the Chris Craft that lay on its side on the beach. The bird seemed to be looking straight at her. "Oh, Grandpa—"

"Pride goeth before destruction and a haughty spirit before a fall." The old man's words from the Book of Proverbs

seemed to be coming from the bird. She had been proud and she had been haughty. *Grandpa?* Had he come to help her in her time of tribulation? Or was this the winged Death come to release her from her misery?

The rays of the sun bounced off the ocean in dazzling prisms of light, distorting her vision so that she did not see Norris Burnside until he touched her hand.

As kidnappings went, Lou Dexter gave this one high marks. It was courteous. It was amiable. It was cushioned in comfort and luxury. No blindfold creasing his eyeballs. No stiletto up his nose threatening terminal sinusitis. No tutti-frutti rag stuffed in his mouth or gun in his gut. Or the problems of personal hygiene in a locked closet.

This time, as the adrenaline of fear cleared the bourbon from his brain, he could see this was clearly a first-class abduction. With a tense and silent Jennie Bliss Sternholdt beside him in the backseat of the limousine, he waited for the two men on the facing jump seats to speak. The curtains were drawn but his New York body was well enough attuned to the New York streets to feel them swing onto the East Side Drive heading north, an instinct that was confirmed when the heavy vehicle veered left and up a ramp, rounding a ninety-degree curve to the Triborough Bridge and stopping exactly where he expected a stop to pay the toll.

A bit further along, at the point where a left turn meant The Bronx and potentially New England, they turned right, toward the borough of Queens and the two New York City airports.

"What kind of a plane do you have?" Lou took a chance.

"An Aero Commander," Norris Burnside replied. "I think you'll find it comfortable."

"Where are we going?" Jennie demanded.

"It's like taking a Bengal tiger for a walk, kiddo; we're going wherever they take us. Although," he appealed to Tom Jennings, "as a southern gentleman, you realize Miss Sternholdt has nothing to do with this. Why don't we just go wherever it is we're going and send her home in a cab?"

"I have no objection to that—"

"Well, I do!" Jennie clutched Lou's arm. "I'm your woman and I'm sticking with you. 'Whither thou goest, I will go,' just like in the Bible."

"You've got it wrong."

"It's in the *Bible*. 'Whither thou goest—' "

"Yes, but it's not a woman saying it to a man. It's Ruth saying it to Naomi. To her mother-in-law. It's not romantic—"

"Well, I don't care. Whither thou is going, I am going—and don't either of you try to put me in a cab! I'm warning you."

The Aero Commander was ready and waiting for takeoff on a deserted runway some distance from the brightly lit commercial area. The interior was the jet age equivalent of the private railroad car for industrialists of an earlier time. They entered a heavily paneled and carpeted sitting room furnished with deep sofas, desk, dining area, and a communications cupboard discreetly housing phones, telex, ticker tape, and a miniature electric typewriter.

"Perhaps you would be more comfortable in here." Norris Burnside conducted them past the galley, where a steward was at work, to another compartment. "I think it will be best if I lock you in. Please ring when you require some refreshment. Sanders will be ready with some food shortly."

The President of the United States could not have had a more comfortable bedroom on *Air Force One*. The broad bed was covered in a handsome geometric design with matching curtains on the windows. There were two armchairs facing each other across a round table, storage built-ins, and a bathroom with stall shower.

"Oh, Lou—what's going to happen?"

The plane was beginning to move. The FASTEN SEAT BELT sign flashed on and off. "Oh, they'll probably take us a hundred miles out to sea and dump us."

"In the *water*—" All that was woman disappeared from her face, leaving behind the wide-eyed panic of the child.

"Jennie—stop that. I was only kidding." He sat down in one of the armchairs and indicated the other to her. "Fasten your seat belt."

"I'll sit with you." She sat herself in his lap and fastened the belt across them. "What a time to regress. Do I remind you of your daughter?"

He held her tight against him. "No you do not."

"That's good."

"My daughter is sexier than you—"

The plane stopped taxiing.

"Something's up."

"Maybe it's the police."

There were sounds they could not identify, some flashing lights Lou thought might be a car's headlights, and then they were moving again faster and faster until the cabin tipped upward and they were soaring into the night sky.

"This is what you get for chasing old men," he whispered into the small of her neck.

"I wasn't chasing old men. I was looking for you. To warn you."

"About what?"

"About—them! When I left you—I was so goddam mad—and then I got downstairs and there was Norris in the corner pretending he wasn't watching the elevator so I thought he probably doesn't know me so I sat down at a nearby table to see what he was doing. And then you came down—"

"You were in the cocktail lounge—"

"And then Tom Jennings ran in and said you found the copy and they had to find you and then I thought you were probably at the Stodge so I called you and they said you weren't there!"

"Don't you know better than to call a man at a bar? It's boys' rules. They always say he just left."

"I didn't know you were still a boy. I thought you were a man! If you had taken my call, we wouldn't be in this mess!"

Lou's mind was on the diary. "What I can't figure out is what was Connie Michelin doing with a Xerox copy of the diary? A diary I did not have a chance to examine more closely—"

"I'm sorry, Lou. Really. I shouldn't have torn it up—"

"If Marva Burnside married Hitler, then that's the big story Dorrie was chasing down when she—disappeared. She must have gotten ahold of that diary and it must have been with her at Trancas."

"Maybe it burned up in the fire."

"Or maybe the killer took it—"

"But Marva and Norris Burnside were Dorrie Bridges's best friends! Did they kill her to keep her quiet?"

Gently unseating her from his lap, Lou began to pace in the

confined space. "That diary could destroy their lives. Just the hint of a sexual association much less a marriage with the most depraved monster of the century—can't you just see the banner headlines, the television news, *People, New York, New West*—they'd be hounded to death—"

"But Tom Jennings was Dorrie's oldest friend. He discovered her. Remember what he said at the memorial service? He loved her. He couldn't be involved in her murder—"

"Maybe he wasn't involved in her death but he's heavily involved with the Burnside interests. I did a little probing there and I discovered Tom Jennings is planning to run for governor of the state of Tennessee, backed by—"

"—Norris Burnside. But what about Connie Michelin? Where does she fit in?"

"Connie is Tom's old friend, too. Remember that Tom sent Dorrie to *Newsmagazine*. That's where she first hit the big time with the Pia Melanaiki piece and the Toni Dean exposé. And Connie never forgave her for leaving. Connie's lost her touch. *Newsmagazine* is in trouble. Losing circulation and advertising. The last issue was so thin you could see through it. She's a bitter old broad and I've heard stories about her bad-mouthing Dorrie, telling anyone who'd listen she taught Dorrie everything she knows and what an ungrateful bitch she was—"

"You think Connie was involved, too?"

"Maybe not with the murder. But involved. I've been thinking about it all. Trying to put the pieces together. The way I see it is the Burnsides found out that Dorrie had somehow got this diary. They—or maybe just Norris—found her alone at the beach house. With the diary. They—disposed of her and the diary. And then I come along, putting together the puzzle of Dorrie's death—and they get worried maybe I'll find out about the diary—"

"That's why Connie offers you a book contract. So they can find out what you found out—"

"But what's she doing with a copy of the diary?"

"Maybe—" An idea was forming in Jennie's mind.

"What—please—anything—"

"Maybe she didn't know it was in her dressing room. I always used to hide stuff in my mother's dressing table."

"Maybe that's it. Maybe they went to her and offered to back her in a book-publishing venture starting with a book about Dorrie Bridges—"

"Maybe you're right and maybe they thought Connie's office was the safest place to hide the copy—"

"I don't know. That part doesn't ring true. If only I could talk to Connie—"

A rap on the door announced Sanders the steward. "A light supper," he said, rolling a laden cart into the room.

"We'll serve ourselves, thank you," Lou said, ushering him out.

"Why'd you do that? If this is our last meal, I'd like it to be in style."

"I thought I saw someone when he came in. I wanted to get the door open again and fast before she moved."

"She?"

"Connie Michelin is in the other compartment. That must be why we stopped."

He tried the door. It was locked. He looked out the window. "Well, I don't think they're going to dump us in the ocean. It looks like mountains down there."

"Which ones?"

"How the hell do I know?"

"Well, up yours, too." She pushed aside a plate of sandwiches untouched. "I'm not hungry." She threw herself across the bed facedown.

"I'm sorry, Jen. I really don't know which mountains they are—"

"So what? So you don't know! So you're all hung up about a man is supposed to know everything. A walking encyclopedia. You're always talking about shelves, how you can't put up shelves. How your wife the princess keeps wanting you to put up shelves. You're really guilty as hell because you really do think you should be able to do everything and know everything—like you're biting my head off because you don't know what mountains they are. What's the difference? You think I love you because you know everything?"

Her face was in the bed covering. He could not hear her crying but he could see her heaving shoulders.

"Jennie?" he whispered, sitting gingerly on the edge of the bed.

Her shoulders continued their silent convulsion.

"Jennie, please—" With awkward movements, as if his hands were connected to his arms with rusty bolts, he patted her back several times before taking her by the shoulders to turn her over. "Please don't cry, darling—"

With an abrupt movement, she flipped over on her back and pulled him down on top of her. "Gotcha!" Her arms and legs clamped him tight to her body in an outburst of triumph. "Fooled you. Now, you're mine, mine, *mine!*"

He was as helpless as a fly in the arms of a spider. A feeble struggle and then he lay limp. "Please—" he gasped.

"Mine—" She bounced them on the bed. "Mine, all *mine.*"

"Don't, Jennie—I'm not kidding—I can't breathe—"

A wary pause. "Lou?"

"—You!" he croaked, barely audible.

Her tentacles relaxed. Her loving hands crawled to his face. "You okay? What is it, darling—?" This Florence Nightingale phase of their relationship was short-lived. The sweet hands poised to give succor were seized by the wrists and forced back flat on the bed. "What are you doing?"

From his dominant position high in the straddle, Lou Dexter smiled. "If you don't know, then maybe I'm not doing it right. What movie is that from and who said it to whom. Get that, *whom?*"

"Fuck you."

"Oh, come now. I thought you were such a movie buff. For a year's supply of kosher dog food, who said that? I'll give you a hint. He's in an elevator with her and he kisses her." He demonstrated. "And then she says, 'What're you doing?'" He did his best to mimic the breathy belligerence of Judy Holliday in *Born Yesterday*.

"William Holden in *Born Yesterday*. Let me up. You don't play fair."

"What man plays fair? If only I could disabuse you of that notion, you've be a happy, well-adjusted woman."

She mouthed the ever popular "Fuck you!" and made a production of closing her eyes and mouth tight shut, locking him out.

"What? What was that?"

The angry mouth repeated the earlier message.

"You really must learn to speak up." He trembled the tip of his tongue across her zipped lips. "Come on, Sweet Lips. No pouting. Gimme tongue. Come on. *Gimme*. Just a little. That's a good girl—"

She opened just wide enough to say, "I don't like this movie."

"What movie?"

"This movie. The one we're doing now. You're directing it the way you want to direct it. I want something new. I want a new kind of movie."

"There is no new kind of movie. Everything that's ever happened in the history of the world was a movie. *Beowulf* was the first art movie. Homer the Great Blind Bard—in his vision, *The Odyssey* was one hell of a movie! And what about Christianity, the longest running movie of all time, right? A cast of millions.

"Listen to me, Jennie. You're working your butt off to be a movie director, right?"

She nodded.

"Can't you see, we're all movie directors. All of what we know of the great universe is just one long, continuing motion picture. We all write, direct, produce, star, and—"

The plane banked severely, rolling them off the bed. The

FASTEN SEAT BELTS light was flashing. They crawled to the armchairs and strapped themselves in. Pale morning light seeped through the windows on the left side. "We're heading south," Lou explained. "Assuming the sun still rises in the east."

The small airfield looked like graham crackers as dawn spilled over the easternmost mountain ridges and washed across the broad valley like a flood of pink lemonade. Lou Dexter's earliest conditioning to nature was a fusion of the Museum of Natural History and F.A.O. Schwarz. Whereas the museum and the toy store interpreted nature in specific and prejudiced ways, they were his first impressions and therefore the bases for comparison when later in life he encountered the real thing.

Foreign travel had muted but not totally erased this subliminal feeling that a Bloomingdale's window designer or Disneyland genius had done the Grand Canyon or laid out the Cotswolds or trucked in all that grass-by-the-yard and china cows and chocolate chalets to Switzerland.

He had been teasing Jennie Bliss Sternholdt, but as often happened, the thought was the father of the truth. In certain absolute ways, he did believe the world was a motion picture. To be a movie director meant trying to exert some passing control over the story of your life and the roles you played. That was why so many people Jennie's age were into directing. In his generation the newsman was the movie director, creating the daily drama of events according to a preconceived scenario based on personal criteria of good and bad.

In the fifties and sixties, the foreign correspondent was by style and definition a movie star, a loner-philosopher searching the Hemingway-tinted world for truth, adventure, and the company of good comrades and soft women. As this movie began to lose its audience, the 1970s remake began with Dorrie Bridges as the leading superstar, the multimedia personality committed to truth but with one basic difference.

From all he had discovered about Dorrie Bridges, the single

characteristic that set her apart from him was this: she was totally without sentimentality. She was direct. She was honest. She kept her word. She told things as she saw them and let the shits fall where they may. Nowhere, he realized, was there a sentimental weakness such as the one that brought him to grief with Sonya Boris.

Truth was her god and her religion. In that sense, perhaps she had died in that fire like Joan of Arc or in some equally painful manner at the hands of someone less attracted to sacrifice.

Set in forest-green velvet bolsters was a blue mirror lake, its perfect manicured shores disrupted by a vast stone house and dock. Moored for the night were boats of various sizes, power and sail, and a candy-striped seaplane.

"Do I look all right?" Jennie asked.

"Very young and very pretty." Without makeup and with her face fresh-scrubbed and with only his kisses to activate the capillary dance, she looked more lovely and more lovable than he had ever seen her.

Tom and Norris had merely nodded before leading the way to the house. Connie was not to be seen.

"Nice place. Who lives here?" Lou addressed their retreating backs.

"You'll see," Tom said.

The path led along the fence separating two fields through a clump of trees behind the house.

"A graveyard!" Jennie signaled him with her elbow. Three neat rows of headstones glistened with dew.

"Why would they wait to get us here to kill us? They could have dumped us anywhere, right?"

"Look at that window, Lou."

A hand holding a steaming mug raised it to a face hidden in shadow.

Parked on the side of the house were vehicles ranging from Jeeps and Hondas to a weathered old pickup. "Tennessee,"

Lou said. "We must be in Tennessee. All the license plates are Tennessee."

"So? They could have done it to trick us." Jennie grinned at him. She was beginning to feel better. Maybe they could slip out and swim to freedom across the lake. Maybe she could seduce the steward and get him to call the authorities.

The front of the house was one enormous room furnished in chintz and wicker and light woods, with a fireplace tall enough for a man to stand in and wide enough to spit-roast a calf. The remains of the night's fire glowed. Norris Burnside signaled them to stay where they were. He tiptoed to the hearth and carefully poked the embers before adding two fresh logs.

The illumination revealed a woman asleep in a mound of pillows on a wide davenport. He knelt beside her and kissed her hand. "We're back, dear."

It must be Marva Burnside. According to that diary, the first Frau Hitler. Lou tried to envisage what this frail and sickly woman must have looked like in 1937 at the Berghof.

"Would you-all care for some coffee? I've got some nice hot cornbread, fresh out of the oven." A plump pretty woman in a pink double knit pants suit with matching pink plastic bracelets and necklace stood in the kitchen door.

"Thanks, Mallie dear, we'll have it right here beside the fire." Marva's voice had the old-money ring of authority.

"We don't want to tire you," Tom Jennings said.

The invalid looked past him and her husband to Lou and Jennie. "Those two are the ones looking tired to me. Come closer. You must be Lou Dexter."

"At your service—"

"And the young woman? Norris, you didn't mention a young woman."

"This is Jennie Bliss Sternholdt, a young filmmaker." Lou did the honors, suddenly sorry that he had not sent her home in a cab.

"I—" Sick or not, the woman had a talent for getting everyone's attention. "I—am Marva Burnside." She smiled wanly at Lou. "Sit by me. Perhaps I should have said I am Marva Von Schmidt Burnside."

"It's a privilege to meet you, Mrs. Burnside. You've given much happiness and help to other people. Museums. Concerts. Hospitals—"

"Summer camps. Canteens for senior citizens—" Norris Burnside's pride could not be contained.

"You're a famous writer, Mr. Dexter." Marva ignored the tributes.

"A writer—" Lou protested modestly.

"Writing a book, I hear."

"Gathering the material for it."

"It appears that I am a writer, too—"

"Is that so—?"

"It appears that I was a child prodigy. That I wrote a diary—" Her voice broke. Perspiration drenched her face. She fell back in the pillows.

"Marva—" Norris rubbed her hands.

"It's all right. It's the hot coffee. Lou, I have a question for you."

"And I have a question for you."

"You know about my diary?"

Lou nodded.

"You've seen the contents, I understand."

"Only the Xerox copy I found in Connie's office and that my friend here tore to shreds." Jennie stuffed a whole corn muffin in her mouth. Lou turned to Norris Burnside. "What I want to know is what the hell was Connie Michelin doing with it? How did she get the copy?"

Tom sighed. "We gave it to her. We needed her help. She's an old and trusted friend and experienced news executive. We hoped she could help us find out who would perpetrate this obscene hoax."

"Is it a hoax?" Lou asked.

"That's what we were hoping you would be able to prove. That's why we asked Connie to commission your book—"

"Wait a minute. Just one minute. First I want to know where Connie Michelin is. She was on the plane, wasn't she?"

"How—?" Norris stammered in amazement.

"She's here?" Marva demanded. "You know I can't bear that woman!"

"That's why we suggested she might want to have a little rest in the guesthouse." Norris appealed to his wife for understanding.

Tom explained that when he called her to say Lou had found the copy and they were taking him to the Jennings country estate in Tennessee, Connie had insisted on coming, too.

"Which leads me to my question," Lou said.

The kitchen door swung open. The woman returned with fresh coffee. There was something about her that was very familiar, as if he had met her somewhere before. On the other hand, with her small even features, despite the double chin, she looked like every friendly overripe waitress he had ever seen.

"Where is Dorrie Bridges?"

The tray fell to the floor. "Sweet Jesus!" Mallie Bridges left the mess where it was and fled to the kitchen.

"You killed her!" Jennie Bliss Sternholdt cried in a fine fury. Norris threw himself across his wife as if to protect her from a hail of bullets. Tom Jennings leapt to his feet as if electrocuted. All Lou Dexter could do was age twenty years in a single moan. "Jen-nieeee." If this woman were ever a diplomat, say hello to World War III.

"I don't care. I'm tired of all this. Dorrie Bridges. Dorrie Bridges. Morning, noon, and night. She's in my life. She's in my bed. She's in my hair. She's old news now. Nobody cares what happened to her except him. He's got to find out what happened. He won't rest till he knows, and if he can't rest, I can't rest. So, for God's sake, what happened? Is Dorrie Bridges dead?"

In the ensuing hush, the figures in the room froze, as if posing for a group portrait like the signing of the Declaration of Independence or the Marines raising Old Glory on Iwo Jima.

"Yes. Dorrie Bridges is dead—" The soft, caressing voice drifted across the room from the open kitchen door like fresh bread baking. "In a manner of speaking, that is—"

"Dorrie—?" Lou's voice trembled.

"Momma just told me we're having visitors." With her sorrel hair grown long and hanging loose around her shoulders and the faded Bibs and Fruit of the Loom T-shirt, she could have passed for near half of her thirty years. "You must be Lou Dexter. I'm proud to make your acquaintance."

Like a drowning man, Lou's lifetime experiences of women flashed through his mind. Women had always made him clumsy. On his first adolescent date he had put his elbow in the ketchup and knocked over a strawberry malted. On his suede shoes. That first Moscow morning with Sonya Boris he was singing with such erotic abandon that he squeezed hair cream on his toothbrush. Worst of all was the time his ex-wife the princess screamed threats at him through the bathroom door that so rattled him, he zipped the tip of his tie into his fly and had to be cut out of his hunched-over predicament.

Finding Dorrie Bridges alive and well was like none of the above. Or even all of the above. In the multiple-choice testings of his emotions, this was something entirely new. He could not think. He could only feel a wild exultation. "You're alive!" He took her by the hands and whirled her around. "Alive! I can't believe it."

"Please—" Her cheeks cherry-red from the exertion, she broke free and sat herself down with Marva. "I have to see to my patient."

"I'm fine, dear. Better every day," Marva assured them all.

"Dorrie—" Lou could feel Jennie's eyes on him and he knew he must be hurting her feelings but he couldn't help himself. Maybe she had been right all along. Maybe it was *Laura* all over again. Maybe he had fallen in love with a dead woman and here she was alive. He had lusted for Gene Tierney and envied Dana Andrews. Maybe the same thing was happening to him—

"Dora June, if you don't mind. Dorrie died in that fire."

"Tell me, for God's sake. Tell me what happened."

Marva had collapsed from nervous exhaustion and made Norris promise to tell nobody, not even Dorrie. "She said she didn't want to jeopardize the fund-raising for the hospital and all the other charities she was involved in." He shook his fist at her with mock anger. "She didn't tell me word one about the diary. Kept it all to herself. No wonder she couldn't sleep. Crying fits. Dropping hot coffee all over herself. Finally, she said let's go up to Big Sur—we've got a little house there— and then when Maria found her unconscious on the bathroom floor—"

"It was all my fault. I'll never forgive myself as long as I live," Dorrie sighed.

Norris picked up the narrative. "Maria was so hysterical, I had the chauffeur take her back to Beverly Hills. To her, anyone unconscious is dead. Marva came around quickly, and that's when she told me about the diary and Dorrie."

Marva continued. "I wanted to see Dorrie. I knew she wouldn't hurt me. I knew she'd been doing everything possible to find out who perpetrated this terrible thing."

Norris had called Dorrie and learned she was at the beach house. There being no phone, he had flown his little Piper Super Cub seaplane down the coast to get her.

"Marva needs you!" he had assured the frightened young woman. "Don't say a thing. She's told me everything."

They were aboard the tiny plane and making their ascent

for the return trip to Big Sur when Dorrie saw smoke and flames coming from her house. "I remembered having a pot of coffee on the kerosene stove. Maybe the kitchen curtains caught fire. We'll never know."

Norris flew in low. Within seconds the small edifice exploded like a tinderbox. Norris flew out across the water in a wide circle and prepared to land. "No, it's too late," Dorrie had told him. That was when the idea of disappearing for a while had come to her.

"For one thing,"—she grinned as she refilled Lou's coffee cup—"it meant I didn't have to go to my birthday party. And for another"—her serious face returned—"I could devote myself to getting Marva on her feet and I could spend some time examining my own life."

"You needed a little space?" Jennie sympathized.

"That's what I needed. Space—"

Lou ignored Jennie's obvious reference to her own need for space the night of the birthday party. "The column you wrote about reaching thirty was very sad," he prompted Dorrie.

"I felt sad, Lou. I was starting to realize that Marva was right. I was full of myself."

"No, dear," Marva protested.

"I was so intent on digging out the truth about everyone else, I was ignoring the truth about myself."

"And what was that?" Lou asked softly.

"That I was leading other people's lives instead of my own. That power does corrupt even if you think you're not corruptible. Power isolates. Power dulls the senses. Power makes you feel entitled to ride around in a chauffeur-driven car. Power is a wall between you and the real world. It separates you from the courtesies of life and the natural affections of love."

"But what about the fame and the fortune?"

Dorrie sighed. "The cliché is true. It is lonely at the top."

Lou Dexter was deeply moved. There was something ineffable about her, the brave little chin, the fearless set of her eyes that somehow reminded him of his own daughter. He felt ten feet tall and protective as hell. "You poor kid. What happened next?"

At Big Sur, her reunion with Marva was tempered by the reports of Dorrie Bridges's fiery death. They telephoned Tom Jennings and all agreed to keep the secret for the time being.

"That was the first I knew about the diary," Tom explained. "With Dorrie 'missing,' we figured it would give us some time to find out who would want to do such a terrible thing to Marva. And why?"

"And that's where you came in," Dorrie reminded Lou.

"Me?"

"We were on tenterhooks. I believed what that woman said. Every day I expected to see the story, 'Hitler's Bride Lives in Beverly Hills—' "

" 'Torrid Teen-age Sexpot in Secret Nazi Marriage,' " Tom chimed in.

"The *Enquirer, The Star, The Midnight Globe*—they'd hock their grandmothers for a story like that."

"That," said Dorrie, "was when we realized that my mysterious visitor had a special grudge against Marva and me. And that's why I was so tickled when I heard tell that the great Lou Dexter was getting ready to do a book on me. I thought, sure enough, if any one person can track down this woman and find out her motives, it would be you."

Lou's chest swelled like a Boy Scout receiving a merit badge. "Is the diary here?"

"Please. It's too upsetting for Marva—" Norris begged.

"I'm fine, sweetheart. Let him see it."

The rich red leather and heavy vellum paper made the grotesque contents seem even more obscene than in Xerox. "The handwriting is the key," he said. "The culprit is someone clever enough to research the facts about Hitler in 1937. Someone with access to Marva's handwriting. And someone who—"

"Someone who what?" Connie Michelin strode into the

house wearing a vampire cape given to her by George Hamilton and a wide-brimmed hat.

"—who is sick with hatred and jealousy, Connie!" Dorrie Bridges cried accusingly.

"What? What are you talking about?"

"Connie—how could you? I should have recognized you. The hat. The cape—"

Connie's face turned Nixon gray as she realized the enormity of her mistake but nonetheless was going to brazen it out. She tossed the hat and cape into a chair. "What is this, some kind of a joke? Not funny at all."

"No wonder you were so antsy about Lou Dexter!" Tom said. "You knew he was a pro. That he'd find out the truth."

In the first display of physical violence anyone had ever seen, Norris Burnside slapped Connie Michelin's face. "You almost killed my wife!"

Connie stood her ground. "I've had just about enough of you. All of you. I'm sick of your smug superiority. *Your* lives. *Your* friendships. *Your* rich bitch wife. What the hell does Marva Burnside know of life! Everything came easy. Wealth. Social position. A loving husband. Everything on a silver platter. Stories on the Society Page. Isn't Marva Burnside wonderful to open her house to a charity tour, to lend her name to a new hospital? What's the big deal? What else has she got to do? When did she earn five cents? When did she take a chance or build up a business—?"

She directed her next words to Dorrie. "I gave you everything. Opportunity. Fame. Friendship. And what did you do? You left me holding the dirty end of the stick. You style yourself as a living saint, but you're a whore. You left me for the first person who offered you more money—"

"That's a lie and you know it!" Tom was apoplectic.

"It's all right. I can take care of this," Dorrie said. "I didn't realize you felt so betrayed, Connie—"

"You were so special to me. I thought we could at least

continue our friendship. But you preferred Lady Bountiful to me."

"We could have been friends, all of us. Women need each other."

"Not that woman. She hates me. I'm not classy enough for her. Unless she wants some coverage in *Newsmagazine*. Then she's all lovey-dovey. Then the sweet little personal note arrives telling me about some fancy ball or celebrity sand-kicking contest. The handwritten note. My secretary files everything. I must have fifty of them."

Of all those present, Tom Jennings was the most incredulous. He had known Connie longer than any of them. With all of her faults, how could she do such a despicable thing? "How did it start, Connie? Where did you get such an idea?" He held up the diary. "It must have taken hours and hours of painstaking labor to do this."

"You really want to know?" For all evil-doers, however secretive, there is the sublime moment of triumph when they stand alone in the spotlight, revealing all to a breathless audience. "I was reading through some psychiatric reports on survivors of the Holocaust. There was one poor woman who had recurring nightmares about marrying Adolf Hitler, about having a passionate physical obsession with him. A horrible case. She masturbated constantly, screaming his name, again and again, and then her guilt was so intense, she tried to perform a clitorectomy on herself."

"Oh, my God—" Marva gasped.

"Connie, really—"

"The truth ain't always pretty, right, Dorrie?"

"Go on," Dorrie said.

"I was thinking that if we went with the story, we should run it with a roundup of pictures of *der Führer* smiling."

"Smiling? It sounds like *Springtime for Hitler*!" Jennie said.

"Think of the drama of it all. Instead of the usual scream-ing maniac, I wanted to show him kissing babies, patting puppy dogs, lovable Adolf Hitler just going about his business. A chilling contrast to this poor woman's story. I had my researcher round up all the pictures he could find from every source, the old *Herald-Tribune* files, the defunct German-American Photo Service—and there you were, Marva. That old photograph of you and your father with *der Führer* himself. You were very pretty, my dear."

Marva merely nodded, unable to respond to the compliment.

"That's when I got the idea for the diary. I keep everything, you know. The original shopping-bag lady. Every piece of paper. Every little handwritten note in that disgusting green ink that you ever sent me, Marva. It took me weeks of diligent concentration. Checking out every detail, every nuance. Now I know how Clifford Irving felt. It was the most exciting thing I've ever done. A perfect work of art!"

"Not quite perfect," Dorrie said.

"It's a tissue of lies!" Norris chimed in.

"Facts are a matter of opinion. We all know that. William Shakespeare said Richard Plantagenet was a hunchback. Contemporary reports said otherwise. The diary is a masterpiece because everything in it could have happened."

"Not quite," Dorrie repeated. "What about George Gershwin."

Connie smiled. "I thought that was a good touch. I know how crazy you are about Gershwin. One of your sweet little notes invited me to your Gershwin concert for the benefit of slum children."

"George Gershwin died in July of 1937."

"So?" The mocking smile froze and melted. She fumbled in her bag. "Cigarette! Somebody give me a fucking cigarette!"

Dorrie tapped out some Bull Durham from her battered Tiffany box into a leaf of e-z wider, rolled the cigarette firm, and licked it neat in a dazzling display of manual dexterity. "Have one of mine."

Connie placed her hand on Dorrie's as the latter lit the

cigarette for her. "What are you going to do, send me to the chair?"

"You deserve worse than that," Norris Burnside bristled. "I'll see that you're sent to prison. I'll get our lawyers and—"

"Norris, calm down. The last thing we want is publicity." Tom had regained his equilibrium. "Right?"

Norris pounded his fists in frustration. "Right. So what do we do?"

"Here's what I'm thinking. Connie—"

"Take me to court. I'll plead temporary insanity."

"Tell me something. Would you like to spend the next ten years of your life in a psychiatric hospital where you belong? Or—"

"Or—?"

"Or living abroad, anywhere you like, in considerable luxury!" Tom's eyes begged Norris to hear him out.

"What would I have to do?"

"Sign over all your *Newsmagazine* holdings to Norris for their true market value and sign a statement confessing your malicious intent as regards the diary. We will see to it that your retirement is announced with suitable style. You will be accorded the respect and honors of your profession. Does all this sound practical to you, Norris? After all, it's your money I'm spending."

"I assure you. It will be the best investment I ever made," the industrialist said fervently. "If Miss Michelin agrees to our terms."

All eyes focused on Connie. As a last act of defiance, she dropped her cigarette on the floor and ground it out with her stiletto heel. "I was getting tired of New York and tired of *Newsmagazine,* if you really want to know. Good luck. Who are you going to get to run it?"

First Tom, then Norris, then Dorrie, and finally all those in the room turned toward Lou Dexter. "Lou? Would you consider a desk job?" Tom smiled.

He had seen enough jackpot winners to know how he

should be acting. Jumping up and down. Slapping himself on the head. Hugging the nearest breathing object. The star spotlight had switched from Connie to him. It felt good to have all of them smiling warmly. *Are you somebody?* For a split second, he wished the little Pube with the autograph book were here.

"It's right where you belong, Lou." Dorrie's smile was warmest of all, the famous eyes sparkling with encouragement.

"Maybe—" The incredible thought was forming in his mind. "Maybe Dora June and I could run it together." He looked to Tom and Norris for agreement. "What a team we'd make. Think what we could do with *Newsmagazine!*" He took Dorrie's hands and brought them up to his lips. "The two of us. What a combination. What do you say, Dorrie?"

He could feel Jennie's stricken stare and the astonishment of the others. Dorrie gazed into his eyes with calm curiosity. "Lou—"

"How about it? We'll make history together."

"That's a mighty flattering offer, and I thank you kindly for making it, but—"

"But nothing. Think about it. Think what we could do together!"

"But"—she looked expectantly at the door as a young man entered with a string of catfish still dancing on the line—"I'm getting married, you see. This is Jim Ed Loomis."

"Congratulations!" Jennie Bliss Sternholdt cried and swung the astonished bride off her feet in a whirl of exultation.

"Getting married shouldn't stop you from working. Other wives work!" Lou tried to cover his embarrassment. For a glittering moment, he and Dorrie Bridges had ruled the world and made it safe for truth and love.

A more practical plan was worked out over an enormous mountain breakfast of fresh ham, fried eggs, grits, and peas. Lou Dexter would assume editorship of *Newsmagazine*. His first exclusive story would be Dorrie Bridges alive and well and starting a new life at age thirty in Tennessee.

"You're right, Lou. Getting married won't stop me working. Jim Ed and I are going to build up the *Roper Valley Echo* into the biggest weekly paper in all of Tennessee. We're going to try to have two children as quick as God and nature lets us and then, well, maybe we'll move into other things, like maybe make us a movie. That is, if Jennie here maybe might give us some professional advice on the subject."

"How did you know I was into film?" Jennie asked meekly. Lou's disaffection had ruined her appetite. What she really wanted to do was cry. After all she and Lou had been through together, he would have left her for Dorrie Bridges without so much as a backward glance.

"Now, Jennie, don't go screwing your mouth up like that. It's going to freeze that way. When I heard Lou Dexter was trying to find out all about me, I found out all I could about him. And that includes you. From everything I've learned, you are a talented and resourceful—and loyal—young woman. Lou's damned lucky to have you."

"Thank you." Jennie brightened up considerably and helped herself to some ham.

"Then you won't mind—"

"Mind what?"

"Mind if I talk to Lou alone?"

With her mouth full, all Jennie could do was nod.

Outside on the grassy slope leading down to the lake, Dora June said, "I feel a connection to you, Lou. Like we're kissing kin. I don't know how to explain it."

"I feel the same way."

"Maybe it's because we share the same views about reporting. You know, I admire the way you've protected Sonya Boris."

His mouth dropped open like a cartoon. It took considerable will to shut it.

"I know all about it, Lou. Why you never tried to explain what happened and clear your name. Your little boy is nearly four. He's bright and healthy and her husband thinks it's his."

"Why didn't you run with it?"

"Because I wasn't a hundred percent certain of my facts. I thought I'd talk to you about it at my birthday party. Was it a good party?"

"Not very."

She took his arm and leaned against him. "I want to thank you for everything you've done."

Emotion got the best of him. He gathered her into his arms and held her close against him, his face buried in her sweet silken hair. "I love you, Dora June."

"I love you, Lou Dexter. And that's the truth."

"Dora June! Folks are getting ready to leave," Mallie called out to them from the house. The earlier twinge of recognition hit him again. "You look familiar," he said when they reached the house.

"That so?" Mallie fluttered her eyelids, promising herself to start wearing the glasses Jerry Lee had bought for her when her vision started to go. "You're too vain for your own good," he had said. And he was right, but she just couldn't stand to wear glasses like some old spinster librarian.

The events of the past few days were doubtless affecting his brain. It was just that there was something about Mallie that reminded him of all those pretty little southern girls who flocked to New York on the Trailways bus in the first years after World War II. He was fresh out of The Bronx himself with his high school diploma and too young for a G.I. Bill to pay for college.

He had run errands for a Broadway press agent, sold gags to Walter Winchell, and finally got a job as a copyboy on the *Daily News,* which impressed all the girls. Especially that one southern dish. Such a sweet kid, wanting to be an actress or a cover girl like all the rest. He wondered whatever happened to her.

A bizarre Dickensian thought crossed his mind. That Mallie was that sappy little southern roundheels and Dorrie Bridges was his daughter. *Oedipus schmedipus,* as long as you love your father. The idea was so outrageous, he burst out laughing.

"You're feeling pretty feisty for a dirty old man!" Jennie Bliss Sternholdt sniffed.

"You don't know the half of it." He was still chortling as they walked across the field to the Aero Commander.

"Lou—"

"You!" He kissed her on the nose. "Cheer up. Everything's going to be fine."

"Let's—" She grinned at him.

"Let's what?"

"Let's say it's day for night." The airstrip lay ahead.

"What do you mean?"

"It's the final scene of *Casablanca,* right?"

"Right."

All was well. They were doing movies. "The sun's out so we have to use a special neutral density filter to get the night effect."

"Okay. You're Ingrid Bergman and I'm Humphrey Bogart."

"Well—no!"

"No? Then who the hell am I, Sidney Greenstreet?"

"No. You see, I've been doing a lot of thinking about *Casablanca.* And the way I see it, the real love affair is between Rick and Captain Renault."

Suddenly he realized how fine it was to be with Jennie Bliss Sternholdt. "You're nuts. You mean you're going to be Claude Rains?"

"No, turkey—you're going to be Claude Rains."

"But I'm Humphrey Bogart. You've always said I'm Humphrey Bogart."

"Not this time. This time"—she grimaced—"I'm Humphrey Bogart!"

"You're a girl."

"Trust me. Remember the end of the picture? Miss Ilsa finally takes off in the fog with Victor Lazlo, right?"

They had reached the airstrip.

"Right."

"Leaving behind—"

"Rick and Captain Renault."

"And a box of Mars Bars to you." She took his arm as they walked toward the plane. "And what's the final line in the movie?" With her best Bogart speech impediment, Jennie Bliss Sternholdt growled. " 'Louie—' "

"That's me."

" 'Louie, I think this is the beginning of a beautiful friendship.' "

AFTERWORD

Fun is good, Truth is still better, and Love is best of all.

—William Makepeace Thackeray